# The
# Awesome Girl's Guide
## to Dating Extraordinary Men

ALSO BY ERNESSA T. CARTER

*32 Candles*

# The
# Awesome Girl's Guide
# to Dating Extraordinary Men

*A Novel*

Ernessa T. Carter

**amazon** publishing

The characters and events portrayed in this book are fictitious. Any similarity to real persons, living or dead, is coincidental and not intended by the author.

Printed in the United States of America.

Published by Amazon Publishing

PO Box 400818
Las Vegas, NV 89140

ISBN-13: 9781612182827
ISBN-10: 1612182828

To Monique King-Viehland, the first person I met at BRIDGE. Sorry darlin', if I'd known we were going to be best friends forever, I would have been a lot nicer.

# August 2010

If you say you want to find an extraordinary man, and you've got a habit of turning down social invitations, I mean any social invitation at all, then I just plain don't believe you're serious in this endeavor. When you're searching for true love, you had best take every invitation you get, because for all you know, somebody's handing you an Invitation to Extraordinary.

—*The Awesome Girl's Guide to Dating Extraordinary Men* by Davie Farrell

# THURSDAY

*H*i, my name is Thursday. You don't think you know me, but trust me, you do. Maybe you've talked about me behind my back or maybe you've said, "Nice to meet you" at the party of a mutual acquaintance. Maybe you've heard a lot about me, but you wouldn't go as far as to say you know me. Semantics. I get it.

But technically you know me. And by me, I mean somebody just like me. Because though women like me come off as enigmatic, we're all pretty much the same. I'm going to give you a list of my qualities, and then I'm going to let you flip through your mental contact list until you find the person in your friend or friend-of-friends group who's just like me. This person you know is:

1. Neurotic.
2. Constantly sabotaging herself.
3. From a privileged background, but because of #2, broke now that she's an adult.
4. The victim of some really sad pre-adulthood experience. Boo-hoo-hoo, something tragic happened to her or someone very close to her before she turned twenty-one. Cue the fucked-upness for life.
5. Attractive—not gorgeous, mind you—just attractive. Easy on the eyes, easy to like at first glance. In my case, I have a set of killer dimples and a lion's mane of long dreadlocks.
6. A complete screwup.

And most baffling of all:

7. Really good at boys. I mean, really good at them. Like if she was taking a class in getting boys to like her, she'd have an A+, and you'd

be hissing at her for throwing off the curve. He's just not that into you, but for whatever reason, he's into her.

Well, that woman you all know, the one who has a different guy in tow every time you run into her—that's me—or I guess I should say now, that was me.

"What's your secret?" I'm sure you've always wanted to ask the version of me that you know. "Hey Thursday-like person? You're a screwup, you sabotage everything you touch, and you're not exceedingly hot. How do you attract so many guys?"

I have two words for you: Ridiculous Honesty. When I'm out and about at a club, event, or party, I simply walk up to whatever guy I would like to sleep with that night and introduce myself. A couple of drinks later, I'll say something like, "You're a really nice guy, but I've got so many reasons not to date you."

Then he'll get mad, saying, "But I haven't even asked you out."

And I'll yell over whatever loud music is blasting, "But you will. I'm fucked up and emotionally unavailable. Guys love me."

And he'll say, "But . . . "

And I'll say, "But you will."

And it'll go on like that until he does in fact ask for my number. Because (here's the big secret) if you have the mammaries to pull it off, there's nothing like announcing to a guy that you're completely fucked up and a challenge. They should walk away, but they never do. After that it's an all-access pass to thirty days or so of mutually satisfying sex, until that month's guy realizes that I was totally serious about being fucked up and emotionally unavailable. Then comes the breakup in a flood of angry recriminations, in which the guy of the month accuses me of being exactly who I told him I was.

So yeah, the breakup part's not so great, but I'm not going to lie to you about the rest of it. Being that woman was a lot of fun. I never got bored with guys, because I never stayed with them that long. In fact, Risa, one of my best friends, came up with the perfect term for the way I dated: "one-month stands." I dated guys, and then I ditched them when they caught feelings. No love, just leave. That was my standard MO. And I *loved* this MO. I was a struggling comedian with a career to attend to, so one-month stands were perfect for me.

But then came the summer of 2010, when I started having The Dream. At least once, sometimes two or three times a month, I'd find myself walking through a crowded farmers market I didn't recognize, feeling bad for reasons I didn't understand. There was a man, standing a few yards in front of me, but I could only see the back of his head, which was covered with some kind of hat. A fedora maybe. I was pushing through the thick crowd, trying to get to him.

Then I'd yell, "Okay, okay, I'll marry you."

He stopped. And I stopped, too, until finally, he turns around, and—

Bam! Then the alarm would go off. *Every single freaking time.*

"I keep on having this dream and it's driving me crazy," I told Risa, Sharita, and Tammy the only time all of us managed to get together for brunch that entire summer. "Basically, I'm following some guy I can't really see through a farmers market, and then I'm all like, 'Okay, okay, I'll marry you.' And he's about to turn around so I can see his face, but then I wake up. What do you think that means?"

"Maybe it's a vision from the future," Tammy, the dreamy, light-skinned model with perfectly dyed honey-blonde hair, answered.

"Maybe you saw a movie and it's replaying in your dreams," Sharita, the adorably chubby and super-practical accountant, said.

But Risa glared at me as if I had been taken over by a body snatcher. "You want to get married," she said. "You have the itch."

"No," I said, feeling like I had just been accused of having an STD. "I love being single. I want to be single forever."

"What's wrong with wanting to get married?" Sharita, who wanted nothing more than to get married, asked.

But Risa just shook her head at me, her face mournful like I had just told her I had a terminal disease. "Dude, I thought you were different. I thought you wouldn't lose your mind and want to get married as soon as you turned thirty. But turns out, you're just like all the other single ladies, living the stereotype."

"I'm not living the stereotype," I said. "It's just a dream, I swear."

"Why are you acting like it's against the law to want to settle down?" Sharita asked Risa. "Day can't sleep around forever. And, you know, marriage to the right person would probably improve her financial picture. You should see how many of my clients have jumped to higher income brackets within a few years after getting married. As an institution, marriage really is good for your wallet."

Sharita gave me a nod of approval. "I think this decision to get married is probably the best one you've made since moving out here to L.A."

Risa folded her arms and pouted. "So now I've got two friends living the stereotype."

"I'm not living the stereotype," I said, trying to rein them back in. "It's just a dream."

Risa's accusation and Sharita's approval felt insulting to me. I was Thursday, as bohemian as my name. As staunch a feminist as a struggling comedian with a low-paying day job could be. I had never needed contracts or vows or commitments before.

"Oh, that reminds me," Tammy said. She pulled two books out of her white Gucci crocodile leather bag and handed them to Sharita and me. "I brought along copies of my sister-in-law's new book."

I glanced at the title: *The Awesome Girl's Guide to Dating Extraordinary Men*. "Is this a dating book? I thought your sister-in-law was a career coach."

"She is, but she says she has to give a lot of relationship advice, so she decided to write it all down. Isn't that a fun idea for a book?"

Sharita flipped through it. "Is there anything in here about how she managed to land your fine brother? Because that's the kind of advice I need."

In Sharita's opinion, Tammy's sister-in-law, Davie Farrell, was exceptional not because of her mega-success as a life and career coach to the rich and famous, but because she had managed to date and keep a good black man. And the only thing that Sharita wanted more than making partner at her accounting firm was to date and keep a good black man. "Heck, at this point I'll settle for decent," she'd told me after her last breakup. "A decent guy with a regular job who takes me out every once in a while."

Sharita, I knew, would do anything to figure out how Davie Farrell ended up with a black dreamboat like Tammy's brother, James Farrell.

"No," Tammy said with an apologetic frown. "It's more like a general relationship advice book. What to look for in a man. How to be your best self. That kind of thing."

"Oh," Sharita said, setting the book aside. "Well, if I'm going to make partner by Christmas 2011, I won't have a lot of free time to read."

I also set the book aside, not because I didn't have time to read it, but because I couldn't see me, the queen of dating, reading a dating book just so I could land a husband.

"You didn't bring me a copy?" Risa asked, all snarky half smile. Risa was, in her own words, "too cool to date men."

"Like you'd actually stop pining over The One long enough to read a dating book anyway," I said. "When was it you two broke up, anyway? Eight years ago?"

"I think it's been nine," Sharita said.

"Wow, you've been mooning over someone who dumped you at the beginning of the decade. A woman who's never even met your best friends."

Risa, having become used to us giving her a hard time about The One, took another sip of her coffee, which she drank in lieu of actually eating food whenever we all met for brunch. "If you knew her, you'd think she was worth it, too."

Tammy started looking all distressed, like she did whenever any of us Smithies teased another one too hard. She hadn't gone to Smith College with us and couldn't really be called an honorary Smithie, either, since nothing about her old-money, Texas-accented, debutante background read "modern black Smithie" in any way. But she and Risa had become friends before Sharita and I had moved to Los Angeles, and though Risa, Sharita, and I were officially the Smith College best-friend trio, somehow Tammy, a former USC cheerleader, multi-millionaire heiress, and the current spokesmodel for Farrell Cosmetics, had been absorbed into our little clique. From what we could figure, the only reason she continued to hang out with us was because we were maybe the only group of black girlfriends in the entire Los Angeles metro area willing to fully embrace a way-too-blessed spokesmodel who could double in looks and temperament for a Disney princess.

Still, Tammy was a sweet girl. And with a trio as opinionated and loudmouthed as Sharita, Risa, and me, it didn't hurt to have a natural mediator in our fold.

"C'mon guys, stop picking on Risa," she said, in that good-girl way of hers. "Let's just enjoy our lunch together."

This, of course, only made Sharita and me turn on Tammy and start grilling her about her own love life. "So you're recommending your sister-in-law's book," I said. "Does that mean . . . "

". . . you're going to start dating again?" Sharita finished.

Other than being exceedingly rich and beautiful, plus unfailingly polite and kind, here was the most interesting thing about Tammy: she used to date Mike Barker. Yeah, *that* Mike Barker. Before he became a huge movie star, he was actually engaged to Tammy, until he dumped her for some random cocktail waitress he met in Vegas. Tammy was destroyed and hadn't dated since. So though Risa and she were as different as night and day, they had this one thing in common—a crippling inability to get over the assholes who had broken their hearts.

But Tammy shook her head at our nosy questions. "No, I enjoyed the book and I want to support Davie by spreading the word, but I think I'm going to stick with being single for now."

"Yeah," Risa said, smirking at me. "Not everybody's dying to get married like you."

"It was just a dream," I said again, nearly shouting the words this time.

But at that point it was already too late. The movie *Inception* had been the sleeper hit of summer 2010 and Risa's words had planted an idea, so to speak.

The next night, I went to an L.A. Derby Dolls game with an "aspiring director" (in L.A. terms this meant that he hadn't actually gone to film school or made anything, but he had dreams and a day job as an assistant at a production company). I'd been one-month standing this guy for twenty-eight days, so we'd gotten to the point where we were just cozy enough to attend multiple events within the same date night. After the game we hit an after-party for a small play one of his friends had starred in for a three-week run. Then we went back to his Echo Park one-bedroom, all smoothed out on Tecate and free wine, for a Woody Allen movie viewing that got interrupted by a sudden, but not unexpected, bout of couch sex.

"That was great," he said, when we both fell back against opposite arms of the couch, spent and out of breath. He ran a hand through his now very tousled black hair and smiled at me in that moony way that guys smile at women like me after almost a month of dating, even though I had said at the Fourth of July party where we'd met that he didn't want to date me, because I was fucked up and emotionally unavailable.

Normally, I would have let this play out. Stopped returning his phone calls until the inevitable confrontation where I'd have to flat out tell him that I had no interest in seeing him again. I used to try to let guys down easier than this, but I had learned the hard way that saying things like "I'm not in a place to date anyone seriously right now" or "It's not you, it's me" or "I think we should pull back" only led to the last one-month stand calling me over and over again, leaving voicemails begging for "closure," while I was trying to hook up with the next one-month stand, until I was forced to have an even harsher, "I don't want to see you anymore" conversation to get him to stop.

This, I had found during my many years of one-month standing, was the main problem with dating white boys exclusively. They were totally up for dating the girl that wore her emotional ineptitude on her sleeve, but they didn't tolerate lighthearted breakups, and when they start to like that girl, in a way that's about more than lust and wicked smiles and having fun, they don't have the good sense to hide it.

So yeah, when the aspiring director smiled at me all goofy and happy, I knew it was time to implement the first phase of the one-month stand breakup and not answer the phone the next few times he called. But at that moment, looking into the eyes of yet another guy who liked me but wasn't right for me, a powerful need to, for once, not have the complete emotionally disconnected upper hand in a relationship came over me. I wanted to have a guy like me and like him back—not like him back well enough, but really like him back in a way that made me smile at him the way the aspiring director was smiling at me.

It occurred to me that as much fun as being me had been up to this point, I had become sick of being me. I was tired of having so much fun. I wanted to take someone seriously.

I scrambled off the aspiring director's IKEA couch and pulled back on my bra, my soft and faded Sweet Janes T-shirt, and the prairie skirt I'd tossed aside less than thirty minutes ago.

"Where are you going?" he asked.

"Listen," I said, tugging on my panties. "I feel really bad about this, because technically, you should have gotten two or three more days before I dumped you. But I'm just going to stop this now. I don't want to see you anymore."

The aspiring director looked from side to side. "Was it something I did in bed?"

"No," I said. "The truth is I don't like you enough to want to see you anymore, and I think it's time for me to start going out with guys I can see myself spending more than a month with." I thought about that statement as it came out of my mouth and agreed with myself. "Yeah, it's definitely time. You're basically witnessing a big epiphany here."

He blinked like I had just slapped him. "Wow, this conversation is really harsh."

"Yeah, I know. It totally is, right? Really sorry about that," I said, fighting the persistent, feminine urge to over-explain myself.

I opened up a can of Tecate from the six-pack we had purchased before coming back to his place. "Here, drink this," I said. "It'll make you feel better."

This last line seemed like a good compromise between my suburban upbringing, which taught me to never say what was on my mind, and my undergrad education, which had insisted I speak my truth always, even if it made others uncomfortable. Then I hightailed it out of there.

Maybe I was simply curious about what Davie Farrell would have to say about finding lasting love or maybe I was looking for answers to why my one-month stands had, as of this particular night, made me start to dislike myself. But for whatever reason, I opened the book when I got home. I only meant to read the first page, but I stayed up all night, enthralled by the dating advice within. And when I finished the book in the wee hours of the morning, it seemed to me that the Universe was trying to tell me something.

I had started having this weird dream in June; *Inception,* a movie all about weird dreams, had come out in mid-July. On the last day of July, Risa had informed me that I had an itch to get married. And then on the first day of August, I had read a dating book that actually made sense.

That couldn't all be coincidence. Could it?

I must have dozed off, because the next thing I knew, I was back in the farmers market, chasing after my literal dream guy again . . .

"Okay, okay, I'll marry you," I said.

He stopped, turned around, and—

My alarm clock went off with a loud, dream-destroying electronic bleat. I hit the snooze button. I had been planning to wash my hair that day and possibly retwist my dreadlocks, a beauty task I'd been meaning to check off my mental list since the Friday before, but in the cold, harsh light of Monday morning, I decided that it would have to wait for ten more minutes. Then another ten minutes when I pushed the snooze button again. And when my alarm went off a third time, I decided to just wear a knit tam to work and pushed "snooze" again.

Almost as soon as I did, though, a fist pounded on my closed bedroom door, causing it to rattle inside its jamb. "Either get your lazy bag of bones out of bed or shut off the bleeding alarm clock," a man's voice yelled on the other side of my door.

At least that's what I thought he said. Benny, my temporary roommate, was Scottish—and not Scottish in the clever, charming way depicted in romance novels set in the Highlands. No, he was some overly large grumpy troll version of a Scotsman, who spoke a garbled plaid patois that I couldn't even begin to understand.

This hadn't been so much of a problem when he had just been dating my English roommate, Abigail, and I only saw him in passing. Back then I smiled and nodded sort of vacantly whenever he spoke to me, which kept our conversations short. But then Abigail got a production assistant gig on a World War II movie filming in Prague for three months, and she and Benny decided to move in together when she got back. And since his lease was up on his Koreatown one-bedroom, he figured it would be cheaper to sublet Abigail's room in our North Hollywood apartment while she worked in Prague. He and Abigail wanted to save up first and last month's rent on a bigger, better apartment in Los Feliz, which they would be renting as soon as Abigail came back from Europe.

At least, that's how Abigail had explained it to me. But I didn't really buy it. I was fairly sure that Benny was subletting for the street parking. Abigail had confessed in the earliest months of their relationship that the reason he always opted to sleep over at our apartment (even though he lived alone and maybe should have been hosting Abigail) was because most nights neither of them felt up to a "desperate parking-space search," followed up by a possible one- to three-mile hike back to his apartment in Koreatown.

Still, I couldn't complain too much. I got to put off searching for a new roommate until Abigail came back. And Benny had become the best alarm clock I'd ever had. Even if I couldn't understand a word he said.

"I'm getting up," I yelled back.

He said something else in Scottish, before clomping away from the door in the Doc Marten boots he wore to work as opposed to sneakers like every other production assistant in Los Angeles. I stretched once, twice, let out a big yawn, and finally got up, pulling on some black yoga pants to go underneath the gray-and-blue Smith College T-shirt that I wore to bed every night. I took my scarf off and ran my hands through my locks to give them some volume, still thinking about the dream, which had seemed especially vivid this time.

*Why did the alarm clock always have to go off right before I got to the good part?* I wondered as I padded into the kitchen. I found Benny at the table, eating a bowl of Trader Joe's cornflakes and reading the *Los Angeles Times*. This had become a somewhat familiar sight, since Abigail used to do the same thing every morning.

After four years of living in L.A., from what I could tell, the only people who ever read the paper version of the *Los Angeles Times* were either in the AARP set or from the U.K. They had this cultural thing about reading actual newspapers, and on Sunday mornings I would often find both Abigail and Benny with a pile of them scattered on the kitchen table, including the *LAT*, the *Guardian*, the *Wall Street Journal*, and a couple of gossipy trades from England, like the *Daily Mail* and the *Sun*.

Sometimes I joined them at the table, but I read the *New York Times* on my laptop. Like most East Coast transplants, I considered the *NYT* a vastly superior newspaper. Also, I didn't get the appeal of having to sort through unwieldy pages and varied sections just to read the same stuff that I could peruse way more efficiently in hyperlink form and with a few simple clicks on my laptop's trackpad.

I grabbed an unopened box of Kashi cereal out of the cupboard, and when I went to the refrigerator for some milk, Benny garbled something in Scottish behind me. Something that sounded like, "A baby yandin dah arrow plain row aitch. Carro coh wittoo picker oop?"

"You know I can't understand a thing you say," I answered. I tapped the magnetic notepad hanging on the freezer door. "If it's important, write it down."

If I sounded surly, it was because we'd already had this conversation, like, three hundred times that summer, and he kept trying to act like what was coming out of his mouth was actual English, when we both knew it wasn't. Benny grumbled some more in Scottish but got up to write something down on the notepad before throwing his dishes in the sink and heading off to work at some movie filming on the Warner Brothers lot in nearby Burbank.

I finished making my cereal before checking the note, which read, "Would you like to come with me in two weeks to the airport to pick up Abby? She's got a mate traveling with her who she thinks you'll like."

My first instinct was to say no. I'd learned the hard way never to let my white friends set me up, because they were usually trying to pair you with the only other black person they knew.

So there was that.

But this was a social invitation—even if it was a really lame "come with me to the airport" one. So technically, I had to take it. *The Awesome Girl's Guide to Dating Extraordinary Men* had, like, a whole chapter on how women looking to get married should never turn down any kind of social invite. And since I'd apparently made some kind of dream-fueled jump onto the "trying to get married" wagon . . .

I grabbed my phone and texted Benny. "Down to go to the airport. Please thank Abigail for the invite."

# RISA

Ⓘf I were asked to write a book on how to be a future rock star, I would say, "Can't be learned. The shit only comes naturally. And the world knows when you're just pretending."

But if they threw a bunch of money at me and were like, "Pretty please," I'd probably do it. Mostly because I could use the dough.

The first chapter would be all about the rock star schedule, which basically goes like this:

**Noon:** Wake up. Give yourself about ten to fifteen minutes to adjust to your hangover, then roll over and tell last night's girl she needs to bounce. Like most future rock stars, you have a "night job." That is, a job with an odd schedule that provides you with funds while you pursue your future rock stardom. You practice and compose in the late afternoon, then join the ranks of struggling musicians who tend bar in Silver Lake at night. (Every Silver Lake bartender is a struggling musician. It's, like, the law.) In any case, you've picked up many a tattooed girl after drinking on an empty stomach.

**12:30:** Have breakfast: Shot of whisky for the hangover, sugar-free Red Bull for the energy, handful of Cheerios eaten dry and straight out the box for the nausea, protein shake for the nutrients. You're done. Don't bitch if you're still hungry, that's how rock stars stay crazy-thin.

**12:50:** Listen to NPR in the shower. If you stay in till one p.m., when they do the news rundown, you'll learn just enough to sound smart and current the next time you're trying to pull some heavily tattooed girl. It's not hard to sound smart and current in L.A. People usually don't ask follow-up questions.

**1:05:** Do your hair. If it takes you under a half hour to do your hair, you ain't a rock star. You've got to commit to a hairstyle that will get you noticed, and hairstyles that get you noticed never take less than thirty minutes. Right now you're rocking a Mohawk with the sides of your head shaved down and the middle relaxed and dyed purple—yeah, purple. The shit is badass. So you need to get out the product and spend at least thirty minutes to an hour styling it in a way that makes it look both spiky and haphazard at the same time.

**2:00:** Put on your makeup. If you don't have a gig that night, then you can probably get away with lip gloss, blue mascara, and blue eyeliner, smudged to look like you slept in the shit.

**2:30:** Throw on some clothes. And by "throw on," of course, I mean scour your closet for just the right outfit combination that looks both hot-to-def and like you're not really trying. It might take you up to an hour to "throw on" vintage orange-checkered Bermuda shorts, a faded black Mötley Crüe T-shirt, and a green rhinestone skull ring.

**3:30:** Call one of the local promoters you know to check in. Until you manage to actually score a record deal to match your rock star status, it's a good idea to keep in regular touch with the people that get you gigs around town. Mumble that you just got up, but wanted to say thank you for getting you on the bill for Space Camp (a club in Silver Lake) in October. It's crap pay, but, hey, at least it's in the neighborhood. While you have this

suck-up conversation, go out on your balcony and smoke a
cigarette, not because you're addicted to nicotine, but because
smoking kills your taste buds and makes everything taste like
fucking dirt and keeps you skinny. If anyone ever tells you that
smoking causes cancer, answer, "It also keeps me skinny, you fat
bitch"—but only say that if the person you're talking to is a
friend and/or really skinny. If neither of those apply, just say, "I
love cancer. I can't wait for it to kill me." Then stare back at them
like, "Yeah, I said it." People will both love you and hate you for
saying shit like this.

So that was my usual routine. But this day was different. This was the
day that a promoter finally gave me the good news I'd been hoping to get for
years.

He said, "Yeah, I was just about to call you myself. One of the A&R
guys from Gravestone e-mailed me and asked about you specifically. He's
coming out to the show."

I nearly dropped my cigarette. Gravestone Records was one of the biggest indie labels in L.A., and unlike every other indie label, they didn't already have a black female artist in their stable—it was like some kind of
quota with these labels and they all claimed they could only have one, like
they were all *Highlander* and shit.

"That's fucking fantastic," I said. "If you were here in person, I'd suck
your dick so hard."

He chuckled because he knew I was kidding. The rumor around town
was that I burned down the closet door with a flamethrower when I was,
like, seven and had been a hardcore lesbian ever since. Not exactly true. I
didn't officially come out to my parents until I was twenty-one, right after
I announced that I was dropping out of college—not a pretty conversation.
I liked the rumored version of my backstory much better.

"Just work on that set list and make sure it's perfect," the promoter said.

I assured him that I would and hung up. Then I opened my wallet and looked at the picture of The One that got away. Also, The One that turned me off marriage in general after she turned down my proposal when it was legal for like a second back in 2008. A small pang of guilt pinched me in the heart. The two of us weren't together anymore—not officially anyway, but I still felt guilty whenever I slept with other girls, since she was The One.

I began to imagine the kind of crowds I would start getting if I were signed to an actual label. I imagined her standing in that crowd, looking up at me and swaying with it. I imagined coming off the stage and finding her outside my dressing room looking fucking amazing and making all the other groupies standing outside my door read like skanks.

And I imagined kissing her in front of all of them and her kissing me back, not caring who saw.

And then I took another drag off my cigarette and wondered if November's show was the first step to making that scenario happen. The scenario I'd been playing over and over in my head since the first time we broke up back in 2002. I sure as Hell hoped so.

# SHARITA

*H*ere's what I needed after a weekend filled with a food drive sponsored by my accounting firm, a brunch with my three closest girlfriends, a half dozen complicated tax returns filed for a client who had "forgotten" to pay his taxes for six years straight, and a lock-in for fifty church-going-but-horny-as-heck middle schoolers: sleep, sleep, and more sleep.

But here's what I got—a phone ringing at six on Monday morning. I picked it up without looking at the caller ID, thinking something had to be burning to the ground if anyone was calling me this early. "Hello, this is Sharita," I said, sitting up on one arm.

"Sharita, it's Nicole." My sister's voice came trembling down the line, shaky and sad.

Now I really sat up in bed. "Nicole? What's wrong?"

"I didn't get the Verizon commercial," Nicole said.

I would've put some effort into comforting my sister, but the thing was Nicole was an actress. Which meant that at least two or three times a month, somebody turned her down for something. And the other thing was, "It's six in the morning. I thought it was an emergency."

"It's an existential emergency," Nicole said. "I can't even land the non-speaking role of Girl #2 in the salon? Why am I even doing this? I don't know. I don't know . . ."

Then she started crying. Not sobbing, of course—she was a graduate of the Yale School of Drama and that would have been too melodramatic for her training to bear—but she hiccupped loud enough for me to hear the tears in her voice.

"Maybe you should come out to Los Angeles," I said. "Like we talked about. You could stay with me for a while and audition out here."

"I couldn't leave the theater behind," Nicole said.

I resisted the urge to point out that Nicole had been in New York for five years and had yet to land a part in anything but the most off-off-Broadway of plays. Instead I said, "Well, the theater isn't exactly paying the bills right now."

"That's because all of your city's untrained actresses come here and steal our roles."

Every time any Hollywood actress landed a role in a Broadway play, Nicole acted like the part had been straight snatched right out of her hands.

I tried again. "Maybe if you came out here, then you could become a Hollywood actress and go back to New York theater after you got famous."

"Why are you always trying to stage-manage my life?" Nicole asked. The tears disappeared and her tone cooled.

"I'm not trying to stage-manage your life."

"No, you are. You think I'm a problem that needs to be solved like your shady clients' taxes."

"They're not shady. We serve a very sophisticated clientele at Foxman & Carroll. They just need help with their taxes."

"Then help me instead of trying to control me."

"I'm not trying to control you . . ." I trailed off. "Have I mentioned that it's six in the morning?"

"I'm sorry," Nicole said, her voice suddenly softened and went pliant again. "It's nine out here and I didn't think before calling you. I'm sorry I woke you; I'm just so upset. My rent's due in two days and I really needed to get this Verizon spot. The director even called my agent to get my number; we thought I had it for sure. I guess I'm going to have to pay my landlord late and hope that I can find some kind of job before he evicts me."

I reached over and took my laptop off the nearby side table. "That's not a good idea, Nic. How much do you need to make rent?"

"No, I don't want any more money from you. You're my little sister, and I'm a grown woman. I shouldn't have to keep asking you for money. I wish Mom . . ."

Our mom didn't make a lot of money at her job as a concessions worker at Busch Stadium in St. Louis, so asking her for help was never an option.

"I wouldn't offer if I didn't mean it," I said. "How much?"

"Eleven hundred," Nicole said. "And I'll pay you back as soon as I find a waitressing job or something."

I typed in my bank account's password. I had paid all my bills for the month and put money in my savings, but I only had $1,200 to get me through until I got paid at the end of the month. Still, Nicole needed the money.

"I'm transferring it into our joint account now," I said.

A couple of years ago, when I had visited Nicole in Astoria, Queens, I had gone ahead and opened up a joint bank account in both our names. I figured it would make it easier and cheaper to get Nicole money when she needed it.

Maybe I had seen the writing on the wall, because Nicole had needed a lot of money since then. My sister had a problem with keeping day jobs. She would start off in an office or a waitressing job easily enough, but then it would turn out that her boss was a micromanager or working in an office made her feel claustrophobic or the receptionist hated her. And the next thing I knew, Nicole would be wailing to me over the phone that she went out for lunch and never came back because she couldn't stay in that place a minute longer.

Funny that Nicole had never quit a play, though. A director had slapped her once and told her she couldn't come back to rehearsal until she had "screwed someone's brains out," because obviously she didn't understand how to portray a sexually evolved woman on stage. Nicole had not only not quit, but had also screwed the director's brains out that night, then praised him to me as the man that helped her break through to a higher level of acting.

Mind you, this was for a staged reading.

"Thanks so much, my darling sister. I really appreciate it," Nicole said, all traces of tears gone from her voice. "How are you these days?"

I pushed the authorize button on the transfer. "Good. Tired. Girl, I've got a million things to do for Foxman & Carroll this week. I've been volunteering for a lot of extra work lately because I've decided to have that partner conversation next year. I know, I know. I've only been working there eight years, and normally it takes ten to twelve before you can move from senior manager to partner, but I was praying on it the other day, and it was like God sent the message direct to my heart. I really think I'm ready to take the next step in my career."

"Mmm-hmm," Nicole said. She never seemed very interested in hearing about my job. And this morning didn't prove any different. "Are you seeing anybody?" she asked without any transition.

"No, not really," I answered. "How about you?"

Nicole launched into a story about a bohemian actor she'd met on the subway. He'd gone to NYU, and had just booked a part on *The Good Wife*, playing some sort of gang member. "He must be a really good actor, because you could just feel this positive light coming off of him."

Nicole was very attracted to "positive" people, which I translated as "people who also flitted from job to job and didn't have any sort of practical plan for their lives"—or "people like Nicole." It was like she insisted on dating her own dang self over and over again. But I kept my mouth shut, since my own dating life wasn't going much better. I'd met a few guys during my eight years in Los Angeles, and every relationship had gone the same route. Serious for a few months, then it would fizzle out. L.A. guys were funny like that.

"You need to start dating out," Thursday had told me. "Black guys in L.A. are the worst. All they do is string you along and play games and make you feel bad about yourself because you don't look like Halle Berry."

Thursday herself only dated white guys, which often came as a surprise to people, since she had dreadlocks down her back and was the daughter of Rick T, one of the most political black rappers in the history of hip-hop. She also got way more dates than I did.

But I couldn't bring myself to take her advice. I had grown up in the black community, had seen black love with my own eyes. Supposedly my parents had it before my father's alcoholism forced them apart. Plus, my friend Tammy had a brother named James Farrell. He was not only fine, intelligent, and black, but he had also married a black woman. So I still had faith it would happen for me. I could see myself standing at the altar in a white dress with a strong brother who loved me. I wanted that. Wanted it so bad, I prayed on it every night. Thursday was wrong. My future black husband was out there.

It was just a matter of finding him.

# September 2010

Trying to find love gets a bad rap these days. A lot of my clients come in apologizing for daring to be about finding a man. But you have to understand, love ain't politics. It's completely natural, and there's nothing wrong with seeking it out for yourself. So put in some effort already.

—*The Awesome Girl's Guide to Dating Extraordinary Men* by Davie Farrell

# THURSDAY

*A* Rick T song came on the radio right as I was about to turn into the parking lot for MTS Systems, the armored car company where I work. The song was "Smells Like Bacon," a surprisingly catchy number from 1987 about cops beating project kids in Brooklyn for committing the crime of "walkin' black, talkin' black."

I grew up in Stamford, Connecticut, an upper-middle-class, mostly white city with suburbs as far as the eye can see—the same city that my father grew up in. He left the suburbs as Ricky Turner and returned as Rick T, a rapper that the *New York Times* dubbed "the voice of the modern black power movement." Neither the music critics nor his many fans seemed to mind that his street preaching didn't come from the actual streets. And sometimes I wondered if I was the only one in the entire world who saw Rick T for what he really was—a complete hypocrite.

I turned off the radio as soon as I recognized the song, but it was already too late. Hearing even a little bit of one of my father's songs meant my day was off to a bad start. A cloud of gloom followed me out of my pale-blue 1999 Toyota Echo and into the two-floor concrete building where I toiled not very hard as a contracts administrator.

A couple of minutes later, I entered my beige cubicle, plopped down at my desk, and checked my work e-mail. Nothing important. It took me less than two minutes to clean out my inbox. I then checked my personal e-mail. One of my best friends from grad school, who also had a day job but on the opposite coast, asked me if I wanted to come out to see the world premiere of her play in New York. "Tickets are so cheap between L.A. and New York right now. And you could stay on my couch."

I loved this friend dearly and loved trips to New York even more, but I'd already given up the dream of writing scripts, and the thought of sitting in a theater watching the work of someone else who hadn't given up that dream yet made me feel itchy, like I had come into contact with an infectious disease.

I told my friend that even if tickets were cheap, I still wouldn't be able to afford it, which was true. I lived paycheck to paycheck, with barely enough left over to make student loan payments, car payments, and for the occasional brunch after I paid my half of the rent.

When I went to get myself some coffee, I found a group of my Latina co-workers at one of the small lunchroom's two round faux-wood tables, laughing and talking over savory-smelling chorizo and eggs. I had to squeeze past them to get to the coffeepot. If I were being a really good former-writer-turned-comedian, I would have paid attention to them, taken mental notes on their mannerisms and the way they carried themselves so that I could use them in one of my stand-up routines or at least have them on hand, just in case an executive ever asked me if I had any ideas for a workplace comedy in a pitch meeting. But I wasn't that kind of wide-eyed comedian anymore. I didn't take real-life dialogue notes as my teachers had taught me or even file situations away to use later in my writing.

Over four years ago, I'd stepped off a cross-country flight with a fresh and shiny MFA in dramatic writing from NYU and dreams of eventually out-earning my famous father as a sitcom writer. Fast-forward to now: I was making more money than I ever had in my entire life—thirteen dollars an hour for eight hours a weekday spent doing the mind-numbing work of contract administrating, which was corporate speak for logging and sending out work agreements—a job that was pretty much the exact opposite of getting paid a lot to entertain people.

Out of frustration, I had abandoned the physical act of writing two years ago and had switched to stand-up comedy, which was, according to a few other writers-turned-comedians I'd met, the best way to land a sitcom writing job if, like me, you didn't know a lot of people and weren't, you know, particularly charming outside of the bedroom. But many improv and stand-up classes later, I hadn't even gotten my proverbial pitch meeting with the hypothetical exec who wanted to hear my ideas for a workplace comedy. And I still owed more than seventy thousand dollars in grad school loans for a now really dusty MFA.

I was only twenty-nine but, career-wise, I felt like an eighty-year-old. Lately, I had become tired. Tired of my dead-end day job, tired of constantly struggling to make it in a city where seemingly everybody under thirty was struggling to make it. So no, I didn't pay attention to the dialogue of the common people as I'd been taught to do at NYU. Instead, I poured myself a cup of coffee, grabbed a yogurt out of the refrigerator, and made my way back to my desk.

Truth be told, I was insanely jealous of my Latina co-workers. They had office friendships, spoke in excited Spanglish over the breakfast they shared every morning like one big happy family. They truly seemed content with working eight a.m. to five p.m. in a concrete building. It must be nice, I thought as I trudged back to my cubicle, to be content with living your little slice of life for as long as you had on this earth.

By the time I finished my yogurt it was eight-thirty, which meant that I had successfully wasted an entire half hour, so I figured I should get to work. I started with logging the five work agreements I still had on my desk from the day before. I made notes in all five of the clients' file folders. Then I printed out a list of twenty-five clients that needed to have their new work agreements logged. Grabbing the already-logged client folders, I followed the blue carpet to the rows of taupe metal filing cabinets, and I put away the finished contracts before beginning the task of pulling the twenty-five folders that I would try to complete that day.

At five-foot-three, I wasn't a tall woman, so I had to get up on a short stool to get to one client's folder, Ole Sporting Goods. And when my fingers made contact with the warm-but-dead folders, a not-so-new thought tapped me on the shoulder: I could go up on the roof and throw myself off. My skin prickled as I envisioned my body falling through the air, dressed in the paisley print maxi dress and green cardigan that I was wearing now. For a moment I stared into space, mesmerized by the lovely image of it ending, ending, ending.

But then again, my office building was only two floors tall. I could end up breaking every important bone in my body, but not dying. Then, in addition to my education debts, I'd accumulate a ton of medical bills and I'd have to go live with my sister, Janine, in Joliet, Illinois.

No, I thought, better to overdose on something or hang myself or go down to the Metro station near my apartment and jump in front of one of the aluminum trains.

It occurred to me then that settling down might not have been the best idea I'd ever had, even if Sharita kept assuring me it was. Without the distraction of sex or the thrill of a new boy hunt, the other parts of my life, which hadn't been going well for years, had started to cast a rather morbid shadow over my day-to-day existence. I missed the thrill of seeing a guy across the room and hooking him like a fish. I missed sex on the first date, sometimes on the first meet. I also missed always having a pre-coitus outing to look forward to on the weekends. Figuring out whether I liked a boy before I slept with him was so freaking boring.

Of the three dates I'd gone on since dumping my last one-month stand, no guy had sparked anything in me above the waist. I'd yet to meet anyone I could see myself chasing after in a farmers market and agreeing to marry.

On mornings like this, when I heard Rick T songs on my commute and continued to use my ill-advised MFA to do glorified paperwork and got to contemplating suicide while pulling files—it was hard for me to breathe, much less shove myself through my zombie workday.

But maybe, I thought, perking up, this was a good thing. Tonight Abigail would be introducing me to her friend from her Prague shoot, so maybe my miserable morning was setting me up for a big win later in the evening. Tammy, being one of those really rich, overly optimistic people, had a theory that when things weren't going well and when a person got to feeling sad, that usually meant something really good was about to happen.

"I broke my arm skiing the week before Farrell Cosmetics offered me my spokesmodel contract," she told me once. "Now I look for bad signs whenever I'm hoping for something good to happen." Only Tammy could find silver linings in broken arms.

I closed the file cabinet. "Listen," I whispered to the Universe, which may or may not have been trying to tell me something with the recurring dreams it had been sending me all summer. "If you're planning something big for me, please let it happen now. I really need a win."

I waited for an answer, and the Universe stared back at me, silent as a happy Buddha statue.

That night after work, I stripped out of my work clothes and threw on a denim skirt and a purple tank top. No makeup and simple accessories: a long necklace and the turtle studs that my sister had gotten me as a souvenir when she and her family went to Hawaii. I didn't even bother to do anything cute with my hair.

Four years of casual dating in L.A. had taught me that I should never go all out on a first meet. In fact, I tried to understate. That way I didn't risk attracting guys that valued looks over everything else. Avoiding shallow guys hadn't been a problem in any other city I had lived in before moving to Los Angeles. But the City of Angels was rotten with them and under-dressing was the only way to preempt getting asked out by someone who expected you to keep everything cleanly shaven and/or waxed at all times and for you to never leave the house in anything less than full hair and makeup.

But as I was getting ready to leave, I reconsidered my stance on never looking my best on a first meet. My relationship quest had begun because I was tired of being myself and wanted to be someone else now, someone who didn't trade in guys every month and didn't have visions of throwing herself off the top of her office every workday.

Also, hadn't Davie Farrell said there wasn't anything wrong with putting in some effort when it came to seeking out love?

I braided my hair into a neat rope down my back. Then I applied some lip gloss and eyeliner that made my large brown eyes pop above my dimples. I looked different, I decided, surveying myself in the mirror after I finished with my mild makeover, like a woman who knew how to be in a long-term relationship. Like the woman I wanted to be now.

Benny pounded on my door then, yelling something in Scottish that I assumed meant it was time to leave, and I grabbed my green vinyl purse thinking, *Here we go . . .*

About forty minutes later, Benny and I stood at one of the places where the escalators deposited newly arrived plane passengers, watching Abigail scroll down the automated stairs. Her English Rose pastiness made her stand out in the crowd of tanned and/or brown Californians waiting for their friends and loved ones.

A tall and shaggy guy with sandy-brown hair stood beside her on the escalator and then followed close behind her as she made her way over to us. He wore large, tortoiseshell seventies-era glasses, but he wasn't rail thin like a hipster—who is just a high-maintenance guy in ironic disguise. No, this guy looked to be kind, considerate, affable . . . like someone I could see myself running down in a crowded farmers market and yelling, "Okay, okay, I'll marry you."

When Abigail got to us, she pecked Benny on the lips and said, "Oh, I'm glad to see you." Then she kissed me on the cheek. "And you, too, mate."

I kissed her rosy cheek, English style, deeply aware of the shaggy guy as I did so. When we were done with our greeting, Abigail said, "This is Caleb, the music supervisor on our film. Is it okay if we give him a ride downtown? It's not too far out of our way, is it?"

Downtown L.A. was actually way out of our way. Completely different freeways, and it would add at least thirty minutes, maybe forty, to our return trip. But before Benny could answer, I put on a happy-go-lucky smile and said, "No problem."

Then I stuck out my hand and instead of announcing that he wouldn't want to date me because I was fucked up and emotionally unavailable, I said, "Hi, I'm Thursday."

My offer of a handshake caught him by surprise, just as he was squirming out of the lightweight brown sweater that he'd worn on the plane. When he pulled it off, he revealed that he was wearing a faded Sweet Janes T-shirt underneath.

I lit up with the delight of already having something so big in common. "You like the Sweet Janes?" I asked him.

"They're one of the most underappreciated bands of the decade," he answered in the authoritative way that white guys with good taste in music often have. By the way, I adored authoritative white guys with good taste in music.

"The lead guitarist is one of my best friends," I said.

"Risa Merriweather? Are you serious?" he asked. "I heard she had some kind of solo project going these days. I've been meaning to go out and see her."

"Maybe you can come with me to her next show," I said with a friendly smile.

At least that's what I said on the outside. Inside I said, *Thank you, Universe, thank you, Universe, thank you, Universe!* Because this guy Caleb definitely felt like a win.

# RISA

*O*ne of the Top Ten Rules in my Future Rock Star Manifesto: Never let anybody outside of you dictate your playlist.

That's exactly what I told the manager at Space Camp when he called to make sure that I'd be playing the classics at my October show.

And by the classics, he didn't mean Joan Jett, even though I did a pretty bitchin' cover of "I Hate Myself for Loving You." He meant the Sweet Janes classics.

I happened to be standing in front of the cover art for the first and only Sweet Janes album when he asked me this question. It was eleven years ago, and everybody in my old band looked so much younger than they did now. Ramen noodle–diet thin and dewy fresh, the four of us lay naked on a red circular bed, with nothing but guitars, hair, and other band members' body parts to cover up the money shots.

I was wearing a long, neon-green wig and my eyes were aglitter with defiant anger. Why was I so angry? I had a contract, and money in my pocket, and buzz. Sweet buzz. Where the hell did I get off being angry about anything? But there I lay, full of piss and vinegar.

A lot of people thought I was the lead singer of the Sweet Janes back then. But of course I wasn't. Somebody had to handle lead guitar, let the guy bands know through hard-driving riffs that my group wasn't one to be fucked with. No, the lead singer was Samanthe, a posh and daring pixie-cut of a woman, who preferred boys but let me kiss and grope her in front of the cameras, claiming a connection with me that went beyond her heretofore-stated heterosexuality.

The year was 2001. *Will & Grace* was the highest-rated sitcom among adults eighteen to forty-nine. Rosie O'Donnell hadn't left her popular talk show yet. Lesbians were supposed to be the next big thing, until they weren't.

One album. That was all the Sweet Janes got. Every rock station played it. The record company sent us everywhere, and that's how I met The One. She lived in L.A. at the time but, funnily enough, I met her at a New York movie premiere. The two of us locked eyes across the room, and that was it. A U2 concert went off in my soul, full of lights and special effects all screaming, "She's The One!" I'd never forget that first look.

I moved in with her a few months later. We were happy. We were in love. We were successful. And that's when everything began to fall apart.

Samanthe didn't turn out to be on the same page regarding our relationship. I had thought she was faking it, while she had thought she was in love. Maybe she was. Sharing copious amounts of coke and ecstasy with a person. Drinking out of the same bottle when you take that Jack Daniels straight to the head. That might be love. I'd heard of relationships based on less.

Recording the second album didn't go so well. There were disagreements and a lot of "I just worry that" grinded out between clenched teeth. I eventually had to pull Samanthe aside to have a long talk in the parking lot outside of the recording studio. But what I had expected to be a reasonable conversation turned into Samanthe sending the record company an e-mail announcing that she no longer wanted to be in the band due to creative differences with me. I knew this was what she said, because she cc'd me on the e-mail.

I went home from the studio and wrapped myself around The One's warm body, telling her everything was going to be fine. I had done most of the writing for the band anyway. I could take over the singing duties, too—I'd been wanting to take the band in a more acoustic direction anyway, blah, blah, blah. Somehow I spun it like our lead singer quitting was the best thing that could have possibly happened to the Sweet Janes.

Looking back on it now, though, it felt like the album had flopped even before the reassuring words were out my mouth. Actually, I can't say it flopped, because the record company didn't hear a single "single" on the album of thoughtful love songs I turned in. Progressive rock, which had been so hot in the late nineties, had begun to death spiral. Indie bands couldn't sound thoughtful or fall in love anymore. They had to be ironic. Electric.

Even though they weren't on the same label as me, my A&R guy had the Strokes playing on low in the background as he explained this to me.

And so the Sweet Janes broke up, meandering off in different directions. I put away my acoustic guitar for good and started playing around with my electric guitar, using my synthesizer as backup, and I decided that I liked that sound way better. And maybe that would have been the end of the story. But I checked my bank account a few months later, and it only had a couple hundred dollars in it. That's when all the crumpled receipts for withdrawals and my charge statements came marching out of the trash cans that I had thrown them in. They piled up behind me, snickering and pointing while I stared at the ATM's balance screen, mouth hanging open.

When I got home from that ATM train wreck, I said to The One, "Let's go out tonight. I need to get wasted so bad."

But The One answered that she wanted to stay home because she had to get up early the next day.

And at that moment I decided I was sick of her bullshit. She still hadn't told her family about us, and she never wanted to go anywhere, even when I promised not to touch her in public. She said she didn't believe me. There was that time a few months ago, when the third single off the original Sweet Janes album premiered on KROQ while we were idling at a red light with her in the passenger seat. I had smacked her on the lips with a huge "Mwah!" and she had been embarrassed. Had insisted that our relationship stay indoors ever since.

That arrangement had been all right when I was on the road. But I was going stir-crazy in the place we shared. I let her know that she needed to come out with me that night or I was going to accidentally fuck somebody else. "That's the way it works with musicians," I told her. "You either keep an eye on us or you lose us."

I'd always been really good at saying the wrong things. People usually laughed when I said things the way I said them. But not this time.

The One's face flashed from hurt to fear to anger before she said, "I don't think this is working."

And so, less than two years after dropping out of Smith College and moving to Los Angeles for a record deal, I found myself broke, with no label and no girlfriend, living in the shittiest apartment complex that Silver Lake had to offer.

Samanthe changed her name back to Samantha and got married to some insurance company executive. She grew out her hair, and she now lived in Plano, according to her Facebook account. I didn't hate her. But I also didn't sing Sweet Janes songs on demand just because some clueless club manager asked me to.

"You engaged Supa Dupa, not the Sweet Janes," I told him, going out to my balcony and lighting a cigarette. Supa Dupa is what I called myself, even though my act consisted of me, a mic, an electric guitar, and a synthesizer. Much like Owl City, Passion Pit, and Five for Fighting, I considered myself more of a "project" than a solo singer. Also, not-so-secret industry secret, it was easier to book shows if people thought you were in a band.

"Yeah, but you know how it goes," he said. "A lot of people are buying advance tickets, and I don't want them to be disappointed."

Not for the first time, I found myself jealous of Dave Grohl, Nirvana's former drummer and the current lead singer of the Foo Fighters. His follow-up band was still going strong; he made lots of money and lived in a nice house. And most of all, he didn't have to deal with any club managers trying to dick around with his set list.

"Listen, let's have a conversation about this. I'll swing by the club," I said. "I'll come by tonight before work."

After I hung up with him, an unexpected loneliness set in. Yes, this was business, but I didn't want to go to Space Camp by myself. I need some backup. So on my way out the door, I called up my posse to see who could come out. I called Tammy first, because, let's be brutal here, if I was going to be seen out with anybody in L.A, I wanted it to be with somebody at least semi-famous. But she didn't pick up. So I tried Thursday, who was a better choice anyway, since she liked indie music.

"I've got to pick my roommate up from the airport," Thursday said. "And we might be doing something with this guy she wants me to meet afterwards, so I don't know. Let me call you later."

Okay, so I tried Sharita, even though I knew that was a longer than long shot.

"I'm already in for the night," she said.

"Put away the ice cream and turn off *The Big Bang Theory* and come out anyway," I answered.

Guilty silence, then: "It's the season premiere."

"For fuck's sake, Sharita," I said, swinging a leg over my Harley-Davidson Heritage Softail Classic, which, unlike the Corvette I used to drive, somehow survived my post–Sweet Janes money woes and subsequent repossessions. "I swear to God, all you need is a cat to be more fucking boring."

"I've got to go," Sharita said. "They're back from commercial break."

"And get a fucking DVR. You're the only person on the face of the earth who still doesn't have one," I said, but I couldn't be sure if she heard me before she hung up.

I hope she did, because even though Sharita had never been one to go anywhere that wasn't work- or church-related on the impromptu, I really did feel mad at her as I started up my bike, put on my helmet and goggles, and pulled on my motorcycle gloves.

Now I was feeling even lonelier, like I was one of those sad people who didn't have any real friends. All of my close lesbian friends had moved on without me, acquiring in a cult-like block lifelong partners and kids made from cocktails of determination, helpful fertility specialists, and donor sperm. My few remaining single friends—my supposed best friends—never wanted to do what I wanted to do at the last minute anymore.

And you know what the only difference between a rock star and a has-been is, right? Entourage.

# SHARITA

While attending Smith, a college with a deserved reputation for staunch feminism, I had been told over and over again that I didn't need a man to live a happy and fulfilled life. *But how about if I really, really wanted one?* That was the question I had been asking myself lately.

Sometimes I'd be watching television, or reading a book, or making something truly delicious to eat and I'd think, "Wouldn't it be nice to have someone to share this with?"

I'd be turning thirty next year and it felt like I had Everything But.

Everything But the guy.

I thought about my desert of good man prospects that day while calculating the amount of Social Security one of my firm's clients, a political candidate, would need to back pay the dog walker he hadn't declared on his 2009 taxes—a fact that his political opponent had gleefully pointed to during their last debate. Figuring out the payment had been tricky because the dog walker was in the process of getting his green card and was not completely legal yet, but eventually I came up with the correct amount. However, when I went to type the numbers into my tax program, I realized that my computer screen needed a cleaning.

I had been about to call Rhonda, our receptionist and the only other black woman working at Foxman & Carroll, when I remembered that Rhonda was on her lunch break. Which was how I came to be sifting through Rhonda's desk, searching for the screen-cleaning solution, when a deep voice said above me, "What you looking for, girl?"

I looked up to see a big, strapping brother in a short-sleeved brown shirt and shorts. "Hi," I said.

His friendly smile disappeared when he saw my face. "Oh sorry, I thought you was Rhonda. I didn't mean to be so forward, sister."

He called me "sister." So few men did that anymore. I adjusted my satin work blouse and smoothed a strand of my shoulder-length bob behind my ear.

"Rhonda's on lunch break," I said. "Can I help you?"

"Sure, just sign here," he said. He handed me a bulky envelope with an associate accountant's name on it. Then he put out a little brown electronic box for me to sign with a plastic stylus.

"Thank you," I said, daring to meet his eyes for a second when I handed him back the signing box.

He lingered, despite our business being done. "You have a nice voice," he said. "It's soft and high. Real feminine. I like that."

I lowered my eyes, a little embarrassed. In my opinion my baby voice, as my mama called it, was my worst feature. Still I said, "Thanks," again.

"You Rhonda's replacement or something?" he asked.

"No, I'm just kind of filling in for her while she's at lunch," I answered, figuring it was simpler to say that than to explain that I was an accountant at the firm.

"Oh," he said. "Well, just in case I don't see you here again, why don't you give me your number? You like happy hour?"

In truth, I wasn't a big drinker, but this guy was way too cute and chocolaty to admit that. "Um, sure. A drink after work is nice sometimes."

I wrote my number and name down in clear, precise strokes on a Post-it note and handed it to him.

He nodded. "Sharita. Nice to meet you. I'm going to call you, okay?"

"Okay," I said, and something fluttered in my heart. It felt like the first time Teri met Damon in that old Showtime series, *Soul Food*, except Teri and Damon were both really light-skinned, whereas this guy and me were both really dark. Still, I was already getting a vision of the two bright-eyed little boys this fine specimen of a man and I could produce together.

This sometimes happened when I met new guys—a Crystal Ball Vision of the life we could have together played out in my head. And at that moment, I could see this brother and me in a park, sitting on a bench while our children tossed a football back and forth.

"Hey, son," I heard him calling out to our oldest boy. "You've got to put some spin on that ball when you throw it. Let me show you . . ."

But in real life, the father of my future children was turning to go. I thought to ask, "Hey, what's your name? So I know who it is if you call me."

He turned around, walking backwards to say, "*When* I call you, and it's Marcus."

Marcus kept his promise. That night, right after I hung up on Risa, who was being stank about me not coming out to some random rock club I had never even heard of, the phone rang with a blocked number.

"Hello?" I answered, thinking it might be a telemarketer that I'd have to ask to take my number off their list.

"Sharita? It's Marcus."

*The Big Bang Theory* had come back from break, but suddenly I didn't care. Seriously, was there anything more romantic than a man calling you when he said he would?

I muted the television. "Hi, Marcus. How are you?"

# October 2010

If a guy takes your number and doesn't call you within two weeks, then don't return his call if and when he does finally call you. I don't care if this guy is Obama's smarter cousin, fine as a sunset, and richer than a Saudi Arabian oil heir, you need to let him go. If he doesn't call you in a timely manner, he is not extraordinary.

—*The Awesome Girl's Guide to Dating Extraordinary Men* by Davie Farrell

# THURSDAY

I realized two things when I woke up that morning:

First of all: Caleb. Still. Hadn't. Called. And according to *The Awesome Girl's Guide*, today was his deadline to do so.

Second of all: It was the tenth anniversary of my mother's death.

I had been in China on my junior year abroad program, taking an oral language exam, which consisted of my heavily jowled Oral Chinese *laoshi* (teacher) and me having a conversation about what I had done over fall vacation.

I had signed up to go to China for my junior year abroad, not because I was particularly interested in China, but because China had been one of the few places that I had never traveled to with Rick T. He was huge in Japan and we'd made it over there quite a few times, but China, having surprisingly cheesy music taste (think Lionel Richie as opposed to Bob Marley), had never embraced Rick T's music, much less invited him over for a concert. My trip to China was supposed to be a lark, something to do just to do it. Growing up the privileged daughter of a popular rapper hadn't done me any favors as far as the real world was concerned. And deciding to study a language I already knew I wouldn't have any use for after college, just for the hell of it, turned out to be the first in a long line of impractical decisions that would eventually land me in Los Angeles with a dead-end job and zero career prospects.

During my time in the ancient country, I had found out the hard way that speaking Chinese was really difficult—like, really, really difficult— especially if you weren't motivated by the prospect of future business deals or teaching Chinese history or being able to speak to your older relatives, like my other program mates, who had all chosen to come to China for much less fun reasons than I had.

"Why you study Chinese?" my Oral *laoshi* asked, switching to exasperated English after I said, *"Ting bu dong,"* or "I listen, but I don't understand," to the fourth question in a row. "You are arrogant," she said to me before I could answer. "I cannot pass if you do not do your best."

I realized at that moment that I had made a horrible mistake. I wasn't just bad at speaking and understanding Chinese, I was actually in the process of failing my midterm. And unless some kind of miracle happened, I, the daughter of Rick T, a girl whose cumulative education up to then had cost more than many people made over a lifetime, would receive her first F just because she thought going to China might be fun.

Shame overtook me, making it hard to defend myself against my teacher's assessment. I opened my mouth to say, "I'll try harder on the next test," and beg her not to fail me, but then a tap sounded on the door, and the director of the program entered the classroom. He said a few words to the *laoshi* in Chinese before saying to me in English, "I need you to come with me to the school's office."

"Am I in trouble?" I asked, wondering if this was some kind of "your Chinese sucks" intervention.

My Oral *laoshi* surprised me by answering for the professor. "No trouble," she said. "And do not worry about test. It will not be on final grade."

I looked between the professor and the *laoshi*, confused and wishing again that I had bothered to learn the language.

# RISA

9had one of those alarm clocks that not only told the time, but also the weather and the day's date. It was a gift from Sharita, and when I received it, I somehow managed not to say, "Do I look like the kind of uptight bitch that uses an alarm clock? And who needs to know the weather in L.A.? It's either sunny or it's raining."

It was Christmas, so I let her get away with another one of her way-too-practical gifts and I even worked it into the mess on my crowded nightstand, so that she could see I was using it when she swung by for *Stargate Universe* nights. *Stargate Universe* was what we were watching for our weekly sci-fi night until *Dr. Who* came back in the spring.

However, that particular day, when I woke up at one p.m. and glanced at Sharita's clock, I saw the date and thought, "Oh shit, it's the day Thursday's mom died." And I ended up lying there in bed, remembering . . .

I'd been practicing on my acoustic guitar, hoping to get in some songwriting before quiet hours began in Baldwin House, when my phone rang, beeping twice to signal an off-campus call.

"Waaaaaassup!" I said, because that was how everybody answered the phone that year thanks to those idiot Budweiser commercials.

"Lisa?" a voice on the other line said—oh yeah, pause the flashback: I forgot to mention my real name is Lisa, but name one rock star named Lisa. Yeah, that's why I changed it. Getting back to what happened . . .

"Lisa?" came Thursday's voice.

"Thursday?" I said, confused, because, "Aren't you in China?"

"Yes, but I'm about to get on a plane now. My mom was in a car accident. A really bad one. And they don't know if she's going to be okay."

There was naked terror in her voice and I didn't know what to say. I wished she'd called Sharita instead, because Sharita wasn't the daughter of stern immigrant Republicans who didn't believe in saying "I love you." I asked her, "Did you call Sharita? You should call Sharita."

"She wasn't in her room."

"Well, fuck, then I guess all I can say is I'm sorry, dude. I hope she's okay."

Thursday sounded more confused than sad, like she was trying to figure out how her otherwise charmed life had taken this turn. "Yeah," she said. "Me, too. I've got to go. They just made the boarding announcement. Thanks, Lisa."

Then she hung up and I wondered why she thanked me, since I'm fucking useless in a crisis. I felt a little mad at myself then, a microcosmic preview of how I would feel three years later when I blew it with The One.

This call happened just two months before the Sweet Janes, my high school band from Orange County, scored a record deal, two months before I came out to my parents, and two months before I dropped out of Smith College.

# SHARITA

**9** wished Marcus had given me his e-mail address, because I had been playing phone tag with him ever since the first night he called. It seemed like every time I decided to turn off my ringer to get work done, that's when he would decide to call.

And then when I got his message and called him back, I'd get his voice-mail. Real frustrating, and we still hadn't been able to schedule happy hour drinks.

So when my phone rang in the middle of lunch, which I was eating at my desk, I picked it up on the first ring, hoping it was him. But it was Risa.

"Hey, girl," I said, picking up. "You're not canceling for *Stargate* on Tuesday, are you?"

"No, we're still on," Risa said. "What you eating for lunch today?"

"I'm not going to tell you," I answered.

"McDonalds?" Risa asked. "Burger King?"

"No," I said, feeling more than a little accused. Being friends with Risa was like being friends with the food police.

"What else is over by where you work?" Then she remembered. "Eww! You're eating Boston Market? That's, like, a million calories. Gross."

I stabbed at my Boston Market macaroni, taking another bite anyway. I could and usually did point out that Risa's habit of smoking was more gross and would kill her a lot quicker than my own thirty or so extra pounds, but I needed to get back to work, so I just asked, "Is there a reason you're calling?"

"Yeah, I was counting the shit on my fingers, and did you know that today isn't just the anniversary of Thursday's mom's death, but it's, like, the tenth anniversary?"

"We should do something for her," I said, putting my fork down.

"Yeah, but what do you do for the tenth anniversary of a death? You can't exactly pick up a gift for that shit, right?"

We'd had a similar conversation ten years before when Risa had shown up at the front door of Tyler House. I had been watching *ER*, sitting in one of the living room's sofa chairs with many of my housemates sprawled out around me on the floor and the two couches. Most of the houses at Smith were converted mansions and, therefore, when people came to visit they had to ring a doorbell. But we'd all been surprised when it sounded that night.

"Who's ringing the doorbell during *ER*?" one of the Asian pre-meds asked. *ER* hour was sacrosanct among the pre-med students and often the only time they came away from their constant studying to do something even halfway social.

"I'm on door duty," a square-faced blonde said from her position on the second couch. She was still wearing her riding boots from her after-dinner horse ride on the chestnut she kept stabled at Smith. They thunked against the hardwood floors when she jogged to answer the door.

"Sharita, it's Lisa!" the girl who answered the door called out.

A few schoolgirl giggles rose up around me. Whip thin with a spiky hairstyle that made her look like the Ghanaian female version of David Bowie, Lisa was what was referred to at our college as a BDOC or a Big Dyke on Campus. And since our first year, my fellow Smithies had treated her like the rock star she fully intended to become someday.

In fact, it surprised me to see Lisa standing in the hallway outside the living room without her guitar, which she carried around with her everywhere mostly for effect. Her band was still back in California, but she claimed that carrying the guitar made girls both lesbian and LUG (lesbian until graduation) swoon.

"Hello, white girls!" Lisa called out from the hallway, even though there were also two Asian women in the small crowd of Smithies watching the TV.

Lisa was a whiz at delivering an insulting line in a way that only produced giggles from her insultees. "Hi, Lisa!" they all called back.

Mind you, these were the women who would grow up to become some of our nation's most respected leaders and power-listers. But all pajamaed up in front of *ER*, they were reduced to giggling fans when Lisa entered the scene.

I got up to go talk with her in the hallway.

"What are you doing here?" I asked. "*ER*'s on."

"Sorry I'm making you miss your doctor show, but Thursday just called. Her mom's in the hospital. It's bad. Like, really bad."

"Oh," I said, thoroughly chastened. "We should do something."

"Yeah, I know," Lisa agreed. "But what?"

# THURSDAY

$\mathcal{S}$o this was how I spent the anniversary of my mother's death: checking my cell phone. I checked my phone when I came back from pouring my morning coffee in the lunchroom; I checked my phone when I returned from my morning constitutional in the restroom. Then I went to ask my co-worker for a file that he needed for insurance purposes but that I also needed to update a contract. We talked over the problem for a full two minutes before he agreed to hand deliver it to my cubicle when he was finished with it. And as soon as I touched back down at my desk, I checked my phone again, but Caleb still hadn't called.

"Oh no, it sounded like he liked you," my sister, Janine, said when I called her after work on my drive back to North Hollywood. We always called each other on the anniversary of our mother's death, but we never spoke about it or admitted that this was why we were calling. Talking to each other about our mother was just too painful, and we had come to a silent agreement not to bring her up anymore.

"But I'm surprised by your reaction," my sister said. "It's not like you to sweat a guy."

"I'm not sweating him," I said. "I'm just ready for something more, and I thought he liked me. He laughed at all my jokes and said that he wanted to come see me perform."

"Well, don't let him see your routine," Janine said. "All your jokes are about how bad black men are. That's not a good look."

"Whatever, Janine," I said. "*The Awesome Girl's Guide* says there's nothing wrong with aggressively being yourself."

"I'm not saying don't be yourself, I'm just saying—where are you going, Gavin? Come back . . . S-word, Bem! Bem, can you come watch your son?"

I could hear Gavin burst into tears on the other side of the line. "Mama!" he said, wailing like he was auditioning for one of the kids in *Sophie's Choice*. "I want Mama! No! No! Mama!"

"Mama's talking to Auntie Day, honey," Janine answered, her voice pleasant enough, but then she yelled even louder. "Bem! Can you come down here?"

More crying from Gavin, but no answer from her husband, Bem.

Janine had simpered and cooked her way into the heart of her Nigerian fellow chemical-engineering major back in college and was now married with two kids. She often complained bitterly about how though she and her husband were at the exact same place in their careers, she was still doing all of the cooking plus most of the child rearing and housework, while Bem sat around "decompressing" after work.

"Get a divorce lawyer and serve him," I said right after Gavin had been born and Bem informed Janine that the men in his family didn't change diapers. "What's the point of having a husband if he's not changing diapers? He's basically a sperm donor who also expects you to cook his dinner for the rest of his life." But Janine didn't listen to me and now look at her.

"For F-word sake," Janine said with a heavy sigh. "I have to pick him up or he'll be all traumatized because I didn't comfort him within five minutes or whatever. Gotta go, sorry."

She hung up before I could answer, which left me feeling a little bewildered as I tossed my cell and hands-free earphone back into my purse. I mean, if I could listen to that exchange and still feel my relatively new desire for a husband and family of my own burning strong, then maybe I really was ready to settle down.

If only Caleb would call. I started rummaging around my purse to dig my cell back out and check my messages again. I could just feel the phone on the tips of my fingers when—

*Don't be pathetic.* Unbidden, my mother's voice sprang into my head. No, not her voice, but her words. Her dying words.

The freeway faded into the background, and I could see myself getting off the plane to JFK from Detroit, which was where I had connected after my flight from China. It was early in the afternoon, almost a full day after my father had called to tell me about my mother's accident.

But instead of my father, I found his personal assistant, Brenda, waiting for me at the gate when I walked off the plane. That was back when they still let people wait at the gate for you, just a year before 9/11.

I slowed. "What are you doing here?" I asked her.

Coltishly thin, light-skinned, and perfectly coiffed in a chignon, pantsuit, and expensive perfume, Brenda would strike anyone as the exact opposite of my plump, mud-brown, all-natural, hemp-clothes-wearing former Black Students Alliance president mother, who always smelled faintly of sandalwood oil.

Which is why Janine and I had been so surprised to figure out a few years prior that Brenda was also my father's mistress.

One Monday, not knowing that it was a federal holiday (one of the those only acknowledged by schools, banks, and the post office with days off), my father had come home during the time that my mother usually drove us to Choate. Janine and I had been coming down the stairs for breakfast, still dressed in our pajamas, when we had caught our dad coming through the front door. He reeked of Chanel No. 5, an old-school scent from the generation of perfumes that clung to anything or anyone its wearer touched.

We knew this, because Brenda had hugged us good-bye on plenty of occasions and left us smelling of her.

"Where have you been?" Janine asked him, her voice small.

"At the studio," my father answered. "Here, you two come down, so I can come up. I need a shower and nap bad."

The stairs were too narrow for two sisters and a father to pass in opposite directions.

So we came down and I even said, "Sleep tight, Daddy," as he climbed the stairs, the scent of his lies trailing behind him. My sister and I, despite having caught him together, never talked about our twin realization to each other. I think we both thought that to say it out loud, even just to each other, would only widen the rift between our parents, perhaps even destroy our family. We didn't know back then that our family unit had already been tagged for demolition.

"Rick is at the hospital with your sister," Brenda informed me, brusque and business-like. "He didn't want to leave your mother's side."

If she was bitter about that, she didn't let it show on her face.

"Fine," I said. "I don't have any other way to get to the hospital, so let's just go, I guess."

"Rick wants me to take you home first. He needs you to pick up a few things for your mother," Brenda said.

I wanted to ask, "What things?" because I couldn't think of anything that would be more important than seeing my mother. But distaste and hope argued with me. Distaste put forth that I didn't want to have a conversation with my father's mistress about my mother. It felt wrong in every way. And hope pointed out that my mother must be out of the ICU if my father wanted me to bring a few of her things to the hospital.

"Fine," I said again. I spotted my Tumi suitcase coming around on the baggage belt.

We arrived at the house that I grew up in an hour later. The sight of the five-bedroom pale-yellow colonial sitting in the middle of our little cul-de-sac filled me with relief, a familiar touchstone on an overcast day.

A dull rainbow of not-quite-dead leaves had fallen from the neighbors' trees onto our lawn, and that made the house look even more normal from the outside. In no way did it announce itself as the home of rap legend Rick T.

The inside of the house, however, told the true story. If the framed posters of black leaders from Malcolm X to Angela Davis, and wood and soapstone African statues scattered throughout the house didn't clue visitors in, the semi-permanent smell of dark and brooding incense let them know that a *conscious* black family lived here. However, having learned the art of political discourse at Smith, our home decor had begun to ring false to me.

"I just wonder if home decoration is a completely truthful vessel for political intentions. Isn't that the job of actions?" I'd asked my mother on my last visit, before leaving for China.

My mother had laughed at me. "Yeah, I came home speaking big after I went away to college, too. That will go away after a couple of years in the real world."

I had swollen up with irritation and accused my mother of being "dismissive" back then, but when I entered our home for what would turn out to be the last time, I felt nothing but guilt. The smug shutters fell off my eyes and I could now see in the decorations how hard Mom had worked to make our home worthy of a great rap star.

I left my suitcase at the bottom of the stairs and headed toward my parents' bedroom, asking Brenda, "What does Dad want me to bring?"

But I stopped when I saw that the door to my parents' bedroom was closed. As far back as I could remember, my mother had demanded an open house. No closed doors unless somebody was inside the room, sleeping or doing homework. That had been her policy. And as a teenager, I had often been annoyed when I closed my bedroom door before leaving for school, only to find it wide open when I returned home.

But now the door to my parents' bedroom stood closed. And though no ticking sound emanated from the other side of the door, I somehow knew there was a bomb inside that room.

"Don't," something whispered inside of me, unsettled.

But I did, dismissing the subconscious warning and turning the round, scratched-up brass knob anyway, like a girl in a horror film; then I found something truly horrible inside.

First of all, there was my mother's gold wedding band, defiant in its simplicity, refusing to speak to Rick T's later success.

Second of all, there was what the ring lay on top of. A piece of white paper, which had probably come from the printer downstairs.

I approached the note the same way that I would have approached a dead body. Fearful, but needing to see it for myself. In many ways, this note was my mother's dead body, which, in the back of my heart, I now knew was lying in the hospital's morgue.

I picked up the ring, then picked up the note.

My mother liked to talk. Later, at the funeral, both Janine and I would recall how often she would give hour-long answers to simple questions like, "Where did you get that refrigerator magnet from?" or "What's a hernia?" The reason we were both so great at research, we told fellow funeral-goers, was because we had learned early to look things up ourselves rather than risk a lengthy answer from our mother.

But on paper she had always been economical with her words. In the early days, when she was still writing all of Rick T's lyrics, the unknowing critics had praised him (and therefore my mother) for the spare yet effective way she managed to paint a picture of the projects where she (not Rick T) had grown up, with poetry beating like a diamond in her heart.

*Thursday and Janine—*

*I know you will find this, because your father doesn't come into this room anymore. You are my daughters. Do better. Don't be pathetic. Don't ever be pathetic like me. I love you from the top of your heads to the bottom of your toes.*

And that was it. No signature. Of course it didn't need one. She knew we would know who wrote this note. I sat there—for a few seconds, for a couple of hours, I would never be sure. All I knew was that an uncertain portion of time later, someone said, "Thursday."

And when I looked up, my father was standing in the doorway. My father, tall and attractive not in the true sense, but in the showbiz sense. He had a face that people could look at for a long time because he reminded them of somebody they knew. Somebody they liked. A cousin, a brother, a friend, a father.

Right before his own father had died, Rick T had driven us to visit our paternal grandparents for the first time. Their house had only been a few neighborhoods over, and I had been surprised to find out that they lived so nearby. My grandmother opened the door, dressed in what my mother called a church suit, even though it was Wednesday.

"Oh Ricky, I'm glad you're here," she said.

He started to hug her, but she shooed him away. "No, no, get upstairs to your father. He wants to see you bad."

My father took the stairs three at a time, running to meet a man he hadn't spoken to in almost fifteen years, of whom I'd never even seen a picture.

"Mom, I have to go to the bathroom," my ten-year-old sister tended to address all of her needs and wants to my mother back then, even the ones with which she had nothing to do.

"It's right down this hallway, through the kitchen," my grandmother told Janine.

"I remember where it is. I'll show you," my mother said, also to Janine.

For the rest of the short visit, the two women would continue to talk through Janine and me, never addressing each other directly, not even to say good-bye when my father came storming down the stairs fifteen minutes after we arrived and said with a face made of angry stone, "Let's go. Let's go now."

While we were alone in the living room together, waiting for my mom and Janine to come back, my grandmother smiled at me and said, "You are the pretty girl twin of your father. Down to the eyes. The only thing that's not his on you are these adorable dimples." She squeezed my cheeks, even though I was twelve, too old for cheek pinching.

I preened, happy to be compared to my father and resenting my dimples, which I had inherited from my mother's mother, a salty old woman who refused to move from the projects and would spend most of our visits saying things like, "Ain't you smart? I bet them white people be falling all over you the way you talk. You probably think you one of them. Well, you gonna find out when you get older. You ain't that special." And then just a few minutes later, "I don't know why your mama don't bring you round here to visit more often."

"Where'd you get these dimples?" my pleasant and pretty grandmother asked me, her preacher's wife eyes taking me in like I was a delight just for existing.

"I don't know," I answered, not wanting to bring my other grandmother into the conversation, or even my own mother, who I could already tell she disliked. She did not, I discerned over the short amount of time we spent together, think my project-born mother was good enough for my suburb-raised father. She would later not even attend my mother's funeral. And by denying my dimples, I had implicitly agreed with her. I would think about this small betrayal often in the guilty years following my mother's death. But back then, like all children of the famous, I idolized the parent who spent the least amount of time with me, and took the one I saw every day for granted.

That is, I took her for granted until that night, when I read her suicide note, and looked up from it to find my father standing in the doorway.

He had been one of the first artists to make it big off the rap game, but in the year 2000, the year my mother died, he was in his early forties and it was beginning to show—not on his face, but in the fashion choices he made to hide the signs of his advancing age. Back in the nineties, during the height of his career, he had worn a beard, but then gray hairs had started popping up, springy steel harbingers of the trajectory of his career. And now he shaved every day, wearing a variety of baseball caps to cover his head and its receding hairline.

I had teased him about this, the last time I saw him before I left for China. He had laughed with me, all good-natured, and told me that he was planning to get some track pants, too, to cover up his gut. "I'm going to wear them like those old men playing chess in the park."

I had laughed, Janine had laughed, my mother had laughed. We had all laughed together, my mother especially, pretending that we were what we appeared to be: a happy family.

And now my father stood in the doorway in his baseball cap and track pants, worn with a baggy "ENYCE" T-shirt that, yes, masked his gut.

I put it together in those moments. My mother hadn't been in a car accident, swerving to avoid an animal or another car, as originally believed. She had barged through that divider and driven herself over the cliff. *Thelma and Louise* style. When I had stepped onto the plane, my mother had still been alive, undergoing hours of surgery to save the failing organs that had been beaten to death when her car had crashed into the divider and then rolled down the steep hill beyond it. But when I stepped off the plane, my mother was dead, having refused to go along with the lifesaving procedures, her life spirit tugging and tugging against the surgeons' efforts until they let her go and called her time of death.

Rick T, stuck in a mire of Janine's tears and paperwork that needed to be signed after my mother's body had been processed, sent Brenda to pick me up and keep me at the house until he got there and could tell me the news himself. He had not known about my mother's letter because, as my mother had said, he did not come in this room anymore.

Janine hadn't made the trip upstairs with him. And neither had Brenda. However, I could sense that my father's mistress was still downstairs, face appropriately sorrowful, but her heart hovering. Like a vulture.

Waiting, waiting, and smiling on the inside because my mother was dead, and she would finally have Rick T out in the open and all for herself.

The wedding band dropped out of my hand to the ground, bouncing with a metallic clink before rolling under the bed.

"Is that your mama's ring?" my father asked.

With a running start, I jumped on my six-foot-tall father and raked my fingernails across his face. "Why did you send your mistress to pick me up? How could you let her come into our home?" I asked him, shrieking every word. "You arrogant, narcissistic, cheating son of a bitch!"

I had never gotten in a fight in my entire life, but Sharita was only five-two and had grown up in Kinloch, which, according to her, was one of the rougher neighborhoods in St. Louis, rife with large, mean black girls who wanted to fight her after issuing accusations like "You think you all that" and "You think you better than me, but you ain't shit."

"The secret," Sharita told me at Smith College's BRIDGE orientation program for students of color, "is to always go for their head. Doesn't matter how big they are, they all got soft heads. Don't be noble. You got to be willing to throw dirt in their eyes if it comes to that."

My father and I fell sideways, rolling across the floor like my mother's car had rolled down that hill. Despite my head attack, he managed to push me off of him and get to his feet, confused and disoriented. And my father, the king of "It Wasn't Me," lied to me like I had heard him lie to my mother. "Brenda's not my—"

I didn't let him finish. I took a glass from the nearby nightstand and threw it at his head with a vicious sideswipe. He screamed, grabbing the side of his head where the glass had shattered against it. Blood streamed through his fingers as Rick T made wounded animal sounds.

"Thursday, stop," Janine said from the doorway.

When I saw my little sister at the door, standing behind my bleeding father, I did what she said. I came to a panting stop, only to have the house turn against me. It pushed me out of the room, stumbling by my father, rushing past Janine, and running by Brenda downstairs before it spit me out the front door, where I violently threw up in my mother's flowering bush.

How the hell was I supposed to live without a mother? My father was all career, sharp flow, and surface charm. He didn't know a damn thing about love. He had funded the whole venture, but it had been my mother that had made the four of us into a family, and now, for all intents and purposes, it was just Janine and me.

I should have started crying then, with the kitchen-sink melodrama that I had left inside the house and the taste of recently ejected airplane food still in my mouth. However, my eyes remained a desert of anger and recrimination when I looked out onto the cul-de-sac.

But then a car pulled up to the curb and two people who looked like Risa and Sharita climbed out. And as they walked toward me, I began to realize that it really was them.

That's when the tears finally came. My two best friends blurred in front of me and they caught me in their arms when I fell toward them. They held me; my taller friend, Risa, keeping me steady from above, and my shorter friend, Sharita, propping me up from below.

"What are you doing here?" I asked. "It's midterms. You can't be here."

Risa shrugged. "We told our professors we had to go see about our girl. We were all, like, 'Fuck your tests, bitches.'"

"We asked nicely to take them later so that we could come see you," Sharita translated.

Which only made me cry harder.

Brenda drove Rick T to the emergency room. I didn't know what he told the people who sewed up his stitches so soon after tending to his dead wife. Didn't care, either. I only saw him once more at the funeral. Then I went back to China to finish out my semester. From then on, I managed to find other places to stay during the holidays and school breaks. And Rick T didn't invite me to the wedding when he and Brenda got married an appropriate-enough year later.

And ten years after the day my mother died, I found myself remembering her written words. *Don't be pathetic.* I removed my hand from my purse and didn't check to see if Caleb had called again. And when I arrived home, I found my two best friends, Risa in a skimpy jumpsuit and Sharita in a gray business suit, waiting for me outside my apartment building.

I parked at the curb right in front of them. "I love you guys," I said as I got out of the car and I pulled them into my arms. "You two are the best friends ever."

"I know, how fucking amazing are we with this friendship shit?" Risa asked.

"So amazing," I answered.

We had all finished hugging when my "Tightrope" ringtone went off.

I pulled out my cell and checked the caller ID. It was a 917 number. New York. It must be Caleb. He had mentioned still needing to get his number changed, even though he had moved from Brooklyn to L.A. over six months ago.

He was finally calling me.

"Who is it?" Sharita asked.

I pushed the "Ignore" option and tossed the phone back into my bag, letting Caleb go to voicemail. "Some boy," I answered. "Want to order a pizza and watch a movie? Benny and Abigail won't be home until late."

"I got the black *Karate Kid* on DVD," Sharita said, pulling a red Netflix envelope out of her large black leather purse.

"Are you serious? How old are we, talking about watching the *Karate Kid*?" Risa asked. "And why are you carrying around Netflix in your purse?"

"It was a good movie. I keep on telling you . . ."

"I kind of wanted to see that," I said, since Tammy wasn't there to play her usual role of Sharita-Risa fight diffuser.

"Okay, fine, if Thursday wants to watch a kid's movie, too, then I guess I can deal," Risa said, stringing a skinny arm around my shoulders. She gave me a little squeeze as we all walked into my apartment building.

# November 2010

Yes, marriage is work, but that's marriage. The first six months of a relationship shouldn't be hard going, and they most certainly shouldn't be a lot of work. If the first six months of your relationship isn't mostly a Hallmark card, get out. If he's not enthusiastic about you or doesn't treat you right, or if you find you're not all that enthusiastic about him or you're not treating him right, dump him. Because if you two can't get the easy part right, how the heck do you think you guys are going to handle the hard stuff?

—*The Awesome Girl's Guide to Dating Extraordinary Men* by Davie Farrell

# THURSDAY

I had been best friends with Sharita for over a decade. Sharita skipped her midterms to be by my side when my mother died. Sharita even loaned me money to move to Los Angeles after grad school. But at that moment, I was truly considering dumping Sharita as a friend.

"What do you mean you can't come to my show?" I would have yelled this question, but I had taken the call at work. "You're seriously bailing on me at the last minute?"

"Marcus just called and he's got an extra ticket to the Earth, Wind & Fire concert at the Staples Center. Girl, you know how much I love me some Earth, Wind & Fire."

"Yes, you and my grandma," I said. "You promised. Bring him along if you want."

"I know I promised, and I would bring him, except he's black, and your whole show is about how trifling black men are," she said, like her ditching me was all my fault.

Reason #1 I didn't date black men. Black comedians and rappers could throw shade at black women all day, and black men not only laughed, but also gave them enough money to buy mansions, cars, and even more women for them to make fun of in their routines and songs. But let a black woman do a routine about how crazy black men are—suddenly everybody gets offended.

"I mean, some of your points are funny, but black men already have so many people attacking them. It just feels like you're ganging up on them," Sharita said after my first show.

Funny that she never seemed to feel like black men were attacking black women when she bought rap albums back in college or liked black comedians on Facebook who did routines about how crazy black women were.

"Can I ask why you're dating a guy that takes himself so seriously that you can't bring him to the show you promised me you would attend?"

"Did you invite Caleb to the show?" Sharita asked, her voice the sharpest pencil in the making-a-valid-point bucket.

"No, but only because nobody gets invited to see me perform if we haven't been dating for at least three months."

"Nobody's ever made it to three months."

"Sharita," I said, hand to brow. "Do you understand that you're really letting me down here? You promised me you'd come out this time."

"I'll make it up to you," Sharita answered.

My fifteen-minute break had come and gone and I could tell that I wasn't going to be able to make Sharita budge. Have you ever met one of those borderline-autistic genius types that could tell you how much 1,623,426 times 30,748,642 was without blinking an eye but couldn't, like, tie his shoe? That's kind of how Sharita was. She was brilliant with money but just plain stupid when it came to men. And she could become weirdly blind to the feelings of her friends when an eligible black man came sniffing around.

"I expect you to come to my next show with three guests," I told her.

"One," Sharita countered. This wasn't our first negotiation. "It's hard to get anyone out to anything with a two-drink minimum. Those drinks are so overpriced."

"You're accountants. You can afford it," I shot back.

"We're accountants, so we know when we're being gypped."

"Two. Final offer."

"Fine," Sharita said.

"Fine," I echoed back. Then I mumbled, "Love you," even though I didn't really feel like saying it. But my mother's death had taught me that the last thing you said to loved ones should always be "I love you." Because those might be the last words you ever got to say to them.

"Love you, too, girl," Sharita answered before hanging up.

# RISA

Thursday called me to complain about Sharita on her lunch hour. I wasn't surprised to hear she flaked on Thursday's show. Sharita is the queen of doing the things she wants to do and finding a reason not to do the things she doesn't want to do.

On one hand I felt bad for Thursday, since I wouldn't be there either because of my Space Camp show. On the other hand, during my many years as a lesbian with straight friends, I'd noticed that straight girls tended to fall out with each other when one or both of them got into a new relationship. Things they didn't mind about each other before suddenly became major problems, which usually didn't get resolved until one or both of them broke up with whomever they were dating and decided that the other wasn't so bad after all. Half the time, Thursday and Sharita couldn't remember what they got so mad about a few weeks later. I'd have to remind them, just because I like instigating shit.

But the lunchtime bitch session took my mind off that night's show for an hour. It also gave me the chance to smoke five Parliaments on my balcony, which killed a little bit of the hunger and anxiety chewing up my stomach.

I was still trying to figure out the set list. Should I play all new stuff or should I make some room for a couple of the Sweet Janes hits like the Space Camp manager wanted? It might remind the Gravestone Records guy that I used to be a rock star.

Used to be.

On one hand, the reminder might seem desperate. On the other hand, it might be needed.

After I got off the phone with Thursday, I decided to spend the next two hours choosing an outfit while eating a Luna bar really slowly. Risa Rule: I only ate food-food between the hours of one a.m. and five a.m., but I always nibbled down a couple of energy bars on show days, because if I didn't I might get too weak to perform and then faint on stage. I found that one out the hard way a few years ago, and was still paying off the E.R. bill since I didn't have insurance.

After settling on a rainbow-striped bikini top and neon-green skinny jeans worn under my illegal R2D2 hoodie (which I snagged off Etsy before Lucas's lawyers came in and shut the designer down), I was still no closer to a set-list decision.

So I called Tammy. Voicemail. Why wasn't she ever there when I needed her? The two of us were supposed to be friends. I even introduced her to Thursday and Sharita after she made that common pretty-girl complaint that she didn't have any female friends, and now she was all cozy inside my group. But she rarely picked up the phone these days. I considered texting her to explain that "friends" don't always send "friends" to fucking voicemail.

But I really did need help with this set-list issue, so I called Thursday back. She told me to play the Sweet Janes songs. I said that it kind of went against my principles.

She said, "We're too old to still have principles. I would kill for the chance to sell out."

Then she made me hold on while she wrote that one down to use in a future routine.

# THURSDAY

The comedy business was an interesting one, because toward the beginning of a career, small comedy club owners didn't really care how good a comedian was. Small comedy clubs weren't really looking for the next Adam Sandler or Wanda Sykes. They wanted to get butts in the seats. So it didn't matter how badly a comic performed. If they had at least ten people in the two-drink minimum audience, then they'd always be invited back.

Thanks to my grad school connections, I had gotten over fifty people to come out the first time I played the Laugh Out Loud in North Hollywood. But tonight I had exactly zero guests on my roster. After arriving at the club, I avoided Louis, the Laugh Out Loud's squat and buttoned-up owner, and slunk back to the green room, which was actually painted dark blue and outfitted with a mishmash of furniture repurposed from trash-collection curbs all over the city.

"Hey, Thursday," most of the other guys called out when I came in.

There weren't a lot of female comics who lasted more than a few months in the harsh world of L.A. stand-up and there were even fewer black females. So when I walked into any comedy club's dingy not-actually-green room, the other inhabitants usually knew me, even if I couldn't return the greeting properly since they were all mostly Jewish or Italian and either really skinny or really overweight. And though I had learned many of their names at one point, I had ceased being able to tell them apart and had resorted to labeling them by their acts. Like Former Drug Addict Comic, who was running his routine under his breath in the corner, and Still Lives With His Mother Comic, who sat on one of the few couches without springs sticking out, with his head between his knees—probably trying not to hyperventilate. More than any other profession, I thought, stand-up came with the most stage fright. Yes, even more stage fright than acting. After all, actors didn't have to worry about their audiences heckling them.

"Hey, guys," I said, keeping my greeting vague. "Looks like a good house." The better-than-average turnout made me feel less guilty about not having anyone in the audience myself.

"Nobody big, though," Extreme Physical Comedy Comic said.

By "nobody big," he meant no agents, no head writers, no A-list comedians looking for writers, nobody who could take you from struggling to making a decent living with just one nod.

But then Bug-Eyed Can't Get A Date Comic came in and said, "Hey, did you hear yet? Mike Barker just walked in."

We all stared at him. It should be noted that Mike Barker was considered the black late-thirtysomething equivalent of George Clooney, thanks to his clean-cut, accessible good looks combined with considerable acting skills. He had enough clout to assign his own rewriter to all of his scripts. And though he usually stuck to action and Oscar-bait dramas these days, he had started off in romantic comedies, so he occasionally decided to do a winter one for his original fans. But if he was at the Laugh Out Loud, "occasionally" must be now.

I knew for sure, though, that Mike Barker wouldn't be tapping me. In the world of comedy, men hired men to do all of their writing. And even black actors would skip straight to a white male writer if no good black male writers were to be found. For everybody else in the room, though, Mike Barker's walking in was a writer-comedian's wet dream come true.

Right on cue, Still Lives With His Mother Comic started hyperventilating.

# RISA

9 thought about forcing myself to throw up to dislodge the fear rumbling in my stomach, but then I decided not to, because I needed those three Luna bars to get through the show.

The first two bands on the bill had come and played, and I was the last act. It had been over fifteen minutes since the previous band walked off, and indie crowds didn't get restless but club managers did, so I knew I had better get out there before the Space Camp guy came knocking on the dressing room door.

But I didn't move. Instead I stared at myself in the foggy mirror, willing Lisa to go away and Risa to take over. Lisa was the one in charge of fussing over my clothes and my weight and my image. Lisa always felt like she was betraying The One whenever she slept with a groupie or somebody she met while bartending. Risa, however, didn't give a fuck. Risa played the guitar hard and ate whatever she wanted to from one a.m. to five a.m., and if a cute chick gave Risa the eye, she took that cute chick home.

I was a Gemini. And at that moment I was waiting for my better, badder twin to take over.

"What the fuck are we waiting for? Let's do this," a voice said inside my head.

And I smiled. There she was.

That night, I played my electric guitar like NASCAR and ripped through lyrics like the Hulk. It felt like only ten minutes had passed, but pretty soon I'd gone through my entire Supa Dupa set list and there was only one thing left to decide: my last song was always a cover—but would it be a Sweet Janes cover?

My body was bathed in sweat. I could even feel the wetness inside my high-top vintage Adidas. It squished in between my toes as I stepped up to the mic.

I dipped my chin to my chest, and I waited for it.

Then I hit the pre-recorded drum track on my synthesizer and strummed out the opening riff to "Party Hard" by Andrew W.K.

There were only three females on the whole planet who could sing a metal song better than the original guy who sang it: Joan Jett, Courtney Love, and muthafuckin' me.

The Gravestone rep, who was half leaning on the bar in his short-sleeved shirt and skinny tie with a vodka on the rocks in his hand, finally stood up and took some interest. I stared him down so hard, he turned his body fully toward the stage. Toward me. I was a future rock star. And if he didn't know it before, he for damn sure knew it then.

# SHARITA

The problem, I had found, with being a giver is that you can never give enough. It seemed to me that every time I got in a good place and started making headway with a guy, that was when my friends started accusing me of being a bad girlfriend, forgetting everything I had done for them with a drop of a disappointed dime.

My conversation with Thursday lingered in my head as I parked in the ridiculously overpriced garage beneath L.A. Live, an outdoor mall of expensive restaurants and nightclubs that had sprouted up around the Nokia Theater and Staples Center a couple of years ago.

The expense of parking made it even more annoying when I got to the venue right at seven, only to find that Marcus hadn't arrived yet. However, when he came jogging up to me twenty minutes later, he looked so good in his dark denim jeans and gray blazer that I felt something release in my stomach. My heart's crystal ball filled me with another vision of those two strong baby boys inside of him, inside of me, inside of our possible future together. I forgave him for being late even before he kissed me on the cheek and said, "Hey, baby."

I'd loved Earth, Wind & Fire ever since my mama introduced them to me via a scratchy LP back when I was a little girl. But the best part of the concert was when Marcus pulled me in front of him during "I Think About Lovin' You" and rocked us both from side to side, swaying to the beat.

Afterward, we ended up at the Yard House, a sports bar/restaurant hybrid, for a late dinner—a really late dinner, as it turned out, since the Yard House didn't take reservations. Marcus hadn't chosen a place that took reservations and then made one, like I would have if I had been in charge of the date. But I wasn't, so, according to the hostess, we would have to wait outside the popular restaurant "for at least twenty minutes."

"Are you cold?" he asked when we got back outside. "I can give you my blazer."

I scooted a little closer to him and nuzzled my nose into his thick bicep. "No, I'm fine."

"Have I mentioned how good you look tonight?" he asked me.

My heart fluttered and I looked down at my black, empire-waist date dress, which hugged my ample chest but flared out to mask my stomach. It had been a while since a man had told me I looked good. "Thanks," I said.

He stroked my arms. "You've got goose bumps," he said. "Here . . ."

He leaned forward and kissed me, his juicy lips exploring mine a little before his tongue slipped into my mouth. It was a good kiss. A very good kiss. I had no idea how long it lasted, only that when he pulled back I felt like he had stopped too soon.

"Hey, you want to skip dinner and go back to your place?"

The romantic Earth, Wind & Fire ballad that had been playing in my head ever since we had floated out of the concert came to an abrupt halt as I pulled out my mental date calculator. This was our third date. I liked to wait for at least the fifth before I had sex; also, I had skipped lunch, so I was pretty hungry.

But Marcus looked even hungrier. For me.

"Okay," I said. "Let's go."

# THURSDAY

M y last time on stage as a stand-up comedian began like all of my others. I walked out and took the mic, my movements stiff with a nauseous mix of fear and dread. I wondered, as I always did, how my father and Risa did this so naturally. How could they feel comfortable performing in a room full of people, most of which they couldn't see, but knew were out there, staring at them, waiting to be entertained?

I shoved the fear away and with a great amount of effort opened my mouth to say, "First of all: Hello. Second of all: How about this black love stuff? Isn't that a crock of shit?"

As usual, a stunned silence met my opening line. From the start, my bohemian appearance and my delivery had been the two things that hurt my comedy career the most. I had never been able to bring myself to "coon it up," as my mother used to call employing a quote-unquote black accent while performing, as opposed to speaking as one does in day-to-day life. My father had been lucky. Having grown up the son of a preacher, he inherited a ringing voice that made him sound like the love child of Dr. Martin Luther King and Nikki Giovanni. But me—how can I put this?—I sounded white, exactly like my nasally Connecticut upbringing. When I opened my mouth, all my good schooling and New England background came spilling out.

At the same time, with my long green sundress, dreadlocks, and dimples, I didn't exactly look like someone who didn't believe in black love. My opening line was never, ever greeted with anything but a few uncomfortable chuckles while the audience scrambled to catch up.

"Let me tell you something. Here's what black love got me." I ticked it off on my fingers. "A bunch of his bills that I had to pay before he could take me out, a bunch of late-night phone calls from a very classy woman named LaQuanda Green."

I then went on to do a pretty terrible impression of LaQuanda insisting that I had stolen her man, even though he and LaQuanda had only dated for two weeks. And then I launched into the subsequent arguments with my fictional boyfriend, who kept insisting that if I would just pay his cell phone bill, he could not only call LaQuanda and tell her to stop bothering me, but also take me to a nice dinner. A really nice dinner . . . at Applebee's.

Strike three against black love, I told the crowd, had been the chlamydia. "It was itchy," I wailed. "I was like, 'This is TOO MUCH DRAMA. I've got to get myself a white boy!'"

Despite my appearance and the fact that my impressions of LaQuanda and my broke boyfriend didn't sound anywhere near authentic, the writing in my routine was usually strong enough to garner a few laughs. Not tonight, though. Tonight the audience was silent, save for a few whispered conversations, ice tinkling around in glasses as people drank to get through my routine, and one guy laughing uproariously in the back. He was probably drunk and his solo laughing somehow made the rest of the audience's non-response that much more noticeable.

The Laugh Out Loud manager gave me the cue to wrap it up, and I brought my routine to its painful conclusion. "Heeeeey. I notice there are a lot of white boys in here. Come see me after the show. The chlamydia is all cleared up. I'm single and ready to mingle."

I came out of my shtick with a forced laugh and stilted wave to the audience. "My name is Thursday, but I'm about the comedy every day. Thanks, guys."

I jogged off the stage, my underarms slick with sweat, the burn of the stage lights replaced by the burn of my own embarrassment. This was the first show I'd ever done without any friends whatsoever in the audience and

I had bombed. I mean bombed bad. I fully expected to soon be receiving condolence letters from Hiroshima survivors, I had gone down so bad.

*I'm not funny.*

The thought appeared clear and bright, shining with truth in the back-stage dark.

There had been an awkward moment a few months ago when Sharita, Tammy, Risa, and I had been at brunch. Risa had said something particularly biting, and we had all laughed, with Sharita declaring after it was all done, "Girl, you are a trip. You are the funniest person I know."

"Me too," Tammy said with clasped hands, trilling with laughter.

I stopped laughing. "I thought I was the funniest person you know," I said to them.

*That was the moment*, I thought now, walking through the backstage wing, which led to the green room. I should have paid more attention. Because the laughter had died in my friends' throats and after much hemming and hawing, Tammy came up with, "Day, you're more technically funny, while Risa's more improv funny."

And I, who had never had to worry about being cool before, because being the daughter of a music star had come with the privilege of being able to dress and act however I wanted for my entire life without worrying about such non-music-progeny concerns as "cool," felt an entirely new emotion: jealousy. For the first time, I looked at Risa, the first-generation daughter of Catholic Ghanaians, and compared myself to her. I wished that I could say whatever I wanted and get away with it. I wished that when I got up on stage, it made random people want to take me home and sleep with me.

I eventually decided that if I studied cool the way Risa did, taking forever to get dressed, cackling as opposed to laughing, claiming to be unavailable by reason of brooding over The One, Heathcliff style, tapping my carton of cigarettes on the table and walking away without a word as opposed to saying, "Excuse me, I'm going to go smoke a cigarette now." If I did that, I would be cool, too. But I didn't want to be cool like that. I was happy being myself, I insisted. Back then, it had seemed like a beautiful moment of self-acceptance.

But now I could see that my cool factor hadn't been what I should have been worried about. When Friend A says to a comedian's Friend B that she is the funniest person she knows, and Friend C agrees, causing the comedian to take exception with that, the best way to prove this isn't true is to say something funny. But I had just gotten offended. Which was the opposite of funny. Because the truth was, I wasn't funny. I had been kidding myself, I realized, for over two years now, chasing a dream that my limited talent set wasn't capable of fulfilling.

My parents had sent me to the best schools; I'd been granted so many luxuries growing up, with the expectation that I would eventually make something of myself. But I was useless. Worse than useless. I was, I realized at that moment, a negative deficit of a woman, unable to make my dreams come true, no matter how hard I tried. And all that money and effort that had gone toward helping me fulfill my potential had been wasted.

A picture of me throwing up in the bushes after finding my mother's suicide note came back to me then. I thought of her, rotting away in her grave while I rotted away in my life, and the shame of it all became unbearable. Much like the night I had dumped my last one-month stand, I was overcome with the desire to be somebody else, anybody else but me. And entering the hallway, which was full of comics waiting to go on after me, only made the shame worse. Some of them gave me sympathetic looks. Most of them ignored me, concentrating on their own lines, probably hoping that my lack of talent couldn't be transferred like an airborne illness.

I had to kill myself, I thought. Anything to escape this shame. I could drive myself to San Francisco, throw myself off their most famous bridge. I got so caught up in the image of my body sailing through the air before it hit the cold water, canceling this hot shame forever, that I walked straight into Caleb, who was waiting outside the green room.

And here I had thought the night couldn't get any worse.

"Hey," I said, both surprised and chagrined. I definitely wouldn't have told the chlamydia joke if I'd known he was in the audience. "What are you doing here?"

He gave me a sly smile. "A little birdie named Abigail might have told me you were performing tonight."

"Oh . . ." So the one laughing guy hadn't been drunk. It was Caleb, giving me pity laughs.

I desperately wanted to tell him that I had based that set on an old boyfriend of Sharita's, that I'd never had chlamydia, and, moreover, hadn't decided to only start dating white guys exclusively because of the imaginary LaQuanda Green. But I didn't know how to say all of that without bringing up my copious daddy issues. It would sound like I was lying or, even worse, sweating him so hard that I really cared what he thought. Dating in L.A. was a beast-versus-beast kind of situation. A woman couldn't afford to let a guy she liked think she cared about him too early in a relationship. It was the exact same thing as exposing your neck to a circling lion.

So I stood there, frying in a pan of embarrassment and yearning for the Golden Gate Bridge. "Well, thanks for coming out," I said.

But if the chlamydia joke bothered him, he didn't show it. "You were great. Funny," he said, rubbing my arm.

"Thanks," I said, thinking that he had already morphed into an Angeleno. It had become a cosmic and continuously surprising mystery as to who was going to go on to be somebody someday, so no one in Los Angeles ever gave you their true opinions about a performance unless they really, really enjoyed it. Consequently, if L.A. audiences were to be believed, every single actor, comedian, and musician had been great in every single thing they had ever done.

After our initial exchange, Caleb and I stood there awkwardly. The problem with being a "sex on the first date" sort of person was that I had no idea how the actual courting process was supposed to go. Usually if I was attracted to a guy, I slept with him. Then when things got too deep on his part, I left him. But I was turning over a new leaf with Caleb. So far we'd been on three dates that ended in awkward-but-sweet kisses and a promise on his part to call.

Him showing up at what I had just minutes ago decided would be the last show in my ill-considered comedy career, which had been meant to replace my ill-considered screenwriting career, threw me off my new version of game. How did one conduct one's self when one wasn't trying to negotiate a guy straight into bed?

"That set didn't go so hot," I said, giving a tentative poke at the truth.

Caleb was polite enough, but apparently he wasn't a liar either. "Yeah, the audience was kind of dead," he said, choosing his words so carefully that I could almost see the consideration that each one had been given as it came out his mouth.

"You know what?" I told him. "I think I'm over comedy. I mean it was fun, but it's time for me to pursue something else."

"Something else like what?" he asked.

"I don't know yet. Something that makes me feel like a worthy person, less tired of being me all the time. I want to be better than this, you know?"

I could see him struggling to come up with an appropriate answer and knew that I had taken this conversation too far. It was too early in our relationship to let him see that I wasn't as breezy and confident as I came off on our first few dates. I had exposed my neck.

But I covered it with a wave of my hand. "Hey," I said, switching my tone of voice back to the Thursday I had been with him up until now, the fun and happy woman who didn't have a ton of issues and wouldn't be dumping him at our thirty-day mark. "Let's go get a drink or something. Want to go get a drink?"

He considered my offer for a beat or two, but then said, "Sure."

I vowed to correct the damage I'd done. We'd get drinks and I'd invite him back to my place and we'd have sex for the first time. When he looked back on this night, that's what he'd remember. Not the routine that failed, not me whining about wanting to be a better person, but our first night of fabulous sex, the continuation of the honeymoon that was our first six months.

But, then, Caleb went still, his eyes wandering toward something over my shoulder.

"Mike Barker is headed this way," he whispered, right before putting on his best nonchalant face. He really was becoming a true Angeleno. In New York, people would honk and call out to celebs on the street, but the one super-big rule in Los Angeles was that you should never let a celebrity catch you staring, even if that celebrity was as huge as Mike Barker.

I tried to look over my shoulder as casually as possible, dying to know which comic Mike Barker had come back here to see. Probably Still Lives With His Mother. His dating life was a mess waiting to be exploited for some bad man-child romantic comedy.

"You know he used to go with a friend of mine," I said. "Strung her along for, like, a year, asked her to marry him, then one day he dumped her out of the blue. Left her for some actress."

Caleb frowned and said, "I don't want to harsh on your story or anything, but I'm not big on gossip. I feel it brings the wrong kind of energy to a conversation."

"Oh," I said, feeling like I had put my foot in my mouth for the third time that night. "I was telling you, because there was that weird connection."

"Yeah, I understand. No worries," he said, rubbing my arm again. And I relaxed. One of the things I liked most about Caleb was his ability to make others instantly feel at ease. It was like dating a non-celibate version of the Dalai Lama. I thought to myself, *Yes, this is what I need. Not a career in comedy but a relationship with someone who challenges me to be better person.*

For a moment, I forgot all about Mike Barker, and for the first time in my entire dating life, I smiled at a guy in goofy way. "I really like you," I told him.

He pulled me in close. "I really like you, too."

"Hey, sorry for interrupting," a voice said above us.

We looked up to see Mike Barker standing there in a vintage terry-cloth, short-sleeved button-up shirt and designer jeans.

"Sorry," I said, thinking he wanted us to get out of the way, since we were blocking the entrance to the green room. I stepped back from Caleb to give him space to pass.

"No, I'm here to see you. Hi . . ." he said, shaking Caleb's hand first and then mine. "I'm Mike Barker."

See, this is what I don't like about actors: they were always acting. You should have seen Mike Barker. Ridiculously tall and handsome, but radiating humbleness, like there was even a remote chance that Caleb and I didn't know who he was.

"Hey," Caleb answered, playing along.

But it felt too silly to play his introduction game, so I kept my mouth closed, waiting for an explanation as to why a movie star like him would be seeking out a female comedian who had just bombed on stage.

"That was, uh . . . a really interesting five minutes," he said to me, obviously biting back laughter at my expense. "Not what I expected at all from you."

Okay, it wasn't exactly true that no one in Los Angeles said what they really thought of your performance. Once you got to a certain level of fame, you could pretty much say whatever you wanted. And in Los Angeles speak, "interesting" was the equivalent of "awful."

"I know it's really far from Beverly Hills, so that was so nice of you to come all the way out here to tell me my set was 'interesting.'"

Mike did not miss my sarcasm, and to his credit he backpedaled a little bit. "No, not interesting-bad. I think the reason you bombed was because of delivery. The way you say things—especially listening to it as a black man—comes off as pretty insulting. And really angry . . ."

Did I forget to mention that I hate when black men accuse black women of being angry? No? Oh, well, I should tell you now then. I hate that so . . .

"You didn't like my set because I was angry? So was every other comic that came before me," I pointed out. "You see, comedians are kind of in the business of being angry and insulting. Maybe it's that you don't like when black women in particular are angry toward black men, because you are, in fact, a typical, double-standardy black male."

Mike stared at me. Hard. And something glinted in the back of his eyes. I met his gaze, letting him know that I wasn't afraid of him, that I didn't care what he thought of me. But then, the stare-off ended just as abruptly as it had begun. Like a Greek stage player, Mike changed out his straight-face mask for a smiling one.

"Listen," he said. "I feel like we're getting off on the wrong foot. I'm here because I'm producing and starring in a new biopic about your father."

I did a double take. "A biopic. About my father," I repeated. "You, Mike Barker, are planning to play my father in a film."

"Yes, he's an amazing man and I think it's time he got his due."

Reason #2 that I didn't date black guys: They were dumb. I mean soooo dumb. For example, they were forever choosing the worst men and making them their heroes. Name any strutting basketball star, swaggering rapper, or unevolved football player, and you'll find a black man hustling to be just like him. I could only stare at this actor who had stomped all over Tammy's good heart, who had just told me that my father deserved a biopic because he was a great man.

"I want to ask you a few questions about your dad, and possibly bring you in as a script vet," he said. "Call me."

He pressed a business card into my hand, and I continued to stare at him, the shock of what he had told me rooting my tongue in my mouth. I watched him shake Caleb's hand again and murmur something. Then, with a squeeze of my shoulder and a blindingly white smile, he was gone.

Leaving Caleb to turn to me with a very confused look on his face. "Who's your father? And why does Mike Barker want to play him in a movie?"

# December 2010

Why continue to date a guy who's not excited about being with you? If the enthusiasm ain't there now, it definitely won't be there later.

—*The Awesome Girl's Guide to Dating Extraordinary Men* by Davie Farrell

# EVERYBODY

The majority of Americans list Christmas as their favorite holiday, but this isn't the case in Los Angeles. As anyone who has lived in the city for even a couple of years could attest, Halloween is the absolute number one holiday. Angelenos take it very seriously, spending enormous amounts of time planning their costumes and coming up with overly considered, precious party themes like "Silent Movie Stars Who Died Too Young" or "Zombie Pirates" or "Jimmy Buffet Was Here."

There was no holiday Los Angeles took more seriously than Halloween. Which was why, in many ways, New Year's Eve, the second most popular holiday in Los Angeles, was considerably more fun for everybody involved. Like clockwork, a hysterical optimism took over the city, with every model, former comedian, musician, and accounting partner alike believing that the coming year would be the one in which everything they had previously hoped for in the current year would HAPPEN! in caps and with a big exclamation mark.

2011 was also the year that Risa, Sharita, and Thursday would all be turning thirty, so their hopes and dreams were kicked into overdrive by the prospect of another full decade of their lives having passed them by.

"Your thirties are going to be so great," Tammy, who was thirty-two, assured them throughout 2010. "I remember this calm coming over me when I turned thirty. I didn't feel anxious anymore like I used to in my twenties. And I became so much more accepting of my flaws."

"What flaws are you talking about, exactly?" Thursday asked her. Life was Tammy's silver platter: she had looks, millionaire money, a spokesmodel job for a worldwide brand, and such a friendly, upbeat personality that it was hard for Thursday to begrudge her the first three—even though Tammy had never worked particularly hard to receive any of them.

"Oh, I have them," Tammy said with a tinkling laugh. "I just don't dwell on them. That's why I think my thirties have been going so well. You'll see."

Back then, Thursday had answered Tammy's optimistic prediction with the most cynical of "harrumphs." But when December 31st rolled around, even Thursday, who had recently grown despondent about her career, allowed herself to get caught up in the mass delusion that was a New Year's Eve spent in Los Angeles.

However, as much as their group enjoyed being on the same hopeful page at this time of the year, they found themselves in a familiar quandary every December 31st. They loved each other, but they all had rather different versions of what they preferred to do on New Year's Eve.

Thursday usually went to a party at someone's eastside apartment, where she ended up talking all night with her fellow NYU grad school friends, who didn't dance, didn't do any drugs heavier than pot, and who wouldn't even think of throwing a party without plenty of red wine and gourmet cheese on hand.

Risa, however, would slit her wrists before agreeing to attend some boring grown-up party on New Year's Eve. She liked to be on stage at midnight, leading the crowd in the countdown before ripping into an electric version of "Auld Lang Syne."

Tammy, on the other hand, could most often be found at a sophisticated party on New Year's Eve. Her sister was married to a jazz club owner, and tonight she would don an evening gown and attend the swanky ball that he threw every year, raising her champagne glass with the rest of the well-heeled crowd at midnight.

Sharita preferred to stay home on New Year's Eve. She ordered in from her favorite Italian restaurant, made a list of next year's goals, and (here was the really fun part) wrote an action plan to achieve those goals. Unlike Risa and Thursday, she didn't believe that "putting it out there to the Universe" was enough to get the job done. Most nights she went to bed by nine or ten, so if she stayed up long enough to see Ryan Seacrest countdown to the Times Square ball-drop on New Year's Eve, she considered it a wild enough night.

Accordingly, the four women had made a tradition of catching lunch and a matinee movie at the ArcLight Cinemas in Hollywood on New Year's Eve. That year, after watching a matinee of *Tangled,* the only movie they could even partially agree on, they gathered upstairs at the ArcLight's informal restaurant/bar and ordered champagne for a New Year's Eve Day toast.

"You're Tam Farrell, right?" A tall woman with an asymmetrical bob, dressed all in black, approached their table. Her monochrome clothing choice and direct demeanor screamed New Yorker on vacation.

Tammy, who had been featured on billboards all over NYC and L.A., her honey-blonde hair happily blowing in the wind while she hailed a cab, confirmed that it was she.

"Ooh, I love Farrell Cosmetics. That's all I use. Your family makes the best stuff."

Tammy thanked her for the compliment even though technically her family didn't make the "stuff." They'd sold the company to a French conglomerate years ago, but the buyout went off so seamlessly that unless one was in the habit of reading the business section, most of Farrell Cosmetic's customers still didn't realize that there had been an exchange of ownership.

"And can I also tell you how pissed I was when they replaced you with Naki Okwelo? I mean, you're like American royalty. These African models keep taking all the fashion jobs."

Tammy, who had been feeling as if a tiara had been ripped off her ever since her brother, James Farrell, the new head of marketing at Farrell Cosmetics, had taken her to dinner three months ago and informed her that they would be going in a different, younger direction and therefore wouldn't be needing her services anymore, lowered her eyes.

"Naki is gorgeous, and we're lucky to have her," she said with as much demure humility as she could dredge up from her jealous soul.

The woman thankfully left after a few more awkward exchanges and reassurances that Tammy would always be the face of Farrell Cosmetics in her mind. And when Tammy turned back to the table, she found her three friends staring at her.

"When the hell did you get fired from Farrell Cosmetics?" Risa asked.

"August," Tammy said. "And it's fine. It was time for me to pursue other things."

"Wait," Risa said. "You got fired in August and you're just now telling us about it?"

"Don't be mad, Risa," Tammy said. "You know I don't like being gloomy."

Her explanation was met with stunned silence, everyone at the table intensely aware that none of them had ever known Tammy as anything but the face of Farrell Cosmetics.

Tammy couldn't bear their looks, which were just a few shades away from pity. She rushed to fill the silence with her personal brand of optimism and sunshine. "Plus, I didn't see any reason to tell you until I had something positive to take away from the experience. And now I do. I've decided to transition into acting, I've already booked my first spot, and it's a national one, for a Verizon commercial. Really, I'm so excited about my future right now."

The waiter showed up with their champagne then, and as he poured, Thursday regarded Tammy with open admiration. Only Tammy would lose a job she'd held for over a decade and spin it into a silver lining. She wondered why she herself couldn't ever do that, why she considered jumping off a roof every day now because of her latest career setback, and she quietly resolved not to daydream about killing herself in 2011, to be happier, more optimistic, more like Tammy.

Sharita, on the other hand, made a mental note not to tell her sister, Nicole, who had taken considerable loans to go to grad school at Yale, that Tammy, a former model with no acting experience whatsoever, had booked an ad for the same company that rejected her sister. But out loud, she said to Tammy, "I'm proud of you, girl."

"Thanks," Tammy answered.

"While we're on the subject I've got some good news, too," Risa said. "The A&R guy at Gravestone sent my version of 'Party Hard' to some music supervisor he knows and now they're using it for a teen movie starring one of those kids from some CW show."

"Which one?" Sharita, their television expert, asked. "*Gossip Girl? Vampire Diaries? 90210? Hellcats? Smallville?*"

"Yeah, one of those," Risa said. She watched sci-fi with Sharita, pretty much everything on HBO and Showtime, and sometimes a few DVRed episodes of the Nick Jr. show *Yo Gabba Gabba!* when she got home from bartending, so she had no idea what Sharita was talking about.

Before Sharita could press her further, Thursday chimed in with, "I've also got some good news and . . . some weird news. The good news is Caleb and I have been dating for three months, so you guys can meet him."

Thursday didn't believe in introducing a boy to her friends if she hadn't been dating him for at least three months, and since she used to be a serial one-month stander this meant her friends had yet to meet anyone she'd ever dated. "Since I'm turning thirty next month, I'm going to throw a party at my place and you all can come out and meet him. That means you, too, Sharita."

Sharita's eyes widened. "It's your birthday. Of course I'll come."

"I'm going to remember you said that," Thursday said.

"You should get her to write it down. Like a contract," Risa said.

Sharita swatted Risa's shoulder. "Okay, I'm not that bad. I said I'd come, and I'll be there."

"I believe you," Tammy said.

"Thank you," Sharita told her with pointed looks at both Thursday and Risa. "Why can't ya'll be more like Tammy?" Then, before they could answer with something snide, or worse, true, she said, "Moving on, what's the weird news, Day?"

Thursday fiddled with the stem of her champagne glass. "I kind of don't know how to bring this up, so I guess I'll just say it quick. This actor-slash-producer approached me last month because he's planning to do a biopic about my dad, and I told him I wasn't interested in it because of, you know, me hating Rick T and all that. But he kept on calling me. And finally, he straight up offered me ten thousand dollars just to read the script and give him my notes. Which is great. I have no problems unleashing on a script about my father, and I could really use the money to put a dent in my NYU loans."

Thursday averted her eyes so that she wouldn't have to look at Tammy as she said the next thing. "Only thing is, it's Mike Barker making the movie, so . . . "

She trailed off and peeked sideways at Tammy.

"My ex, Mike Barker, is producing a film about your father?" Tammy asked.

"I know, crazy, right? You two broke up before I met you, but I don't want to go there if it's going to mess up our friendship."

Sharita and Risa's eyes ping-ponged between Thursday and Tammy. Thursday's weird news entered a rather gray area of Girlfriend Law. In the real world outside of Los Angeles, it was somewhat implicitly understood that one didn't date, work with, or really do anything whatsoever with a good friend's ex. But in the City of Angels, getting paid for entertainment work trumped all. For example, if Tammy got an offer to star in a Rick T video, she would have Thursday's blessing. But in this case, neither Sharita nor Risa knew how Tammy would respond to the prospect of Thursday working with Mike Barker.

After a few moments of uncomfortable silence, Tammy plastered on a gentle smile. "Don't worry. Mike is so far in the past, and it's a new day."

Thursday let out a full-body sigh of relief. "Thank you for being so cool about this."

Tammy answered with a weak trill of laughter that didn't sound at all authentic to either Sharita or Risa. "It's not like you two are dating or anything. Right? Hahaha . . ."

Thursday screwed up her nose. "I would never, ever do that," she said. "I mean he's hot or whatever. But he's, like, zero percent substance. And he's dumb. And he's an actor. And he's playing my dad in a movie. And didn't he used to be some kind of gambling addict? Eww."

Not until she was putting all of her vocal might into the word "eww" did Thursday realize that putting down Tammy's ex might verge on putting down Tammy for having dated him in the first place, which caused her to get embarrassed all over again.

But Tammy, who had been raised to remain Southern and graceful under any situation, said, "I wish I'd seen all that bad stuff you see when I met him for the first time." She shook her head. "Seriously, it is no big deal. You have my blessing and my best wishes."

Thursday tipped her glass toward Tammy. "Thank you. My bank account thanks you. My college loan company thanks you—"

This was where Sharita cut her off. "Don't use the money to pay off your college loans. That's good debt and you're not paying that much in interest. Get rid of your credit card debt first, and if you have anything left over after that, put the rest into a rainy-day fund."

"Good advice," Thursday said, not because she agreed, but because she had learned over the years that agreeing with Sharita was the only way to stop a stream of unsolicited money advice.

Tammy asked then, "Sharita, do you have any good news? How's it going with Mark?"

"Marcus," Sharita said, putting her BlackBerry away. "And it's going really great, except . . ." She trailed off.

"Except what?" Thursday asked, sitting forward.

"Except we're kind of in a rut."

"Already?" Risa said. "You've only been dating for, like, two weeks, right?"

"Six weeks," Sharita said. "And we see each other all the time. In fact, we saw each four times last week. The only thing is we don't ever go out anywhere."

"Oh, you need to dump him," Thursday said.

"I KNEW you would say that. That's why I didn't even want to tell you."

"If he's not acting enthusiastic about you, you need to dump him. That's, like, all of chapter five in *The Awesome Girl's Guide*."

"Please stop quoting that book to me, and I'm not a big going-out person anyway."

"Then why did you describe it as a rut?" Risa asked.

"Because I wouldn't mind going out to eat or something every once in a while. Lately he's been coming over to my house and just kind of laying there on the couch while I cook us something, then we watch TV and go to sleep."

Risa laughed. "You're already that domesticated and you've only been dating for six weeks? Why didn't you tell me you were a lesbian?"

"Not really, because most lesbians still go out to eat, right?" Sharita frowned into her champagne glass, her initial defensiveness cross-fading into mild despondency.

But Tammy came to the rescue. "Hey, guys, let's not worry about men or jobs or money for the rest of the day, okay? The point is that 2011 is going to be our Best Year Ever. I can feel it in my bones. Who's with me?"

Sharita couldn't resist Tammy's happy smile. "I am," she said, raising her glass.

"Me, too," Thursday said, raising her own glass.

"Me three," Risa said, bringing her glass straight up into the air above her head.

"To 2011, our Best. Year. Ever," Tammy said.

"Our Best Year Ever!" they all repeated, clinking glasses.

Yes, Los Angeles was a strange and magical place, casting its optimistic spell anew over its inhabitants year after year. When these four women clinked their glasses together, they all truly believed that this would be their Best Year Ever. Little did they know that when the next New Year's Eve rolled around, one of them would describe 2011 as her Worst Year Ever, one of them would describe it as The Year That Everything Changed, one of them would describe it as The Year My Dream Finally Came True, and one of them would describe it as The Year I Learned To Live.

But not one of them would describe 2011 as her Best Year Ever.

# January 2011

A lot of women waste a lot of time worrying about what men want from them, when they should really be figuring out what they want from a man. If you want to be a girlfriend and he just wants to be friends forever and a day, don't bend over backwards to accommodate him. Dump him and get with somebody who's looking for the kind of girlfriend you want to be.

—*The Awesome Girl's Guide to Dating Extraordinary Men* by Davie Farrell

# THURSDAY

The morning of my birthday dawned bright and clear. I turned and looked at the alarm-slash-weather clock that Sharita had given me for Christmas 2009—Sharita always gave Risa and me the exact same gift as if we were siblings who would resent each other if we suspected any favoritism on her part. The gift clock declared in bright-orange numbers a low of sixty-three degrees and a high of seventy-five. In other words, it would be a perfect California winter day.

As if to confirm this, Caleb tugged on my arm and pulled me to him for a kiss, morning breath and all. That was another thing I loved about white guys. They didn't expect you to maintain absurd standards of hygiene. Sharita had been keeping a travel-sized bottle of Scope in her nightstand's drawer ever since one of her exes told her that morning breath turned him off.

I would have answered, "Your ridiculousness turns me off." But of course, Sharita had bought mouthwash and, to this day, faithfully took a swig before kissing any overnight guests, even though Mouthwash Guy had dumped her less than two weeks after she made that concession for him.

"Happy birthday," Caleb said, nuzzling my ear.

"Yes, it is," I agreed, cupping his balls in my hand.

He deepened the kiss, and inside my hand his soldier let me know that he was ready for some birthday sex. Caleb was a good kisser, which, to tell you the truth, wasn't that big of a superlative in L.A. I didn't think there was anything such as a big-city dweller over the age of thirty who wasn't a good kisser. The residual effect of so much dating.

Usually I was a pretty amazing kisser in my own right. But that morning my mind wandered away. I had so much to do. I hadn't picked up any food for my birthday party yet, and it being Friday, I still had to go to work.

I could call in sick, since the new year had delivered with it a fresh batch of sick days, but my office always ordered a cake and decorated your cubicle on birthdays. It was the only day of the year that I didn't want to kill myself while working there and, seriously, was there anything better than sheet cake? I didn't think so. I could ask my boss for an extra-long lunch break, but then I'd have to say why and my boss might be hurt that I hadn't invited her to the party, even though she's, like, fifty and, moreover, my boss. So maybe I should lie and say that I had a doctor's appointment, but who scheduled doctor's appointments on their birthday, unless they were really sick . . . ?

"Are you still awake?" Caleb asked, his voice muffled against my lips.

"Yes, of course," I answered. "Why do you ask?"

"Your hips stopped moving all of a sudden."

"Oh, I'm sorry," I said.

He nestled his dick between my thighs. "Something wrong?" he asked.

"No, I just . . ." I searched for an excuse. "Do you mind a quickie? I'm really horny."

I congratulated myself on this phrasing. It sounded so much better than "My mind's somewhere else and I don't have the energy for a long session of sex." I came off as saucy and sexy, as opposed to lazy and easily distracted.

Caleb rolled on top of me and guided his dick inside me, no questions asked. I bore down on my thoughts and moved my hips against his rhythm, concentrating on my own orgasm, which I had learned over the years was the only way I could ever come with penetration.

Back in my early twenties, I had just laid there, hoping that the guy moving on top of me would spark something off, but letting the guy do all the work most often left him satisfied and me just getting started. So now I put everything I had into making sure I had a good time during sex, too. And as a consequence, I'd garnered a reputation for being good in bed. This wasn't a hard feat to achieve. Despite what women's magazines try to tell you, it only takes two qualities for most guys to label you as good in bed: that you come hard and that you come loud.

And I excelled at both. So with a certain determination, I worked my hips against Caleb's dick, and I could feel myself building up to something good, when—

"Do you think I care if it's a bleeding bargain? There were dodgy rats running round the place." Abigail's English accent came through the thin wall, her voice loud and clear.

Benny yelled something back in Scottish.

Caleb and I stopped rocking, our need to eavesdrop supplanting our need to climax.

"What did he say?" I asked Caleb. He was a lot better at translating Scottish than I was.

But before Caleb could answer, Abigail cried, "Wanting a decent flat doesn't make me a princess. It just means I want a decent flat."

Benny said something else in Scottish. It was like listening to a Charlie Brown cartoon, where the adults spoke jibber-jabber and you could only understand what the children said.

"I don't care if North Hollywood is cheaper. I want to live in Los Feliz, and before you go accusing me of being a sodding princess again, might I remind you that we agreed to Los Feliz when we decided to move in together?"

I could feel Caleb's dick going soft as we listened to Benny's angry, unintelligible response. I couldn't believe that my two roommates were having this argument yet again.

True to their word, they had started looking for apartments as soon as Abigail got back, and more than three months later they still hadn't been able to find anything they both liked. According to Abigail, Benny would want to go see studios in the shadier, ungentrified neighborhoods to the east of Los Feliz, because they were cheaper. Abigail would answer (quite reasonably, in Abigail's opinion) that she didn't want to move in anywhere that didn't have at least two bedrooms or where she didn't feel safe. "Shouldn't we live within our means?" he would ask (according to Abigail). And Abigail would say that they had two very different definitions of living within their means. A few times I had gotten up in the middle of the night to use the bathroom and had found Benny snoring quietly on the couch, wrapped up in the fleece guest blanket, which made me feel bad for both of them.

"Why can't we sleep over at your place again?" I asked Caleb after he settled back down beside me, completely out of the mood. The now-constant bickering between Abigail and Benny reminded me of how my parents used to yell at each other, the volume of their fights getting louder and louder, until one day they started going in reverse, my mother's voice getting quieter, and my father's answers growing shorter.

Caleb lived in what I imagined to be a fantastic loft in one of the revitalized areas of downtown Los Angeles. But I could only imagine it, because he had yet to invite me over.

"That's where I work and I need to keep it clear of sexual energy."

During his time in L.A. Caleb had definitely picked up the Californian tendency to answer practical questions with spiritual answers. For example, when I asked him to go see a movie he didn't want to see, he'd say something like, "I had a bad experience with that director once, and I don't want to invite negative energy." Or if I wanted us to go to brunch at a time that conflicted with his Saturday morning yoga class, he'd say something like, "I'm dealing with an editor who doesn't know what she wants, and I'm afraid if I don't hit yoga first, I'm going to bring angry energy to our meal."

Caleb was very concerned with energy.

But today with William Wallace and King Edward having it out all over again on the other side of the wall, and the failed birthday sex, I found his usual answer unsettling. "Look," I said. "I don't want to press you or anything. I know we haven't had the girlfriend-boyfriend conversation. But I have to ask if you're hiding another woman back at your place."

He gave me a reassuring smile. "No, I'm not hiding anyone in my apartment."

And again that lovely calm came over me. I realized then why people put so much stock in being in relationships for more than a month. Sharita was right—deciding to seek out a life partner had been one of the best decisions I'd made since I moved to L.A.

Then, as if to prove my conclusion, he turned to face me in bed and said, "And maybe we should have that conversation. Mind if I start referring to you as my girlfriend?"

I smiled. "Yeah, you can totally call me your girlfriend," I said.

Then we kissed again, and it all would have been very romantic—if Abigail hadn't chosen that moment to yell, "I'm dead sick of having the same row over and over again. I don't want to see any more flats with you. Let's just call off the search."

# RISA

9t's official, I was fucked. And of course, by "fucked" I meant "stumped," which in the world of music is totally and utterly fucked.

Gravestone loved my demo, they just loved it. They loved it so much, they sent in a sparkly producer named David Gall. David Gall worked on many of Gravestone's other hit albums. He was twenty-five, but he looked like a thirteen-year-old going through puberty with his gangly limbs, sparse beard, and tight jeans worn under a steady stream of T-shirts with misspelled and/or bizarre words on them.

When we met for the first time at the Aroma Café in Los Feliz, he showed up wearing a T-shirt with a shadow-figure stripper swinging around a pole. It said "SLIPPER PORE MISS" in block letters above the image.

"I got it in Japan," he said with studied nonchalance. "I get all my T-shirts in Japan."

Anyway, David Gall (who I assumed changed his name to David Gall like I changed my name from Lisa Amoakohene to Risa Merriweather) was supposed to be wildly original. The only thing was, every time I tried to do my own thing in the studio, he said something like, "Well, when I was producing the Homer & Marge album, we did it like this," or "Yeah, the lead singer of Ipso! Facto! wanted to do that, too, but I convinced him to do this," and so on.

Homer & Marge and Ipso! Facto! were Gravestone's two biggest bands. And it was beginning to feel like David Gall, who told me at the Aroma Café meeting that he loved how different Supa Dupa's music was, wanted me to sound exactly like them, even though they were boy bands in their early twenties, and if I may say so myself, their singers' thin, whiny voices didn't kick nearly as much ass as mine.

I tried not to get angry. My birthday was in June. I would turn thirty. And thirty meant I would officially be old as far as the music business was concerned. Young people didn't like working with old people for a lot of good reasons. Old people complained. Old people didn't move albums, unless they started out when they were young. Old people didn't listen to young people, because they always thought they knew better. The music industry hated old people. They wouldn't even let someone of my advanced years audition for *American Idol*. Not that I wanted to audition for *American Idol*, but still . . . working with David Gall made me feel old.

I shook off this feeling in the studio because I had hopes and dreams and rent riding on getting this album delivered. So I said, "Cool," every time he told me to "try to sound more English" or "let's do it the Ipso! Facto! way here" or Auto-Tuned my voice.

Gravestone told me through David Gall that they thought the album was perfect, except it needed a bitter love song. I said, "Cool, I'll come up with something over the weekend."

I even got out my notepad and sat down to write at my kitchen table on Friday afternoon and . . . nothing. I was stumped. I hadn't been in a real relationship since The One and me broke up, but I could win her back if this album did well, so I couldn't write about her.

I sat and sat at my kitchen table but the song wouldn't come. Then my stomach started grumbling with hunger, so I had some coffee. Then I turned on the television and there was an episode of *Yo Gabba Gabba!* I would kill to be one of the many alternative acts that came through to perform on *Yo Gabba Gabba!* Kill. So I watched the children's show with my grumbling stomach keeping time in the background, and I thought about making another pot of coffee or going outside to smoke another cigarette, but instead my eyes drifted closed.

I dreamed of eating donuts with David Gall and The One. Her arms were draped around my neck as I talked business with my producer. In the background, the *Yo Gabba Gabba!* characters sang their hit song "Don't

Stop, Don't Give Up" as a soft, sincere ballad. And then I said something funny and we all laughed while I picked up another donut and took a huge bite.

When I woke up, DJ Lance Rock was throwing the magic confetti that made the characters freeze and become inanimate toys again at the end of the show and it was time to leave for Thursday's birthday party.

# SHARITA

$\mathcal{I}$t wasn't a difficult day at work for me, but it was long, and not just because I had to stay at the office until after eight p.m. preparing for a consult with an actor who wanted to turn himself into a corporation so that he could launch a production company. The day also felt long because of the incident that happened with Marcus during my lunch hour—the incident that I was blaming on Thursday and Risa.

Two things had been niggling at me since the start of the new year. The first was that I still hadn't found a way to correct Marcus's assumption that I was some kind of backup receptionist as opposed to a senior accountant. The second thing was the no-going-out situation, which had become especially irksome after Thursday and Risa told me to dump him. So in an attempt to be slick, I decided to bring up the not-going-out problem to take some of the edge off my big-omission confession.

The plan had made sense on New Year's Day right before he came over for dinner with two loads of dirty clothes in a laundry bag. I had tried to be as nice as possible about it, waiting until I had put the first load in to say, "Marcus, I love spending time with you, but I was thinking we should try to go out more."

And he had seemed okay with it, nodding and promising to take me out soon. Then he'd kissed me in such a soul-shaking way that I forgot all about my accountant confession.

The next morning, he kissed me good-bye with his bag of clean and folded laundry slung over his shoulder, and afterward I just about floated to my church, whispering an especially joyful "Praise Jesus" after the pastor finished his sermon about new beginnings.

But then . . . nothing. No phone calls, no e-mails. It was like Marcus had fallen off the face of the earth. And the old familiar dread began to creep in. It was happening again: the part where I messed up and then the guy stopped liking me.

And Thursday hadn't been any help. "Good riddance," she said, when I told her about Marcus's disappearing act. "Davie Farrell says you should be grateful when a guy decides to take himself out of the running, because it leaves you clear for somebody who will appreciate you."

"But he did appreciate me. We were getting along fine before I brought up not going out," I said, wringing my hands.

"He wasn't taking you anywhere, then he stopped calling when you asked him to correct his behavior. Yet another black man that doesn't want to put any work into his relationships. That's why your quote-unquote black love doesn't work. Because black men expect black women to do all the work and then they bail the moment you stand up to them."

I loved Thursday, but sometimes I wanted to slap her when she said things like this in that authoritative way of hers, like it was a fact as opposed to some wild theory she had come up with because she had out-of-control daddy issues. I had met Rick T a couple of times before Thursday's mom died. And there had been no other word to describe him except wonderful. He was a huge rap star, but he had remembered my name and had even referred to me as Thursday's stunning sister friend.

Growing up dark-skinned in St. Louis, no boy had ever called me "pretty," much less "stunning." Rick T made me feel like a princess and I still couldn't understand why Thursday had turned on him like that. Yeah, maybe he had cheated on Thursday's mom, but it had been Thursday's mom who had decided to take her own life. That's who Thursday really should have been blaming, in my opinion.

After Thursday had stopped accepting Rick T's calls, he had started calling me every once in a while to check up on his daughter and make sure she was all right. The last call had been right before graduation, and he'd said, "I guess she's really not going to invite me to this graduation, even though I paid for her education." He was right. Thursday pretty much invited everyone in her family except for Rick T. I couldn't believe her audacity. My own mother couldn't come out to graduation unless I paid for it myself and arranged all the travel details. Thursday didn't know how good she had it, could have it if she wasn't so hardheaded about not wanting to have anything to do with her father or any other black man.

I wanted black love for my own reasons, but finding a nice black brother and making a good life with him would come with the bonus of showing Thursday that there was such a thing as a happy black marriage. Until then, I just had to bite my tongue when Thursday said ludicrous things about black men, because if I tried to defend them, she'd run down the list of black men who had done me wrong, using my own dating history to make her case. So instead of arguing with her, I got off the phone, and took to praying that Marcus would come back into my life.

To my surprise, my prayers got answered on Thursday's birthday. Having resolved at New Year's to try to eat better, I had been munching on a homemade salad at my desk. I had just stuffed a huge bite of romaine into my mouth when someone in my open doorway said, "So when was you going to tell me you're an accountant?"

I looked up and froze when I saw Marcus standing there, with a package in his hand. "Rhonda wasn't at her desk again, and I saw it was for you. So I asked, and they sent me back here to your office."

He stressed the word "office," and I could see how this must look to him, as he surveyed my large workspace with its cherry wood furniture and its panoramic view of downtown Los Angeles.

But before I could defend myself, he thrust his brown box at me. "Anyway, sign here."

I put my plastic fork down, feeling silly as I signed on the LED screen's signature line, still chewing like a rabbit.

"You know, if you didn't want to go out with somebody who made less than you, you could have just told me that from the get-go," he said to me.

I swallowed and stood up. "I don't care that you make less than me. I'm not like that. And you're the one that didn't call me, remember?"

"Yeah, because I thought you were different, and it turned out you were like every other sister in L.A. All like, 'What can you do for me? You ain't good enough for me.'"

I felt helpless and hurt when he accused me of this. Like I was on the school playground again, with all the other kids calling me "siddity" because I got As and "talked white."

"I'm not like that," I said. "I just wanted to go out for dinner every once in a while."

Marcus started tapping something into the brown box. "Well, I'm a hard-working brother. I don't have any kids, I don't have any diseases, and I don't have any time for sisters who think they're too good to hang out with me."

"I don't think I'm . . ." I trailed off, knowing that it was useless to try to convince him that he was wrong about me when he obviously had made up his mind. "I'm sorry you feel that way, Marcus. I guess I'll get back to work now."

"Yeah, you do that. Gotta keep earning them dollars, right?"

He tucked his brown box under his arm and left. I was overtaken by guilt before he had even made it to the hallway. Marcus thought I was some kind of gold digger now. Things had been going really well, but like they had warned about in so many R&B songs, I went and listened to my girl-friends and messed up the good thing we had.

All afternoon I thought and thought about what I could have said to defend myself and change his mind about me, but I couldn't come up with anything stronger than "I'm not a gold digger, and I didn't mean to come off that way"—which wasn't exactly an argument that would get me into law school.

I was so confused, but I didn't call Thursday or Risa to talk about it after work. Thursday was messed up when it came to men and Risa didn't even like them. I wouldn't make the mistake of asking either of them for relationship advice ever again.

So I called my sister but got Nicole's voicemail. Again. Which was a little irritating because I had been trying to get in touch with her for over a month now and had gotten nothing but "I'm fine. So busy. Sorry! Sorry! Will call soon!" text messages when I left voicemails about being worried about her.

I had only been fourteen when I had gone to see *Waiting to Exhale* with my mother and Nicole on Christmas Day 1995. But I still remember being surprised that the four girlfriends in the movie seemed to talk on the phone more than they talked in real life. I had wondered if that was how it was when you became an adult. I eventually found out that the movie had understated the phone situation for adult women. Our New Year's Eve lunch had marked only the fourth time that Thursday, Tammy, Risa, and I had all been in the same room that year.

Before *Sex and the City* went off the air, people had called it a fantasy because the four women wore designer clothes all the time and dated all these handsome, rich, and successful men. But in my opinion, the biggest illusion was that four working friends could find the time to meet for brunch once a week all the way into their forties. There was no such thing as a group of working women who could manage this, and I felt that this unprecedented level of friendship was the most unattainable fantasy of them all. In a way I blamed *SATC* for Thursday and Risa's unreasonable expectations. They wanted me to happily show up at all of our events like I was Miranda, but in real life I wondered how Cynthia Nixon's character hit all those glamorous parties at night and managed to make it into work at her law firm the next morning.

When I got home from work that night, I would have given anything to get out of going to Thursday's birthday party. I was tired and wanted nothing more than to set myself up on the couch with a microwave dinner and watch *Supernatural* on the CW. But I had promised Thursday, so I shed my suit jacket and put on a gray silk blouse and vest over my trousers. I was just about to put on my high heels when the doorbell rang.

Wondering who it could be ringing my bell at this time of night, I went to the door and looked out through the peephole.

It was Marcus.

Something opened up in my heart and my wide feet sang a little song of praise and happiness. They would not be getting shoved into heels tonight, they would not have to pretend they weren't in pain while making small talk with Thursday's artist friends, who always wanted to talk about their projects but never asked me anything about my work. My feet wouldn't have to endure at least an hour of standing around, pained and bored. They cheered, because even before I opened the door, they knew that I would not be attending Thursday's birthday party.

# February 2011

I'm always shocked by how few dating books stress this, but for goodness sake, do not compromise your friendships for a man. Your friends are your wealth. Your friends are your insurance. Your friends chose to love you. One of the biggest mistakes that you can make in pursuing a mate is deciding to undervalue your friendships.

—*The Awesome Girl's Guide to Dating Extraordinary Men* by Davie Farrell

# THURSDAY

$\mathcal{B}$ack during my one-month-stand years, Valentine's Day had been awkward territory. It always felt weird, having to go out to a big dinner with a guy I had only known for a short while or would be dumping in a few days. I usually didn't bother with presents, and last year I had even dumped the guy ahead of time, so that I could hang out with Risa after her annual Valentine's blow up with The One. Every year since 2008, when gay marriage became legal for a short time in California, Risa had made a big impassioned plea to The One to marry her on Valentine's Day, even after the law had gotten reversed. And every year Risa got shot down.

"You've got to give up and move on," I told her last year.

"I wish I could," Risa said, pouring herself a third glass of straight vodka behind the bar. Even though it wasn't a great idea to get completely wasted on one of her bar's busiest days of the year, this is what Risa had proceeded to do after every one of her Valentine's Day rejections. Risa did Risa and that's all she knew how to do. And the only reason she hadn't gotten fired for this stunt was that I had been there to keep on serving customers drinks when she no longer could, to lock up the bar at two a.m., to pour her into my car, and to deposit her safely at home to sleep off her copious vodka consumption.

But this year, I had Caleb. I would have asked Sharita to take over Risa duty, but we hadn't spoken since she'd called me at the last minute the month before to say that she wouldn't be attending my birthday party because Marcus had shown up and they "needed to talk."

There were four types of Smithies in this world: Those who had chosen to go to Smith College because it was an institution with a reputation for graduating strong women and, as young feminists, we believed that it was in our best interest to attend a school with like-minded women—that was me. Those who had known in high school that they were lesbians and wanted to go to a school where they would feel comfortable—that was Risa. Those whose female relatives had been going to Smith for generations upon generations, also known as legacies—that was none of us. And those who went to Smith simply because the prestigious women's college had given them the biggest scholarship—and that would be Sharita.

The problem with the latter two kinds of Smithies was that they thought of putting women first as an option as opposed to a "should." And they somehow managed to graduate from Smith having learned few of the tenants of feminism, or even how to treat their female friends with a modicum of respect.

So in many ways it felt like I was repeating a basic lesson to a particularly slow child when I said, "Sharita, I'm your best friend. I'm the one who will still be here when Marcus goes crazy on you. Again. And it's my thirtieth birthday party."

"Tammy and Risa are going to be there, right?"

"That's beside the point."

"And you guys always complain that I don't socialize enough at parties."

"We only complain when you sit in the corner on your BlackBerry and don't even try to talk to people," I said.

"People I don't even know," Sharita said, as if her contempt for socializing with people she hadn't met yet was all my fault. "You'll have more fun without me. You know you will."

True, but . . . "That's beside the point. You promised you'd come."

"Me not coming to your party isn't the end of the world. You know that, I know that. I wish you would just grow up and admit it," Sharita said.

I had simply been annoyed when Sharita had first called, but after she said this, I went from mildly unamused to livid. So I hung up on her. It occurred to me afterwards that turning thirty may have rendered me too old for childish moves like hanging up on people, but whatever.

Since that night, I hadn't answered any of Sharita's calls or returned any of her texts. I hadn't even responded to her brunch invite, which had been proffered on a weekend that Marcus would be out of town visiting his family in Atlanta. Sharita had once again revealed her true (and thoroughly ridiculous) colors, but this time something shifted within me upon seeing them. My love for her gave way to distaste. And it almost didn't hurt to lose her as a friend. Almost.

Unfortunately, the memories got in the way of a good, clean break. I'd be rehashing in my head all the times Sharita had stood me up, but then a little voice would remind me that she'd been the one who had arranged it so that she and Risa could come up to Connecticut to be with me after my mother died. She'd been the one who had called in a separate Town Car for us when I had said that I didn't want to ride in the limo with my father. And she'd also been the one who had taken the train with me to JFK and put me on a plane back to China to finish out the semester.

After that, Sharita had e-mailed me little affirmations and a piece of scripture every day, even though she knew that I didn't deal well with either scripture or cheesiness. But those e-mails had been the best and brightest parts of my days in the dark months that followed my mother's death, and they didn't stop coming until I was back on the Smith College campus. By then, Risa had dropped out and moved to Los Angeles. But Sharita greeted me on the porch of Capen House, where I would be living for the rest of the school year. She'd given me the best hug, tight and fierce, before taking one of my suitcases and helping me move back into the house.

So, yeah, remembering stuff like that made it hard to stay mad at Sharita. Really hard. But how long could I continue to give her credit for things she'd done ten years ago? The problem with becoming friends at an all-women's college was that there was no way of knowing who the people you swore would be your friends for life will become once boys are put into play. I'd thought back then that Sharita was true blue. But putting up with her crap in

L.A. made me wonder if she'd been such a good friend back then simply because there hadn't been any boys in the picture to distract her.

Still, my fingers itched to call her and make sure that one of us would be there for Risa that night. I ended up calling Caleb instead. I explained to him that we were going to have a wonderful dinner and afterwards we could go back to my place and have even better sex . . . but then I had to go attend to Risa in Silver Lake.

"Romantic," he said.

"I know, I know. I'm sorry. It's like this universal rule that in order to be no-drama, you have to have a high-drama friend." This statement set off a tiny ping of guilt in my brain, because while I had certainly been as low-drama as possible for Caleb all of these months, I wasn't exactly no-drama, especially on the inside.

"You're a good friend," he said. "I love that about you."

I hadn't yet told him about my falling out with Sharita, but I accepted the compliment anyway. "Thanks," I said, dwelling on the fact that he had used "I love" and "you" in the same sentence. I wondered how long it would be before he got rid of the "that" and the "about."

# RISA

"Is Thursday not talking to me?" Sharita asked me halfway through lunch at the Daily Grill. And by "lunch" I mean I was drinking coffee while she was eating a huge cheeseburger, so I guessed she'd thrown up the deuces on that New Year's diet already.

By the way, I was starting to fiend for a cigarette when she brought this shit up.

"How are you just now figuring that out?" I asked her. "She hasn't been talking to you since you skipped her birthday party for that boy."

"His name is Marcus. We're not at Smith anymore. You don't have to keep on calling grown men boys just because a few of them call us girls."

I answered this reasonable argument in the same manner that I answered all reasonable arguments—with a rock-star shrug. "Whatevs—boy or man, she's still hella-mad at you for standing her up."

Sharita frowned and tapped her fingers on the table, and I knew the next words out of her mouth would be something about how ungrateful Thursday was.

"You see, this is what I don't like about Thursday. Every time I don't show up to something, she acts like I'm the worst person in the world and forgets all the stuff I've done for her in the past like loaning her money to come to L.A., and calling in a favor to get her that job at MTS Systems, and . . ."

Sharita stopped there, leaving the rest unsaid. Helping Thursday get through the death of her mom was a big fucking deal, but lumping it in with all the other favors wouldn't have been right. Even Sharita, who could come up with a thousand arguments for why she shouldn't get blamed for something she did or for why people shouldn't be asking her to do something she just plain didn't want to do in the first place, wouldn't go there.

I shrugged again, staying out of it. The truth was that Sharita needed to accept that if she promised to do something and then she didn't do it, then people were going to get mad at her ass. And Thursday needed to accept that Sharita was a fucking idiot when it came to men. It was like a disease, and Thursday couldn't hold it against her if she wanted to stay friends with Sharita.

"Can you talk to her?" Sharita asked.

"Hell, no," I answered almost before the words were out of her mouth.

"Seriously, Risa, somebody's got to talk some sense into her. She's so hardheaded."

"Somebody doesn't have to be me," I answered.

"Why not you?" Sharita asked.

I waved her question away, like "shoo fly, don't bother me." She acted like any of this shit really mattered. Here was how I knew our lives would be going down: Thursday would marry her white boy, because Caleb was the complete opposite of Rick T and exactly what Thursday wanted. So she was going to do whatever it took to get a ring off of him and literally make her dreams come true.

Sharita, on the other hand, would continue to be single for the rest of her life, not because she wasn't desirable, but because she couldn't see straight when it came to men and the best she could hope for was some-body who would agree to move in with her so that he could sponge off of her like a parasite—and even then he probably still wouldn't ask her to marry him.

Either way, at the end of the story, this close friendship that the three of us had built since we met at Smith College was reaching its twilight. Soon, neither Thursday nor Sharita would have time to do anything with anyone who didn't either live or have sex with them.

They'd both go away, and if Tammy gave in to her family and found some rich guy to settle down with, then I was going to be left alone with nothing but my career.

And maybe that was why I was so intent on making it happen this year, so that I could finally be the rock star I needed to be for The One to come back to me. Straight talk: my future happiness depended on what I could get done in 2011.

So I shook my head when Sharita tried to wheedle me into calling Thursday and said, "I'm not doing your dirty work. Just keep calling her until she picks up."

Sharita crossed her arms over her chest. "Why is it always on me to make up with her? Why doesn't she ever call me when we get in fights?"

"Are you seriously going to whine all through lunch? Because I got up early for this." I pulled out my iPhone, to show her I was beyond bored with this conversation.

Sharita switched the subject with a coy head tilt and grin. "Guess what I'm making Marcus tonight for Valentine's Day dinner?" she said.

Jesus H. Christ, I needed to find some new friends. There were a ton of single women and men in their thirties in L.A. I didn't have to stick with Sharita just because she was awesome when she wasn't in a relationship, which was most of the time since she never went out and guys pretty much had to stumble upon her in her office like Marcus did, or run into her at Blockbuster like the last boyfriend back in early 2009.

I imagined myself with a set of shiny new friends. Friends who liked electronic rock, friends who didn't mind going out late on weeknights, friends who didn't always want to meet at restaurants, where I'd be tempted to eat. My fantasy of my anti-Sharita friends distracted me for a pretty minute, or I would have noticed the black box that appeared on my iPhone screen sooner.

It was a text message from Tammy, and it said, "S.O.S. I need your help. On bad date at Kate Mantilini. Please save me. Serious 911."

Saved by the urgent text message. I threw back the rest of my cold coffee and said to Sharita, "It's an emergency. I've got to go. Call Thursday and apologize for being you on her voicemail. She'll forgive you eventually."

"I've already called her enough. It's time for her to call me."

"Okay, whatever," I said, then I left, not bothering to put down money for the bill. I only had a coffee and Sharita could afford to pick up my tab.

Tammy's biggest problem could easily be summed up in five words: she was too fucking nice. I knew this because she never stood up to her older sister, Veronica, who kept coming up with increasingly audacious schemes to get Tammy into a relationship with someone other than Mike Barker. Tammy had put up with strange (but successful) men calling her out of the blue because her sister gave them her number, and she often made excuses for why she couldn't go out to dinner with her sister because she suspected Veronica would spring a date on her.

Later in the day, Tammy would tell me that she thought it would be safe to meet her sister at Kate Mantilini, a high-end restaurant in Beverly Hills, since she was driving herself and Veronica was seven months pregnant.

But after a quick hug at the waitress stand, the next thing Tammy knew she was being deposited into a chair across from some entertainment lawyer named Henry. And her sister had grabbed her purse, which had her car keys inside of it, before dashing off.

"I'm just going to go get your car detailed like we talked about," Veronica had said. Like anyone would ever ask a seven-months-pregnant woman to take her car in for detailing while she went out on a date.

"And I couldn't leave," Tammy told me later. "That would have been so rude to Henry." Like Veronica putting her in that position in the first place hadn't been rude as hell anyway.

So because Veronica was an asshole and Tammy was too fucking nice, I end up walking into Kate Mantilini on Valentine's Day and finding Tammy being bored to death by some square-jawed guy who was trying to convince her they should start working out together.

I cracked my knuckles. It was a dirty job being me, but somebody had to do it.

I walked right up to them and slammed my motorcycle helmet on the table. "Hey, are you trying to come on to my girl?"

Both Tammy and Henry looked up at me in all my rocker-grrl glory, looming over the table, and I glared at Henry like I'd just caught him and Tammy having sex or something.

"My girl?" he repeated.

I leaned toward him and bared my teeth. "Yeah, my girl. You got something to say about our lifestyle choice?"

Tammy, who was wearing a very pretty, green A-line dress, covered both her eyes with her hands as if hiding from the entire scene.

"Oh, you two are together? I didn't know." He looked a little cowed, but not so much so that he didn't remember that he was still in the entertainment business, and therefore genetically compelled to say, "How about a threesome?"

I stared at him for a long, hot second, then said, "Yeah, I've got a gun back in my Harley saddlebag and rage issues. Do you really want to go here with me?"

"I'm leaving," Henry said, throwing down his napkin and raising his hands, like I actually had the hypothetical gun trained on him.

"Yeah, walk away," I said. "But leave some money for the bill. Tammy's a lady."

Tammy finally uncovered her eyes long enough to say, "No, Henry, you don't have to."

He threw down a couple of one-hundred-dollar bills and pretty much ran away, looking over his shoulder a few times as he did.

"Well, that was fun," I said, dropping into his abandoned chair.

"I can't believe you did that!" Tammy said as loud as she could without raising her voice.

"What? You sent me a 911."

"I wanted you come in and pretend that there was some kind of emergency or something. Not—not . . ." She couldn't even say it.

"Yeah, you didn't want me to make him think you were gay like me." I widened my eyes to simpering and did a high-pitched impression of Tammy. "And we can't have people thinking I'm gay. That's so gross! Ew!"

"That's not how I feel about it. You know that. But he's going to tell my sister and she's going to flip out."

I shrugged. "Just tell her I did what I had to do to get you out of the date she'd stranded you on. You need to learn how to stand up to your sister anyway."

For a moment, the Disney Princess shutters fell off Tammy's eyes, and she looked at me with real hatred.

"Can you please take me home now?" she asked, her voice strained.

"Sure," I said, deciding not to care about how on edge she was about the scene I'd just created. "Right after I order a cup of coffee."

Then I signaled for a waiter.

# March 2011

If a man really loves you, he's not okay with you being mad at him. On the flipside, if you really love a man, you let him know when you get mad. When I meet with a couple and the guy doesn't get that the girl is seething with pent-up resentment, what I see are two people who really aren't in love with each other like they think they are.

—*The Awesome Girl's Guide to Dating Extraordinary Men* by Davie Farrell

# THURSDAY

On Valentine's Day, Caleb told me he loved me, and I decided to love him back. It wasn't that hard, really. He was everything I wanted: tall, shaggy, only moderately successful (too successful leads to insurmountable ego issues—ask any starter wife about that), nice, gentle, and, most important of all, nothing like my father. He was decent in bed. He called when he said he would call. He never canceled dates. My friends liked him. My sister thought he sounded great. I could see us together in the future, buying a house in Echo Park and raising hip kids with good taste in music and a certain acerbic wit.

He was everything I had ever wanted, except . . .

"The apartment thing is bothering me," I told him one Sunday morning in mid-March.

We were in the kitchen, eating a spinach-and-egg omelet I'd made for us. Caleb was also a vegetarian, so cooking for him felt more like an extension of cooking for myself as opposed to a chore, like it had with my meat-eating one-month stands.

"Is it because of the Benny and Abigail fight?" he asked.

Both of my roommates had left early that morning, Abigail having scored a gig on a one-off March Madness feature show, and the daytime talk show that Benny now worked for having decided to pay everyone union overtime to do a pre–March Madness special. But before leaving for their respective gigs, they'd somehow managed to get into yet another fight about the apartment situation. From what I had been able to figure out from Abigail's half of the conversation, Abigail had been looking for apartments by herself and found a perfect two-bedroom, except that it was about three hundred dollars over their budget. Abigail thought they should fill out a rental application anyway. Benny thought it was too expensive.

At least that's what it had sounded like to me when Abigail had yelled, "Stop saying it's too dear. It's not too dear. You're just a right tight Scottish bastard, aren't you?" I think "dear" meant expensive and "tight" meant cheap, but I couldn't be sure . . .

"Why doesn't she dump him as opposed to arguing with him all time?" Caleb asked, shaking his head. Then: "Do you want me to talk to them?"

"I appreciate the offer, but no," I said, putting down my fork. "What I really want is for you to let me spend the night at your apartment once in a while, so that I don't have to wake up to screaming roommates every morning."

He put his own fork down. "I don't want to fight," he said. "I told you why my apartment is off-limits, and I need you to respect that."

"I do respect your wishes," I answered carefully. "I just want to see where you live."

Neither of us was from California, but it was like we were trying to out–California speak each other with this conversation. I had to tamp down the desire to yell, "Who else doesn't let his girlfriend see his apart-ment? That's freaking crazy."

"Okay," he said, scooting back from the table. "I have to get back to my apartment and do some work. I've got a deadline coming up."

"Are you angry at me?" I asked, feeling a little panicked by his abrupt subject change.

"No," he answered. "Just frustrated that we can't get past this."

He went to the living room and pulled his jacket off the couch, where he had tossed it the night before. I followed him, trying not to come off as all neurotic and scared, but I was neurotic and scared. This was, I could see now that we were inside of it, our first official fight.

"So you're just going to leave?" I asked.

"I'm on deadline for this short documentary project," he said.

"Why didn't you mention this deadline before?" I asked, hating how whiny I sounded even as the words were coming out of my mouth.

"Because it didn't come up." He had made it to the door now, hand on the knob. "Look, I'll call you later tonight, okay?"

Then he left. And though he had at least promised to be in touch before he left, I couldn't help but note that he hadn't kissed me good-bye.

# SHARITA

That afternoon, I found myself trying not to get into a fight with Marcus. Since getting back together after our first fight, we had gotten in two more arguments, both of which had ended with him disappearing for a week before deciding to forgive me. But unfortunately, I didn't see any way to avoid yet another fight that night, especially after Marcus got up an hour before my March Madness bracket-picking party and said, "I'm bouncing."

He had been watching ESPN all day and hadn't offered a helping hand or even a few words of conversation while I set up for the party. Though not social by nature, I had been throwing a bracket party ever since I'd gotten promoted to senior accountant. All of my firm's partners threw at least one party every year. So now, not only did I make sure to dress like the partners, always in a suit as opposed to business casual like some of the less ambitious CPAs at Foxman & Carroll, but I also threw an annual bracket party and invited everyone at the firm and a few of my friends—with a strict warning to Risa to be on her best behavior.

I hadn't minded Marcus not helping with the party particulars. I understood that he had a demanding job and couldn't be expected to do physical labor on the weekends. I understood this because one of our fights had been about a shelf in my bathroom that I had asked him to fix, that he'd never gotten around to. He had disappeared for three days after that argument, and I had ended up fixing it myself with the help of an Internet tutorial. And I wouldn't have minded, except he had been the one who offered to do it in the first place.

"I already went and got ice," I told him, when he made moves to leave. "You don't have to go get it."

"Naw," he said, grabbing his coat and slipping it on. "I'm leaving-leaving."

I stood up straight from the black and gray napkins that I had been fanning out on the side table. "What do you mean 'leaving-leaving'? The party starts in less than an hour."

"Yeah, that's why I'm leaving. I'm gonna let you do your thing with your work friends."

He came over to kiss me good-bye, but I put a hand on his chest. "You're invited, too. I thought you understood that."

He smiled, his dark brown eyes twinkling like I was joking. "You want me to hang out with you and your co-workers while you all pick brackets? I'm going to be doing the same thing tomorrow at my own job."

I felt a little silly for pressing the point when he put it that way. But . . . "I was looking forward to you meeting Tammy and Risa. They're my girl-friends and we've been going out for three months now. You're supposed to meet my girlfriends by the three-month mark, right?"

With a small pang, I thought about how I, myself, hadn't met Thursday's Caleb yet—but that was only because Thursday was being stubborn and still wasn't talking to me.

Marcus shook his head, bemused, like my wanting him to stick around long enough to meet Tammy and Risa was too crazy to even contemplate. "Look, I'm tired. I'll catch your friends some other time."

The part of me that didn't want to get frozen out by him again told me to let it go, but unfortunately that other part of me—the part that had got-ten me into Smith College and was now in position to eventually become my firm's first black female partner—wouldn't let me.

"Can you at least stick around long enough to meet them? I told them you'd be here. They're even coming a little early to help me finish setting up and meet you."

"Why did you tell them to come early to meet me?" Marcus asked, his smile disappearing. "I never agreed to that."

"I didn't think meeting my girlfriends was something you had to agree to. You're here almost every night now anyway, and they're coming over. What's the problem?"

Marcus scratched his arm underneath his lightweight sweater, as if this line of conversation was giving him an allergic reaction. "Like I said, I'm tired. And I don't have time for this. I'll see you later."

He started to leave, but I grabbed his arm. "You don't have time for this?" I said. "Strange, you always seem to have time for me when you want to have sex."

He took back his arm. "Look, girl, I like you, but you can't spring your friends on me then get mad when I say 'No, I don't want to meet them 'cuz I got stuff to do.' This isn't how you treat a hardworking brother if you want to see him again. I haven't cheated on you, I'm with you all the time. If that ain't enough, I don't know what is."

*I don't know what is.* Those five words peeled the shutters off my eyes. The Crystal Ball Vision of the two little boys in our future and the home we could make together fell away. Suddenly I could see through Marcus's chocolate skin and straight white teeth and twinkling brown eyes to who he really was. And I did not like what I saw.

"You know I'm a hardworking sister, right?" I asked.

He shook his head, confused. "What?"

"I said I'm a hardworking sister. Technically I work longer hours than you, but I still find time to cook when you come over here and wash your clothes when you bring them by and then I put on pretty lingerie before we go to bed. I do that because I like you and I appreciate you. But every time I ask you to do anything, you act like I've lost my dang mind. Why can't I have any expectations when it comes to you? That's not how you treat *a hardworking sister* if you want to see her again."

Marcus went back to looking bemused. "Yeah, but good black men, ones without kids or records, are hard to find. Like Kanye said, there's a thousand yous. There's only one of me."

I blinked. "Fool, you think I should be grateful for any scraps you throw me, because you don't have kids or a jail record?"

"You don't have to be grateful, but maybe you need to work a little harder to recognize."

The worst feeling came over me as I realized out loud, "You're a straight-up idiot."

"What?" he said.

"You're an idiot. I'm caring, I cook, I clean, I'm smart, I make a lot of money. I'm a great catch. YOU are barely decent. And I can't believe I let you waste my time like this."

Marcus shook his head, looking almost childish in his confusion. "What you talking about? There are a million sisters in this city exactly like you. I can have another one of you in a second, but no real black man is going to put up with your uppity act."

I went and opened the door. "No real black man would call me uppity because I asked him to take me out to dinner, fix one shelf, and meet my girlfriends. You know what, just get out. I'm feeling too stupid now for putting up with your bullwinkle as long as I did."

Marcus hesitated, like he was trying to think of a strong comeback. And as he walked out the door I was holding open for him, he said, "You know what? You a fat BITCH!"

I slammed the door closed as if I were shoving his words out of my house with him. How had I not seen what a horrible guy he was? How could I have let him use me like that for so long? A feeling of such terribleness washed over me that it nearly knocked me to my knees and, without warning, a sob rose up in the back of my throat. I was too old for this, too old to still be getting used by guys who didn't even really like me. Too old to be called a fat bitch like I was still in high school and had refused to pay attention to the guys catcalling me as I walked home.

I had skipped church that morning to start cooking for my bracket party, but now I went to the couch that Marcus had abandoned and fell to my knees.

"Oh Lord," I prayed. "Please make this awful feeling go away. Please . . ."

I prayed this same thing over and over again, my eyes squeezed shut for long minutes. And when I opened them again, my heart no longer felt shriveled and defeated inside my chest. Something in me lifted and I felt lighter—good. Better than good. Just ten minutes ago, I had been thinking of calling Tammy and Risa and telling them that I needed to call the party off, but now I felt strong, like I could do anything and I couldn't wait to see my friends and co-workers.

Oh, God was good. God was so, so, so good. I got out my BlackBerry and updated my Facebook page to say, "I am grateful to my Lord and Savior. I got down on my knees and He raised me up."

Within twenty minutes I had twelve "Likes" from other friends, including Risa, who showed up at my door a few minutes later.

"You weren't looking at Facebook on your motorcycle, were you?" I asked.

"Long light," she said, handing me a bottle of Yellow Tail. "Open that shit up right now."

Tammy rang the doorbell a few minutes later and she also handed me a bottle of wine—one with a name I didn't recognize, but it was French and looked expensive. I put Tammy's wine on display in an empty part of my bookshelf. Really good wine was an investment that could often be sold for even more money later. I typed a note into my BlackBerry to research the bottle's lineage further and then opened the cheap-but-good-enough Yellow Tail for my guests.

As I led Tammy and Risa into the kitchen where I had been preparing food all morning and early afternoon, I thanked God again for having such good friends. I might not have a man anymore, I thought, but there was no one who could tell me I wasn't truly blessed.

# THURSDAY

*U*sually I loved having the apartment to myself. I could watch whatever I wanted on TV, without anyone asking why I would "watch that crap." Benny wasn't too judgmental (from the little I could understand), but Abigail got particularly snotty when it came to television, sticking to a steady diet of BBC News Programming. So when I got the rare moment alone with our shared television, I adored lying on the couch with a bag of Veggie Pirate Booty, watching whatever cheesy program I happened upon. But tonight, I couldn't get in the mood.

First of all, Caleb still hadn't called, even though he had said he would and, according to Davie Farrell, you weren't supposed to stay with guys who didn't call when they said they would. Second of all, I had dumped enough guys to know the score. Caleb suddenly going cool like that and then rushing out meant that he was already in the process of re-evaluating our relationship, deciding whether or not to dump me. And since he hadn't called yet, he was probably leaning toward getting rid of me as opposed to putting up with me asking to see his apartment, which in all fairness, he had told me from the beginning was off-limits.

And third of all, when I had tried to *not be pathetic* about Caleb and had called Risa to see if we could hang out, Risa had said that both she and Tammy were going over to Sharita's March Madness party. That smarted, because Sharita was like a really good cook. At her last bracket party, she'd made a fake-meat version of these buffalo-wing chicken/cream cheese phyllo-dough appetizers that had made my vegetarian stomach stand up and clap.

But as much as I was tempted, delicious hors d'ouerves were not a good enough reason to resume talking to someone who didn't deserve my friendship anymore. "Well, I guess I'll hang out here alone then," I said.

"Oh, are you guys still not talking?" Risa asked, like she hadn't gotten the newsletter about Sharita and me remaining on the outs. "She's making those cream cheese things you like."

My stomach let out a mutinous grumble, but I gritted my teeth and said, "I'm sick of getting stood up all the time. I wouldn't put up with that behavior from a man, why should I put up with it from her?"

"Because Sharita ain't your man, she's our best friend," Risa answered in a tone that insinuated my stance on this matter was dumb as opposed to principled.

"It's still about basic respect, so call me if you want to do something afterwards."

"Okeydokey fanoke," Risa said before getting off the phone.

And that's when I got to thinking about jumping off the MTS roof again. This would be a good night for it. I seriously had no idea what to do with the rest of my life career-wise. I was about to get dumped by my first real boyfriend. Sharita and I had already broken up. And Risa and Tammy obviously felt no particular loyalty to me whatsoever. For a moment, my brain zoned out as I watched the mesmerizing image of my own body falling through the air.

Then my phone rang, interrupting the fantasy. I came back to the real world and looked at the caller ID. It was Caleb.

"Hello?" I said, bracing myself to get dumped.

"Hey," he said. "This project is out of control, but I can break for a minute. Can you come downtown? I'll meet you outside Drake's."

Oh, I had forgotten that you can't dump someone over the phone when you've been together for over a month. This was going to be an in-person, I realized.

Drake's was a bar that had been refurbished into a speakeasy about two years ago, complete with a password that you had to know to get in for overpriced drinks. It was housed within one of those mixed-use buildings, with shops on the first floor and loft apartments on the top. I had never been, but

Risa had swung by with a few of her hipster musician friends and declared it "cool enough for a minute, until we move on to the next thing."

When I arrived downtown, I found Caleb waiting for me outside.

"Hi," he said. He didn't lean over to give me a peck on the lips as he usually did, and I wondered if he would dump me outside on the curb or wait until we'd had a couple of drinks.

But then he took me by the hand and said, "C'mon," leading me around the building to a set of metal stairs in the back.

"I thought we were going to Drake's," I said.

"We are," he answered, letting go of my hand and climbing the stairs. "But first I wanted to show you something."

I followed him up to the second floor where he pulled open a steel door, revealing a thousand square feet of dark hardwood floors, huge warehouse windows, high vaulted ceilings, and brick walls with an assortment of vintage album covers and framed concert posters hanging on them. A keyboard sat in one corner of the room and a DJ booth posed in another. In the middle room sat a black-and-red carpet with an impressionist-style image of a seventies-era James Brown on it.

The chorus to "It's a Man's World" echoed in my head as I took in the apartment. "Is this . . . ?" I asked.

"Yeah, this is where I live." He pointed to a black partition that separated an unseen space from the rest of the loft. "That's where I work."

"Oh . . ."

"See, it's not that great," he said.

"Are you kidding? This apartment is insane. I can't believe you spent all those nights in my tiny bedroom when you had this to come back to."

He laughed. "You like it?"

I shook my head and walked over to the window, which showcased a view of a slivered crescent moon made blurry by the smoggy L.A. night sky. "No," I answered. "I love it."

He put an arm around my shoulders, and drew me to his side. "More than you love me?"

I turned away from the moon and looked him in the eye, my previous thoughts of suicide retreating to their secret place behind my heart. "No, I love you more," I said.

"I love you more than I love this apartment, too," he said. "That's why I brought you here. Sorry it took so long."

I beamed at him, so very happy that he wasn't about to dump me. "You're not afraid my sexual energy is going to disturb your work energy?"

Caleb took off his glasses and set them on the nightstand. "I'm not going to lie. I was scared about that, but then I got to thinking about it, and I decided I really like your sexual energy." He kissed me before adding, "I mean, I really like it."

He then gave me a gentle push and I fell back onto his soft bed. "My work energy would be honored to share the same space . . ." He bent over me and slipped his hands underneath my loose peasant top. ". . . the same hot space as your sexual energy."

Then, as if the Universe decided to prove that it was definitely on my side, he said, "Oh, and before we get too far into this, do you want to move in with me?"

# April 2011

Don't change your hair. Don't change your personality. Don't change the way you dress. Don't lose weight for anything other than health reasons. And, listen to me well now, don't worry about whether this will affect the number of guys that are attracted to you. For all the guys that reject you because your hair isn't straight, because you laugh too loud, because you prefer flats to heels, because you have hips, there's one guy who's going to adore that about you. And that's the guy you're looking for. So help him find you by staying just the way you are.

—*The Awesome Girl's Guide to Dating Extraordinary Men* by Davie Farrell

# THURSDAY

There were several things that I could have been doing on Easter. For instance, a costume designer friend of Caleb's was having a party in her Mount Washington home, complete with a grown-up Easter egg hunt. And Tammy had invited me to Easter dinner at her brother's house in the Los Feliz hills—a dinner at which I could have finally met Davie Farrell, Tammy's sister-in-law. Before becoming a dating guru, Davie Farrell had gotten her start as a life-coach-slash-career-counselor to people in the entertainment industry, and I could have used some free advice about what to do now that both my writing and stand-up careers had gone bust.

But, on Easter, I wasn't at a dinner party receiving advice from Davie Farrell. And Caleb went to the grown-up Easter egg hunt all by himself, because I was stuck on freaking Catalina Island. Now, normally I would have loved a trip to Catalina Island. I'd been so broke since moving to California that I counted myself lucky if I could make my car payment on time, much less take a vacation. So, really, I should have been thrilled about being on the same island where movie stars like Bob Hope, Cicely Tyson, and Nicolas Cage had vacationed.

However, I wasn't on vacation. I was in a guest suite in Mike Barker's vacation home with one hundred and eighteen pages of pure crap.

I had been able to avoid Mike's many calls and e-mails and put him off for a whole four months, but two weeks before Easter it had all come to a head.

I had been doing data entry and half listening to an audiobook when the receptionist said over the speaker system, "Thursday, please report to reception. You have a visitor."

I had taken out my earbuds, thinking it was Risa (who tended to show up places unannounced whenever she felt like it) or maybe Caleb. He had never come over for lunch before, but who knew? However, I began to suspect who had really come to visit when several phones started ringing throughout the office and then everyone who was anywhere close to reception stood up to stare over their cubicle walls.

But I kept on walking, kept on hoping that it wasn't who I thought it was. However, when I got to the reception area, I found two of my Latina co-workers standing on either side of Mike Barker while the receptionist took their picture. An amendment on that not-staring-at-celebrity rule I mentioned before: Most resident Angelenos refused to stare at celebrities if they were out and about in public. But as soon as celebrities entered some area where they seriously weren't supposed to be, like, say, your ultra-boring place of business, then all unspoken contracts became null and void, and even resident Angelenos felt free to lose their mind.

"Me next!" my boss, Nancy, came running, stopping only to hand her camera to the receptionist, who apparently had been designated the picture-taker.

If all the attention bothered Mike, it didn't show. He even thanked the two women for letting him take a picture with them, and then he slipped an arm around Nancy's shoulders, complimenting her on her pastel-purple business suit.

This move reminded me of my father, who always had a ready smile for fans who approached him on the street. I knew how to operate pretty much any camera made before 2001 because I had taken so many pictures of Rick T and his fans. Back then I had admired him for being popular, for never forgetting the fans who had put him at the top of the charts in the nineties. But watching Mike do the same thing with my office workers, charming them with a few seconds of attention, only made me feel even more cynical toward both him and my father. I promised myself that I would never smile at him the way my boss was smiling at him, just because he said, "Purple is a good color on you."

I looked back over my shoulder. At least half the office was standing there, their eyes all asking me the same question: "How do you know Mike Barker?"

My heart sank. The nice thing about living in California is that there are so many people named so many strange things, that when I introduced myself as a day of the week, people barely blinked. Unlike on the East Coast, where men my age all seemed to know Rick T had a daughter named Thursday, none of my co-workers had figured out yet that Rick T was my father. By showing up at my office unannounced, Mike Barker had caused me a whole slew of problems.

Speaking of which, the movie star himself finally saw me and waved. "Ready for lunch?" he said, like he had actually asked me to go out to eat with him ahead of time.

"Um, sure," I said, playing along. Lunch with Mike might buy me time to come up with a plausible excuse for Mike's visit. "Let me just get my purse."

But Mike waved me forward. "You don't need it. It's my treat."

"Thursday, why didn't you tell us that you were friends with Mike Barker?" my boss asked, seemingly on behalf of everyone in the office.

"Don't tell the trades or anything," he said to Nancy, like they were having a confidential conversation as opposed to talking in an open-plan office with several onlookers. "But I'm playing Thursday's father, Rick T, in an upcoming biopic."

The office exploded into a chorus of gasps and accusatory exclamations: "You're Rick T's daughter? His daughter, really? Why didn't you tell us? I can't believe you didn't tell us."

"Okay, well we should get going," I said to Mike, ignoring their questions.

# The Awesome Girl's Guide to Dating Extraordinary Men

He nodded at the office like they had all become close personal friends in the less than ten minutes he had spent with them. "It was nice to meet all of you."

"Bye," they called back, all smiles for Mike, but side-eyeing me like I had deeply betrayed them with my parental omission.

"Seriously, did you have to tell them I was Rick T's daughter?" I asked after I climbed into the passenger seat of Mike's bright-red Audi R8 Spyder.

Mike pushed a button and turned the key in the ignition. The car came alive with an aggressive roar of its V-10 engine while the top folded down like something out of *Transformers*. "It looks like we're always going to start things off with an argument, so I'll say that I didn't even know you were trying to keep your identity secret. Plus, if you had returned any of my many calls and e-mails, I wouldn't have had to surprise you at your place of work."

I folded my arms. "I've been really busy. I haven't been able to get to the script yet."

Mike pulled out of the parking lot and headed toward downtown Burbank. "It's hard for me to go out to regular restaurants because of the fan issue, but I can do a drive-through."

"You don't have to take me anywhere. I get it. I'm late. I'm sorry. I'm moving in with my boyfriend and it's been crazy busy. But I'll get you my notes and revisions, I promise."

"Okay, when?" he asked.

"When?" I hadn't been ready for that question. I scraped my head for a date that was far enough away that it seemed plausible but close enough to satisfy Mike. "Easter," I said. "We have that Friday off, and I've set aside the entire weekend to read the script and get you notes."

That, of course, was a lie. At that point, I'd already agreed to go to both the grown-up Easter egg hunt and Tammy's family dinner, but I had to buy myself some more time.

"Really, you've set aside the whole weekend?" he said, his voice skeptical.

"Yes, yes I have. I've told everybody that I can't come to their parties, because I feel so bad about not having gotten the script back to you yet."

He nodded. "That's a good idea to take the whole weekend."

"Yes, and I can't wait to tackle this script." Another blatant lie. I had thought ten thousand dollars would be enough to make it worth reading a script that glorified my father. But I'd had to stop after the first five pages, in which my parents meet cute as teenagers in Brooklyn's Marcy Projects with hip-hop unfolding all around them like a graffiti-covered pastoral.

First of all, my mother had lived in those projects, but my father had grown up in Connecticut. Second of all, the only reason they had met as high schoolers was because they had both received college scholarships to Columbia from the same black leadership organization and had been introduced to each other at the awards ceremony in Manhattan.

In the script, my father steps to my mother all poetry and swagger and it's love at first sight. In real life, my mother saw something in my scrawny, nerdy father and gave him a hip-hop makeover. In fact, most of the rhymes on his first record were taken from poems that she had written about growing up in the Marcy Projects.

Reading five pages had enraged me to the point that I had thrown the script across the room, and I hadn't picked it up since. I wished I could just give it back. But it had already gone to paying off my credit cards and my next few months of student loan payments. I had decided to skip the rainy-day fund that Sharita had suggested, since I'd become used to living paycheck-to-paycheck anyway. Why quit now?

"I've got Easter weekend free, too," he said. "Tell you what, I'll pick you up from work and we'll take my boat out to Catalina. I've got a little place there—nice, quiet, peaceful. We'll go. You can read over the script, and we'll bounce some thoughts off each other."

Alarm bells went off in my head as I realized Mike Barker was pulling that old Hollywood trick of sequestering the writer away to get the job done.

"I really don't need anything that serious," I assured him.

But I might as well have saved my breath. "Okay, then, I'll pick you up next Thursday at your office," Mike answered, as if I hadn't put up any protest.

He pulled into my parking lot and unlocked my door. "See you next week."

And that had been that. I got out of the car still trying to figure out what had just happened and how I had been railroaded into spending Easter weekend with Mike Barker.

Then I had to call Tammy to cancel for Easter dinner, which was even worse. After I explained the situation, with a lot of self-deprecating one-liners, letting her know how annoyed I was both at myself and at Mike Barker for putting me in this position, her immediate answer had been, "You're going to be spending three days alone with Mike in his house on Catalina?"

She didn't sound angry, exactly, but she also didn't sound like her usual happy self.

"More like I'm going to spend three days with a script, and he's just going to be around."

Silence, then: "I'm just a little concerned for the big picture of your career here. I really do think you should take this chance to meet Davie. I mean, she's so great at what she does. Get this, I went in for a counseling session with her just last month, and she came up with a whole new career path for me. You're now speaking to the official fitness representative for Farrell Cosmetics. I'll be blogging about fitness, and speaking at high schools around the nation. We're even going to do an exercise DVD, which we'll give away for free with every fifty-dollar Farrell Cosmetics purchase as a New Year's promotion."

Now you have to understand something here. This new career path that Davie Farrell came up with for Tammy wasn't just good, it was perfect. Tammy exercised every day, not because she had to in order to stay model thin, but because according to her, "Exercise is just so much fun!" She was one of those people who would fall on a vegetable tray and say things like, "Mmm, carrots, they taste so fresh and yummy." I was raised a vegetarian and even I wasn't down with vegetables like that. There is nobody in this world who would make a better fitness guru than Tammy. And Davie Farrell had figured that out with just one session.

Resisting the urge to bang my head against the loft's brick wall, I said, "That's awesome, Tammy. I'll be first in line to try out that DVD. But I don't know how I can get out of this. I tried to reason with him, and he totally wouldn't let me off the hook."

"Yeah," Tammy said, letting an uncharacteristic bitter note slip into her voice. "Mike Barker gets what he wants. That's, like, his motto."

"That's why it's better to just get it over with, right?" I said. "Three days and both Mike Barker and his awful script will be out of my life for good."

On the other side of the line, Tammy sighed. "Okay, Day. But I'm going to miss you at Easter dinner. I even made sure you'd get the seat next to Davie."

"Oh, believe me, I'll miss you more," I said, wondering how I could possibly sabotage my career any worse than I had so far this year.

So that was how I found myself on Easter Sunday 2011 in Catalina as opposed to hunting for Easter eggs with Caleb and rubbing elbows with Davie Farrell. And by the way, Mike's "little place" turned out to be a beachfront Mediterranean two-story, seven-bedroom *Architectural Digest*–level masterpiece of a house, with large colonnade windows overlooking a cliff that dropped down to a pebbled beach.

"This place is insane," I told Mike as we walked through the house-shaped masterpiece.

"Yeah, I bought it after I made my comeback a few years ago. Plus, there's no gambling on Catalina, so win-win." He took my carry-on suitcase by the leather handle, and led me up a winding stairwell lined with Catalina tile and an ornate black banister.

I tried to recollect what I'd heard about Mike's gambling addiction. At one point, I knew, it had gotten so bad that he had fallen to C-list status, doing any paycheck movie to make ends meet and fuel his habit, but then a few years ago he'd overcome his addiction, co-starred in an indie drama, and gotten nominated for a Best Supporting Actor Oscar.

"This seems like a good investment in your new life," I said. "I'm trying to get over some of my own BS right now, too."

"Oh yeah?" he said, glancing at me over his shoulder. "How's that going for you?"

I shrugged. "A work in progress."

He reached a white door and opened it. "Well, maybe this will inspire you."

I followed him into a large suite that looked more like a travel brochure than a guest room. Coved ceilings and wicker furniture with creamy white cushions made the space seem even larger and airier than it already was, and though I couldn't see the water from where I stood, if I opened the French patio doors that led out to a balcony, I was sure I'd find nothing less than a spectacular ocean view. I was impressed, but that was before I realized that this room would become my cage for the weekend.

After Mike deposited me in the guest suite, I didn't see him again. The only sign that he might still be on the premises had been the boxes of gourmet takeout from various restaurants that appeared outside my door with a short knock at ten in the morning, one in the afternoon, and six at night every day since I had arrived. Also, the room had no television, no radio, no Internet access, and no cell phone reception.

If I wasn't being kept prisoner, I didn't know what else to call it.

The first night, I read myself to sleep—with a literary mystery, not the script. But I promised myself that I'd pick up the script as soon as I finished my paperback. However, on Friday, when I turned the last page, I figured that I might as well read one more book for pleasure before I had to enter one hundred and eighteen pages of reading hell. I snuck out of my room and found a den filled with leather furniture and lined with bookshelves. The bookshelves boasted first editions and leather-bound copies of classics like *War and Peace* and *Roots* with lots of plays in between. I scoured his shelves, but couldn't find anything by an author who was currently living or even a woman, so I settled on a copy of *The Count of Monte Cristo*. Not exactly light vacation reading, but it was one of those books that I'd always meant to read.

After sneaking back into my room, I played several games of mah-jongg on my phone, read the first three hundred (out of a thousand-plus) pages of *The Count of Monte Cristo*, and went to sleep. So Friday was a wash.

Saturday I decided to shake things up by reading *Monte Cristo* out on the balcony, which, as I'd guessed, looked out on the sparkling blue ocean below. Along with red clay roof houses and the lazy sight stimulations of boats pulling into the bay, it made for the perfect reading view. But by late afternoon the usual depression began to creep in. The main character of *Monte Cristo* had managed to take charge of his life despite fourteen years of imprisonment and I couldn't even figure out how to pay my grad school loan bills with any kind of regularity. I eventually had to go back inside for fear that I might throw myself off the balcony.

I continued reading and eventually, I finished. But by that time, I felt so miserable that I knew I wouldn't be able to fall asleep, so I figured that I might as well read the stupid script. In the biopic version of Rick T's life, my father manages to claw his way to the top of the charts, all by his lonesome, despite hailing from humble beginnings and getting disowned by his father for making pop music as opposed to gospel. Then when he's at the top of his game, his first wife goes crazy on him, losing her mind while he's out on the road, and killing herself. In the screenplay, poor Rick T takes solace in Brenda after my mother's death, and ends up discovering that she's the true love of his life. The movie ends with their beach wedding in Kona, Hawaii, the day after 9/11, Rick T finally at peace after all he's been through. It only took me two hours to finish the script, but I spent three hours filling up ten sheets worth of hotel stationery with notes about why it sucked so very much.

When the next knock sounded on my door, I looked up from my computer screen to see the bright Easter-morning sun shining in through the windows. So I took a break from describing why the upbeat ending insulted both the truth and its audience to retrieve the food . . . only to find Mike Barker standing there, holding a clear plastic container filled with my breakfast.

That was when I remembered with mind-cringing embarrassment that I'd not only skipped showering for the last two days in a row, but had also slept in my clothes. I was still in the same TV on the Radio sweatshirt I'd had on when Mike had picked me up two days ago.

"Wow," he said, looking me up and down and cupping his nose against my smell. "Are you depressed?" he asked. "I only let myself get as bad as you when I'm depressed."

If I hadn't been so full of hate for his script, I might have slammed the door and not come out until I had showered and brushed my teeth, but, as it was, I opened my mouth, from which I could almost feel green fumes emitting, and said, "Yes. Yes, I am depressed. Reading this script has depressed the hell out of me."

He came in and set the plastic container down on the French Provençal desk at which I'd been working. "It's not that bad," he said. "C'mon."

I grabbed the container and started eating the egg-white omelet inside of it with a plastic fork while standing up. "Yeah, it is that bad," I said, my mouth full. "First of all, it's not even true. Second of all, it reads like it was written by somebody who doesn't give a damn about the story and just wants to get paid."

"Ronald Barnes wrote this script. We flew to Hawaii, and spent days consulting with your father on it," Mike said. Ronald Barnes was a renowned screenwriter who commanded a high five figures just to outline your script and about six for the rough. I could imagine Mike, my father, and Ronald Barnes, the white man tapped to write a script about a black man's life, having a boozy great time in the islands, and agreeing to write this piece of crap, which painted my father as an enterprising pioneer, and in the best possible light.

I shook my head at Mike. "Well, you paid that dude a lot of money to get over on you."

Mike picked up the ten pages lying next to my computer. "Are these your notes?"

I nodded. "I was going to type them up for you, but then you knocked on the door."

He skimmed the pages, his brow going tight with anger as he did. "Let me get this straight—you think we should write a Rick T biopic in which he's a cheating asshole with a saint of a wife? I guess he should also have a beautiful and gifted daughter he's estranged from."

"No, I wouldn't want Janine or me to be in it. It would be their story. But I know you're too clean-cut to actually want to play him the way he was. You want to give it the Johnny Cash experience and make it seem like he's this huge, misunderstood star who ended up falling in love with the woman he was really meant to be with. Yet another biopic from the prick's point of view, while the wife, who took care of his children and supported his career only to get dumped when somebody prettier came along, gets shuffled around in the background. Because her life doesn't even count. Right?"

148

"Thursday . . ." he started, tilting his head to the side like I was some poor, confused girl who needed the script mansplained to her.

And I just lost it. "I told you I didn't want to read it. And you offered me money, which I wasn't able to turn down because I'm a complete fuckup, barely getting by, drowning in student-loan payments for a degree I have yet to use. So, no, you definitely shouldn't listen to me. You're right, just pay your crappy writer a lot of money to do another crappy draft. I don't care. But you asked me for my opinion and I gave it to you, so there you go."

Despite my tone, hot tears burned behind my eyes. Where was all this anger coming from? I had been doing so well, faking it until I made it with Caleb, somehow managing to come off as a happy and carefree person despite my fears, general depression, and now-daily thoughts of throwing myself off tall buildings. But five minutes in Mike Barker's company had reduced me to a stereotypical angry black woman, overreacting to a script I shouldn't even care about.

"It's you," I realized out loud.

"What?" he said.

"Something about you brings out the worst in me." I started packing, throwing my computer and my paperback into my small suitcase.

"What are you doing?" he asked.

I would have answered, but I had to use all of my strength to pack and hold back the tears. And the depression. The stupid depression. It felt like it was going to crush me if I said even one more word to stupid Mike Barker about his stupid Rick T script. So I walked out, tugging my wheeled bag behind me.

Once outside in the fresh air, I was able to pull myself together enough to come up with some kind of plan. Mike's vacation home sat on top of a huge hill about three miles up from the Catalina pier. It would take a while, but it was doable. I knew I smelled and didn't want to inflict myself on other passengers, but I also couldn't see myself knocking on Mike's front door and asking if I could take a shower before I left. That wouldn't exactly make for a grand exit.

I had been walking for about ten minutes when Mike pulled up beside me in one of the golf carts that everyone used to get around on the narrow island roads. Of course, his cart was fire-engine red with fifteen-inch chrome wheels and customized to look like an old thirties coupe. Reason #3 that I didn't date black men: They always had to stand out, didn't they?

"Get in the cart," he said from inside his flashy vehicle.

"No," I said, gripping my suitcase's handle even tighter. "I've put in a lot of effort, trying to be a better person, and I'm not going to let you destroy all my good work."

"Just get in the cart. I'll drive you to the pier and take you back to Los Angeles," he said.

I had always wanted to be one of those women who stood my ground and didn't compromise my pride and integrity. But the fact was I had already grown tired of walking, and I was dirty, and as awkward as a boat ride back to Los Angeles with Mike Barker would be, it might be a little better than looking and smelling this bad on a ferry full of people.

So I chose the movie star. I deposited my bag in the cart's trunk and slid onto the buttery leather seat next to Mike, who put the cart in drive.

We puttered down the hill in silence for a while until I said, "Listen, obviously I'm not the right person for this project."

"Obviously," he said, his jaw tight.

"Why don't you call my sister? She's nicer than me and likes our dad a lot more. Between her and your expensive writer, you should be able to come up with something."

Mike glanced over at me. "You're in a relationship, right? With that guy I saw you with at the comedy club?"

I nodded, and he looked out at the road ahead for a long time before saying, "Davie would say you shouldn't be in a relationship until you solve your issues with your father."

I sat up. "First of all, who's Davey? And second of all, how does he think I'm supposed to solve my father? Have you ever tried getting closure from a narcissist?"

Here was the thing about actors: their favorite drink was the Kool-Aid of positivity. It was like their religion, and it made them think that any emotional issue could be surmounted with enough positive thinking. Even the ones like Mike Barker, who could convincingly play smart people on film, thought this way. And it made them hard to talk to because they failed to understand that not every broken thing could be fixed with the mindset.

"Davie Farrell is kind of like my substitute mom, kind of like my life coach," he said.

I looked over at him. "Wait a minute, you know Davie Farrell? I skipped going to dinner with Davie Farrell so that I could come out here and work on your stupid script."

He stared at me for what felt like a full minute before saying, "You told me you had the entire weekend free." He shook his head. "Wow, you're unprofessional."

"I didn't ask for this job," I said, through gritted teeth, trying hard not to completely lose it again, to hold on to the better version of Thursday that I had been working so hard to achieve. "You're the one who insisted I take it. You're the one who wouldn't give up until I took it. Really, you're the one who's being unprofessional."

This only made him chuckle in a way that felt like a small expulsion of anger rather than true amusement. "Well, I tell you what. Mike Barker gets what he wants. And I only get unprofessional when my hand is forced. What's your excuse?"

"You don't think you forced my hand?" I asked him. "You don't think railroading me into a weekend in Catalina with a script I hated wasn't forcing my hand?"

"You didn't hate it, you just didn't agree with it," he said.

"No, I assure you: I hated it," I said. I could see the pier and the shining ocean that led back to Los Angeles in the distance now. "It's a bad script. I'm sorry if you can't admit that, but trust that I did hate it. And quite frankly, I'm beginning to hate you."

He laughed again, and there was an even angrier edge to it this time. "You know what? You need to get on some anger management or something," he said. "Trust me, if you don't get your shit sorted out, you're going to end up alone and broke. And you're going to deserve exactly what you get."

My breath caught. He had said the two things I was most afraid of. Out loud. How did he know? And why would he wish something like that on me? I stared at him, horrified. My co-workers were wrong about Mike Barker. He wasn't nice. He was mean and evil and capable of saying really hurtful things when he didn't get his way.

The wind picked up, and I could hear my parents screaming at each other downstairs in the living room. My father telling my mother that she was lucky to have him, because he was the one who paid all the bills and got us this nice house, and made sure that Janine and I went to the best schools. He yelled that he was stressed and all she did was nag him when he came home. He yelled that he was leaving the house at ten p.m., in fresh clothes, smelling like cologne, because she had pushed him away. He yelled that she deserved to get treated the way he treated her, because of her poor attitude and her mouth, which she just couldn't keep shut when he got home.

All over the United States, I thought, there were black men putting black women down to build themselves up. And I was sick of being a better person.

"I might end up alone and broke, and you might try to ascribe that to some flaw in my personality," I told him then. "But if I do, it won't be because of today. And just because I have issues with my father doesn't mean I'm wrong about your script. It's by the numbers, and it doesn't have any heart. You can put me down as much as you want to, but I'm right about that. And I'm not going to let you mess with my self-esteem. So here's me being a really unprofessional nobody and saying to you, a big-deal somebody, *shut the fuck up.*"

Angry, thick silence. Then Mike didn't say anything else until we got to the pier a few minutes later. He got my bag out of the golf cart's trunk and set it down in front of me.

"There's the office to buy ferry tickets," he said, pointing out a small gray metal building to the right of us. "You can get your own ass home."

And then he was jumping back in his red coupe cart and driving away. I felt outraged, indignant, and righteous at the same time. But as his cart disappeared over the hill, depression set in again. And I started to feel stupid. Yes, maybe Mike Barker was another black man trying to tear the black woman down. But he was rich and driving back to his amazing house in his custom golf cart, both of which he owned. While I was left standing there alone on the dock, about to use the last fifty dollars in my bank account to buy a ticket back to the city, having burned the one and only professional bridge I had managed to make after struggling in Los Angeles for over five years.

*Maybe . . .* I thought. *Maybe Mike Barker was right about me.*

# May 2011

No, you don't have to change yourself to find an extraordinary man, but that doesn't mean you shouldn't strive to be the best version of yourself possible and sometimes that means being open to hearing what people are telling you about yourself. I, myself, am a big believer in not caring what anyone else thinks. But if somebody tells me something about myself that makes me so mad I wanna spit, then maybe I think about what they said a little harder, because they just might be telling me something I need to know.

—*The Awesome Girl's Guide to Dating Extraordinary Men* by Davie Farrell

# SHARITA

9 was sitting at home, reading my Bible, when Risa called, basically using every cuss word the book advised against while some really loud, sad, and angry song screamed along in the background. From what I could put together, the record company not only wanted to use the bitter love song some producer named David Gall had written as the first single off her album, but they also didn't want to release her record until next February.

"They're all, like, 'It's Black History Month! More buzz!' because black people don't have a reputation for being homophobic or anything, and they're really going to want to buy an album from an electronic rock 'project' fronted by a black lesbian out of solidarity. It's the only way to honor Dr. Martin Luther King, right? And why can't they just let me sing dirty, electronic rock and roll anyway? Why does every woman singer have to agree to portray herself as some kind of victim of love if she wants a recording contract? It's so fucking unfair."

"Risa, I can barely hear you," I yelled into the phone.

"You're right," she yelled back. "I should come over. That way we can come up with a game plan that doesn't involve me shooting up the offices of Gravestone Records."

I looked at the clock. "You can come over, but you can only stay for about an hour. I've got my women's Bible-study group at seven-thirty."

"Wait," she said. "Didn't you go to church on Sunday?"

"Yes," I answered.

"And didn't you go to that church book club on Tuesday?"

"Risa, if you're trying to tease me about going to church on a Friday night, then I don't want to hear it. I'm still getting over Marcus, and I need my Savior right now, okay?"

"Okay," she answered, but her voice sounded neutral, almost too neutral. "I'm going to be there in about thirty minutes, alright?"

"Okay," I said, feeling suspicious. Risa usually didn't back down this easily. "See you then."

About forty minutes after I got off the phone with Risa, the doorbell rang and I found her standing on the porch of my little two-bedroom Craftsman . . . with Tammy and Tammy's brother, James Farrell, behind her. I looked down at what I was wearing. I had just changed out of my suit into a pair of sweatpants and my USC Leventhal School of Accounting hoodie. Not exactly what I wanted to be wearing with a fine man showing up on my porch.

But then this mild regret triggered my next question: "What are you all doing here?"

"Sharita, can we come in?" Risa asked, her face grim in the waning evening light.

"Um, sure," I said, stepping back so that they could all come in.

Thank God I was tidy by nature—unlike Risa, whose apartment always looked like it had been hit by a tornado of clutter. I led my unexpected guests into the living room.

"I'm not sure why you're all here. But can I get you something? I've got water, orange juice, diet soda, um, what else?"

Before I could list any more beverage choices, Risa placed two hands on my shoulders and said, "Sharita, this is an intervention."

"What?" I said.

Tammy gasped, her shock both innocent and hurt. "That's why you said that James and I had to meet you at Sharita's house right away? I thought this was an emergency or something."

"It is an emergency," Risa said, not taking her eyes off me.

"Exactly what are we intervening in?" James asked, wrinkling his handsome forehead.

But I already knew the answer to that question. "Wow, Risa. I'm sorry I haven't been able to spend as much time with you lately because I'm trying to get my soul right in church, but this is really extreme. I can't believe you tricked Tammy and her brother into coming here."

Risa said, "Sit down, Sharita."

"No, I'm not going to let you lecture me about loving God."

"This will only take five minutes," she promised. "Sit down."

I ran a small cost-benefit analysis through my head. If I didn't sit down, then I would have to continue to stand here arguing with Risa in front of the finest, richest black man I knew. If I sat down, though, it would only be five minutes worth of embarrassment. The latter got Risa out of my house sooner. So I sat down on my couch and folded my arms across my chest.

Taking on the demeanor of a trial lawyer—if trial lawyers wore white leather leggings and motorcycle jackets—Risa came to stand in front of me. "I am not here to harangue you about going to church. Indeed, there is nothing wrong with staying in touch with your spirituality."

I unfolded my arms, feeling a little less defensive.

"The reason I came here today, the reason we all came here—"

"James and I didn't exactly come here for this," Tammy inserted with an apologetic look. "She tricked us, too."

Risa kept going as if Tammy hadn't said anything. "The reason we all came here is not to prevent you from being a good Christian, but from being a lonely one. For Sharita, the cultural landscape has changed, and there is something that you might not know."

Risa held up a finger and paused for maximum effect before declaring in a tone that would have made a born-again Southern fire-and-brimstone preacher call her overly dramatic, "Sister Sharita, I must inform thee that church is the new cat."

"The new what?" Tammy asked.

"The new cat," Risa repeated, grave as St. Peter.

"Church is the new cat?" I repeated. "What does that even mean?"

"I'm glad you asked, Sharita." Risa folded her hands together in front of her chest. "You know how guys don't mind if a woman has one cat? And maybe if she has two, he'll still go out with her? But if she has three cats, then he figures she's a crazy cat lady and doesn't ask her out again? Well, church is the new cat. You can go once a week, no problem. Twice a week, a guy might think you're a little zealous, but will still date you because you're cute and you've got a banging rack. But three times a week, and that pretty much guarantees the only loving you're going to be getting in your life is from Jesus. By the way, the same rule applies to Facebook statuses, so you might want to keep the 'I love me some Jesus' updates to, like, once or twice a week as opposed to the daily thing you're doing now."

"Wait, let me get this straight," I said. "You all came over here because you honestly believe I won't be able to get a date because of my commitment to God?"

Tammy looked shocked to find her genteel Southern self in this awkward urban situation. "Oh no, Sharita. James and I would never try to make you feel bad about going to church."

"She is correct," Risa said. "I didn't bring Tammy here to take part in this intervention, but to stand forth as state's evidence."

I stared at her. "Do you even know what 'state's evidence' means?"

"No," answered Risa. "But I like the sound of it, and I offer you one Tammy Farrell."

She turned to Tammy. "Tammy, you could get any boy you want, right?"

"Risa . . ."

"You took an oath, you've got to answer the question," Risa said.

"Um, I don't remember taking any oath—"

"Okay, then, just answer the question so that we can get out of here."

Tammy wrung her hands together, her long eyelashes fluttering with pretty awkwardness. "I couldn't get any boy . . ." she said.

"Your humility is admirable, but boys do like you, and if we asked a single guy to take you out, he'd probably say yes. And this is because you don't go to church three times a week."

I had been trying to stay quiet, but I had to point out here, "Tammy's a former *model*. And she's sweet and she's funny. Who wouldn't want to go out with her?"

Tammy blushed. "Aw, thanks, Sharita. That's so kind of you to say."

"I had a feeling you would present that argument, which is why I invited your crush, James Farrell, along to my intervention."

My face went red-hot with embarrassment. As soon as James Farrell was out of sight, I was going to kill Risa. Literally kill her.

"James," Risa said, turning to him. "Does your wife attend church?"

James looked embarrassed for both himself and me. "Occasionally," he answered. "We're more Christmas and Easter kinds of people."

"I see," said Risa, nodding like Matlock before the kill. "And before getting married, did you ever date a woman that went to church more than two times a week?"

James actually thought about it before saying, "No, I guess I didn't."

"And if any of your prospective dates had informed you that they attended church three times a week, would you have asked them out?"

James grimaced, but admitted, "Maybe not. Three times a week is a lot."

"*Three times a week is a lot,*" Risa repeated, pointing at me. "I rest my case."

"Okay, get out of my house," I said.

Risa came out of her lawyer persona with a hurt frown. "Wait, I didn't convince you?"

"By comparing me to a model and making James Farrell admit that he would never have dated me, even if he was single? No, you didn't convince me. Now get out."

I put my hand on Risa's back and started pushing her toward the door.

Tammy followed us, saying, "I'm really sorry about this. If I had known, I would have tried to talk her out of it. But she might have a point about the church thing. Right, James?"

Another handsome grimace from James. "Yeah, I have to admit, she kind of does."

They were ganging up on me now? "No, really, all of you need to get out."

Risa shook her head. "See, I knew I needed a regular-woman example. This would've gone differently if Thursday hadn't refused to come."

I paused in my effort to push Risa out the door. "You told her it was an emergency, and she still refused to come?"

"Well, unlike Tammy, she guessed that it wasn't really an emergency. And then when I told her what it was really about, she agreed with me but said you would be too thick-headed to take the intervention, so I had to make do with Tammy and James."

I held up a hand. "She said WHAT?"

# THURSDAY

*E*ver since having my "better Thursday" project go so freaking off the rails with Mike Barker in Catalina, I had decided to double down on gratitude. For example, instead of missing Sharita, I decided to be grateful that I no longer had to deal with someone I couldn't count on.

Also, sometimes things got a little boring with Caleb. Though we said we were in love with each other and spent most of our non-working hours together, at times it felt like we were somehow shadow-puppeting love, that we were the love equivalent of a cardboard cutout. But after the Mike Barker incident, I'd push those thoughts away and decide just to be grateful I was in my first long-term relationship. We had lots of interests in common, liked the same music, talked easily about our future together, which, in our shared vision, included two kids and a three-bedroom house. *I am grateful for Caleb*, I'd chant to myself when the boredom nudged at me. And I'd thank the Universe over and over again until the boredom went away.

Whenever I got a rejection e-mail for a job that paid more or sounded far more worthwhile than administering contracts at MTS Systems, I focused on how grateful I was to have a job at all in this economy, and used that gratitude to keep myself off the MTS roof.

In fact, that morning when I got a rejection e-mail from the grant-writing department of KPCC, one of Southern California's National Public Radio affiliates, I held myself there as still as I could, clinging to my desk, willing myself to be grateful for the job I currently had as opposed to becoming overwhelmed by searching for a good job in a bad economy.

"Thursday," a voice said above me. "Are you all right?"

I looked up to see my boss, Nancy, standing there. I realized then what I must have looked like, holding on to the edge of my desk, stiff as a stroke victim. "I'm fine. I'm just . . ." I didn't know how to finish that sentence, so I just said it again. "I'm fine."

Her eyes softened, and she gave me the most gentle look. "Can I see you in my office?"

As it turned out, I would no longer have to actively resist the urge to throw myself off the MTS roof, because fifteen minutes later, I could no longer count myself as an employee of MTS Systems. There were lots of reasons for this layoff. My boss had been instructed to cut at least two contract administrators, and though I had done good enough work for the company, in her words, "You don't seem enthusiastic to be here."

No, I hadn't been enthusiastic, not like my co-workers with their cheesy workplace banter, and their scene-by-scene reconstructions of the last episode of *Modern Family*, and their happy breakfasts in the lunchroom. I thought about chorizo and eggs as I packed up my desk in three boxes provided by MTS. I wondered what it tasted like. I had only eaten the fake kind. And by the time I was done collecting the contents of my desk into boxes, under my now-former boss's awkward supervision, I had an official craving for meat.

A few minutes later, I thanked my boss for helping me carry my boxes out to the car and then went straight to In-N-Out, where I ordered a double-double cheeseburger. Being a vegetarian by inheritance was a little different than being a vegetarian by choice. Most of the time, I stuck to the diet I had grown up with, but I didn't feel the need to resist the urge to eat meat. And on the rare occasion that I found myself craving meat, I had a hamburger. No biggie.

I hadn't even tried to explain this reasoning to Caleb, who was a vegetarian by choice. He used words like "moral" and "equality" when talking about his college conversion from midwestern meat eater to a card-carrying member of PETA, which was why I stopped at a CVS and bought a travel bottle of mouthwash. I swished with it before making the trip upstairs with one of my boxes. But I needn't have bothered. Caleb had his headphones on and was deep in a project. He didn't even hear me come in.

Risa called to invite me to Sharita's place as I was making my way down the steps to get my second box. "That's funny," I said, after she admitted that she was staging an intervention. "But it's not going to work. Sharita's way too thick-headed."

I got off the phone laughing, but soon the depression came back. Who gets laid off from her dead-end job? Where did I even go from here? And how was I going to tell Caleb I got fired and could no longer pay my half of the rent? Instead of returning to my car for the third box, I lay down and stared at the loft's high ceiling, trying to find meaning in its exposed pipes.

I was sick of being grateful. Gratitude had gotten me nothing except two weeks' severance. The image of Mike Barker driving away in his custom golf cart came back to me. If I hadn't burnt that bridge I could call Mike now and see if he could get me a production assistant job or something. He could probably snap his fingers and get people jobs just like that. Why, oh why, had I been born a complete screwup?

And so on and so on until Caleb's face appeared above me.

"Are you okay?" he asked.

"Hey," I said, quickly pasting on a smile. "I thought you were working."

"Bathroom break, but then when I was coming back, I saw you laying here with your eyes open. It sort of looked like you were dead."

"I'm sorry," I said, sitting up. "I didn't mean to scare you."

"Are you okay?"

Just then the landline sounded, giving off the two short rings that meant someone was at the downstairs door and wanted to be buzzed up.

"Did you order a pizza?" I asked. Used to working on big projects alone, Caleb often ordered out without consulting with me first.

"No," he said, looking over his shoulder at the retro eighties wall phone. "I'll get it."

"Hello?" he said after picking up the bright green receiver. Then: "Could you hold on?"

He called across the room, "It's Sharita."

# SHARITA

9 can't believe you didn't come to my intervention," I said when Thursday came down the metal stairs that led to the loft she was sharing with Caleb now. I hadn't seen Thursday since December and I was surprised to see her dreadlocks were styled into wavy curls now. I felt a compliment tug at my tongue. Despite everything, I wanted to tell her she looked good, like I would have back when we were still best friends.

But then she said, "I don't believe the intervention actually worked."

"It didn't work," I informed her. "I'm still very much a child of God."

"Then why are you here as opposed to at your Bible study?" she asked.

That stymied me for a second. When I had gotten Thursday's new address from Risa and driven over here, it hadn't occurred to me that I was skipping my Bible study to confront my trifling ex-friend.

But I reset and jabbed my finger at her. "You need to learn about a big thing called forgiveness. It was *one party*."

"First of all, having this conversation with you really is the last thing I need today. Second of all, you can't demand that somebody forgive you," Thursday said, in that irritating, droll academic way of hers that she employed for fights. "Third of all, if I need to learn forgiveness, then you need to learn how to be a real friend first."

"I am a real friend when it counts," I said. "That's what I don't like about you. You don't remember anything. If somebody doesn't do exactly what you want them to do, when you want them to do it, then you go crazy on them. Just like with your father—"

I broke off, because even before Thursday's eyes went cold, I knew that I shouldn't have activated that minefield.

"Oh, what a surprise," Thursday said, her voice as mocking as it could possibly get. "Sharita is taking the side of yet another black man over her friends. In fact, Sharita is so conditioned to put men first that she can't seem to see the pattern in her own behaviors." Thursday broke off to glare at me. "Instead of fixing yourself, you're over here, trying to convince me I'm the crazy one, when you're the one who keeps on doing the same thing over and over again and expecting different results. Well, you got your different results. You canceled on me one time too many and now we're no longer friends."

I saw red. Thursday was one of those black girls who hadn't grown up with other black girls and therefore had never learned that you can't say whatever you want to us. The only thing that kept me from snatching every last lock out of her fool head was the certainty that I would never make partner at my firm if I had an assault arrest on my record.

But even considering that outcome, I was extremely tempted to do it anyway. "You think you're better than me because you're dating a white boy?" I asked. "You're just like those house slaves that lorded it over the field slaves because they were sleeping with the massa."

Thursday rolled her eyes. "Oh my God, minoring in African-American studies doesn't make you an expert on interracial relationships. And really, comparing my relationship to that of masters and slaves only makes everything coming out your mouth sound even more dumb. So I'm going to talk to you like you're as stupid as you sound right now."

Thursday said this next part really slowly, like she was talking to a child. "I don't think I'm better than you because I'm in an interracial relationship. I think I'm better than you because I'm in a healthy and loving relationship with a man who is committed to me *and* because I maintain my friendships despite being in said relationship. Unlike you, who can't even manage this task when you're just hanging out with yet another trifling, no-good Negro."

This time I had to control the impulse to straight-up kill Thursday. "You," I informed Thursday, "are a siddity, racist, and ungrateful bitch. And I can't even believe we were friends as long as we were. I must have been out of my dang mind."

I considered myself a lady and tried not to call people names. But Thursday had pissed me off that bad.

Thursday jutted her chin out, still haughty as she could be. "Well, thank you for coming all the way over here. I've learned so much from your brilliant observations. Good night."

She walked back up her stairs to her apartment, and though I should have felt righteous and vindicated, sadness overtook me as I got back into my Volkswagen Jetta, which I'd parked in the guest spot underneath the stairs. Was this really it? Were we ending our twelve-year friendship over one party?

My phone went off then and part of me hoped it was Thursday, calling to apologize.

But the caller ID lit up with my sister's name. Nicole, who hadn't bothered to do more than text message me since August and who was most likely calling to ask for money yet again.

I picked it up anyway, because at least Nicole was nice and would never accuse me of being stupid. But maybe I shouldn't have, because my annoyance flared up all over again when Nicole said, "Shariiiita! I have a HUGE favor to ask of you."

"Wow," I said. "You couldn't even say hello? The answer's no, okay?"

"But you can't say no," Nicole said. "I really need my little sister."

"I can and I am saying no because guess what? I'm not an ATM, Nic. I know you think I'm rich. But you don't seem to realize that I have money because I work hard for it. And you don't seem to appreciate that giving you money that you always promise to pay back but never do is not helping me maintain my wealth. In fact, you are bad for my wealth. And it would be different if you were really poor. But you have a weave that you manage to maintain even when you know your rent is due, so if you really need money, think about cutting back on your hair-salon bills. How about that? How about taking out the expensive weave that hasn't gotten you any paid roles and using the money you save to pay your own dang rent as opposed to calling me every time you want a handout?"

There was a long moment of silence on the other end. But I refused to apologize. All people did was use me and then dump me when I didn't do what they wanted me to do, and I was done apologizing.

"Sharita," Nicole said, her tone quiet and much less upbeat now. "I wasn't calling for a handout. I'm calling because I've been dating this really nice guy and he just asked me to marry him. I was hoping you would agree to be my maid of honor."

# June 2011

The golden rule applies, especially when it comes to love. Do unto others as you would have others do unto you. I can't tell you how many clients I've had complain about what they're getting, while refusing to give all of themselves.

—*The Awesome Girl's Guide to Dating Extraordinary Men* by Davie Farrell

# SHARITA

$\mathcal{N}$icole was getting married. Nicole, who had majored in theater at Trinity College and had then decided, against my advice, to dig herself even further into the black hole of art by taking on major debt to go to Yale's School of Drama. Nicole, who had insisted on pursuing acting despite having never been paid more than seventy-five bucks a performance to do so. Nicole, who couldn't keep a day job. Nicole, who had dated one useless starving artist after another and squandered all of her brains on a career that did not want her. Nicole, who called her *little sister* every other month to borrow money, was getting married.

And the groom wasn't another starving artist who could barely afford a five-minute wedding at city hall. No, she was marrying the director that had turned her down for the Verizon ad. A few weeks after passing on her for the commercial, he had called her up and asked her out.

"Apparently, they were all set to cast me, but he didn't want there to be a conflict of interest when he asked me out," Nicole explained after I arrived at the apartment that her fiancé and she were now sharing in the East Village.

The apartment was large and stuffed with first-edition books and mid-twentieth-century artwork. Apparently, Graham—that was her fiancé's name—had inherited the apartment from a great aunt. Graham's mother was Jewish, and his father was black. His parents had met at Hamilton College during a non-school-sanctioned meeting of the Revolutionary Communist Youth Brigade. Both the RCYB and his parents' marriage had dissolved by now, but Graham had been able to keep the spoils of both sides of his ancestry. He seemed very cool and of-the-people when he introduced himself to me over dinner at Degustation, an impressively hip tapas bar within walking distance of his and Nicole's apartment. But he had also used family and old private school connections to work his way up the career ladder, managing to become a steadily working commercial director by the age of thirty-eight.

He hadn't dated much before meeting Nicole because he had always been too focused on his career. "But one day, we're casting this commercial and in walks your sister. There was something about her. I loved her vibe. She seemed so happy and carefree, even though she probably could have used the job."

I had to bite my tongue to keep from saying that Nicole was probably "so happy and carefree" because she knew her little sister would bail her out if she didn't book the commercial.

Graham and Nicole glowed together at the restaurant, holding hands over the table, the large diamond in her engagement ring gleaming under the restaurant's lights. Because Graham was left-handed, they could hold on to each other throughout dinner. And when I went for my credit card after the bill came, Nicole said, "Stop it, sis. You know we've got this."

"You know we've got this," she said, like she had ever treated me to dinner in my entire life. And she said "we" like she and Graham were already married.

Furthermore, Nicole was pregnant. Graham had been upfront about wanting children from the beginning of their relationship, and they'd been talking about getting engaged anyway, so Nicole had stopped taking birth control with Graham's consent—a plan I would have heartily advised her against if she'd told me. But *voila*, they got pregnant. Graham made it official with a ring, and he even found an abandoned Friday opening at the Lighthouse at Chelsea Pier (the original groom had gotten cold feet) for the ceremony. And now they were planning a small wedding for late July. According to Nicole, they needed to do it soon, so she wouldn't be showing when she walked down the aisle. Her laughter positively twinkled when she said this.

And that was why I had come to New York in June, to help my sister (who I hadn't even known was dating someone seriously) find a dress.

"Sorry about what I said on the phone the other night," I said when Nicole showed me to the guest room after dinner with Graham. She looked so comfortable in the role of Manhattan wife-to-be, in her pencil skirt and sleeveless satin blouse, as if this acting stuff had been something to pass the time until she met the handsome, rich, and intelligent man of her dreams.

"That's okay," Nicole said, gracious as a party hostess. "I know you didn't mean it."

But that was it. I had meant it. I had meant every single word about Nicole needing to get her act together. I just hadn't expected her to actually do it.

My sister had found the right man, and thanks to his connections, she was booking all kinds of commercials now, even though she didn't really need the money and was already talking about "taking a long break" from acting once the baby came.

I barely got through the weekend of dress shopping with my sister, who didn't even look at price tags before picking wedding gowns to try on. The dress she ended up choosing cost fifteen thousand dollars. I started to point out that fifteen thousand dollars would bear greater fruit throughout the course of their marriage if they invested that money as opposed to spending it on a dress Nicole would wear once. But the first rule of dispensing money advice is that the person you're giving it to has to be poorer than you. And Nicole, in her new designer wardrobe and wearing an even more expensive and swingier weave, wasn't that anymore. So I kept my mouth shut and tried not to choke on my own bitterness.

Because even though I had done everything right and Nicole had done everything wrong, Nicole was the one getting married and about to welcome a child. Nicole, of all people, had become the sterling example of black love. How was that fair?

Perhaps irrationally, my thoughts skittered to Thursday, who'd been a shameless ho since college. Her stand-up routine was vulgar and distasteful. She had daddy issues out the wazoo. She dressed like a dang hippie. She wasn't entirely right in the head. And yet her very first stab at a healthy relationship had netted her a decent boyfriend. *Her very first one.* How was that fair?

I obsessed about this on my flight back to L.A. How was it that both Nicole and Thursday, two of the most ridiculous people I knew, had managed to land stable relationships?

Obviously, good men preferred neurotic basket cases like them as opposed to strong, capable women like me. And I was sick of it. Sick of dating men who didn't appreciate me. Sick of getting used only to be passed over for women who, despite years in the workforce, hadn't even made it into the mid-five-figure range. Even the good guys had awful taste in women, and I couldn't take it anymore.

I made a decision as my JetBlue flight landed at the Burbank Airport. From now on I would date my Career exclusively. My Career paid me compliments and my Career appreciated me. My Career never asked me for loans or got mad if I missed its birthday party. And if I committed to my Career, the most rewarding Love I had ever known, then unlike my relationship with Marcus and my friendship with Thursday, at least I'd have something to show for it. I'd be named a partner by December. That, I swore to myself.

# RISA

One day . . . one day I was going to rock an arena, and The One would be there and she would see me in a new light. Her knees would quiver because my guitar sounded so good, her nipples would harden because she would be surrounded by a crowd of girls who would do anything to get with me, her pussy would get wet because she'd know that she was the only girl I really wanted. She'd call her family and she'd tell them that she is in love with Risa Merriweather. She'd say, "Yes, Risa's a girl. She's a woman, actually. The only woman I have ever loved." And if they threatened to shut her out, she would say, "That's fine." Then she would come to me backstage, and I would kiss her with the electricity of the music still coursing through me. And she'd know she did the right thing, because she might have liked pretending to be a good little straight girl, but no one would ever love her as fucking much as I did.

However, it was kind of fucking hard to get to the arena level when I was being ghettoized in stupid Black History Month. I needed a closer release date and I needed one this year. So I thought on it. Then I thought on it some more. Then I called Sharita because I couldn't come up with anything by myself.

She was in New York with her sister and happier than usual that I called. She said she could use the distraction. "Have you tried talking to the label?" she asked.

"Yeah, but I can only make my feelings so known before I get tagged as 'difficult.'"

"Then it sounds like they need an incentive to put the album out earlier. Maybe if it coordinated with some event. Could you put together a tour or something for the fall?"

"No, they've already got a college tour scheduled for the fall with Ipso! Facto!, Homer & Marge, and Yes, We Are Trying To Cute You To Death. I asked if Supa Dupa could jump on, but they said that's not the vibe they're going for. They act like they're all alternative at Gravestone, but it's such a young white-guy club over there, it's not even funny."

"Hmm . . ." I could just see Sharita on the other side of the phone, turning over the problem in her head. "Well, when I wanted to get noticed by the president of my accounting firm, I joined his wife's book club. I pretended it was a total coincidence and like I was all surprised to see her there. Then I agreed with everything she said and even backed her up with arguments from the book. It only took about two months for the president to 'realize' what an asset I was to the firm and give me a promotion to senior accountant."

"Wow," I said, truly impressed. "That's, like, the most boring intrigue I've ever heard."

"Laugh if you want, Risa," she said. "But often the most direct path to the guy in charge is through his wife."

I got off the phone shaking my head because Sharita had been no help at all, but then I started thinking about it. Maybe she had a point. I got out my laptop and did some research.

Ipso! Facto! was the most successful band on the tour and therefore the ones that got to decide who went out on the road with them. Three of the guys seemed to go through reality starlets like water. But the lead singer had been dating the same woman for three years. And get this—she was an artist. Not a recording artist, but an artist-artist, like with paint.

Now this was important, because almost all fine artists are genetically wired to swing both ways until the age of twenty-eight. Don't ask me why, it's a fact. And another important point: bi chicks loved my ass. I mean, check out my stats: tall, strong personality, broody as hell—total dream dyke. If The Lead Singer's Girlfriend was within age range, I might have an in.

I clicked more links connected to her name and found out she graduated from CalArts two years ago. Which would make her twenty-four. "Gotcha!" I smiled and called Thursday.

"Hey! What's up?" she said. Like Sharita, she sounded a little too excited to get my call.

"Yo, I'm about to text you an address for this event I want to go to. Meet me there at eight, okay?"

"For what?" she asked, sounding a little less excited to be on the phone with me now.

"Does it matter? It's free, and it's not like you have a job or anything."

"I've learned to ask questions," she answered dryly. "The last time I met you no-questions-asked, I woke up in a closet in some random RISD dorm room."

"It was a couple of tabs of ecstasy," I said. "You always tell that story like I let you get roofied or something."

"Are you going to explain what the event is or not?"

"It's an art show. You'll like it."

"Does this have anything to do with The One?" She took my answering silence as a confirmation. "Oh my God, why are you like Wile E. Coyote with this ex, forever hatching questionable plans to get her back?"

"I'm so close. Okay? Closer than I've ever been before. This isn't the usual bullshit—"

"I worry that you're always doing this stuff to win her back when she's not doing anything to get you back. It's kind of like what Davie Farrell says about applying the golden rule to love. Shouldn't both of you be trying to make this relationship work? Why are you always the only one trying to get back together?"

"Thursday . . . don't. I don't want to have this argument with you again. Just be cool and meet me, okay?"

"Okay, I'll come. But only because it's free, and also because I'm bored to death and sadly have nothing better to do," she said. "But I want to go on record as not approving of this latest plan to get with a woman who obviously doesn't appreciate you the way you appreciate her."

"Fine," I say. "Whatever. See you at eight."

# July 2011

I tell you what, I believe in Karma. So no matter who pisses you off, or who you have to dump, try to be as upstanding a dating citizen as you can be. And definitely don't scheme. Take it from me, schemes are no good, and even the cleverest ones will eventually bite you in the butt.

—*The Awesome Girl's Guide to Dating Extraordinary Men* by Davie Farrell

# RISA

*W*ell, that was easy.

That's what I think after I get the call that I've been invited along on Gravestone's "Hide Your Frat Boys" tour as a "special guest" of Ipso! Facto!

I couldn't have been more right about The Lead Singer's Girlfriend. I showed up at her art show with my arm slung around Thursday's shoulder like she was my girlfriend (thanks to the dreadlocks, passing her off as a girlfriend was pretty easy). Then, when Thursday took a break from haranguing me about the real reason I'd invited her to some random art show in Echo Park in order to go to the bathroom, I struck up a conversation with The Lead Singer's Girlfriend. I told her I liked her art, even though I'd seen the exact same hipster photo-realism painting concept at three other gallery shows that year. But whatever, she believed me and thanked me before admitting she recognized me from the wall of new artists at Gravestone Records. "You're Supa Dupa, right?" she said. "I hear your album turned out great."

"Yeah, I heard that, too," I said. "But that might just be a rumor."

She checked me out over her wine glass. "So was that your girlfriend you came in with?"

"Yeah," I lied. "For now. We've been having problems lately."

She leaned in for the gossip. "Oh, really?"

"Yeah, she's a great girl and everything, but I've been wanting to explore the merits of an open relationship and she's more on the let's-rent-a-U-Haul-and-move-in-together tip."

"Oh, really?" The Lead Singer's Girlfriend said again.

And I said, "Yeah, I was like, 'Are we trying to live the lesbian cliché?'"

The Lead Singer's Girlfriend adjusted her green nerd glasses before saying, "My boyfriend and I are sort of in an open relationship."

Now it was my turn to say, "Oh, really?"

The lead singer of Ipso! Facto! didn't have to participate, she told me after a few more glasses of wine and after I'd sent Thursday home to her boyfriend, having served her purpose. But he liked to watch her with other girls. Would I be cool with that?

I pretended to think about it, then went all quiet and sincere. This shit I pulled next was why so many musicians think they can easily cross over into acting: "I've got to tell you the truth. I'm intensely attracted to you, and I would do just about anything to make you mine. The question is, will your boyfriend be cool with that?"

Her eyes flickered, and she moved closer to me. Every woman wanted to believe she was capable of sparking instant, intense attraction in a broody stranger. Every woman had a teenage girl inside of her still yearning to be Catherine to somebody's Heathcliff, Bella to somebody's Edward, The One to somebody's me.

We ended up fucking back at my place. Then the next week we fucked again, twice. And the week after that, she started coming over whenever her boyfriend was at band rehearsal. Somehow the lead singer of Ipso! Facto! never got invited over to watch.

Halfway through July, I said, "After your boyfriend leaves on his fall tour, this will be easier to negotiate."

And she waited a guilty moment before saying, "He wants me to come with him."

And I said, "So you want me to put my need for you on hold for three whole months?"

And she didn't say anything. So the next time she texted me late at night, I told her I couldn't because I had plans with Thursday. And then I swung by her gallery with Thursday in tow and bought a seventeen-hundred-dollar painting, which Sharita would have berated me for cuz that's a lot of record-advance money to spend on what basically amounted to a long grift. So I didn't tell Sharita. And when The Lead Singer's Girlfriend showed up at my door to ask why I'd bought it, I said, "To remember you by."

And she said, "So you're back together with Thursday?" And I said, "I think I might need to start making decisions with my head as opposed to my heart." And, no, I don't know how I came up with this shit.

She got a little weepy then. "No, your heart is beautiful"—dramatic, like we were in a same-sex version of one of those nighttime soaps where the timing's always wrong and the leads keep breaking up until the need for ratings pushes them back together.

We ended up fucking again. Afterwards she cried and said, "I've got to go, but I'll think of something. I promise."

And three days later I got a jovial call from Gravestone, saying that Ipso! Facto! decided some diversity was in order for their tour, so they were inviting me along. Moreover, they were going to put my album out in September so that I'd have something to sell at the shows.

Somehow I managed to sound nonchalant and excited at the same time when I said, "Cool. Sounds good." Rock Star 101.

But when I hung up, I was not as joyful as I thought I would be. Not just because I had to bang some random chick to get a spot on a tour that should have been mine in the first place. But also because, as a lesbian, I never thought I'd have to sleep my way to the top. And mostly because I was deeply in love with The One, and I was beginning to wonder if this would be enough to make her finally realize how much she should love me back.

It was her legs that I imagined draped over my back when I went down on The Lead Singer's Girlfriend. And even though The One and me weren't together anymore, it felt like I was betraying her by pretending to be as obsessed with someone else as I was with her.

But then I snapped out of that sentimental bullshit and decided to call up my girls for a celebration. I started to call Sharita, but then remembered she was at her sister's wedding, and she probably wouldn't have come out anyway. Against all odds, she'd managed to become even more boring lately. Now that she was "dating her Career," I only saw her on *Dr. Who* nights.

So, whatever. I called Thursday, who said she'd love to come out almost before I was even done inviting her. "Caleb's working nonstop on another big project, so I'm all free. And invite Tammy, too," she said. "We'll do a ladies' night."

On one hand I was glad Thursday hadn't gone to the complete dark side and disappeared from our friendship, Sharita style. But on the other hand, every time I called her up, she was available on short notice because Caleb was working. Something wiggled on the right side of my brain, but oh well, I kept my mouth shut.

When I called Tammy, I got her voicemail. "Hey," I said, "I know you've got your fitness video shoot coming up, but Thursday and me are going out tonight, and we need you to come along, you hot bitch." Then remembering how much I'd missed her lately, I said, "Seriously, we haven't seen you in a while. Give me a call back when you get this."

# SHARITA

There were probably worse places I could be, I thought. For example, one of the founding partners at my firm had served in Vietnam, and that didn't sound like much fun. Also, I had read *A Thousand Splendid Suns* by Khaled Hosseini with my church book group a few years ago, and had thought that living in a Taliban-led Afghanistan as the first wife of a tyrannical and abusive husband would be an awful situation to be in. And there was always Hell. Yes, surely Hell must be worse than serving as the maid of honor at my sister's wedding.

First there had been coordinating all of my sister's many artistic friends for the bachelorette party. None of them seemed to have or be willing to spend any money on the bachelorette-night activities, so I had to front the whole thing myself, including a limo. And it would have been different if the four other bridesmaids hadn't been flaky actresses. But they were, and none of them seemed capable of arranging a restaurant for the pre-clubbing dinner or even figuring out which nightclub Nicole would prefer to go to.

So I had been forced to arrange everything pretty much by myself from over three thousand miles away. And then I'd had to work like a fiend to clear off my desk and front-load my August so that I'd be available to Nicole for a whole week before the wedding.

I did all of this, but here was how Nicole greeted me when I arrived at her apartment after having taken a cab from JFK: "Hey sis, great timing. I've got my last fitting, and we can see how the dress looks with Grandma's pearls."

Our grandmother had been the longtime maid for a Jewish surgeon and his wife who had lived in one of the redbrick mansions in University City. In fact, the only reason I had applied to Smith College in the first place was because my grandmother was so fond of the doctor's wife, who had graduated from Smith in the late fifties. The friendship between my grandmother and the doctor's wife grew, despite them coming from two such different backgrounds. And they remained close, even after I went off to college and my grandmother had to retire because her back couldn't handle heavy housework anymore. But even my grandmother hadn't expected the doctor's wife to will her Smith Pearls to her when she died. "Smith Pearls" were the traditional gift from Smithies' parents to their daughters when they graduated. But the doctor's wife only had sons, so she'd left them to my grandmother.

Of course, my grandmother didn't have much use for such an expensive gift. I had advised her to sell them on eBay in order to make her forced retirement a little more comfortable—even back then I'd had my head on straight when it came to finances. But much to my surprise, my grandmother saved the pearls and mailed them to me right before I graduated from Smith.

"I was going to wear my gold cross with my dress, not the pearls," I said. I didn't even want to talk about the gaudy fuchsia bridesmaid dresses that Nicole had picked out. According to my sister, they were supposed to make the wedding "pop"—whatever that meant—but as somebody who preferred conservative colors like gray, black, blue, and maybe a pastel if I was feeling adventurous, the thought of my image being forever preserved in the dress she had chosen gave me the shivers.

Nicole laughed. "Remember, we discussed this a couple of weeks ago?"

I looked at her blankly. "Discussed what?"

"I said I was having trouble finding the perfect jewelry to go with my dress. And you said that was too bad. And I said you should bring Big Momma's pearls because then I could wear them as my something old. And you said okay. Then you had to get off the phone because you said you had work to do."

I could vaguely remember that conversation. But only because that was how all of our conversations went. Nicole would call me in a panic about some aspect of the wedding and I would say that was too bad, while continuing to do my work. And then Nicole would present some crazy solution, and I would say, "Okay," because I had to get back to work and it was easier to just pretend to agree with her than argue. I had pretty much the same policy for my phone conversations with Risa.

"Oh, I forgot," I said. "Sorry."

"How could you forget? They're Big Momma's pearls."

"Sorry," I said again. "You're going to have to go with something else."

Then Nicole started crying. Just out and out bawling.

I was so stunned by this reaction that I didn't know what to do, which is why the seamstress ended up comforting Nicole and quizzing me about the pearls in her thick Russian accent. "You have no boyfriend who can send pearls?"

"No," I answered.

"Roommate? This Los Angeles very expensive, yes?"

"Yes, but I was conservative with my money and was able to buy a house on my own after the market crashed for a really good price."

Normally this was a point of pride for me, but the seamstress was looking at me like I had purposely decided not to make getting the pearl necklace easy.

"You must send friend to your apartment then. She can send necklace."

"My *house*, and I don't think so . . ."

"What? You have no friend either?"

"No, I've got friends," I assured her. "I just haven't given any of them a key."

That wasn't exactly true. Thursday had a key, but we weren't talking.

But like a heat-seeking missile, Nicole zoomed in on my hesitant tone. "Not even Thursday?"

"We're not talking," I said.

"I need Grandma's pearls. They're all I have left of her."

Unlike me, after Nicole had gone away to college she hadn't even bothered to visit home, except for the occasional Christmas. Yes, our childhood home, a one-bedroom house in Kinloch, was dismal and cramped, but if Nicole really cared about my grandmother, she would have made an effort to visit her more often before she died two years ago.

So I lied and said, "Risa told me that Thursday's away on vacation."

"Does she have boyfriend?" the seamstress asked, rubbing Nicole's back. "Maybe he can—"

"No, he can't. He's on vacation, too," I said, deciding to take back control of this spiraling conversation. "Nicole, we're not going to be able to get to Big Momma's pearls. I'll buy you some new wedding jewelry if you want."

"It's not the same," Nicole wailed. "I don't see why you can't send Risa with a locksmith or something."

"I'm not going to have a stranger break into my home just so you can have something old. We can get something from somewhere else."

"No, it's more than that. Wearing them down the aisle would be like having Big Momma here with us for the wedding, and I know she would have wanted to be here for this . . ."

And even more tears came streaming out of Nicole, right on cue.

"We'll find you something else, I promise."

"No, I don't want anything else. Call Risa. Tell her to get a locksmith. This is very important to me."

And so on and so on. We argued about this all week, and it spread to the bachelorette party. Nicole barely thanked me when the stretch Escalade pulled up in front of her apartment to whisk us away for a night that was supposed to be fun. Then Nicole refused to eat at dinner because she didn't want to look poochy for the wedding. "I'm three months pregnant, but if I eat all of this, I'm going to look like I'm eight," she said.

She and all her skinny actress friends laughed, but I wished I had known Nicole wouldn't want to eat before agreeing to pay for her and everyone else's food. Then Nicole hadn't liked the club I had picked based on Yelp reviews. So we ended up at another club that one of her actress friends suggested. And even though I rarely stayed up past ten most nights, I nursed one Diet Coke after another until three a.m., while Nicole and her friends danced sexy with guys they barely knew.

The wedding ceremony itself had gone off without a hitch, but I had to put up with Nicole saying how much better the dress would have looked with our grandmother's pearls as opposed to the diamond pendant that Graham had bought for her because he wanted to relieve her distress over her little sister's betrayal.

Which was why I was now having a hard time figuring out which was worse. Spending a whole week having to revolve around my completely self-absorbed sister or Vietnam, Afghanistan, and Hell.

Our mother, who had not shown up until the day before, and whose plane ticket I had to pay for, and who had decided to wear a lime-green pantsuit ensemble so loud and bright that I found myself reflexively squinting whenever I looked directly at her, wasn't making things any better. I could overhear her now, taking credit for the presents table, which I'd set up myself.

"Yeah, it's nice, ain't it? You know I wanted everything to be perfect for my baby," my mama was saying to one of the relatives that had flown from St. Louis to attend the wedding.

"And don't Nicole look good? She get it from her mama, right?" My mother stomped her yellow-heeled foot and laughed, loud and bawdy. "See, they say they ain't any good black men out there. But look at my baby. I don't know why Sharita can't find a nice man like that. You know, maybe I do. She got that independent head problem. Don't know how to let a man be a man and a woman be a woman. And she picky, too, like all these little girls want to be these days. But at least she getting paid. I thank the Lord for that, poor thing."

That was when Vietnam, Afghanistan, and Hell lost. I switched from Diet Coke to champagne. And what seemed like only a few minutes later it was time for the toasts.

I'd tried to beg off from doing one, since I didn't like speaking in front of large audiences. But Nicole had insisted, so I made my way to the front of the room, a little unsteady on my feet. However, to my surprise, when I started talking, the words flowed out, clear and excited.

It started out as a warm speech about how happy I was to welcome Graham to our family. But then I saw my sister's hand move to her chest, as if to say, "These should have been Big Momma's pearls. Poor me."

The next morning, hungover on the plane back to L.A., I wouldn't remember much about the rest of the speech. Only the words "lucky bitch," "leech," and "ungrateful"—all used more than once.

And now Thursday had some company. Because my sister wasn't talking to me either.

# August 2011

Think about the long run. If you got fat, would this man still want you? If you were diagnosed with some disease and couldn't cook, clean, or have sex for a year or more, would this man stand by you? If anything goes wrong, does this man have your back? If the answer is no, let him go. You know how rappers are always looking for a ride-or-die bitch? You should be looking for one of those, too.

—*The Awesome Girl's Guide to Dating Extraordinary Men* by Davie Farrell

# EVERYBODY

*W*ith less than three weeks until Risa was to leave town, she had become giddy. As in, played certain cheesy songs despite herself, because they were the tracks of her youth: music by Backstreet Boys, Britney Spears, Biggie Smalls, all the Bs of the nineties. They provided an optimistic soundtrack for success while she waited for the "Hide Your Frat Boys" tour to begin.

Instead of packing, she scheduled lunches and watched movies and worked on new songs "for the road." She celebrated quitting her night job to fully pursue her passion with noisy drinks with Thursday and quiet, coffee-soaked brunches with Sharita. Her life felt crazy and full, and she loved it, even though she knew that this was just a dinky little college tour. For the first time since the Sweet Janes broke up, she felt like something was about to happen. Something huge.

When Risa was a teenager in Orange County, she skipped school with a bunch of friends to surf at Huntington Beach. The surf forecast on the radio had said that the waves were supposed to be puny that day, which was why she brought her longboard as opposed to her shortboard. It was more fun to longboard on the smaller waves. But when she paddled out she saw that the next wave was bigger than she'd expected. A hell of a lot bigger. Bigger than anything she had ever surfed on her banged-up Stewart. Her friends stopped when they saw that wave, and then started paddling furiously toward the horizon so as not to get eaten alive by the monster. But Risa didn't. In fact, she turned her board toward the shore and paddled hard to catch it. She was that sure she could handle anything the ocean threw at her.

The ocean thundered around her as she popped up to her feet and rushed down the face of the wave. Next, she was in the barrel of the wave, surrounded by water. For a few moments, all she heard was the sound of ocean, but then there appeared inside her head the opening notes of a song with a hard-driving guitar riff. She eventually shot out of the wave, riding the shoulder of it into calm water, before it crashed onto the sandy beach. And when she looked back to the horizon, she saw her friends in the choppy water, hollering and cheering like she was some kind of superhero. The song the Universe delivered to her inside the wave would later become the lead single and the only Top 40 radio hit on the Sweet Janes' only official album. It still got played on L.A. radio to this day.

Right now, it felt like Risa was paddling out to meet a set of waves, and they looked small, but wait for it . . . the big kahuna was coming to meet her.

There was just one problem. She'd said good-bye to Thursday and she'd said good-bye to Sharita, but Tammy hadn't been returning any of her phone calls. So she hunted her down, motorcycling over to her condo and using the call box outside the front doors to buzz her apartment. Tammy didn't answer. So Risa tried her phone again. Straight to voicemail.

And she started to get a bad feeling, because she hadn't spoken to Tammy directly since Sharita's intervention back in May. She was starting to think that maybe she should call her family, just to make sure they'd seen her lately, when—

"What are you doing here?"

She turned around to see Tammy at the bottom of her steps in a light-pink tracksuit. "You coming back from your afternoon jog?" Risa asked her.

But then she saw the cane Tammy was leaning on with her right hand, and the oversized orthopedic shoe she was wearing on her right foot. And why, she wondered, her brain sluggishly working to catch up, was Tammy wearing a scarf around her head?

"No, I had a doctor's appointment," Tammy said. She looked around, at the tiled steps, at the palm trees, at the sky, at the other people walking by, everywhere but at Risa.

Risa's hands fell to her sides. She didn't want to know. She really didn't want to know. But she had to ask, "Yo, what's up with the cane?"

Sharita didn't know whether to be pleased or annoyed that Risa was the only one calling her for non-work-related reasons these days. On one hand, it was nice that she still had one friend left. On the other hand, Risa never called just to shoot the breeze, which made accepting a call from her feel like the equivalent of opening herself up to an adventure. And she'd never been a very adventurous girl.

Sharita answered anyway. "Hey, Risa."

"I need you to come over to Tammy's. Like, right now."

"Is Thursday going to be there?"

"Yeah, I called her, too, because it's important."

"Another intervention?" Sharita asked, her tone bitter.

"No," Risa said, but she didn't explain any further.

"Risa, I'm in the middle of *Warehouse 13*. And I'm tired. And I don't have time for your games. Especially if they involve Thursday, so can we not do this tonight?"

"Tammy has cancer. Is that important enough? Now get the fuck over here."

Then she hung up before Sharita could answer. Sharita frowned. She had to be joking. Risa had to be joking . . . right?

But just in case, she got her purse and headed out the door.

When Risa called and told Thursday to meet her over at Tammy's because it was important, she suspected it might be a joke, too. But Caleb was working on his latest huge project. He only ever seemed to get assigned huge projects these days. This was good, since Thursday still hadn't been able to find another job and wouldn't be able to pay her half of the rent until further notice, but he never had time to hang out like they used to. So joining Risa for whatever crazy scheme she had up her sleeve this time seemed like a good enough way to spend the evening.

"I'm going out to meet up with Risa and Tammy on the Westside," she called to Caleb.

"Okay," he called back from behind his work partition. "Have fun."

"Love you," she said.

"Love you, too," he said back.

What she had with Caleb was very cozy. She loved their life together and how comfortable they had become with each other. The complete opposite of her father and mother. It was so nice. Nice and cozy, just the way she wanted it.

So why, she wondered as she walked down the stairs to the parking lot, was she so bored?

Maybe this was what healthy love was supposed to feel like. Like one long, lazy afternoon that would never end. She had never been in love before, had never even been in a relationship that lasted this long, so it could be.

The night before, Caleb mentioned in passing that they should do something really special for their one-year anniversary in October. That was what he'd said. Really special.

And a few weeks before that, when they were shopping at Target together, he'd asked her whether she wanted her future husband to pick the ring or if she wanted to pick it out herself.

"I'd let him pick it," she'd said, wondering why her heart hadn't even skipped a beat at that question. "Why do you ask?"

He lifted his eyebrows and answered, "No reason," in a pretty obvious way.

So she and Caleb were definitely on the marriage track. This was good. He was exactly what she wanted, a low-drama, no-crap, incredibly supportive white boy. Maybe, she thought on her way over to Tammy's, I'm trying to sabotage myself with these thoughts of boredom. Yet again. According to Mike Barker, she was really good at that.

She shook her finger at the dark thoughts crouched in the back of her head and let them know, *I'm watching you.*

And later that night, upon her return from Tammy's condo, in a flood of tears, she found herself especially glad that she had beaten back her doubts about Caleb. Caleb, she decided anew, was extraordinary, the kind of guy who wouldn't dump her for any petty reasons, the kind of guy who would stand by her through thick or thin. It was in his arms that she spent much of the night crying, unable to wipe the image of Tammy in her pink tracksuit, sitting on her white couch looking tired and haggard, from her mind.

Tammy didn't actually tell Sharita and Thursday herself. It was Risa, standing behind the couch, who delivered the bad news. Tammy just nodded at the right parts and gave Risa gentle corrections, like, "I only saw four doctors, not five."

She also said, "Yeah, we sorta do," when Sharita said, "But black people don't get skin cancer."

Tammy, however, didn't tell them or Risa the full truth of the cancer: that she stubbed her toe while rushing out of the restaurant after her brother told her she would no longer be a spokesmodel for Farrell Cosmetics, more than a year ago. How she'd covered the black sore that appeared on her toe with black nail polish and had begun opting out of pedicures or bi-monthly spa visits. How when the black sore began to spread beyond the cuticle of her big toe, she had started wearing gladiator sandals as opposed to going to a doctor.

She didn't tell them she spent the past year yearning to be the woman everyone thought she was: beautiful, famous, and carefree. How could she explain that the thought of her doctor, a woman who had been on the USC Song Girls cheerleading squad with her, seeing this ugly mark on her otherwise flawless body filled her with a paralyzing dread?

She didn't tell Thursday, Sharita, or Risa any of this. Instead she made it seem like a flighty oversight: "The only reason I finally got it looked at was that a head-to-toe physical was a condition of my new contract with Farrell Cosmetics. Yes, it was getting kind of gross looking, but I didn't think it would be such a big deal. I mean, my toe didn't even hurt that much."

Sharita and Thursday sat on either side of her to comfort her and tell her that they would all fight this disease with everything they have. Reassurances flew, even though the words "acral lentiginous melanoma" and "aggressive" and "late diagnosis" sent arrows of fear down all of their spines. The truth was black people could get skin cancer. In fact, when black people got skin cancer, it often presented in such late stages that it had a high fatality rate.

Bob Marley, as it turns out, had the exact same cancer as Tammy. He went in to see the doctor about a bruise on his toe that wouldn't heal, and he died a little over a year later.

The doctors cut off Tammy's toe. They cut off her toe! This information sent Thursday's eyes flying to Tammy's orthopedic shoe. She no longer had a right big toe. Thursday found this hard to believe and could not imagine Tammy taking off her shoe to reveal only four toes where there should be five.

"It's okay," Tammy said, looking stricken by Thursday's stricken look. She once again began spinning a silver lining out of nothing. "It doesn't hurt. They gave me these pain pills and I didn't even need them. And it's going to be boot season soon anyway. Plus, I'm okay with flats. They have really cute flats. I see them in shops all the time."

The tired and haggard version of Tammy was just as sweet, which served as further reassurance to Thursday and Sharita that she could beat this strange kind of cancer that none of them had ever heard of before.

Risa stood in the background of this conversation, fists clenching and unclenching, looking like she wanted to go over to Cancer's house and kick its ass. "You should have told us sooner," she said to Tammy.

"I didn't want to worry you," Tammy said. Then she offered to make tea.

Both Sharita and Thursday refused the tea, and they somehow managed to hold on until they got out of the apartment. But they were crying as soon as the door closed behind them.

"Oh, my God. I'd be so pissed," Thursday whispered as they walked to the elevator. "How is she still so infallibly gracious? So Tammy?"

"I don't know," Sharita whispered back.

She took Thursday's hand and held on to it. And that was all it took. Their last argument, as immense as it had seemed, got left inside Tammy's condo, their anger floating away on the ocean that crashed beneath her windows.

# September 2011

Relationships can't be a bed of roses one hundred percent of the time. That's okay as long as they smell sweet *most* of the time.

—*The Awesome Girl's Guide to Dating Extraordinary Men* by Davie Farrell

# THURSDAY

$\mathcal{T}$ammy had undergone a course of chemo before telling us she had cancer, but she still had a couple more to go, and we swore we'd be by her side for those. Risa got Tammy through her first two rounds of the second course of chemo before she left town on her college tour. But before she went, it was decided that I would drive Tammy to the four chemo appointments she had left. And on those days ("Chemo Tuesdays," we called them), Sharita would come over to make Tammy dinner and spend time with her after work.

The first week that I took over, I ended up staying with Tammy until Sharita came. But then Sharita told me that she was making pierogies and matzo ball soup, one of the few meals she could think of that was tasty enough to make Tammy ignore the chemo-induced loss of appetite, yet bland enough not to further trigger her also-chemo-induced nausea. I had never had pierogies, which were basically sauerkraut-and-potato-filled dumplings, before, and as any vegetarian will tell you, we jump at the chance to try new foods that fit within our chosen diets, so I stayed for dinner. The next week, Sharita came in with a Crock-Pot full of meatless, three-bean chili, and I had always loved her chili, so I stayed for that. And then the next week, Sharita brought along three pieces of sweet potato pie, assuming that I would once again be staying, so I did.

If not for the sight of Tammy with a Hermes scarf wrapped around her newly bald head, and if not for Tammy's in-home nurse hovering in the guest bedroom, and if not for the fact that Tammy started nodding off if we stayed past eight, then Chemo Tuesdays would have felt like a girls' night full of good food and lots of laughter.

But Tammy's hair was gone, and even though she napped for a couple of hours before Sharita came over, we still ended up having to carry her over to the couch, which she now preferred to her bed, at the end of each Chemo Tuesday. Sharita had given Tammy the first five seasons of the revamped English sci-fi show *Dr. Who* on DVD, and Tammy spent the days leading up to Chemo Tuesdays watching *Dr. Who* and, to my surprise, nothing but *Dr. Who*.

"I like that people die for no reason whatsoever all the time on this show," Tammy said with a pretty shrug when I asked her about this newfound obsession. "Innocent people. Bad people. It doesn't matter. They all die. Even the main character dies occasionally."

I had thought myself morbid with the constant imaginings of my suicide, but somehow Tammy's insistence on seeing a silver lining in everything that was happening to her began to strike me as even more morbid.

"Chemotherapy is awesome. I had kind of wanted to live before starting it, and it's totally making me see the upside of dying," she said with a self-deprecating smile after an hour of dry heaving into her pink toilet.

And another time over dinner, she said, "Remember when Twinkie got diagnosed with cancer and it was too late for kitty chemo and I was all upset because he died three weeks later and there was nothing I could do about it? I don't so feel guilty about that anymore. Twinkie got out good." Then her thin trickle of a laugh, followed by an awkward changing of the subject by Sharita—usually into yet another discussion about *Dr. Who*.

So yeah, I pretty much broke down in tears every time I left Tammy's condo on Chemo Tuesdays.

Every week, I thought about not going. Tammy, I insisted to myself, was the very embodiment of empathy. She would understand if I begged off, told her I couldn't handle it. Plus, she'd hired a live-out nurse, who could transport her to and from appointments. And it took forever to get from downtown to the Westside in morning rush-hour traffic, and a whole day was a long time to spend with someone who mostly threw up, slept, and watched TV. Also, I hated freaking *Dr. Who.*

Yet I ended up watching it every Tuesday in September, because I never made that call. Just dragged myself out of bed every time for what I knew would be the worst twelve hours of the week. Also, considering my current situation—that I was a well-educated, thirty-year-old feminist, but the only thing standing between me and total destitution was a man—this seemed like the best use of my copious amount of free time. Being called in to take care of someone else, after years of depending on others, made me feel better. Like I wasn't completely useless.

In fact, I was buying ice packs, Tums, and other chemotherapy necessities for Tammy at Target when I ran into my old roommate, Abigail, coming out of the pharmacy aisle.

We hugged, and it surprised me how good it felt to see her again. Before Benny and Caleb had come along, we had been the best of roommates, grabbing drinks after work or talking late into the night about our dreams and aspirations over Two-Buck Chuck.

"I've missed you so much," I said, realizing it was true.

"We missed you, too. How come you haven't given us a ring since you left?"

When my ex-roommate said "we" and "us," she actually meant "I" and "me." Saying "we" and "us" to refer to oneself was an English thing. I thought it might have something to do with how the Queen spoke, but had never been sure.

"How come you haven't given *us* a call," I countered, letting her out of the hug.

"Sadly, I've been out of sorts as of late. Benny and I . . . well, we broke up, didn't we?"

This came as zero surprise to me. Benny had been on the couch, like  every night toward the end of my tenure in our North Hollywood apartment. But I pasted a look of suitable surprise on my face and said the requisite, "Oh no . . ."

"No 'oh nos' required. I'm well shot of him. I mean, he was a right cheap bastard, wasn't he? Refused to see my side of things, and I don't know how we would have managed in a marriage, much less introduced children into it."

It was usually my policy to take the woman's side in an argument, but later that night I said to Caleb, "I don't think he was that cheap. I mean, they're both basically freelancers. He had a point about them maybe not needing to spend a ton of money on an apartment in Silver Lake."

The news about the breakup had been a bit of a boon. Caleb didn't really watch the same TV programs I did, and he didn't do anything much with his free time these days except listen to new music and go to yoga classes. So dinners with him had been a little . . . well, quiet. At least this was something we could talk about over our Indian takeout that night.

"I wouldn't want to live in North Hollywood for the rest of my life, though, just because he didn't want to spend any money," Caleb said. "And they're both working pretty steadily."

"First of all, what's wrong with North Hollywood? I loved living in North Hollywood. Second of all, everybody's a strike or recession away from not being able to pay the rent. I think I'm with Benny on this one."

Caleb frowned. "That's not very nice of you. Abigail's the one that set us up."

"Yeah," I said, spooning more vegetable biryani onto my plate. "But that doesn't mean I have to agree with her in this case."

"You know what," he said. "You don't know anything about what was going on in their relationship. What business is it of yours anyway? Why are we talking about this?"

"I just thought it was a little strange, that's all. They were such a strong couple before she left for Prague but ended up splitting over an apartment."

Caleb pushed his plate away with unexpected violence. "Maybe instead of gossiping about her, you should just be grateful Abigail introduced us in the first place."

I didn't answer, afraid that whatever I said next would just make him even angrier. After what had to be at least five excruciating minutes of thunderous silence, he said, "I'm sorry."

"It's okay," I said.

"The director on this latest project has been driving me up a wall," he said. "I wish I could dump this project."

We both knew that the reason he didn't quit his problem job was because he was supporting the both of us now. Guilt overtook me. *I should have cooked tonight*, I thought, looking down at my half-eaten biryani. And I shouldn't be spending so much time hanging out with my friends, even if I was tired of being cooped up in our apartment all the time. Caleb had been working twice as hard lately, and that was my fault.

"I've got to find a new job," I said to Tammy the next day. "Not being able to support myself was fine when I was in college and grad school and when I first moved out here, but I'm thirty years old now."

Usually, I wouldn't have dumped my domestic problems on someone I was driving to chemo, but she'd asked me what was wrong, and it seemed easier to tell her the truth than lie.

In the passenger seat Tammy thought about my problem with a knuckle pressed to her bow mouth. "I know. I'll call my brother and ask him if they have any openings at Farrell Cosmetics. I'm sure there's something you'd be qualified for. You're so talented."

"Really? Thank you so much, Tammy," I said, touched to my very core that she would take time to ask her brother about giving me a job, even though she was fighting for her life. I seriously wondered if there was anyone else as kind as Tammy on the planet.

The mention of her brother, though, sparked another question. "By the way, how is your family taking all of this?" I asked.

"Fine." She answered so fast that it made me a little suspicious.

"Really?" I said. "Because not that I mind, but I'm surprised that your sister didn't want to take you to these chemotherapy sessions herself. You two are so close."

"Well, she has a five-month-old baby, so she really doesn't have time."

I wrinkled my forehead. "Really? Because Veronica kinda screams 'I have a nanny' to me. I'm surprised she and James wouldn't want to be here with you—"

"Okay, they don't know." Tammy slumped back in her seat, seemingly defeated. Apparently cancer hadn't made our Disney princess any better of a liar.

"You haven't told them?" I said, nearly swerving out of my lane, I was so surprised.

"No, I told them that I had to quit the exercise DVD because I got a better offer. They think I'm in Toronto right now, playing a small role in an indie movie. I just . . . I just don't want them to be unhappy."

"Yeah, but they're going to be pretty unhappy if—" I stopped myself. I had been about to say, "you die," but couldn't bring myself to say the words. "They're going to be pretty unhappy if something happens and they find out that you kept this from them."

"I'll tell them soon, okay? I don't want to be mean, but please don't press me about this. I really can't handle it right now." Tammy sounded annoyed, like my pointing out the obvious, that she should tell her family that she had stage IV cancer, was at the very height of rudeness.

An awkward silence descended, but then my cell phone went off with "Winter in October," my favorite single off of Risa's recently released debut album.

I put in the earpiece on my twenty-dollar-a-month cell phone (which I often felt like a dinosaur for having, as opposed to a smartphone like Tammy, Risa, and Sharita) and answered without checking the caller ID, since I was driving.

"Hello, this is Thursday," I said.

"Thursday, this is Mike."

"Mike who?" I said, flipping through my mental Rolodex of the Mikes that I knew.

"Mike Barker."

My mouth dropped open. "Oh, Mike." I looked sideways at Tammy. "Um, I'm kind of busy right now. Can I call you back tomorrow or something?"

"Sure," he said. "But I need to talk to you, so try to make it sooner than later."

"Okay," I said. "Will do."

I hung up, hoping that Tammy hadn't caught on that it had been her ex, Mike Barker, on the other side of the line. But when I took my earpiece out, Tammy was staring at me with a weirdly intense look on her face. "Was that Mike Barker?" she asked.

I thought about lying. I really did. And I would have done it, too, except, you know, she had cancer, and that seemed wrong, even for me. "Um, yeah."

"I thought you two got in some big argument in Catalina?"

"We did," I assured her. "But now he's calling me."

Tammy continued to stare me down. "Why?"

"I have no idea," I said. "But I won't call him back if you don't want me to, okay?"

Tammy had always been so accommodating that I figured she wouldn't make me follow through on this promise, but then she surprised me by saying, "Okay, I think that's a good idea."

I blinked. "You do?"

"Yes, actually, I do. I should have told you this at our New Year's get-together, but you working with Mike makes me really uncomfortable. That was such a bad breakup for me, I can't deal with the thought of him and you and cancer right now."

"Um, it's not him and me," I pointed out. "It's business. I'm sure it's about the biopic."

"I thought you hated that biopic."

"Yeah, I do," I said.

"Then it's easy. Just don't take his calls, okay?"

"Okay," I said, keeping my voice neutral so that she wouldn't get any more upset.

But then after a few moments of silence, she said, "I think . . . yes, I think I should tell you the full story of how Mike and I broke up."

"You really don't have to."

"No, I do, because I don't want you to think I'm just being a big old meanie. The truth is, he hurt me, Thursday, worse than I've ever let on." She took a deep breath. "You already know that Davie, James, Veronica, and I all went to high school together, but what you don't know is back then I wasn't as nice of a person as I should have been, and Davie was . . . well, she wasn't what she is today either. She was very unpopular, and Veronica and I ended up playing this really evil trick on her. It was so bad, she ran away from home."

"Ran away from home? That must have been some harsh trick." Knowing Tammy, and having met her sister, I doubted that my friend should be taking much credit for this evil trick. Veronica, with her sharp angles and icy beauty, seemed like the kind of person who would prank someone so bad that she would run away from home. And Tammy, who had problems standing up to her sister, seemed like the kind of gentle sheep who would go along with it.

"Yes, it was harsh, and I'll forever regret what we did to her. But the story doesn't stop there. A few years later, Davie sicced Mike on me. She bet him three thousand dollars that he couldn't"—she made air quotes—"land me. So he hit me with his now-famous Mike Barker charm, and I fell head over heels in love with him. I even let him move in with me. And then when someone better came along, he dumped me and got with her, because Mike Barker gets what he wants—that's his motto, and he doesn't care who he hurts in the process."

"Wait," I said. "He went after you because of a bet, then he asked you to marry him, then he cheated on you, then he dumped you?"

"Yes, the cheating would have been bad enough, but I found out about the bet a few years ago when Davie got together with James. I could understand why Davie did it. What we did to her wasn't right, and she's since become a beloved member of our family. But Mike had no excuse for what he did. It took me a long time to get over that."

For a moment she stared out the car window, lost in her memories of Mike. "He's a user, Thursday, and manipulative, and a truly awful person, and it would keep me up at night, knowing that you were mixed up with someone like him."

I shook my head. "You're right," I said to her. "I won't call him back."

# RISA

I don't want to be a bitch or anything, but this was a very, very bad time for Tammy to get cancer. Yeah, I'd been raised Catholic, and though I was no longer practicing, that religious background combined with my ten-year journey to land a second record deal had made me advanced in the skill of clinging to hope—I had become good at believing in miracles.

But between Tammy's cancer, and frat boys chanting "dyke" every time I took the stage at whatever midwestern college I was playing that night, and sleeping on a tour bus, and having to act like I was obsessed with a woman (a girl, really) who insisted on talking about "deep things" after sex, I was starting to feel like it was maybe more than even badass Risa could handle.

The One seemed so far away at that moment that it was becoming hard to imagine that I'd ever be with her. Not in this lifetime, anyway.

I hated the Midwest. I hated sleeping on a twin bunk in a rolling vehicle. I hated waking up with achy bones; it made me feel old. I hated feeling old. I hated talking about *Candide* at length like I was still in college and gave two shits about philosophy, especially after sex. That Peggy Lee song was playing in my head on a fucking loop: *Is that all there is to a fire?*

Strangely enough, the only thing that made me feel better about any of this was calling Tammy, who was now taking any and all of my calls.

"I wish you were still taking me to chemo," she said that night after our Columbus, Ohio, show. "You play depressing music and don't make me feel like I have to pretend to be okay."

"You don't have to talk to Thursday and Sharita. They'd understand if you were, like, 'Hey, I just had a shitload of chemicals pumped into my ass. Can you shut the fuck up?'"

Tammy giggled. "I can't bring myself to do that, I'd feel bad if I did. Not like with you."

"Well, I'm glad you're comfortable putting in absolutely no effort with me."

Tammy giggled again. "See, you make me laugh. That's why I wish you were here." Then out of nowhere: "Mike called Thursday while I was in the car with her."

"I thought they weren't talking or something?"

"They weren't but suddenly now they are. Thursday's on a roll. She and Sharita are friends again. Now Mike's calling her. The next thing we know, she and Rick T are finally going to make up and go to the premiere of his biopic together." Tammy laughed at her own uncharacteristically bitter joke, but then she got quiet again and said, "I have a bad feeling about Mike and Thursday."

"Why? She hates him. And she's in love with Caleb."

"It sounds to me like she and Caleb are having some problems, and I know she hates Mike. But it's like she hates him too much, like it could flip and become love and then . . ."

Tammy started crying, which had ceased alarming me. In movies, people dying of cancer always kept a stiff upper lip until they were either cured or had to say good-bye to the ones they loved. But in real life, any emotion could set Tammy off. Last Chemo Tuesday, she had answered the phone crying after watching the original *Breakin'*—a rare departure from *Dr. Who*. But it had been playing on the TV when Tammy woke up. Sharita and Thursday had left the remote on top of the television out of reaching distance, and Tammy hadn't felt like getting up. So she had watched it. "They were so happy at the end," she told me. "So young and happy."

Now she was saying, "I can't deal with this. With them. I shouldn't have to."

"You won't. I promise." And I made a mental note to call Thursday and make sure she stayed the fuck away from fucking Mike Barker for Tammy's sake.

"I hate that I'm crying over this."

"It's okay."

"I hate that they're seeing me like this. Risa, I look so bad. I'm swollen, and all my hair is gone. I've got this skin rash—it's so ugly." She started crying again.

"No, no," I told her. "Don't say that. You're beautiful."

"I don't want Sharita and Thursday to see me this way."

"It's okay, Tammy. They think you're beautiful, too. No matter what. Everybody does."

Tammy's soft crying died down to a few sniffles. "Well, at least I won't have to put up with them next Tuesday," she said.

My call-waiting clicked. It was The Lead Singer's Girlfriend. I pushed the "Ignore" button. "Yeah, today was your last day for this round of chemo. How did it go?"

"Not so great, maybe. The doctor called me into his office before to-day's round to talk about the results from my last MRI. He said the cancer isn't responding at all and, also, it's spread into a couple of organs, so he's suggesting we start a new kind of chemo in a few weeks." She said this casually, like it was an afterthought and not all that important.

"Jesus, why didn't you lead with that?" I asked, my heart thick in my throat. "And they think this new chemo will work?"

"No, not exactly. It's more for palliative reasons."

"What does 'palliative' mean?" I ask.

"It means making me more comfortable, so that there's not too much pain," she said. "I've got my at-home nurse, so I won't need Sharita and Thursday to come over anymore. Do you mind telling them that for me? They've been so sweet, and I don't want to hurt their feelings."

A few moments of me not answering went by and she said, "Are you crying?"

And I said no, but the "no" came out strained, because of course I was crying. How could I fucking not be?

# October 2011

Let me give you a little bit of a warning beforehand. While you're out there searching for extraordinary, you're going to want to give up. You're gonna wanna give up bad. In fact, what you really want to do is wait for that moment when you say, "I can't do this anymore," because that's EXACTLY when you should redouble your efforts. By the way, this works for exercise plans, too. Just letting you know.

—*The Awesome Girl's Guide to Dating Extraordinary Men* by Davie Farrell

# SHARITA

Risa said that Tammy said she didn't need Thursday and me to take her to chemotherapy or bring her food anymore. Risa said that Tammy said she was fine with her live-out nurse. Risa said that Tammy said she didn't need company and, in fact, wanted to be alone.

But Risa was on the road, and though I'd been dating my Career for a few months now, I missed having someone to watch *Dr. Who* with. Thursday, though available, insisted on watching only "shows that make sense," and according to her, *Dr. Who* didn't qualify.

So the first Saturday after Tammy got the news that her cancer was terminal, I worked a full day of unpaid overtime at my firm, then I sat in traffic for over an hour and showed up at Tammy's condo with Chinese takeout for us to eat in front of *Dr. Who*.

Tammy didn't turn me away. She buzzed me up, opened the door, and let me ladle some fried rice onto a plate for her. And even though she sometimes only picked at her food while we watched the latest season of *Dr. Who*, we settled into a comfortable routine.

Tammy didn't complain about me defying her wishes as expressed through Risa. Every Saturday, she greeted me on the intercom and said, "Come on up." Still, I couldn't shake the feeling that I was intruding on Tammy, as opposed to keeping her company.

Other than her short hair, which wasn't growing back very fast, it wouldn't have been obvious from looking at her that Tammy had cancer. Her face appeared a little swollen and maybe her body wasn't as toned as it used to be, since she'd stopped exercising. But other than that, it'd be easy to think that she was perfectly healthy and that she had ten toes underneath the thick socks she wore around the condo.

Except she had stopped going outside. Except the curtains were all drawn on her gorgeous ocean view. Except she kept the lights low, which made it very hard to see in her living room. Except the TV was always on now, the volume turned up loud enough to be heard as far away as the back bathroom, like Tammy couldn't bear to be alone with her own thoughts even on the toilet. Except both Tammy's BlackBerry and her home phone kept on ringing, and she'd check the caller ID, but never bothered to answer it unless it was Risa. Except I suspected that she still hadn't told her family how sick she was. Except when I suggested we take a walk on the beach lying right outside her building's back door, Tammy always said, "Not right now." Except she randomly broke down crying and never wanted to talk about it.

So I started bringing Tammy books: cancer memoirs, spiritual memoirs, books with beautiful heroines who died with their heads held high, romance novels that had nothing to do with cancer to take her mind off her situation.

Tammy thanked me for all these books with a gracious smile, and put them on the end table where she kept her mail. They stayed there, and nothing changed except the height of the stack, because Tammy wasn't reading them.

I offered to read them with her. "Like a book club," I said.

Tammy shook her head. "Thank you so much for that offer, but I'm a little tired. Do you mind just watching *Dr. Who*?" Tammy was always tired. She always had an excuse for not doing something. She always only wanted to watch *Dr. Who*.

And I wouldn't have minded. But while keeping Tammy company on the Saturday night before Halloween, which would fall on a Monday that year, I looked over at Tammy lying on the couch with a scarf wrapped around her head. And as the television blasted and cast a bluish light over my friend's face, I realized something:

Since beginning my quest to make partner by the end of the year, I myself only went outside to work and to visit Tammy. If one of my programs was on and a friend or family member called, I checked the caller ID but usually didn't answer it. And though a junior accountant had invited me to his Halloween party that night, I had turned down his invitation. And that Davie Farrell book that Tammy had given me last year? Well, it was still sitting on my bookshelf unopened.

I myself always felt tired lately. I myself always had an excuse for not doing something. I myself only wanted to watch *Dr. Who* on Saturday nights.

I realized that if I wasn't with Tammy at that moment, I would be lying on my couch, a scarf around my head, with nothing but the light of a sci-fi show illuminating my night.

But the thing was, I wasn't dying of cancer.

"I have to go," I said out loud.

"Okay," Tammy said. And that was all she said. She didn't take her eyes off the large flat-screen or ask where I was going, or why it was suddenly so important that I leave now. She just watched the TV, already dead, already not living, because the doctors declared her terminal.

*What time did Halloween stores close?* I wondered. The accountant lived in Culver City. Maybe I could pick up a costume on the way there. Maybe I could go as Martha, the first black assistant on *Dr. Who*. Or maybe I could go as an accountant, since I was already wearing a gray suit. So many possibilities. My life, unlike Tammy's, I realized, was wide open. I could do anything, go anywhere, and, and . . .

"I don't want to make partner at my firm," I said, when Thursday unexpectedly called me in my car a few minutes later. This was how I answered the phone.

"What?" Thursday asked. "What happened?"

"It's already a lot of work to be a senior accountant. And if I want to take a vacation, I won't be able to because I'm so busy trying to prove that I deserve to be partner. When you make it out of the hood, people act like it's your duty to grab the highest possible ring." Every word I said to Thursday felt like a new fact being downloaded into my head from God above. "But I'm sick of working on Saturdays, and you know what, I really want to take a vacation, Day. Hey, do you want to take a vacation with me?"

Thursday laughed. "Am I still talking to Sharita? *Sharita*-Sharita?"

"Let's go to Jamaica. Or better yet, Europe. They've got great churches over there, right? Let's go next month as soon as I can get off. How long does it take to get a passport?"

"First of all, it takes more than a month to get a passport, especially this close to Christmas. Second of all, I can't afford to go with you. I'm unemployed, remember?"

"Oh," I thought about that. "Then I guess I'm going to have to go by myself. I really want to take a vacation, but I'm not going to loan you money to come with me."

"Okay," Thursday said.

"Normally I would, but I don't think I should be loaning anybody money anymore. It makes me too resentful."

"I think you're right about that," Thursday said, sounding amused.

"I'm serious, Day," I said. "I hope things work out with you and Caleb, and I hope even more that you set up a rainy-day account with that Mike Barker money like I told you to back in December, just in case things don't work out with him. But either way, I'm not bailing you out anymore, even if it means you're going to get mad and stop talking to me again."

Thursday surprised me by answering, "Okay, that's fine. I hope you do take that vacation, and I'm proud of you for finally standing up for yourself."

Now I became confused. "Didn't you get mad at me before because you didn't think I was being a good enough friend?"

Thursday sighed. "I've just now realized that I wasn't mad at you for not being a good enough friend. You're a great friend, and you've always been there when it really counted. What made me mad was that you weren't being a good friend to yourself. Skipping my party in order to hang out with some dude who didn't respect you or treat you well, you were doing yourself more of a disservice than you were doing me. You're a great person, and I just want you to manifest that in relationships. Come to things I invite you to or don't come. I don't care anymore. Just make sure that if you don't come, you're not coming for the right reasons, okay?"

I became overwhelmed with love for my friend, and I couldn't believe I had wasted a whole eight months being mad at someone who had only ever had my best interests at heart.

"Thursday," I said. "Thank you. You're a good friend. I've never said that to you, but you know that you're a good friend, too, right?"

"Thanks, Sharita," she said. "I love you."

"I love you, too, girl." And I got off the phone feeling brand new.

# THURSDAY

$\mathcal{G}$ should've felt all warm and fuzzy when I got off the phone with Sharita; I should have felt like I was telling the truth when I said that I only wanted what was best for her. I should have been so very proud of her for finally growing a backbone and learning to put herself first. I would have liked to have felt all of those things, except in this case it was just really—seriously, I could not stress this "really" hard enough—*really* bad timing. Because less than an hour before Sharita had her epiphany, this was what happened to me:

First of all, Caleb's and my one-year anniversary had come and gone. He had taken me to Ethiopian Row to eat at Rosalind's, the same restaurant where we'd had our first date. The food was great, and I loved the fact that we were cool enough to celebrate our anniversary at an unpretentious hole in the wall, but all we did was eat dinner, and then we left.

We had a nice (if a bit perfunctory) round of sex when we got home, and then he kissed me and rolled over. And that had been it. No proposal.

This shouldn't have upset me. Unlike my parents, who promised to be together forever within six weeks of meeting each other, most people didn't get engaged before they even knew each other's middle names. But . . .

Tammy had never called me back about that job at Farrell Cosmetics, and this weird feeling had begun to dog me as of late. It felt like I should be doing something other than what I was doing. Back in college and grad school, it had always been hard for me to go out to parties with Risa when I had a big assignment due. My homework would nag at me, infringing upon my good time, until I called it a night and finally just returned to my room to do the assignment.

I had been out of grad school for over five years at that point, but for whatever reason, this huge homework-assignment feeling had been looming over my life, setting me on edge, making it hard for me to be the happy, free-spirited woman I wanted to be for Caleb—who hadn't asked me to marry him on our anniversary as I thought he would.

But I had no right to be angry, I told myself in the weeks that came after our anticlimatic anniversary dinner. Caleb was still the nicest guy I had ever dated and he'd been supporting me for almost six months at that point. Why couldn't I just be grateful for that? However, instead of doubling down on my gratitude for having a great boyfriend, the pending-homework feeling grew into a burning sensation in my gut.

*Don't be pathetic, don't be pathetic, don't be pathetic!* My mother's words circled around my head, whenever I thought of bringing up the topic of marriage with Caleb.

*Throw yourself off the roof, throw yourself off the roof!* An uglier voice said. If I couldn't do the homework, it asked, why did I insist on taking up space on this planet?

I didn't tell Caleb that I was leaving the apartment on the Saturday night before Halloween. He was on the phone with someone—a client, judging from the careful way he spoke. Also, he would have asked me where I was going. My emotions had gotten so thin inside my heart, making it harder to hide the depression. If he'd asked, I might have confessed that I was getting away from him and to low ground, so that I wouldn't turn *pathetic, pathetic, pathetic,* so that I wouldn't *throw myself off the roof, throw myself off the roof.*

So I left without telling Caleb and walked around downtown. I found it inspiring to walk around an area of town that had been a grocery-store-less pit when I had first moved to Los Angeles in 2006. Back then, no one but homeless people, drug addicts, and the most starving of artists had lived on this block; in other words, only the completely desperate had this address.

But then developers had come in, the Nokia Center had been built, and a grocery store opened. In a surprisingly short time, the area went from special-ed wallflower to goth girl homecoming princess. It would never be the most popular girl at school like Beverly Hills, or even the most beautiful like the Westside, or the coolest like Silver Lake, but it was starting to make its own kind of splash in the sprawling high school that was Los Angeles.

And at the risk of wearing this metaphor thin, I had taken to roaming the streets outside of our loft in the hopes that I could figure out how to make myself over in the same vein.

*Don't be pathetic! Don't be pathetic! Throw yourself off a roof!*

A good main character, I had learned in grad school, was supposed to have a strong want. But what did I want? I had a great guy already. What else could I possibly ask for?

The answer came to me so suddenly that I stopped in my tracks.

This strong but vague yearning—maybe that's what it felt like when you were ready for kids. Caleb, I knew, was ready for kids. Though he considered himself a feminist (as nearly all white men who went to liberal arts colleges in the nineties considered themselves to be feminists), his own mother had been a stay-at-home, and he had even hinted once or twice that he wouldn't mind supporting a wife and kids.

This new road built itself with neat, perfectly straight gray bricks. Like a gift, it laid itself out in front of me. I could see a three-bedroom house in my future, with a yard and a fence. I could see myself being that fun mom who played with my kids and cracked them up with sly jokes. I could, I thought, make myself be happy. I could decide to be grateful for the writing and comedy careers that had gone nowhere, because they had led me to this man who didn't yell at me, didn't put me down, and would never embarrass me in front of my daughters by leaving to go out with his mistress every weekend and often not coming home until the next Monday.

Yes, I could see it now. My real future glistened under the bright lights of downtown L.A. And who cared if it was boring? It was mine. And it was real and, unlike day jobs or writing or comedy, motherhood wouldn't leave me depressed and wanting to kill myself all the time.

I turned around and ran back to the loft, my cheap flip-flops slapping the pavement. Aflame with the need to tell Caleb how much I loved him, I tore up the building's metal stairs. I was a feminist. I could ask *him* to marry *me*, I realized. Then, when he accepted, I'd let him know how excited I was about our future together, a future in which I wouldn't be depressed anymore because I would be too busy attending to the important work of motherhood.

"Caleb!" I called as soon as I came in the front door. I jogged over to the office partition, but he was no longer in his workspace. His Sennheiser headphones lay abandoned on his not-quite-vintage art deco desk, with music still bumping out of them.

Maybe he was in the bathroom, I thought, but then he called my name from somewhere else in the apartment. "Thursday," he said. His voice sounded frightened. And I felt guilty for not telling him where I was going before just disappearing like that.

I deposited my house keys on his desk and came out from the office partition. I found Caleb sitting on our black velvet couch. Only . . . Abigail was sitting there with him.

They both had their hands folded, and Abigail had eyeliner smudges under her eyes. She was one of those women who wore lots and lots of eyeliner, like she was in a Middle Eastern harem or taking part in a French New Wave movie. The result being that I could always tell when she had been crying, because her eye makeup got all askew, like she was posing for the inevitable painted portrait of a pale woman who had been crying that all art students seemed to have at least one of in their portfolios.

I had seen this look on Abigail often, back when we had been roommates and Benny and she had been slowly but steadily imploding. I'd come home to find Abigail sniffling in front of an HGTV apartment-hunting program and she'd say something like, "I really do hate him sometimes. You're so lucky to have a good one like Caleb."

And we'd talk for a little bit, but then inevitably either Benny or Caleb would come in and we'd have to stop. It felt to me like every important conversation that my friends and I attempted to have these days got interrupted by boyfriends, by children, by jobs, by the start of an event, by life. My thirties had basically been a graveyard of unfinished conversations so far, and I had already begun to fear that I would never have a full and meaningful one again.

But that was beside the point in this case. After a few puzzled seconds, it occurred to me to ask, "Abigail, what are you doing here?"

"I'm . . ." she trailed off. "Oh my God." Abigail turned left then right like she was searching for something to cry into, before just going ahead and plunging her face into Caleb's shoulder and full-on wailing.

Then Caleb said the seven words that would change my life forever. "Thursday, we didn't mean to hurt you."

Apparently, Abigail and Caleb had been more than friends when they had worked on that movie together in Prague. Apparently, they had flirted and hinted and hugged and done everything but physically kiss, because Abigail had a boyfriend waiting for her back in Los Angeles. Apparently, Abigail had been so unsettled by her attraction to Caleb that she had invited me to the airport because she had known that we would get along. And though it pained her to see me with him, she wanted him to be happy.

But then they had kept in touch after I moved out. A phone call here, a lunch there. And when she had broken up with Benny, Caleb had called to tell her how sorry he was to hear about it. This had led to more phone calls and lunches. "That was it," Abigail assured me.

However, that original attraction they had felt while in Prague—it was still there. But this time Caleb was the one in a serious relationship.

They were so drawn to each other, and Caleb didn't want to cheat on me—he knew how much that would hurt me . . . "But I can't settle for you, when I'm in love with her."

I remember how he had assured me that he wasn't hiding a girl at his apartment back when he wouldn't allow me to come over, and my eyes narrowed. "Wait a minute, you were hiding a girl. But you weren't hiding her in your apartment; you were hiding her in mine. The reason you always wanted to spend the night was because you wanted to be closer to her."

From the way both of their faces turned red, I could see that I was right. And even more pieces fell into place. "That's why you invited me to move in with you out of the blue, wasn't it? You told her to leave Benny, and when she refused, you invited me to move in. Like a punishment. You were pretending to love me to get back at her."

"No," he said, standing up. "It wasn't like that. I decided to see what I could have with you because you were available and into me. I had no idea this would happen down the line."

Caleb had tears in his eyes, like having to do this was hurting him way more than it was hurting me. Abigail, who hadn't met my eyes since I'd walked in, stood up and rubbed his back.

*Funny*, I thought in the long silence that followed this tortured reveal. I had been so desperate to never let a man disrespect me or cheat on me that I hadn't ever considered the other possibility: getting thrown away. I'd had some vague notion that white men did this. Black men often cheated on their wives, like my father did, or refused to marry their long-suffering girlfriends and babies' mamas, yes. But I had heard stories about white men coming home to the sixty-year-old woman who had raised his children and informing her that he was trading her in for a woman half her age and size. Black men treated you like trash, but white men actually threw you away—I hadn't calculated this fact into my "not getting hurt" formula.

I opened my mouth, but nothing came out. In that moment, when I could feel an earthquake running from my stomach to my heart, breaking it apart, I had no idea what to say.

I should have cursed them out. Black women were good at cursing people out. Everyone knew that. But my anger was having a hard time shoving past the hurt and surprise. I could have cried, but then, Abigail was crying and it seemed too awkward to do the same.

Then it hit me: the perfect response. Our loft was on the fourth floor. I could go out to the metal stairway and throw myself over the railing and plummet down to the concrete below.

A better person would want them to be happy. I did not want them to be happy. I wanted them both to suffer like I had suffered after my mother's suicide. And I wanted them to suffer apart.

There was no way Caleb and Abigail were going to be able to build a happy relationship on top of my dead (or, at the very least, quadriplegic) body. I could ruin both of their lives with just one leap. Unlike my father, they would always feel the weight of their actions, would always know that guilt, would never be able to move on from what they had done to me.

So without a word, I opened the heavy steel door and let it close behind me with a bang. I went over to the railing and gripped it. The parking lot was perfect right now. There was no one standing below, no guest cars parked at the bottom of the stairway to possibly cushion my fall.

Now all I had to do was jump.

But ten minutes later, I was still gripping the rail.

I heard the door open behind me.

"We're going to go now. I'm staying with Abigail until the end of the month to give you time to find another apartment. Okay?"

Caleb informed me that he would be moving into my old North Hollywood apartment in hushed tones, like I was a friend's widow as opposed to the ex-girlfriend he had totally betrayed.

Now would be the perfect time. I congratulated myself for waiting, because it would be even better to fall to my death in front of them. But I didn't, couldn't move. After a hesitant moment, I heard Abigail and Caleb make their way down the stairs. Abigail went to her Chevy Aveo and Caleb went to his Prius.

*Do it now! Do it now!* the ugly voice inside me screamed.

The mechanical gate opened with a noisy jangle to let them out.

*Do it now while they can still see you in the rearview mirror.* But the ugly voice was no longer screaming. It was a bitter, whimpering thing now, making a suggestion that it knew I wouldn't go along with, because the truth was that it wasn't just black men that had a problem with not being able to let black women go. My life was crap. My money situation, my boy situation, my career situation—it was all one big old pile of crap.

But it was *my* steaming pile of crap. The only pile I had at that moment, and I was unwilling to throw it away. I had been disappointed with myself before. There had been times when I could have gotten better grades if I had put in more effort, times that I'd miss payments on something because I bought something else that I shouldn't have. But I had never been as disappointed in myself as I was when I finally admitted that, though I had been dreaming about committing suicide for years now, I didn't actually have what it took to kill myself.

I wasn't half as determined as my mother.

So I was going to have to live with myself. Even though at that moment I couldn't think of a person I'd rather not have to live with.

I let go of the railing, my fingers sore from having gripped it so long. I went to the door, deciding that I could salvage some of my pride. I'd pack and go stay with Sharita until I could find a new job and a new apartment.

But when I reached into my pocket for my keys, I felt nothing but my cell phone, an old pack of Listerine breath strips, and some pocket lint.

The image of me dropping my keys onto Caleb's desk twenty minutes ago when he called my name came back to me in a flash and I cursed. I was locked out of my ex-boyfriend's apartment and if I wanted to get back in, I'd have to call him. Or maybe Sharita could call him for me and, while she was at it, come over and help me sort this mess out . . .

I grabbed my cell phone out of my sweater's pocket and called my most dependable friend.

But then Sharita surprised me by answering the phone with, "I don't want to make partner at my firm."

Sharita, I found out over the next ten minutes, had finally had the epiphany that I had been trying to nudge her toward for the entirety of our post-college dating life. And it didn't seem like a good time to say, "Hey, Sharita, I know you've just vowed to stop being a mule, but wanna put me up for a month or so and maybe help me find another job, since I got fired from the last one you finagled for me?"

After I put on a cheery front and hung up with Sharita, I sat down on the metal stairs, trying to decide what to do. The thought of throwing myself over the railing came to me again, but it was toying with me now, teasing me about what I couldn't have.

Risa was out on tour and Tammy was dying. If this breakup had happened to me in my twenties, I would have had no shortage of friends to stay with. But now everyone I used to able to couch surf with had disapproving husbands and, in many cases, innocent babies who were too young to be exposed to a thirty-year-old woman who couldn't get her act together.

Below me I could hear feet on metal, someone coming up the stairs. Probably our downstairs neighbor, a neat and vesty freelance editor who would call and complain whenever Caleb tried to play music without headphones. Music even at the lowest volume echoed through to the downstairs lofts and made it hard for him to concentrate, he claimed. Caleb hated the downstairs editor and had been talking about us moving because of him. But now he and Abigail would move together. Maybe to a hip apartment in Los Feliz like she had always wanted.

A fresh wave of hate and anger washed over me.

This is the place where I would have expected the tears to come, and to their credit, the tears did think about it, lingering behind my dry eyes, offering to give me something to do while I figured out how to proceed now that my future path had crumpled in front of me. But before I could give in,

I noticed three strange things about the guy who was now standing on the third-floor landing below me.

First of all, it wasn't my downstairs neighbor. Second of all, he was looking up at me. Third of all, it was Mike Barker.

"Thursday?" he said. "What are you doing sitting up there?"

"What are you doing standing down there?" I asked, swimming out of my fog of confusion and shock. Then, remembering an *E! True Hollywood Story* I had seen one night long ago which had detailed Mike Barker's rise from drug-dealing project kid to highly sought-after actor, I asked, "Hey, you used to be a drug dealer or something, right? Do you know how to pick a lock?"

# November 2011

A lot of women advise other women not to wait, to find a husband as soon as they possibly can. The sooner the better—especially if you want a successful man. But there's often a big difference between what you want and what you need and, then again, sometimes there's no difference at all. My point is that it takes a while to figure all of this out. I've yet to meet a woman who's on top of things at twenty-two, and I remain unconvinced that any woman has any business whatsoever getting married before the age of twenty-seven. In fact, if you're under twenty-seven, put this book down, stop worrying about finding a husband, and make sure you have lots of fun while fun is to be had. As quiet as it's kept, women need to sow their wild oats, too.

—*The Awesome Girl's Guide to Dating Extraordinary Men* by Davie Farrell

# SHARITA

*I* had been cutting back at work. I hadn't been taking on any extra projects, and when the partners asked me if I could stay late to work on their cases, I gave them excuses: I had a play to attend. I had plans with friends. I had already bought my tickets to a seven o'clock movie.

And the crazy thing was that all my excuses were true. Whenever I tried to turn on the TV, I would see Tammy dying on her couch and then I wouldn't be able to sit down long enough to enjoy my program. So I went out to the movies. And when I had seen everything I wanted to see at the theater, I started watching the ones that only played at art houses. And when I had seen all the art films, I got a copy of *L.A. Weekly* and started going to plays and book signings. But then another movie would come out that I wanted to see, so I'd go to that. Then someone on Facebook would invite me to a party, so I'd go to that, taking Thursday with me so that I didn't feel so awkward and alone.

Thursday was great at talking to people she didn't know. And since Caleb had dumped her, in the surprise move of the year, she now had even more time to go to a bunch of things with me—especially if they were free. To accommodate Thursday's financial situation, I had started hitting up art gallery openings and pay-what-you-can nights, and the next thing I knew, I was booked up every night of the week. No time to take on extra projects at work.

At one point, John Worthington, the only black partner in my firm, called me into his office. "You should decide if you want to have a social life or if you want to be partner."

John had been nice to me from the start, taking me under his wing when I got hired and not seeming to hold it against me that I was younger and smarter, so I answered him straight. "I'm reevaluating if I need to be partner. I like being a senior accountant, but my social life hasn't been going nearly as well as my career. So I'm concentrating on that right now."

John stroked his salt-and-pepper beard. "I've been at this firm for over twenty years. I've given that career-versus-social-life advice more times than I can remember, and I've never had an accountant pick 'social life.'" He nodded thoughtfully. "Good for you. Wish I'd been smart enough to pick social life when I was your age. Maybe things would have turned out different."

It was common knowledge around the office that John's wife, Dorothea, had served him with divorce papers. He had two daughters, but they were both in college, so, much like me, John had been sleeping in an empty bed every night.

"Listen," he said. "Do you want to have a drink with me after work?"

I had always had what Risa called an "optimism problem" when it came to guys. Every time a guy showed an interest in me, I got struck with a vision of our potential future together. I'd see us walking down the aisle after getting married or envision what our children would look like. I'd say things to my friends like, "He's got these soft brown eyes. I could see how pretty they'd be on a little girl."

So when John asked me out and I got zapped with a vision of my future with him, that wasn't unexpected. What surprised the bejeezus out of me was what the vision contained: I saw myself going out with John, enjoying the company of a man who was both old enough to be my father and wise enough to teach me a few things. I'd agree to a longer dinner date. Then eventually we'd go to bed. He'd talk about us getting married after his divorce was finalized. We'd discuss the possibility of more children.

But the divorce would never get finalized. At first it would be because divorces take time. But then Dorothea would decide that she no longer wanted a divorce, and though he would insist he had stopped loving her when he started loving me, he would claim to feel bad about abandoning her and suddenly he'd have moved back in with his wife, just for a little while.

Four years. That's how long it would take for me to realize that John was never going to leave his wife and marry me. And at the end of those four years, I would be extremely bitter that I had wasted so much time on this man who had never loved me as much as he said he did. I saw all of this in the few seconds after John asked me out. It was like a crystal ball had opened up in my mind. And it felt real, like God was whispering my future in my ear.

"I don't think that would be a good idea," I said to John. Handsome, successful, black man John. I said, "Workplace romances can get weird."

John suddenly became very interested in his computer. "Understood," he said, and started typing. Which I guessed meant I was dismissed.

I got up and left. And I wouldn't have thought so much about that unusual vision, except it kept on happening. A few weeks later, I bumped into Marcus after coming back into the office after a lunchtime walk. Usually, we avoided eye contact when we crossed paths, but he must have been feeling romantic that day, because he said, "Hey, Sharita."

"Hi," I answered.

He thrust out his brown signing box at me. "Rhonda's not here again."

"Sure, no problem," I said, taking the stylus and signing for the many large envelopes he had placed in Rhonda's mail basket.

Then he said, "I've been meaning to apologize for how things ended with us."

That was all he said, but another vision hit me with a zap of mental electricity. His apology would be followed by a dinner invitation. We'd go out a few more times, he'd even agree to meet my friends, but then . . . the exact same thing would happen. He would start accusing me of being uppity whenever I asked him to do anything he didn't want to do, and when I dared to ask where he saw our relationship going, he would dump me again. Six months. This latest resurrection of our relationship would last six months, with him getting a half year's worth of sex, cooking, and laundry and me getting . . . nothing. Absolutely nothing.

"You're a nurture digger," I realized out loud.

"What?" he said, screwing up his face.

"You know how guys are always accusing women of being gold diggers? You, Marcus, are a nurture digger. You want all the benefits of dating a woman who knows how to take care of her man, but you don't want to do anything for her in return." I thought about this for a second. "What you might want to do is start using your discretionary income on a maid. That way you wouldn't have to do your own domestic work, and then you could just hire hookers for sex."

"What?" he said again.

"Isn't that what you want? Somebody to have sex with and do all the domestic stuff, without you having to give her anything in return? Your problem is that you're looking for all of that in one woman. What you need to do is outsource your domestic and your sex separately."

"What are you talking about?" he said. "I don't have to pay for sex."

"See, Marcus, that's where you go wrong. Being a black man with a job doesn't mean you qualify for some type of entitlement program. Nothing is free. You either have to pay a monetary cost or an emotional cost to get what you really want. But you've got to pay."

Marcus's handsome face had been so smooth and affable when he said hello, but now it was contorted into the cruel lines that I remembered from their last encounter. "You a crazy bitch," he said. "Fuck you."

I handed him back his brown box. "Outsourcing is definitely the way to go for you. Remember I said that when you're fifty and alone."

"I ain't the one who need to be worried about being old and alone. You fat, you black, you crazy—ain't nobody going to want your ass. And I got bitches coming at me ALL DAY."

I shrugged. "I also seem to have bitches coming at me all day. But the thing is, I'm not trying to get with a bitch like you. So good-bye, Marcus."

I turned and left, with Marcus cussing me every which way. But I just waved over my head and said it again, this time in a jaunty singsong. "Good-bye, Marcus."

And the Crystal Ball didn't stop there. The next few weeks brought run-ins with guys at events. I met a light-skinned guy with dreadlocks and dreams of becoming a progressive-rock star at a gallery show. The Crystal Ball told me that he would date me until his parents threatened to cut him off unless he got rid of his dreads, dumped his girlfriend, and came back east to work for his father's company. And there was a Latino IT guy I met while in line for an action movie who was really affable. But the Crystal Ball told me we had nothing in common. He liked watching UFC fights while I liked watching *Dr. Who*. Neither of us had ever seen even one episode of what the other liked the most. And it would make for two very awkward dates. I ended up turning both guys down.

The Crystal Ball also showed up at one of my co-worker's birthday parties. A tall brother from New Orleans introduced himself to me. He was fine and had that same Southern gentleman quality that I admired in James Farrell, not to mention the fact that he was a tax attorney, which meant he had to be making at least six figures a year. When I took his card, I suddenly saw us hitting it off, getting married, having children. But then the vision turned sour. He'd seem like the perfect husband, but he would keep a mistress on the side. His father had a mistress, as did his grandfather and the grandfather before that. That was what the men in his family did; it could almost be qualified as a tradition. Except he wouldn't tell me about this tradition until after I found the secret credit card bill with all of the gifts he had bought for his other woman.

The rest of his life. That's how long that relationship would last. First I wouldn't leave him because of the kids. Then I wouldn't leave him because I was too scared to be alone. Either way, he would die happy, and then I would die several years later feeling like I had wasted my life with the last in a long line of men who didn't truly love me.

This was when the Crystal Ball Visions began to feel a little crazy. John, Marcus, the light-skinned guy, and the Latino guy were one thing, but this was a fine successful brother, who had graduated from law school and he was asking for my card.

"Did your father have a mistress?" I asked him, feeling stupid.

"Excuse me?" he said.

"It's just something I have to know before I give you my card," I said.

He shook his head. "I don't understand. Why does my father's mistress matter?"

His Southern accent was so sexy, I wanted to slap myself and these stupid visions I'd been having lately. But I had always been a believer, and something inside me believed in the new version of the Crystal Ball one hundred percent. "So he does have a mistress," I said.

"Yes, but . . ." The tax attorney looked comically baffled now. "What does it matter?"

I sighed. "You know, you should be upfront about that with whoever you marry. You should tell her from the get-go that you plan to keep a mistress. It's only fair."

I had expected him to deny his intention to acquire a mistress after getting married, but instead he looked shaken. "Are you—?" He started and stopped, but then started again. "You see, I'm from New Orleans, so I have to wonder, are you some kind of seer?"

"I'm thinking I might have become one." I pressed his business card back into his hand. "At least when it involves seeing through guys that want to date me."

# THURSDAY

$\mathcal{S}$itting on the steps outside my ex-boyfriend's apartment, I thought for sure that October would go down as the worst month of 2011 for me. But, as it turned out, October had nothing on November. The messiest chapter in the soap opera that had become my life began with Mike Barker showing up on the metal stairs that led up to my soon-to-be-former apartment.

"Hey, you used to be a drug dealer or something, right?" I asked when I saw him standing there at the bottom of the stairs. "Do you know how to pick a lock?"

Without even asking how I had managed to lock myself out of my apartment, he jogged up the stairs, inspected the door and said, "Yeah, this is easy."

Then he'd reached into his pocket and pulled out his iPhone. "Mrs. Murphy," he said a few seconds later. "This is Mike. Can you send a locksmith ASAP to this address?" He gave her the loft's address and hung up. "He should be here within the hour."

"Thanks," I said. Then thinking about my small bank account, which would no longer be subsidized by Caleb, I asked, "Just how much does a locksmith that comes within the hour cost?"

"I got it," he said. "Part of my apology."

I lifted my eyebrows. "Your apology?"

Mike ran a hand over the back of his neck. "Yeah, Davie thinks that maybe I overreacted to your feedback and she's been encouraging me to make some sort of atonement with you. She's big on atonement, but you never called me back, so I had to ambush you. Again."

I nearly forgot about my newly broke-and-boyfriendless state, I was so amused by Mike's apology. "First of all, *maybe* you overreacted? You left me on the dock. Second of all, what are you? Like, forty? Does it bother you even a little that somebody else has to tell you when your behavior sucks? It's like you don't have any agency of your own. Third of all, you didn't have to ambush me. Nobody has to show up anyplace unannounced. You chose to come over here."

My point made, I sat back down on the stairs to wait for Mike's locksmith.

Mike came to sit down beside me on the stairs. "Okay, fine, I'm sorry for leaving you at the dock. That was uncalled for. You're obviously not as enlightened or as much of an adult as I am, so I should have taken the high road with you."

I looked over at him. "Wait, are you calling me a child?"

"Yes, yes, I am," he said. Then, before I could respond to that: "And, by the way, it's not that I don't have my own agency, it's that I don't necessarily trust my own agency, because it's let me down in the past. Recovering addicts don't have the luxury of trusting themselves all the time. So, yes, I touch base with Davie every month. You can make fun of me for that if you want to, but it's kept me off the table now for three years and counting."

Well, that shut me up. "I'm not making fun of you," I said after a few mortified seconds. "I'm glad you were able to get your life together. Really I'm jealous that you can afford a really good life coach. I could totally use one of those right now."

Mike smiled at me then, full wattage, putting all of his movie star looks behind it. And I would have liked to have remained myself, the woman that didn't fall for any of the famous-people tricks because I had grown up with one. But I had just been dumped. And the nicest thing a guy like Mike could bestow on someone like me at a moment like that was the gift of his smile, which even I had to admit was totally gorgeous.

I smiled back at him.

"Look at us," he said. "We're smiling at each other."

"Yeah, I know, crazy, right?"

"I like your dimples. Do me a favor and keep on smiling, okay?"

"Okay," I said, though suspicion started to creep into my smile.

"I didn't apologize on your machine because that isn't exactly the kind of thing you can leave on somebody's voicemail. I felt like I owed you an in-person."

"Okay," I said, still smiling. "As long as we're being honest, I shouldn't have cussed you out in Catalina. I was tired and hungry and I wasn't exactly in my right mind."

"This is really good," Mike said. "Now don't stop smiling when I say this next thing."

He didn't wait for me to agree to his request before continuing. "I've been thinking about what you said, and the thing is, you were right about the script. It's not where it needs to be. And I've been meeting with other writers, trying to figure out how to fix it, but I keep on coming back to one solution: you need to write it."

I immediately stopped smiling. "I assume you're joking."

He maintained eye contact even though I was now staring at him like he was insane. "Hear me out," he said. "You have an MFA in dramatic writing, right?"

"Yeah, but my thesis was a sitcom pilot," I reminded him.

"Okay, understood, but I've worked with a lot of dramatic screenwriters since getting serious about my career, and the one thing I've noticed is that the great ones also have a great sense of humor. I think you have a great sense of humor, too. I mean, your delivery sucks, but your content—that's on point. And, quiet as it's kept, comedy is way harder than drama."

I believed that myself. It was easy to pull on people's strings and make them cry, but making people laugh, now that was a whole different level of effort. Still . . . "You would hate my version of my father's life," I said. "You wouldn't be able to handle playing a dick."

Mike shook his head. "I don't think you hate your father as much as you think you do."

I gave him a frank look that said he was wrong about that.

"Okay," he said. "Okay, say that you really do hate him and you write a script where he's a total villain. Then I'll play him that way. Denzel Washington got an Oscar for playing a bad guy. If that's my path, then that's my path. But I don't think that's how this is going to go down. I think you're going to write this script, and I think you're going to tell the truth, and I think the truth is going to set you free."

I stared at him. Stared at this idiot who was sitting next to me, daring to psychoanalyze me and my writing, even though he didn't know either. And whatever sunshine he had brought into the getting-dumped-by-Caleb situation with his movie-star smile disappeared. "Fine," I said. "I want the Writer's Guild standard for writing the script."

"I'll give you twenty thousand, and if my production company can get it green-lit, then I'll give you the standard on top of your upfront fee."

I thought about that offer, which was actually halfway decent for an unproven screenwriter. Then I thought about my current homelessness. "You probably have a big house, right? One of those splashy mansions?"

Mike's eyes narrowed. "Yeah, and . . . ?"

"I need a place to stay until I can find a new apartment."

"I thought . . ."

"He dumped me," I said. "As it turned out, he was in love with my old roommate, so he dumped me, like, fifteen minutes before you showed up. And I came out here to commit suicide by throwing myself over the railing, but then I couldn't do it, so I tried to go back into the apartment to get my things, and that's when I discovered that I had locked myself out."

Mike whistled. "Wow."

"Yeah, it's been a hell of a day."

"So when this locksmith comes, you're not going to try to burn the place down or trash it or anything like that, right? Because that's the kind of stuff that would land me in the tabloids."

"That's actually a really good idea," I said. "But I don't think I have the energy. I'm just going to pack. But seriously, can I crash with you?"

So that was how I came to be living in the pool house behind Mike Barker's mansion.

It wasn't so bad. No TV, but at least I had Wi-Fi this time, unlike on Catalina. When I fell into bed that first night, a tiny sliver of hope started to radiate underneath my demolished heart. Maybe I would wake up the next morning and feel better about myself and my future.

But instead, I had a nightmare about throwing myself off of the MTS roof, even though I didn't work there anymore. Only Risa, Sharita, and my sister attended my funeral, because Tammy was mad at me for moving in with Mike Barker. And directly after the service, Caleb and Abigail got married in front of my coffin.

I awoke, my brain racing, my heart feeling like a dead gray thing in my chest. I had heard people talking about things that kept them awake at night. But I had never truly understood that idiom until I woke up at three in the morning afraid to go back to sleep, because I never, ever wanted to have another dream like that. This thing Caleb and Abigail had done, it was going to keep me awake at night. Tonight and maybe every night into the foreseeable future. And I didn't even want to think about where I was at the moment.

First of all, as the fact that Mike Barker had sold Tammy out for money had proven, he was a liar. He would never play my father as he really was. And second of all, even if he was willing to, he would never get it green-lit, because Rick T was a rap idol. No studio exec would want to give Mike millions of dollars to play Rick T as a ridiculous narcissist. Third of all, twenty thousand wouldn't last me very long, especially after 1099 deductions. When Mike kicked me out of his pool house, I'd still need to find a new soul-killing job and, worse, I'd actually have to do it without the fun option of suicide to get me through the day.

Fourth of all, how was I going to explain the Mike Barker situation to Tammy? I had promised not to have any further contact with him. And when Risa called me two days later and said the exact words "You need to stay the fuck away from Mike Barker," I had promised again that I wouldn't take any more of his calls. But now I was living in his pool house.

Fifth of all, was there something wrong with even the best version of me that Caleb had been able to toss me away so easily?

Sixth of all, was anybody else ever going to love me again?

Seventh of all, was I going to be wandering around directionless for the rest of my life? Because if that was the case, the rest of my life was going to suck. Really suck . . .

I sobbed into my pillow. I missed Caleb, missed having someone stable in my life who I could depend on. Just the thought of having to start dating all over again made me cry harder.

In between my racking sobs, I heard a noise. A *thump-thump-thump*. Somebody knocking on the door, I realized after a few moments.

"Who is it?" I asked, my voice still wet from the crying.

"Ah . . . it's me. Mike. I came down for a swim and I heard you crying."

Obviously this day didn't want to end until it had wrung every bit of humiliation that it possibly could out of this situation.

"Sorry," I said, trying to get my tears in check. "Sorry for interrupting your swim."

"Do you want something to drink? I have a poolside bar. Fully stocked."

I hadn't known how very badly I wanted a drink until he offered me one.

"Okay." I pulled on some sweatpants to go underneath my Smith College T-shirt. Then I stepped into the cool October evening and found Mike right outside my door . . . wearing a purple sarong around his waist.

Mike wasn't skinny like Caleb. And he wasn't completely ripped, either, like he'd been back in his younger days. Still, there was something about him under the fairy lights that surrounded the pool. He seemed so confident, so comfortable in his own skin. Seriously, how many guys could pull off a sarong with a straight face?

I followed him over to the poolside bar, which had large tiki lights running across the top. As promised, it was fully stocked.

"What do you want?" he asked, walking behind the bar.

"I don't know," I said. "Wine?"

He grabbed a bottle of some red wine with a white label and uncorked it with an electric bottle opener. "Cabernet okay?" he asked, because he was the kind of guy who asked if things were okay after he did them. The kind of guy who got women to agree to cabernet even when they, like me, preferred shiraz.

*"Mike Barker gets what he wants,"* I remembered Tammy saying just a few weeks ago.

"I don't need the glass." I took the bottle from him and took three large swigs straight from the head. Then I said, "You don't have to stay here with me. You can go have your swim."

He took the wine bottle from me and poured his cabernet, which he preferred over shiraz, into a wineglass of his own. "I could, but that might be a little weird for you. I swim naked."

He didn't look at me when he said this, but somehow it felt to me like he was staring at me. Staring at me hard.

A certain electricity rose up between us, crackling beneath the tiki lamps. And my breasts swelled underneath my T-shirt as a hard rock guitar went off in my ovaries.

This right here, I realized, was a boy-girl moment. And the one thing that I had always excelled at, before deciding to mess it up because I had a recurring dream about agreeing to a marriage proposal at a farmers market and saw the movie *Inception* during the summer of 2010, was boy-girl moments.

The warm red wine sloshed around in my empty stomach, and I thought about that section of *The Awesome Girl's Guide* where Davie Farrell talks about making sure you sow all of your wild oats before you settle down into a relationship. I watched Mike's Adam's apple go up and down as he took a drink from his wineglass, and I thought, *Mike Barker looks to me exactly like a wild oat, like a boy in need of a good sowing.*

I blinked, and my poor-Thursday red eyes got exchanged for the heavy-lidded sensuality I had employed so well in my twenties as I took the wine bottle back from him. "You mean you don't have anything on underneath that sarong?"

"No, I thought you'd be asleep, and I needed a swim. This is what I do when . . ."

He trailed off.

"When what?" I asked.

"When I'm tempted to gamble. I swim instead."

Recalling this story, I would have liked to believe that there was a moment of pause here on my part. I'd love to think that when presented with further evidence of his gambling past, I stopped and thought of a broken-hearted Tammy, who had been one of the first victims of his addiction to games of chance.

I would like to believe that reservations came up, but the only thing I can remember saying for sure is, "You swim naked?"

"Usually there's no one else here."

Mike Barker was an actor. Mike Barker was a black man. In fact, Mike Barker was a black actor who was set on playing my father in a film. Of all the men on earth, I couldn't think of one man who I should be less attracted to than Mike Barker.

"Is the pool heated?" I asked.

He nodded, and his eyes met mine.

"Fine," I said, putting the bottle aside. "I'll go swimming with you."

And even though my breasts weren't pert with silicone and even though I hadn't shaved my bikini line since August, I pulled my T-shirt off, over my head.

Mike's gaze stayed on me, hungry and prodding me on until I also came out of my fleece sweatpants and stood there in nothing but my underwear.

When Mike came around the bar, I thought he was going to take off the sarong, but instead, he grabbed my hand and led me past the pool, back into the house, and up the stairs.

"This is my bedroom," he said, opening a door on the second-floor landing.

"So you don't want to swim?" I said. I shivered, not just because of the situation, but also because I was standing in Mike Barker's doorway in nothing but my cotton panties.

In fact, it felt like Mike was doing me a favor when he cupped each of my breasts in his large warm hands and pressed me into the wall beside the door.

He didn't kiss me, just fondled my breasts as he explained, "We could have taken a swim first, but I don't think I would have made it more than a minute or two without going after you. And I don't have any condoms downstairs, so it wouldn't have been safe. I prefer we be safe."

Oh, his hands felt good. "Well, I'm glad you put our safety first," I said, feeling my sense of humor coming back for the first time that day.

But then Mike took one of my breasts into his mouth, and his sarong came off, and the time for jokes quickly passed.

Now, I wasn't one of those people that believed that actors were gods, capable of slow-mo movie sex as soon as you said, "Action!" Also, this wasn't my first rodeo. I had slept with dozens of guys, both good in bed and not. I had thought I knew all there was to know about sex.

But I had never had sex like the sex I had with Mike Barker that night.

246

First of all, there was the intensity. I had a fleeting moment of thought for Tammy, who'd had her heart broken by this man, but then the moment passed, and it seemed to me that the train had already left the station, running over my friendships, personal tastes, and standards as Mike sucked on my breasts while pushing me against the wall.

Second of all, there was Mike himself. Both weird and sexy at the same time. Sexy because he was aggressive, picking me up like a caveman after a few moments spent with each breast. Weird because he jumped into the bed with me like we were kids.

Third of all, there were the compliments.

"No way," he said when he pulled down my panties. "Real bush! I haven't seen real bush since the nineties." He stroked my hair-covered mons like it was a wonderful new pet. "I love this," he said, sticking two fingers into me. "I'm going to get it nice and wet and ready for me." Then: "Oh, wait, you're already there."

He turned me over with a gentle-but-firm instruction to get on my knees. Then he said, "Your dreads aren't extensions, right? They're real. If they're real, you've made my night, my month, my whole year."

"They're real," I said, confused. "But why does it mat—"

He entered me and, without warning, yanked my hair. Hard.

It was completely unexpected, and so freaking hot I nearly came right there.

"Your hair is beautiful," he said. "Long enough to pull, but I don't have to worry about pulling it out." He held on to my dreads, seeming to know instinctively when to pull them and how hard for maximum pleasure.

Fourth of all, there was the tracking of my orgasm. "Are you close?" he asked me a few times. "Tell me when you get close."

There were some false alarms, a few times when I thought I was moving close to the edge, but then Mike would do something different . . .

Fifth of all, Mike was a very distracting lover. Sex with him didn't resemble anything I had ever experienced before, so I had trouble concentrating on making sure that I got mine. But in the end, I didn't even have to tell him when I started getting really close, because he seemed to know.

He pulled out and flipped me over. It was a simple missionary, nothing new, but the way he slow-grinded into me, hitting my clit every time he came to the top of the circle, you would have thought he reinvented the position.

My breaths started coming out in short bursts. And I could feel the orgasm rising up in my pelvis like a storm.

And that's when he finally kissed me. Connected his delicious lips to mine and rode and rode me until I was screaming into his mouth with pleasure. It had never been like this, shouldn't be like this. It was too much. And when he came, it was like he pushed a button and flooded me with a wave of pleasure so strong that there was no afterglow, just aftermath: me pressing my face into his shoulder and crying, and him comforting me like he had accidentally hurt me as opposed to gifting me with the best sex of my life. I felt like somebody else, an entirely new person. So very, very good!

I meant to say "Thank you," but I felt too weak to speak. So instead I held on to him, while Mike whispered into my ear, "It's all right. That was intense, huh? But it was good. We were good. I really enjoyed that. Don't worry about crying. Just feel it, okay?"

I nodded, not seeing how I had much choice but to feel it.

Eventually, he moved out of me. "I've just got to get rid of the condom," he said.

But then he came right back and pulled the covers over both of us. "One last position," he said. "Turn on your side, away from me."

To my surprise, he wrapped me in his arms, spooning me from behind. He smoothed my hair and said, "Let's try to go to sleep, okay?"

Going to sleep was pretty easy this time. I closed my eyes, the sex still swirling around inside of me, and the real world faded away, giving way to dreams tinted purple and hazy with the emotions that Mike had stirred up, Caleb far from my mind.

It was waking up the next morning that was hard.

Because as soon as I opened my eyes to the harsh morning light, I no longer felt warm and sensual. No, in the morning I remembered how brazen I had been, how I had stripped for Mike Barker, Tammy's ex-boyfriend, like a groupie. What had I done? Shame washed over me in bigger waves than my climax had the night before.

We had fallen asleep with him wrapped around me, but we had drifted over to separate sides of the bed during the night. So with one last fleeting look at Mike, who was lying on his back on the other side of the large bed, I ran out of there. I slowed only to grab the sarong that he had discarded near the door and wrap it around my naked body before running into the hallway.

I should have been looking where I was going, but then again, how was I supposed to know there would be a middle-aged woman standing on the landing with a tray of food?

I tried to stop but it was too late. I ran right into the woman, smacking into her so hard that we were both head-butted backward and the tray of food went flying over the railing.

"What the . . ." The poor gray-haired woman sat up, dazed and confused.

And I groaned, cupping my nose. It wasn't broken or anything, but man did accidental head-butting hurt.

"Are you two okay?" Mike asked.

I looked up to see him standing above us in the doorway of his room, dressed in nothing but a pair of hastily thrown-on gym shorts. So much for the stealth getaway.

"Michael, I was bringing you your breakfast, because Frederic had already dished it up and you hadn't come down. I thought you were having a lie-in. Is this your guest?" She glanced over at me, but then looked away again so quickly that I didn't have to be told that Mike's sarong hadn't stayed closed after the collision.

Sure enough, I looked down to see that I was pretty much naked from the waist up.

"I'm sorry," I said again, covering myself up. "I didn't see you when I came out." I scrambled to my own feet as Mike helped the woman to hers.

"Thursday, this is my personal assistant, Harriet Murphy. Harriet, this is Thursday."

"Oh, you're Thursday, the woman who has been giving Michael so many problems with his biopic." Harriet's lips set and I could tell she was recasting me from clueless hussy to stubborn-brat hussy.

"I'm just going to go now," I said, really wishing that I'd had the courage to throw myself over that railing yesterday.

"Wanna have breakfast?" Mike asked.

Harriet glared at me. "Yes, we can ask Frederic to whip up a whole new breakfast, since you ruined the first one."

As lovely as that sounded, I said, "Um, no, I think I'll go. Thanks, though."

I gave a little wave, and beat a hasty exit down the stairs.

Back in the pool house, I had to sit on the bed and hyperventilate for a little bit. This was terrible. What had I done? Betrayed my dying friend, and for what? Just to feel better about myself for a little while? I had suspected that I was starting to lean toward the wrong side of selfish for a while now, but this had confirmed it.

I felt horrible, dirty-in-a-bad-way to my very core. And not even the ice-cold shower that I took in the outdoor fixture behind Mike's pool house made me feel clean again. I had to get out of Mike Barker's house, I realized while drying off back inside the pool house. But I didn't have any money to get out of his house. Without the twenty thousand that he had promised me for a finished script, I would be stuck in this pool house for the conceivable future. But I couldn't get the twenty thousand without a script.

I looked at the messenger bag that held my laptop, then toward the small wooden desk sitting underneath the pool house's one window and made a decision. I fished out some sweatpants and one of my purple NYU T-shirts from my suitcase, put them on, and started writing.

It was like riding a bicycle. Well, a rusty bicycle. It definitely felt strange to open my screenwriting program, Final Draft, for the first time in over three years, but after a few starts and stops it all came back to me, and I managed to clock twenty pages before my stomach switched from mildly asking to full-on demanding that I eat something. I didn't want to go back into the main house, but I also didn't want to faint, as my body was threatening it would do if I didn't get something to eat soon. In the end, I decided to risk it, promising myself that I would go and get a microwave and a bunch of non-perishable groceries as soon as I finished the day's writing.

I knew that the chance of Mike or his hostile personal assistant being in the kitchen at three in the afternoon was little to none. Still, I felt rather unsettled as I made my way back into the house. And it wasn't just because of the possibility of running into Mike again. It was the screenplay, which was already sort of getting away from me. I had opened my version of the Rick T biopic with scenes from both my mother's and my father's lives. Juxtaposing my mother's upbringing in the Marcy Projects of New York with six brothers and sisters against my father's suburban life in upstate Connecticut as the only child of a solidly middle-class preacher and his kindergarten teacher wife.

It was meant to show what a fraud Rick T was, but instead, when he and my mother met at an awards banquet for Columbia University scholarship winners, it read more like a great love story. Opposites attract and all of that. Like they both had something that the other needed. And the montage that happened after he discovered her journal of poetry was feeling less like watching a poser try to be something he wasn't and more like a genuine transformation of a formerly middle-class kid into a political dynamo.

Rick T wasn't coming off as a saint, but he definitely wasn't the villain of the piece, as originally intended. At least not yet, I reminded myself, coming in through the kitchen's back door. The screenplay might not have started off as strong as I wanted it to, but Rick T would definitely get his before the end.

I opened the refrigerator door and found nothing but an assortment of juices, milk, salad ingredients, and fresh vegetables. Ugh, Mike was obviously one of those health nazis. I closed the fridge and grabbed an apple out of the fruit bowl (by far the sweetest thing in the entire kitchen) and took an unsatisfying bite.

Apple in mouth, I looked through the cabinets and, after a protracted search, found some shredded wheat. Shredded wheat and skim milk didn't sound like the best lunch ever, but it would do until I got to the grocery store. So I fixed myself a bowl of cereal and poured myself a cup of grapefruit juice. Then I gathered it all up to take back to the pool house. But just as I was nearing the door, someone said behind me, "So you're going to sneak out without talking to me?"

I nearly dropped the bowl and the glass, I was so surprised to hear Mike's voice. I turned around to see what I had missed when I came in. The kitchen wasn't a rectangle, but a backwards L. And if you were distracted, it was perhaps easy to miss the other half of the kitchen around the corner from the fridge, where a large breakfast nook could be found with what looked like a genuine diner booth, big enough to seat six.

Mike was sitting at the booth with an iPad in front of him.

"Mike," I said. "I didn't see you there."

He gave me a look like, *Sure you didn't*, and stood up. "We need to talk," he said.

"Actually, I'm on a writing roll with this Rick T script, so I should really be getting back," I said.

"Thursday." And that was all he said, but the look on his face said the rest. I didn't know how to feel at that moment, torn as I was between guilt and the determination not to get sucked into his charm trap again.

"My shredded wheat is getting soggy," I said. "Can we talk later?"

I didn't wait for him to agree, just opened the door with my free hand and backed out of the kitchen. But his eyes were on me as I left, hot and steady and all-knowing. Like a wolf sizing up its prey.

There is a story that screenwriters love to retell, and it goes like this: Sylvester Stallone wrote the screenplay for *Rocky* in three and a half days.

That's it. Pure and simple. But it's the biggest and most enduring screenwriting legend in Hollywood, the one repeated by the most writers and in the most screenwriting books.

There had been a lot of back and forth throughout the years about whether this story was fact or fiction. And to my knowledge, no one had ever asked Stallone publicly whether he rewrote before actually showing it to anyone. But the legend endured, a shining beacon to all would-be screenwriters, its promise oh-so-alluring in its ease. And deep down every wannabe writer wanted to think up a story so good that a concise one-hundred-and-twenty-page script could come tumbling out of her or him in eighty-four passion-fueled hours.

Well, I was ready to call bullshit on that legend. Unlike Stallone, I actually had an MFA, experience writing, and a laptop as opposed to a typewriter. And it still took me no less than five days of barely eating or sleeping to write the Rick T biopic. Then it took me two more days of editing to make the thing comprehensible.

But when I was done, Stallone was all I could think about. Was this how he had felt when he finished *Rocky*, buzzed up with the adrenaline of a story that needed to be told, wanting to show it to everybody and nobody at the same time?

It hadn't turned out how I expected. I had put everything I had known about my father's career and my parents' relationship into the screenplay, including the mistress-turned-wife and the real story of my mother's suicide. Some ugly, ugly stuff made it on to the page. But then there was also the good stuff. The years when MTV was playing his singles, the spate of black nineties movie soundtracks that had included his songs. And the whole thing ended with him getting inducted into the Rock and Roll Hall of Fame back in 2008.

That had been the last invitation I had received from Rick T, and it went unanswered. But I had watched the rebroadcast on VH1 and had been struck by how well he still performed, how he delivered on stage, but also how he seemed to realize that this supposed honor marked the end of an era and made him the last of a dying breed of rappers who actually had something worthwhile to say and could make money saying it.

The final scene in the script was the speech he made at that ceremony about the responsibility of musicians to leave behind some information for future generations, to make an impact while they could. "Because no one listens to you when you're old. So if you've got something to say, say it now and say it bold. And if everything you have to say has already been said before, consider doing us all a favor, and keep that noise to yourself."

Classic Rick T. A few younger rappers had made comments about him being old, about him being jealous because he never had their kind of record sales, even at the height of his fame. Maybe they were right. But maybe Rick T was right, too.

I was so tired, I didn't know what was right and what was wrong anymore.

I typed Mike's e-mail address into a new message window, attached the script, and in the subject line wrote, "Let me know when I can pick up my check."

I pushed "Send," and as soon as I did, all the story energy that had kept me going with minimal sleep and food for the last week seemed to drain right out of me. I desperately needed a shower, but I couldn't imagine standing in one. So I slept, and then I slept some more, and when I woke up, it was many hours later and nighttime.

The outside shower only emitted cold water, which was hard to put up with during the day when it was warm, and basically impossible to wrap your mind around at night when it was cold. So I crept into one of the downstairs bathrooms in the house and took the longest shower known to man, making sure to get my dreads, too, with a really fantastic-smelling shampoo that I had found unopened in the guest shower. I nearly sang, the shampoo and water felt so good on my itchy and dirty scalp. And I felt like a new woman when I climbed out of the shower and piled my wet dreads on top of my head in a messy bird's nest of a bun. Glad that I had taken this risk to get clean, I pulled on a pair of socks and a robe and prepared to sneak back to the pool house . . .

. . . and of course I found Mike waiting for me when I opened the bathroom door. I would have jumped, but why bother to act surprised? It now felt like I had known the entire time that Mike would be standing there when I opened the door, waiting.

We stared at each other.

"I read the screenplay," he said. "As soon as I got it."

"And . . ." I said. My heart surprised me by speeding up in anticipation of his feedback, even though I wasn't supposed to care about the screenplay or what Mike Barker thought, only about the money that I would receive for writing it.

He said this next thing so slowly that there was no mistaking his sincerity. "It's the best thing I have ever read."

Now, it should be noted here that I did have a staunch policy against messing around with my friends' exes. I really did. But the thing is, it goes against the laws of physics for a writer not to have sex with any pretty person who says something like, "It's the best thing I've ever read."

Listen, the narrator of *The Kite Runner married* the first girl that ap-preciated his writing. So after hearing a thing like that, in what universe would it have even been possible for me *not* to pull Mike Barker's face down to mine and kiss the living daylights out of him? Was there really any other action that I could have taken other than pushing him to the floor and rid-ing him with my robe open, not even questioning it when, before I got on top of him, he took a condom out of his pocket and put it on, like he had come down there expecting this reaction?

I had been struggling in Los Angeles for a long time. A very long time. And the truth was I had needed a win like a movie star simply saying he really liked what I wrote. Receiving a sincere compliment, one that came without caveats or a "but, sorry, it's just not for us"—well, that just over-whelmed my senses. I could not be blamed for screwing Mike Barker a sec-ond time, even though I had promised myself (and Tammy, in my heart) that it would never happen again.

Mike came first, and I climaxed right after him, falling against his chest when I finished.

I rolled off of him and stared up at the ceiling. This time the wave of shame didn't wait until the next morning. It suffused me in place of an af-terglow. "I can't believe I did that again."

He turned over on his side to face me, his pants still around his ankles. "I thought we'd at least make it to a couch."

I scrambled to my knees, tying my robe around my waist as tightly as I could. "You think this is funny? This isn't funny."

"Baby, we just had sex outside the guest bathroom on the hard tile floor. It's definitely funny. I thought I was getting too old for stuff like that."

"You really don't get how bad this is, do you?"

He stood and pulled up his designer jeans in one smooth move. "It's not bad. It's extremely good. Come to bed with me. We'll talk, we'll figure this out, I promise."

He reached out for me, and I certainly felt something in me being tugged toward something in him, but I held up my hands and stepped away.

"Tammy is my friend. And I'm not the type of person who sleeps with my friend's exes. That's not me."

His face went from amused to annoyed. "Thursday," he said, "Forget about Tammy. She was nothing. And it was a long time ago."

I went completely still when he said that, and it felt like a cold front came over my heart. "She was nothing?" I said. "Tammy was nothing to you?"

"No, not nothing. 'Nothing' is obviously the wrong word."

"Obviously."

"But I wasn't—it wasn't as big of a deal as you think it was. Tammy and me are cool. Me and her have nothing to do with you and me."

"Wow, you are just like my father. Leaving wreckage in your wake and never wanting to take responsibility for it."

Mike rubbed his temples like this entire conversation was giving him an inconvenient headache. "I'm not responsible for Tammy—"

"You asked her to *marry you*, then you cheated on her and dumped her in an extremely callous way. And she was devastated. You left her unable to love again. Do you understand this? She hasn't dated anyone since you, and guess what? Now she's dying alone, because she was all messed up over you and never found anyone else—"

I cursed, realizing I had just said too much.

Mike stood there, stunned. "Tammy's dying?"

"I shouldn't have told you that. It's a secret. Don't tell anybody else."

"I won't, but . . ." Mike shook his head. "I'm sorry to hear that. But I'm not the reason she's dying alone."

"Yeah, but you are, Mike, and I'm a really horrible person for sleeping with you. I mean, really horrible. The only real thing that I've ever had going for me is my fierce sense of loyalty to the women I love. And now I don't even have that anymore, because I let myself get tangled up with you."

He reached for me again as if his movie-star touch could make what he did, what we had now both done, to Tammy just disappear.

"Seriously, don't touch me," I said. Then, I didn't walk but ran back to the pool house.

# December 2011

Never put your life on hold for a guy. Your life is your biggest project and it should always be your number-one priority.

—*The Awesome Girl's Guide to Dating Extraordinary Men* by Davie Farrell

# THURSDAY

$\mathcal{I}$t should be noted that after my second round of sex with Mike Barker, I reset with the absolute best of intentions. The very next day, I looked up studio apartments on Craigslist and started e-mailing their landlords and leasers, making appointments to see them. Then I spent the rest of November looking for a reasonably priced apartment that I could afford even after the twenty thousand ran out. Part of me wanted to take the first thing that was available and decent, but Sharita advised me to rent practically, not emotionally.

"You want a place that you can stand living in for the next year or two," she said. "Don't move into anything because you want to get out of your friend's hair."

Though I had been spending way more time with Sharita lately, I still hadn't figured out a way to admit that I was staying with Mike Barker without also admitting that I had sexed him two times, so I had lied about staying in a grad school friend's spare room. I wanted to ignore Sharita's advice and do anything to get out of Mike's pool house, where, despite my better instincts, I still found myself tempted to go to him. I had woken up from a few dirty dreams so sick with lust that it made me miss the recurring farmers market dream—the one that had never come true, no matter how many L.A.-area farmers markets I had dragged Caleb to for reasons I could never quite explain to him without coming off like a psycho.

But Sharita did have a point. I wanted to get to a place where I was dependent on no one but myself, and the only person I knew like that was Sharita. I figured maybe I should start making decisions the way she would. So I took my housing search slow, asking questions, checking landlords' names out online, and eventually I found a little green studio guesthouse in

Eagle Rock. It was tiny, with a shower that put me in mind of a coffin, but it was cheap and within walking distance of the main drag of Colorado. Most of all, when I looked at the bright yellow main room, I could see myself living there for a long time . . . and being happy.

Mike Barker, I admitted while surveying this space, had thrown me for a loop. He was pretty much everything I didn't want in a guy, plus he was off-limits according to basic girlfriend code. But I couldn't stop thinking about him and that deeply disturbed me. I'd always been a free spirit when it came to sex, but if that meant sleeping with someone I should despise, then maybe what I needed was some time alone to get my head right before I pursued any other relationships.

"I'll take it," I said to the landlord, who lived in the front house. Then I wrote him a check for the first and last months' rent that just about wiped out what little money I had managed to hold onto since getting fired.

I needed the twenty thousand that Mike had promised me, so even though I'd been avoiding him for almost three weeks, I went looking for him the first week of December. He wasn't in the kitchen, but he also wasn't in his bedroom. I might not have found him in the large house if I hadn't heard the muffled sound of his voice while walking past a closed door.

I could hear Mike on the other side of the door saying, "I don't care what I signed. This is causing me huge problems. You've got to. No, you've got to. Don't hang up on me. Seriously, don't hang up on me—*goddammit!*"

I assumed whoever it was had hung up on him, despite his command not to do so. I knocked on the door, and there was a long pause before he said, "Mrs. Murphy?"

"No, it's Thursday," I said.

The sound of footsteps, and he opened the door himself, beaming down at me. "Hey, long time no see. Come in, come in."

When I walked in, I saw that his office looked exactly like a rich person's office would look . . . in the seventies. All dark woods and heavy but brightly colored furniture. The only things that indicated this space belonged to Mike were several framed movie posters from recent years lining the walls.

"I didn't know you had an office," I said.

"Yeah, I don't use it much," he said.

I took a seat in one of the two bright-orange chairs in front of his desk. "It doesn't look like the rest of the house."

"No," he said. "I had an interior designer, but then my gambling debts ballooned and my checks started bouncing, so he never got around to this room. But you know what, it's my favorite. Lately I've been thinking about redecorating the rest of the house to match the office."

I nodded. "Yeah, I really like this room, too."

He dropped into his high-backed leather desk chair. "So we have aesthetic tastes in common, too." Then he leaned back and smiled at me. Just smiled at me. Like we were back on the steps outside Caleb's apartment.

I had to remind myself that he acted for a living and he had been nominated for an Oscar, so he was very, very good at what he did. It was probably easy for him to radiate the kind of energy that made even women as cynical as me feel weak in the knees.

"Did you have a nice Thanksgiving?" he asked.

"Not really," I answered. "Usually I try to visit my sister, but I was super-broke this year, so I ended up making myself a microwave dinner. I really want to see her for Christmas, though." I said, hoping he'd catch the hint and segue into the matter of my check.

"I'd always thought that would be nice," he said. "Having a sibling. Makes it a little easier to be in the dead mothers club."

"Oh," I said, derailed from my hoped-for segue by this new information. "Your mom's dead, too?" I had only seen the first ten minutes of his *E! True Hollywood Story.*

"Yeah, she overdosed when I was a sophomore in college. Crack."

"I'm sorry," I said, remembering how it had felt to lose my own mom that early. "What was her name?"

Mike squinted at me, obviously confused by the question.

"No one ever asks me my mother's name," I explained. "It makes telling people she's dead so vague. Like it's this thing that happened, but . . ."

". . . Maybe you just imagined it," he said, filling in the gaps of my explanation. "I'm forty-one. My mom's been dead for longer than I knew her alive. Sometimes it feels like she's just a sentence in my biography. Like my publicist made her up."

"Exactly," I said. "You should tell people her name when you talk about her. It makes her more real."

"I don't talk about her. I mean, I never talk about her with women I've slept—" He didn't finish that sentence. Just stopped and said, "Her name was Delores."

"I'm sorry Delores died on you. That sucks," I said.

"I'm sorry Valerie died on you," he said. "She was my favorite part of your script."

We looked at each other, me so unused to hearing my mother's name come out of anyone's mouth. Even Caleb and I hadn't talked about her much. I had told him she had died in a car accident when I was twenty on our second official date and that was it.

"Um, thanks," I said. Then: "Awkward subject change: I found an apartment, and I need the money you owe me so that I can move."

"I don't have it yet," he said, leaning back in his chair.

"It's been three weeks. And you said 'upon delivery.'"

He sighed. "Okay, I've had too much therapy to sit here and lie to you, so I'll say this straight out. I don't want you to go yet."

I determinedly ignored the warm rush of blood to my heart. "I respect your honesty, but I'm trying to turn over a new leaf here, and I can't sponge off of you forever."

"Well, how about for now?"

"How about you give me my money like you said you would?"

"How about you stay here and deal with whatever is going on between us?"

"How about you realize that Tammy is one of my dearest friends?"

He clenched his jaw. "Like I said the other night, Tammy and I were a long time ago. You and me are happening right now."

I leaned forward and asked, "Has it occurred to you that you only want me to stay because you can't have me? If I was all over you like one of your usual cocktail waitresses, you wouldn't be able to wait to get rid of me."

"I don't sleep with cocktail waitresses anymore," he said. He opened up his dresser drawer and pulled out a checkbook. "Not since I stopped gambling. I think you're judging me by what you've read in the tabloids as opposed to getting to know me for who I am today."

I shook my head. "Mike, we're not getting to know each other. We're a two-night stand kind of situation, and I only slept with you those two times because I was desperate and lonely and pretty much the worst feminist in the world."

Mike grabbed a fountain pen out of a wooden cup on his desk. "You slept with me because you were desperate and lonely," he repeated.

"Yes," I said. "And I'm sorry I did. Now can I pretty please have my money?"

He put on a pair of reading glasses and wrote out the check. But when he tore it off, he peered over the top of his glasses and said, "You're lying to me. But I'm not mad, because I know you're also lying to yourself. You've got feelings for me, and I'm not going to let you get away with not feeling them. Here's your check."

His desk was so large and wide that I had to stand up to take the check and when I reached for it, he caught me by the wrist. "Thursday," he said. And that was all he said.

Less than two minutes later I discovered what it felt like to have sex in a leather chair, bouncing up and down on his lap until we both came and wilted into each other.

When it was over, I got off of him and scrambled to put my jeans back on.

"The landlord says I can move in on December 15th," I said, grabbing the check from where I had dropped it, when Mike pulled me across his desk. I met Mike's eyes for one horrified second and then I left.

I subsisted on snack food and fruit for the next week, refusing to come out of the pool house for any reason. Not even when I woke up to the sound of him swimming laps in the pool that night. And the night after that. And the night after that. Until finally it was December 15th and it was time to pack up my car.

Mike had helped me move in, but on that cold (for L.A.) winter day when I moved out, I did so all by myself. It only took me an hour, since I didn't have much. After a few trips to my Echo, which I'd left parked in the circular driveway in front of Mike's house, I was ready to go. I decided against saying good-bye to Mike. The check fiasco had taught me it wouldn't be safe.

But just as I was about to start the engine to leave, a sharp rap sounded on my passenger window. It was Mike.

"Thursday," he said. "Roll down the window."

I really didn't think I should roll down the window.

"Roll down the window or I'll stop payment on that check. It couldn't have cleared yet."

Okay, fine. It was true that the bank hadn't released the mandatory seven-day hold on my check yet, so I rolled down the window and said, "What?"

He shook his head at me.

"What?" I said again, knots of terror forming inside my stomach for no reason that I could explain.

"Thursday . . ." he said. He lowered his eyes to the steering wheel and stared at it for the longest time before saying, "I wish you were braver. That's all. Have a nice life."

That said, he stepped back from the car and stood there. Just stood there.

It was a challenge. A challenge for me to stay. A challenge for me to betray Tammy. A challenge to prove that I was indeed brave. But the truth was I wasn't brave. And the truth was that I knew that he knew that if I got out of this car, we'd kiss and I'd let him take me up to his bedroom and maybe I'd never leave.

"I was madly in love with him," my mother had once told me, when I was younger and would ask her to tell me over and over how she and my father got together. "I thought he was the whole earth, and I have never wanted to be somebody's moon so bad."

What I'd had with Caleb had been nice, I realized, missing my ex-boyfriend with a bitter ache. There had been none of this all-consuming passion. When he was away, I never had problems sleeping like my mother had when my father was on tour, especially later when he started taking his mistress with him on the road, leaving her to ramble around our house at night like the insomniac ghost of her former self. Caleb had been comfortable and low-key and boring. I wanted boring. I deserved boring.

Just talking to Mike Barker felt like driving off a cliff to me.

"*Don't be pathetic*," my mother's corpse whispered over and over again. "*Don't be pathetic*."

I didn't roll back up the window, just stuck my key in the ignition and drove away. It was the right thing to do, but I checked the rearview anyway.

And yes, Mike Barker was still standing there, hands in pockets, watching me go.

I had thought that was the end of it. I moved into my little green guesthouse and kept on looking for a job. I also went to all sorts of holiday parties and random events with Sharita and visited Janine for Christmas. It was the first time she hadn't had to pay for my ticket, and that felt good. I still hadn't worked up the courage to visit Tammy, but I maintained hope that one day, I'd be able to face her again.

As I flew back into Los Angeles on December 30th, I decided to label 2011 as the Year That Everything Changed.

But it all came to a head on December 31st with a sharp knock on my door. I was pulling on a shiny red dress, one that fell a bit shorter than I liked, but hey, it was New Year's Eve. When I heard the knock, I sighed, because I still had to dig my electric blue heels out of the back of my closet and Sharita was over forty-five minutes early.

Los Angeles was a town that didn't appreciate people showing up on time. And early was just rude. I had loved these social rules and had adjusted to them accordingly, but Sharita, being an accountant, had never gotten hip to the game. Eight years after her arrival in this West Coast metropolis, she had yet to be anything less than fifteen minutes early to every event that she attended.

But forty-five minutes—that was ridiculous. And I would have told Sharita that when I opened the door. Except it wasn't Sharita standing there, it was Mike, dressed in a very non-New-Years-y jeans-and-light-sweater ensemble.

"Um . . ." I said.

"I'm sick of swimming," he said. "I've been swimming every night, and it's not working. I'm sick of it."

He was looking at me like this was all my fault.

"If you're having that much trouble with wanting to gamble," I said, "you should talk to Davie."

Something ticked in his jaw. "Davie can't help with this. In fact, Davie's part of the problem. I'm swimming because of you, because I want to be with you, but that stops tonight. You can come along if you feel like it."

I had no intention of going anywhere with him, but I had to ask, "Go where?"

"To Tammy's," he said. "We're going to get her permission to date."

Then, without waiting for my answer, he turned around and started walking toward his Audi, which was idling in the driveway.

# RISA

So they released Supa Dupa's first self-titled album. It was doing okay. Not great, not terrible. Just okay. I did a couple of interviews with alternative weeklies, went on a couple of radio shows. The thirteen- to twenty-five-year-olds, Gravestone's key market, weren't rabid about me or anything, but they wouldn't kick me out of bed.

My A&R guy thought Gravestone might offer me a second album deal. But I didn't care.

I was finding it hard to care about much these days. The road had become such a grind. It was all tour buses and a motel every two or three days. That was the only time I could take a decent shower and sleep in a non-cot-sized bed. Lots of acts write their best albums on the road. I was not one of those acts.

Maybe if I were able to pull pussy at every college like the younger guys in the other bands, I would have been able to enjoy it more. But, no, I had to service The Lead Singer's Girlfriend. And when she couldn't get away, I had to act like I was pining for her. The situation was so old it was decrepit. It was in a nursing home, on an oxygen machine. And my heart called out, "Euthanasia!" every time she knocked on my motel room door.

Most of the other guys on tour told me I was lucky, because I was the only woman, which meant I didn't have to share a hotel room. I didn't tell them that I'd rather share a hotel room than have to pretend to be excited about fucking the same girl I didn't even like every night.

After falling in love with The One all those years ago, I kind of swore off hanging out with any single girl for more than a week or two. It was either her or nobody long term. So this thing with The Lead Singer's Girlfriend really went against my nature. And by the time New Year's Eve rolled around, I was in a pretty shitty mood. I missed my L.A. apartment, I missed The One, I missed my friends. This was the first time in four years that we hadn't met up for our annual New Year's Eve matinee. If I were still in town, I would have dragged Thursday and Sharita over to Tammy's with a DVD. But I wasn't in town, so . . .

. . . the night of New Year's Eve, I was on the East Coast, scheduled to play a corporate party as the opener along with Yes, We Are Trying To Cute You To Death (Yes, We Are for short). This started out as an Ipso! Facto! gig. But the label threw Yes, We Are and Supa Dupa into the deal so that we could get some more exposure. Whatever that meant.

I went on after Yes, We Are, and the suits weren't exactly rocking out to my set. One corporate drone even plugged the ear closest to the stage with a finger as he networked over his champagne. I started to feel rather stupid in my green patent leather pants and my string bikini top, which had "20" written over one breast and "12" over the other. And I was relieved when the set was through.

The guys from Yes, We Are asked if I wanted to go somewhere, somewhere *real* to celebrate New Year's. I had already played, and I didn't have to stick around till midnight. But I couldn't tell if they were serious about the invite or being nice since I was standing right there when they started tossing around plans. A couple of years ago this wouldn't have even been a question. I hated, hated, hated my thirties.

I told them sure, give me a second. And then I went into the bathroom and did a line of coke. I was not cliché enough to be a cokehead (anymore), but I was also not young enough to get through a whole New Year's Eve of hard partying without a little help from my powdery friend. I stared at myself in the corporate mirror while I waited for the coke to do its thing. The track lighting in the bathroom made it look like I had on too much makeup. Garish. Old. That was how I looked.

And I kind of felt like crying then, because I'd never wanted to be anything but a rock star. But I was starting to realize, at the age of thirty, that being a rock star isn't all that great. And I really wished I'd had this epiphany earlier, before coming out to my parents and getting disowned, before dropping out of Smith College in the spring semester of my junior year, before spending the last nine years acquiring exactly zero transferrable skills.

Instead, this was the Year I Finally Achieved My Dream . . . only to find out that my dream sucked and, moreover, I was now too old to truly enjoy it. I didn't want to go back to school. I didn't want to start getting up before two in the afternoon. But The One . . . well, that wasn't going to happen, was it? Not with my tepid record sales, not with her still refusing to love me back the way I loved her.

*What was taking this coke so fucking long to work already?* I was about to line up another rail of powder when my phone rang.

I checked the caller ID. It was Tammy. So I answered it, because if she was going to bring me down with her terminal cancer, then I wanted to save the other line of coke for after the phone call. "What's up, Tammy-Tam," I said.

"Thursday," Tammy was crying so hard, I could barely make out what she was saying. "Thursday and Mike Barker are together. And they came over here. And they . . . And they . . . This is The Worst Year Ever."

Tammy was crazy sobbing now, worse than when the whole Mike Barker situation went down in the first place, worse than when she told me she had cancer.

"Tammy, calm down," I said, trying to keep my voice steady, even though the first line was starting to kick in and I definitely didn't feel steady. "Just tell me what happened."

# January 2012

If you can, try to meet someone during the summer. It's a downright lovely time to fall in like . . .

—*The Awesome Girl's Guide to Dating Extraordinary Men* by Davie Farrell

# THURSDAY

I ran after Mike, although my dress was still unzipped at the back and I didn't have on any shoes. "Wait," I said. "You can't bother Tammy with this. She's *dying.*"

"I realize that," he said. "And I've been trying to figure out how to solve us without going over to her place, but I can't, so I'm going to have to confront her. You don't have to come with me if you don't want to."

"First of all, there is no 'us.' Second of all, I'm not volunteering to come with you, I'm trying to stop you from further traumatizing a very sick woman. Third of all, this right here is why I kind of hate actors. You are being so unnecessarily overdramatic."

Mike came to an abrupt stop. "Wait," he said. "Can you say that 'first of all' one again?"

Standing in the concrete driveway, I had to cycle back in my memory before restating my first point. "There is no us," I said.

He smiled and stepped closer. "Say that again."

"There is no us," I repeated, taking a step back because I didn't like the gleam in his eyes.

"Yes!" he said, pumping his fist. "I've seen all these movies where the main character says 'There is no us,' and do you know what they all have in common?"

"Cliché?" I guessed, honestly baffled by this new line of conversation.

"The characters always end up together at the end. *Always.* Because there was in fact an 'us,' the manifestation of which was one of the characters denying it."

He turned and started walking again.

"You know we're not in a movie, right?" I asked his back.

"Like I said, you don't have to come with, but I'm going to do this thing. Mike Barker gets what he wants."

He acted like I had a choice, but I did have to come—for damage control, at the very least. Also, how was I supposed to enjoy two New Year's parties with Sharita, knowing that Mike was telling Tammy everything?

"Fine," I said. "Can I at least have time to zip up my dress and get some shoes and my phone?"

Mike was at his car now. "I can zip up your dress for you, but I'm done with waiting. I'm leaving right now, with or without you."

Scared that he'd really leave without me, I jogged and jumped into the car before he put it in drive.

"How about the part about me not liking you?" I asked, pulling on my seat belt.

"I'm a pretty likeable guy, Thursday. I think it might be that you think you don't like me because you haven't gotten to know me yet. We definitely had sex too soon."

"You can't have casual sex too soon," I said. "That's why it's called 'casual sex,' because it doesn't mean anything. It's something you do and then you get on with your life. How are you not getting this part?"

"That's a fascinating perspective. We should talk more about it on our first date."

"I can't date you because you're my friend's ex-boyfriend. Also, because I don't want to. I just got out of a relationship and I've decided to take a long break from dating. So you see, we really don't have to go to Tammy with this."

"Okay," he said. "I'm going to get rid of one of your excuses, and if you still don't want to date me after that, then you don't have to. I can't force you to give me a chance, but I can clear away the obstacles so that you can see what a good idea it would be to have me in your life."

"Let me guess, Davie Farrell told you to say that. Word for word."

He shrugged, "If it makes you feel more powerful and in control to make fun of the fact that I consult with Davie about relationships and my mental well-being, go ahead. I know it's going to be hard for you to be with someone who has already done the work when you yourself haven't."

"Wait, are you seriously putting me down for not having had a ton of therapy that I can't afford?"

"No, I'm putting you down for not doing the work that you need to do and for choosing hate over forgiveness and for backing away from me because I challenge you. That's why I'm putting you down."

For the first time in my life I got how Sharita must feel whenever we got into fights. There was something icky and cold about being on the receiving end of an argument that was way more intelligent than your own. It made me feel both angry and desperate at the same time.

How was I supposed to answer him? Saying, "You don't challenge me," would not only be a lie, but would also prove his point. And going with my impulse to just up and smack him would be dangerous because he was driving.

"I only watched the first ten minutes of your *E! True Hollywood Story*, but . . . you're not dumb, are you?" I said, phrasing it as more of an accusation than a question.

"No," he said. "If you had watched the part beyond my high school stint as a drug dealer, you would have seen that I went to Amherst. Right up the road from Smith."

I looked at him sideways. "Oh, please don't tell me you were one of those Amherst guys. You were the absolute worst—so cocky, like you were God's gift to women, just because you had a seven-girls-to-one-guy ratio going on."

He chuckled. "Well, you Smithies were always talking down to us, like we were idiots because we were guys."

"*Guys who went to Amherst*," I corrected, as if that proved my whole argument.

276

He laughed, sounding way happier than he should have while driving in a car with an unwilling love interest as his passenger, about to confront an ex-girlfriend who was dying of cancer.

"The other day I was watching this old movie on TCM, and I was thinking, that's what's missing from rom-coms these days. There's not enough banter anymore. And you know, I think it's reflective of society. Men and women, we don't appreciate wordplay as much as we used to. This is good. I love that we can do this."

I wanted to point out that we weren't in a relationship, but he had already shut down that line of argument with his "There is no us" thesis, so I just folded my arms and looked out the window, giving him silence as opposed to banter until we got to Santa Monica.

Sadly, there was a bunch of available street parking outside of Tammy's building, so my dream of Mike giving up this mission due to parking frustration quickly evaporated.

I set to hoping that Tammy didn't answer her buzzer. She had become a recluse since getting her terminal diagnosis, and according to Sharita, these days if her nurse wasn't around to answer the buzzer, then it didn't get answered.

But as (bad) luck would have it, some guy dressed in a tux was coming out of Tammy's building as we were approaching the front door. And if he had any questions about the fact that I wasn't wearing shoes, they were eclipsed by Mike's star presence.

"Loved you in *Adults at Play*," he said, holding the door open for Mike and me. "I really thought that you should have gotten the Oscar for that one."

"Thanks, man," Mike said with a smile and a wave. He took my hand as we walked through the door, and kept on holding it in the elevator.

I allowed this small intimacy, but only because I needed something to hold onto to get through the worst elevator ride ever. I was going to lose Tammy tonight. It was inevitable, and though I could try to cushion Tammy against the hurt of my betrayal, there wouldn't be much I could do to salvage the friendship. I knew that, and I could only hope that my friendships with Risa and Sharita wouldn't also be damaged in the process.

I once again found myself missing Caleb, who had been so nice and non-confrontational. Really, WASPy guys were the best. I hoped Abigail appreciated that about him.

The elevator dinged and the next thing I knew, Mike was knocking on Tammy's door. Then knocking on Tammy's door some more when she didn't answer the first set of pounds.

"Tammy," he called. "It's Mike Barker. And I'm not going away until you open this door."

We waited, me very much hoping that Tammy would leave him standing out there as long as it took for him to give up and go away.

But no, the door opened a few seconds later, and I was more than a little aghast when I saw Tammy. Sharita's description hadn't done her new appearance justice. Her eyes had sunken in, and she was hunched over in a leopard-print Snuggie, her short hair a frizzy and tangled mess. I could just about smell the cancer coming off of her.

To his credit, Mike did hesitate before saying, "Tammy, we have to talk."

Tammy's eyes went from Mike to me and back to Mike. "I'm sorry. I hate to be rude, but I'm not up for visitors," she said, her soft accent as gentle as a cotillion tea. "The only reason I opened the door was to ask you politely not to make a scene. Again, I'm sorry I can't invite you in, but I'm feeling poorly, and I should return to bed now."

With her eyes cast down in demure embarrassment for not being the perfect hostess, she then tried to close the door in our faces. But Mike caught it. In her weak, Snuggie-hampered state, she was no match for him and eventually had no choice but to step back when he forced his way in, pulling me (who felt a few steps down from a rat with bubonic plague) in with him.

"I'm sorry, Tammy," I said, trying to take control of the situation. "I tried to keep him from coming here, but he wouldn't listen to me. This is all my fault. I shouldn't have slept with him, and I'm so ashamed."

Tammy blinked. "You slept with him?" she said. "You promised me you wouldn't have any further contact with him, and then you slept with him? Thursday, I know you've always taken a liberal attitude toward relations, which I've tried to respect—to each her own. But in this case, I have to say that I'm hurt, and that I expected better of you as a supposed feminist. I thought we were friends."

I grew up not believing in Hell, because my mother had told me it was a concept made up by the powers that be to keep their sheep in line. But in that moment, I reconsidered my belief because it felt like I was burning alive in a Hell made up of guilt. "Tammy, I'm sorry," I whispered again.

She regarded me with her large, solemn anime eyes and said, "I'm sorry, too. I'm sorry that our friendship had to end this way. Now, please go." She pinned me with a look akin to a child begging in the streets. "Please just leave."

I wanted to grant her wish, I wanted more than anything to leave Tammy in peace. But Mike stepped in front of me. "Don't guilt trip her like that," he said. "Look, Tammy, you're sick. I can see that. And I wanted to avoid this, but you stopped returning my phone calls, and you refused to be reasonable when I asked you for permission to date Thursday the first few times."

"Wait," I said, "You already told her?" And just when I thought my opinion of him or myself for sexing him three times couldn't get any lower, it plummeted off a cliff.

"Yes," Tammy said, clamping her lips together. "Mike's been calling ever since Thanksgiving, begging me for the go-ahead so that he could date you."

Something dropped in my stomach. "Oh, Tammy, I'm so sorry he bothered you."

Tammy covered her mouth with her two hands and shook her head once, twice, as if trying to ward off a coming tide of tears. "I just want to be left alone," she said. "I just want to die with some dignity."

Okay, I had thought beforehand that this scene would be bad, but this was even worse than anything I could have possibly imagined. "Let's go," I said, tugging on Mike's hand.

But to my surprise, Mike refused to budge. "Tammy," he said. "You're killing her with guilt. She's upset because she doesn't want to hurt you. And I'd let it go, but I'm in love with her, so you've got to tell her it's okay."

"In love with me?" I said. "No, no, no, you can't be." Then, to Tammy: "He's just being overdramatic again. He barely knows me."

"Tell her, Tammy," he said.

"No," Tammy said, her eyes soft with tears. "I just want you to go."

"Tell her!" he yelled.

"Oh my God," I said, yanking my hand away from Mike's. "You can't make somebody stop being upset that you've screwed her over. You can't make someone be okay with us seeing each other just because you want her to be. I'm never going to be okay with my father's homewrecker second wife, and Tammy's never going to be okay with this."

Mike turned to me, his eyes ablaze. "This is nothing like your father and his mistress."

"It's exactly like that," I said. "And I'm on Team Tammy."

Mike rubbed his forehead like he had that headache again and said, "Tammy, this is getting really frustrating. Either you tell her or I will."

Tammy sniffled. "I don't want to be the kind of person that sues for breach of contract, but please know, I'll do what I have to do to make sure that you honor your promise."

"Sue?" I said. Then, upon further review of their exchange, I asked, "Tell me what, exactly?"

"Tammy?" he said.

"Mike, don't," she said, her tears gone, replaced by a wild, fearful look that put me in mind of a cornered animal.

I let go of Tammy, deeply unsettled. "Seriously, what's going on?" I asked.

Silence.

And then Mike said, "You know what? I guess I really am in love with you, Thursday, because I'd rather give up my money than let her game you like this."

"No!" Tammy screamed. Then she ran away. Yes, just ran away, nearly tripping over her Snuggie a few times before her bedroom door slammed behind her.

"What the . . ." I said, watching her go.

"I'm assuming that she told you Davie Farrell bet me three thousand dollars to get with Tammy because she knew that I would eventually break her heart?"

"Yeah . . ."

"Well, it's not exactly true. What really happened is, Davie bet me. I tracked down Tammy and did my best charm offensive, only to discover that she wasn't interested. But I owed a guy a lot of money and I really needed the three thousand. It was either that or a broken arm, according to him. So I went to Tammy with a direct appeal. I told her about the bet with Davie and asked if she could at least pretend to be with me, so that I could collect on it.

"She agreed and did me one better. She told me I could move into her condo and have a room, I just had to pretend to be her boyfriend until further notice. So I dumped my then-girlfriend Chloe—not cool, I know, but we were already having major problems anyway. I moved in and I pretended to be Tammy's boyfriend for the next year and a half."

I shook my head. "I don't understand. Why would you do that? Tammy could have had any guy she wanted. She doesn't need someone to pretend to be her boyfriend."

"Tammy could have had any guy she wanted, but she didn't want any guy. She wanted Risa. So she hired me as cover. And she paid me extra to fake a proposal at her family's Christmas dinner. Her idea was for us to be engaged for at least three more years—I have no idea what she planned to do after that. But then Risa started talking about Tammy coming out of the closet. That's when Tammy dumped her and created our breakup cover story to explain why she wasn't dating any guys. From what I can tell, she and Risa have been off and on ever since."

"Wait," I said the puzzle pieces finally all coming together to form one hell of a surprise picture. "Tammy's 'The One'? The girl that Risa's been mooning over this entire time?"

Mike nodded. Then he said, "We should go."

In a daze, I let Mike lead me out of Tammy's condo.

And when we got back to his place, for the first time our sex wasn't frenzied and awash with shame and guilt. That night, Mike took his time with me, turning me toward him and pumping into me, nice and slow, completely silent, except when he woke me up two times to do it again.

"You know, I used to sell drugs to the guys you dated in high school," he said, as we were coming down from the third time.

"What?" I said, even though sleep was already calling me back to its dream-filled shores.

"People always talk about the fact that I used to be a drug dealer, but they never talk about who I would sell to. I wasn't on the corner. The real money was delivering to the rich kids' parties. Weed, coke, ecstasy, sometimes heroin. There were these two private high schools I serviced. I got fake school IDs made for both of them, told kids from one that I was on scholarship at the other one. That's how I figured out I was good at acting. For real, that was my first role. These white guys I sold to, they always had these girlfriends, these smart girls in plaid skirts with rich daddies. Sometimes they'd want to get with me, but I'd have to say 'naw' because I didn't want to mess up my business relationships with their boyfriends."

I gave him a sleepy smile, too tired and sated to take my usual offense. "So this is all about your latent private schoolgirl fetish."

He cupped my face in one hand, pressing his thumb into my left dimple. "No, I just wanted you to know something else about me, something you wouldn't have guessed. I like telling you stuff. That's all."

"I'll file it away for future reference." Then I kissed his temple and said, "Good night," before drifting back to sleep.

And when I opened my eyes on New Year's Day, I rolled over and for once, wasn't unhappy to see Mike Barker. Who always got what he wanted.

But then I remembered something else: "Oh no, Sharita!"

Sharita was the kind of person who had the numbers of all her close friends and relatives memorized, even though those were all collected in contact lists on phones these days. I, unfortunately, was not that kind of person. I had to use Mike's landline to call my cell and get my messages. My mailbox was full—first with several messages from Sharita, asking where I was. I had thought Sharita sounded as mad as a person could possibly get . . . but then the messages from Risa came rolling in.

# SHARITA

$9$ was not amused when I got to Thursday's house on New Year's Eve and she wasn't there. I could hear an old Janet Jackson album playing behind the closed door of the little guesthouse, but no Thursday.

Thursday had an utter disregard for timeliness that had always irritated me, but this went above and beyond her usual hijinks. I hadn't expected Thursday to be ready or anything, but I had at least expected her to be, you know—there. I sat on Thursday's stoop and answered a few work e-mails on my BlackBerry. Then I called Thursday to get an ETA, but no answer.

Annoying. And the annoyance grew into out-and-out anger when an hour had gone by. The Janet Jackson album had long since stopped playing, and still no Thursday.

I checked my watch. It was ten o'clock, and I had two parties to hit before midnight. I'd just have to go without Thursday and deal with her tomorrow.

Risa called just as I was getting back into my car. "Happy New Year," I said when I picked up the phone, since Risa was on the East Coast and three hours ahead.

"Do you know where the hell Thursday is? She's not answering her phone."

"No, we were supposed to meet at her place an hour ago, but she's not here."

"Yeah, well, I've got to go," Risa said.

"What's going on?" I asked. "Why are you looking for Thursday?"

"I'm sure she'll have told you everything by tomorrow," Risa answered.

"What's 'everything'?" I asked.

"Gotta go." And this time she hung up before I could ask any more questions.

Weird.

Obviously something was going down involving Risa and Thursday, but what could it be? For someone who ran her mouth the way Risa did, she had never been one for real fights. As far as I could tell, Thursday and Risa had never gotten into one.

The question of what was going on between my two best friends nagged at me even as I hit my first party in Burbank. This one was being thrown by a guy that I had gone to USC with, and apparently kids had been invited, which made me feel out of place in my strapless, sparkly red dress with its bosom-enhancing sweetheart neckline. The dress wasn't quite my style. I was more of an elegant, bosom-cloaking black dress sort of woman. But when Thursday and I had gone shopping at the Beverly Center the day before, she had persuaded me to buy it, insisting that we would look so cute if we both wore sparkly red dresses on New Year's Eve.

When I'd gone off character and agreed to buy it, I had felt like I was a part of an adventurous duo. But now, as children ran around a party of jean-clad moms and dads, I felt silly. I had to hightail it to make it to the next party, which was being thrown by one of the partners at his house in Hancock Park, by eleven-thirty.

I got to the party on time, but when I entered the partner's Greek Revivalist mansion, I felt even more out of place, because everyone here was dressed up in evening gowns and tuxedos. That was the problem with L.A. It was way too easy to over- or under-dress for parties. It only took a few glimpses of other senior accountants in long, tasteful black evening gowns to let me know that I'd need a drink to summon up the courage to face anyone at this party.

I was putting a dollar in the bar's tip jar when someone said to me, "Nice dress."

I turned around to see a tall, brown-haired guy with a mustache and full beard. He had an odd accent that made it sound like he was rolling his

"Rs" when he said "dress." Also, he was wearing jeans and a nice shirt, so he, like me, seemed very out of place at the party.

"Are you Welsh?" I asked him, thinking that he sort of sounded like the gap-toothed Gwen from *Torchwood*.

"Close, but not quite. Scottish."

"Oh," I said. "My girlfriend used to have a Scottish roommate, but she couldn't understand a thing he said."

The Scot chuckled. "I've heard tell that's a problem for you Yanks, and I've been told meself that my own accent is a bit of a bear."

"No," I said. "You're easy to understand, not like my girlfriend's roommate at all."

"So I've noticed this odd phrasing in the States, and I wouldn't bring it up, except I don't want to find myself barking up the wrong tree here. When you say 'girlfriend,' do you mean your lover or do you mean your friend?"

"I mean my friend," I said, laughing. "That's kind of how black women refer to their friends here. I went to an all-women's college and I was so confused the first year about which of the black women were lesbians and which ones were just referring to their friends."

He laughed. "I imagine that would be rather confusing."

"Yeah, it was," I said.

Then I waited to get struck with a Crystal Ball Vision of my dismal future with this guy. And waited . . . but nothing.

"So, are you an accountant?" I asked, stalling while I waited for my vision.

"Not exactly," he answered. "I did a degree in business studies at uni, and I thought I might do something with it when I came to the States, but then I got a production assistant job and found I've a knack for organizing people. So now I'm an AD on the show that Tracey directs. She invited me at the last minute, though I'm sure she's regretting it now that I've shown up in my Steve McQueens to her posh party."

Tracey was the name of the partner's wife, but . . . "Steve McQueens?"

"That's slang for jeans."

"Oh, an AD?"

"That's short for assistant director."

"And what does an assistant director do?" I asked, feeling like we were having a conversation in a different language, even though we were both speaking English.

"If you're familiar with the theater, we're somewhat like stage managers—just bossier."

I found myself smiling again. "I always said that if I were going to go into the entertainment business I would want to be some sort of stage manager. My sister's always accusing me of trying to stage-manage her life."

"So's mine. I think she's glad I moved here and now have other people to boss. AD'ing is a nice gig if you like loads of organizing and telling tedious people what to do."

"That's kind of like accounting, except we're telling people what they can and can't do with their money."

He nodded. "I suppose it is. What did you say your name was again?"

I was about to tell him my name when the office manager, Rhonda, came running over with two silver noisemakers in her hand. "There you are, girl. I've been looking for you everywhere. We're all over here."

If Rhonda saw the Scot, she didn't put it together that we'd been talking. Before I could protest, the audience was counting down and I was being pulled away to where Rhonda and three other black accountants were standing with their girlfriends and wives.

The Scot got swallowed up by the crowd, and even though I looked for him after the countdown, I didn't see him again in the whole hour that I spent at the party. Maybe that was why I hadn't gotten a vision, I thought. The meeting must have been a nonstarter. People from two very different worlds colliding for a curious-but-brief moment in time, never to be repeated.

However, the next morning I came out of the shower to the sound of the *Dr. Who* TARDIS landing, which was my ringtone. I picked up my BlackBerry to see an 818 number that I didn't know. "Hello, this is Sharita Anderson," I said.

"Sharita, this is the Scot you met at Tracey's party last night."

"Hi," I said, unable to keep the shock out of my voice. "How did you get my number?"

"I couldn't find you again after the midnight toast, could I? So I asked Tracey about the beautiful woman in the red dress, saying that I wanted to ring you to ask you out. Lucky you wore that dress, hey, because Tracey knew of whom I was speaking right away."

"Yeah, lucky," I said, amazed because I had never heard the word "lucky" and my dating life referenced in the same conversation.

"I've not dated an American before, but from what I've been given to understand, you lassies like formal dates in which the man pays, correct? You're not ones for a meet-up at the local and a bit of a hangout, am I right?"

If by "right" he meant utterly charming, then I agreed. "Yeah, that's a pretty good assessment of American dating habits."

"Alright then, in that case would you care to have brunch with me?"

Again I waited for some kind of Crystal Ball Vision—anything. But my mind remained stubbornly blank, so I had to wing it and say, "Okay, when?"

"Ah, well, it's ten o'clock now, so how about eleven? I'm in Burbank, where are you?"

"Windsor Hills. It's near Leimert Park. But I've always thought Burbank might be a nice place to live."

"I like it here," he said. "The rents are quite reasonable, and where I am is within walking distance of the movie theater and only a short ride to the studio where our show tapes, so I don't end up spending so much on petrol."

"That's very practical."

"Well, ADs are a rather practical lot."

"So are accountants, but back to the dating rules. You know, in America you're supposed to wait two days before calling, then schedule a date for, like, a future day, right?"

"I'll admit that I've heard that," he said. "But I've a real desire to see you again sooner rather than later, if that's all right with you, Sharita."

Thursday had once quoted something she had read somewhere in reference to a guy I wasn't sure liked me or not. It basically went, "If you're confused, then he's just not that into you."

And though this Scottish assistant director wasn't the black man I had been dreaming of all of my life, he intrigued me and, perhaps more importantly, for the first time since I'd started dating after graduating from Smith College, I wasn't confused. Like, at all.

"Okay," I said. "How about meeting at the Granville Café at eleven?"

# RISA

On New Year's morning, I woke up in some box of a Manhattan hotel room, took a piss, opened a window, and lit a cig. I grabbed my phone and left my kajillionth message for Thursday between puffs. "Motherfucking call me back already," I said. Then just in case she wasn't getting how incredibly pissed off I was: "Way to keep your promise to stay away from Mike Barker. You're a truly loyal friend and I can see why you stayed mad at Sharita so long for not living up to your impeccable standards. Motherfucking call me back already."

Then I hung up.

This was not good. Not good at all. A small panic squeezed my heart. Tammy was so upset with Thursday, and Thursday was my best friend, so that meant she was upset with me. Tammy almost never got upset, but on the rare occasion when she did, she put me through the "maybe we shouldn't see each other anymore" drill.

That was exactly what happened last Valentine's Day after I saved her from the entertainment lawyer at Kate Mantilini. I took her home on my Harley, and when I went to help her off the bike, she surprised me by kissing me in the parking garage, not quite in public, but not behind the closed doors of her condo, either, as she usually insisted.

Tammy was so fucking pretty, so well put together, it always seemed like a privilege when she allowed me to mess her up. I smeared her lipstick with my kiss, and I wrinkled the skirt of her cute green dress when I slipped my hand underneath it and pushed aside the crotch of her frilly pink panties. And I disproved Thursday's theory that Tammy did not possess sweat glands when I made her come on top of my bike.

But then I went and fucked it all up by saying afterwards, "You know if you came out to your family, then you wouldn't have to put up with your sister springing dates on you."

And she morphed into Public Tammy again. She smoothed her hair and looked around to make sure no one had come into the garage and seen us. Then she pulled out blotting papers to remove the sweat from her face, because heaven forbid someone see her looking less than her best on the elevator ride to her condo.

"I don't want to hurt you, Risa," she said, pulling out her compact and lipstick to fix her makeup. "I always feel like I'm hurting you by trying to stay friends with you. Maybe we shouldn't see each other anymore."

"You're not hurting me," I said because the truth was it went beyond hurt. Sometimes it felt like she was slowly killing me with her refusal to come back to me on a permanent basis. "I'm just saying . . . I fucking love you. I never loved anybody like I love you."

Tammy lowered her eyes. "I can't choose between you and my family," she said quietly. "I understand if that means you need to move on and find somebody else. I know you've got all kinds of girls throwing themselves at you."

"No, I don't want anybody else. Just you. We could be so good together."

And we went on and on like that until I asked her to marry me again.

"I have to go before I start crying," Tammy said after I asked her that.

And then she didn't accept my calls for a while, which wasn't so unusual after we got into an argument about her coming out.

I pretty much staged the whole Sharita intervention so that I could see Tammy again. But of course that only made it worse, because not only was her sister mad at me for springing Tammy out of her Valentine's Day trap, but now her brother thought I was a little crazy. I knew this because he said, "You're a little crazy, aren't you?" as we were all leaving Sharita's house.

By the time I showed up at her apartment, yet again prepared to do anything to convince her that we could remain friends and that I wouldn't try to pressure her into something more, she went off script and told me she had cancer.

So yeah, by the time Thursday called back, I was practically foaming at the mouth. "What the fuck?" That was how I answered the phone. "What the fuckity-fuck-fuck-fuck?"

"Risa . . ." she said.

"Don't 'Risa' me. You had no right. You promised."

"I did," she said. "And I'm sorry—"

"Apologize to Tammy, you feckless bitch," I said. Aside: The only word I love more than "bitch" is "feckless," and the only thing I liked about this situation was the fact that Thursday had provided me with a reason to use both.

"Whoa, first of all . . ." she said, "I'm not a bitch like you've been Tammy's bitch for all of these years."

That's when I realized that Thursday was speaking to me in the same tone of voice that I was speaking to her. "Hold up, how are you going to be mad at me? After what you did?"

Thursday sighed. "I'm not mad at you, but I am feeling a little testy after listening to you do nothing but curse me out on, like, ten different voicemails. The only thing that's keeping me from cursing you right back out is that I feel sorry for you."

This sent me into a full-on sputter. "How the fuck are you feeling sorry for me?"

"Risa . . ." she said. "You shouldn't have introduced Tammy to us as your friend. You should have told us who she really was because, if I had known, I never would have let her into our friend group. I knew you before The One. And I knew you after. She used you and she strung you along, and she made you complicit in hiding her from your two best friends. But worst of all, she really fucked you up."

I didn't know where this was coming from. I told her, "I'm not fucked up; I just have a strong personality."

"First of all, you haven't dated anyone seriously but her, and it's been ten years. Second of all, you didn't smoke or have an eating disorder before the first breakup."

"It's not an eating disorder."

"Risa. If I look up 'eating disorder' in the medical dictionary it reads *'Exactly what Risa has.'* Third of all, she damaged your self-esteem to the point that you think you're nothing unless you can get her back. Fourth of all, she hid you. And, Risa, you are too awesome to be anybody's secret girlfriend."

For the first time in maybe the history of Risa, I didn't have a smart comeback.

In the ensuing silence, Thursday asked, "Why didn't you tell us?" She sounded so disappointed in me.

And for some reason I couldn't answer her. The old panic that I'd come to associate with Tammy came back and clogged up my throat.

"Risa, why did you introduce her to us as your friend? Why did you cover for her like that?"

The box of a hotel room had become unbearably hot, but I kept on sucking on my cigarette. "It was the only way I could keep her," I said. This answer sounded logical in my head, but when I said it out loud . . . not so much.

Thursday sighed again, like this entire situation was too tragic for words. "I know there isn't a ton of dating advice out there for lesbians, and even if there was you wouldn't read it, so I'm just going to give you the synopsis: What Tammy has been doing is called 'stringing you along.' She does just enough to keep you available, so that she can hook up with you whenever she wants and then leave again because you two aren't really in a relationship, and she technically doesn't owe you anything. She's holding you hostage with crumbs of affection, and worst of all, she's somehow convinced you to keep up her cover story with those crumbs. Quote-unquote nice guys do this all the time. Tammy has pretended to be a nice girl this whole time, when in actuality she's a coward who won't stand up for herself or you even though she's dying. And I'm not going to let your lying to me ruin our friendship because I can see that you have the love equivalent of Stockholm syndrome."

"No," I said. "You don't understand. We got in this big fight. And then everything started going wrong with the Sweet Janes and I said some really shitty things to her. Then I ran out of money. But if I could have made this music career work and if she hadn't gotten cancer—"

"What? What do you think would have happened if you'd become the biggest rock star on earth before Tammy got cancer?"

"She would have come back to me. We could have made it work."

Thursday was silent so long, I thought maybe we'd lost the connection, but then she finally said, "First of all, she would have been an asshole if she only came back to you because you got famous. But that doesn't matter, because it was never about the fame or the money. Tammy already has fame and money. More money than most rock stars. It was about Tammy. Nothing you could have done would have gotten her to commit, because in Tammy's universe, being a lesbian isn't a good look, and she's all about looks."

The truth of Thursday's words radiated inside the hotel room. And for the first time since meeting Tammy, I didn't see myself as the brooding hero of this story. Instead I felt weak, like the hunter that got caught by the prey.

Thursday mistook my silence for anger.

"Okay," she said. "I'm your best friend and I will represent for how awesome you are until the day I die. When you come to your senses and realize who's been on your side this entire time, feel free to call me back. Till then, I'm going to be having lots of hot sex with Mike Barker."

Then she hung up on me, even though I was by all rights supposed to be the one hanging up on her.

A few moments later, my phone went off again. I looked at the caller ID. It was Tammy.

I'd loved her since I was twenty-one, and I would fucking do anything for her, and sometimes it felt like when she died I would no longer have any reason to go on . . . but I didn't answer the phone.

I just didn't.

# February 2012

Sometimes opposites attract. But if you meet one of these "opposite" couples who have been together for a while, and dig a little deeper, you'll find two people that may not look or act alike, but have the important things in common.

—*The Awesome Girl's Guide to Dating Extraordinary Men* by Davie Farrell

# THURSDAY

*L*ast Valentine's Day, Caleb and I went to Cliff's Edge, a romantic restaurant in Silver Lake. I gave him a gift certificate for a Bikram yoga class, which is a kind of yoga done in a very hot room. And Caleb gave me a T-shirt that said, "THURSDAY IS THE BEST DAY OF THE WEEK." Then we went back to my place, where we had perfectly nice Valentine's Day sex, after which he said, "I love you," and I said, "I love you, too." After that, I'd driven back to Silver Lake and pretended I knew how to bartend while Risa got increasingly drunk. "Don't bother," she kept on telling me. "I'm about to quit this job anyway." Then in the wee hours of the morning, I closed the bar and drove her back to her apartment, where her landlord helped me carry her up the stairs—she had passed out during the five-minute drive, in the middle of a slurred sentence about how next year The One would accept her proposal because she was going to be famous.

"We'll fly to Massachusetts. Do it at Smith," she told me. "You can come, too."

"Oh, I don't think The One will want me there," I said, furious that this woman shattered Risa's heart every year, leaving me to pick up the pieces.

"No, she will," Risa said. "Trust me."

This year, Valentine's Day was completely different. I had no idea what to get for Mike, because Mike was a superstar, and from what I could see, if Mike Barker wanted something, he got it. Period. From the latest 3-D television set to the most reluctant girlfriend he had probably ever pursued. What exactly did one get for somebody like that?

"Maybe you could make him dinner," Sharita suggested. "Guys like it when you cook for them."

"Maybe you could make him dinner *naked*," Risa said later, when she heard about Sharita's suggestion.

298

I had thought that it would take Risa a while to want to speak to me again. But less than a week after our argument, she had called me from the road to talk about a "particularly fucking lame show at the frat boy-est college in the United fucking States" like nothing had changed.

And then, just like before, we called each other at least once a week when the mood struck us, neither of us bringing up Tammy. Though, from what I could glean, Risa wouldn't be asking for her hand in marriage this Valentine's Day, which meant I had even more mental free time to worry about what to get Mike.

First of all, he already had a personal chef. *From France.* Second of all, I had no idea what Mike and I were. Caleb and I had done things right, and we'd already had the boyfriend-girlfriend convo when we went out last Valentine's Day. But Mike and I were in some nebulous state that neither of us was trying to define. He hadn't brought up the word "love" again since the scene in Tammy's apartment—which was good. I knew that actors liked to fall in love within a month of knowing each other, but I was a little too practical for that kind of thing.

Mike, by definition of being my complete opposite, was definitely in the "one-month stand" category, but three months had passed since the first time we had slept together. If he were a real boyfriend it would be time for him to meet my friends, but he was a movie star, so . . .

So I had no idea where we were going with this or what to get him for Valentine's Day. The only thing he really wanted was to get the Rick T biopic green-lit, but so far, as I had predicted, there had been no takers.

"It's easy to get bad stuff made in Hollywood," Mike had explained a few weeks earlier, while we were watching a particularly terrible summer blockbuster in his entertainment room. "If our script had sixteen explosions and some thin-ass plotline, it would have gotten picked up already with my name attached. But since it's about something deep, it's got studios scared."

"Then why not start off with producing an action movie or a rom-com like you used to do back in the day?" I asked. "Maybe try to get the biopic made later?"

But Mike shook his head. "I'm sick of action films. Acting-wise, an action film is the most boring thing you can make. It's all hitting your cues and having some director shout at you to do it again—but faster. I want to produce something meaty, something that allows me to practice my craft and gives me more of an adrenaline rush than gambling. I need this biopic to get made."

I didn't like to think too much about the script. On one hand, I wanted it to get green-lit, because then that would mean a lot of extra money going into my bank account. On the other hand, it felt like Mike was gambling. And that scared me.

"I'm swimming because of you," he had told me on New Year's Eve. It made me wonder if he was really attracted to me, or to the rush of my being hard to get. Mike definitely wasn't used to hard-to-get. He could easily mistake it for love. Yet another gray area in an already complicated relationship.

So I kept on applying for jobs. Contract administrator jobs, receptionist jobs. I even signed up with a few temp agencies. Like Davie Farrell had said in her book, I had to make my own life my number one priority, so that when this thing with Mike came to its inevitable end, for once I'd be able to stand on my own two feet.

But there hadn't been one bite on my résumé. And by the time Valentine's Day rolled around, I had become way too dependent on Mike. Since I didn't have any new money coming in, it seemed silly to hang out at my own place, where I had to pay for all of my own food and utility bills. Mike had a big bed, a six-hundred-square-foot entertainment room, and a personal chef who didn't mind making my vegetarian dishes to order.

So, though I still didn't know exactly what I was doing with Mike, I hadn't actually been back to my own place to do anything more than collect my mail and drop off my rent check since New Year's Day.

And though I eventually managed to pick out a two-part Valentine's Day present for my . . . whatever Mike was, I presented the first part to him with a bit of reluctance on Valentine's Day morning, not sure if it was good enough—or even appropriate.

"What's this?" he asked, when I set down four clear plastic containers, each with a piece of cake inside of it, beside the healthy breakfast and wheatgrass smoothie that Frederic had whipped up for him.

"Happy Valentine's Day," I said, sitting down in the chair next to his. "It's cake from Aroma in Silver Lake. I got you carrot, coconut-lemon, red velvet, and German chocolate. I figured since actors are always on a diet, it's probably been a while since you've had a nice piece of cake, but I wasn't sure what kind you liked."

He stared at the containers, his mouth hanging open.

"I'm sorry," I said. "This was stupid. I should have gotten you something else—"

"Ssh!" he said, holding up his hand for silence. "I need a few moments."

And a few moments was what he took. His eyes bounced from container to container for several seconds. Then he picked up the red velvet cake and opened the box. His eyes fluttered closed as he took several deep breaths through his nose, waving his hand over the cake so that he could inhale even more of its scent.

By this time, Frederic had turned from the stove to see what was going on.

Mike then opened the piece of German chocolate cake and did the same thing, with a blissed-out smile on his face. After giving the carrot cake and the coconut-lemon cake the same treatment, he pushed aside his much healthier breakfast and lined them all up in a row in front of him.

Then he picked up his fork and broke off a bite of the German chocolate cake with a trembling hand before bringing the piece of cake to his mouth.

He slammed his hand on the table no less than three times as he chewed and swallowed. Then he took a bite of the coconut-lemon, and after that a bite of the carrot cake, and after that a bite of the red velvet.

"Cake! Caaaaake!" he said, in the same way that Celie's long-lost son had said, "Mama!" after being reunited with her over twenty years later in the movie version of *The Color Purple*. "It's been so long," Mike whispered. Then he looked at me with wonder-filled eyes. "This is the best gift I have ever received. Thank you," he said.

I glanced at the willowy Frederic, who stood at the Viking stove with his arms crossed, looking very much offended.

"Um, you're welcome?" I said to Mike, feeling a little bit like an intruder in what had obviously become a very profound and tender reunion.

He took another bite of carrot cake. "The only problem is, I doubt my gift's going to compare to yours. It's in my office. You can go get it while I enjoy this beautiful, beautiful cake."

I rushed out of there, eager to escape the glaring Frederic, who said to Mike as I left, "I, too, can make the cake recipes. I did not, because you say you are afraid of attracting the belly."

Happy to get out before that argument really got started, I opened the door to Mike's study and saw that I had also received the best Valentine's Day present ever.

Because sitting behind Mike Barker's desk was a very dark-skinned woman with a large afro, wearing a Strokes T-shirt and a big smile.

"Hi," Davie Farrell said. "Mike tells me you need some help with your career."

# SHARITA

*L*ast Valentine's Day, I had taken off work early and cooked a huge dinner for Marcus with all of his favorite foods. He said, "Thanks, baby," after dinner and gave me a drugstore-brand box of chocolates. Not exactly a match for my gift, but I'd appreciated it required a little forethought, which had been way more effort than Marcus had put into our relationship up until that point.

But this Valentine's Day, the Scot and me argued about dinner duties. "You cook all the time, woman. It's time for you to stand down and let me at the stove," he said.

I giggled. "I like cooking for you."

"And I love your cooking, but a man ought to be able to make his woman a nice meal every now and then. It's only fair."

His woman? I allowed my heart to thrill a little at those two words. Our first breakfast date had lasted so long that he had offered to buy me a late lunch "at the Korean place across the street." Then that lunch had lasted so long that he had asked if I'd like to go to a movie.

And then after the movie it had been, "Well, then, we might as well grab a bit of dinner." And after dinner, he told me it was only fair that I join him for "a couple at the pub"—which had translated into a glass of wine for each of us at the Burbank Bar & Grille before he walked me back to my car, which was still parked in front of the Granville Café, where we'd eaten brunch.

I had expected him to kiss me, but he just said, "I've consulted with a number of my American friends, and they say we're not supposed to see each other again until the weekend next. But can't we negotiate that down to say this Wednesday coming? That's two whole days."

More than a bit mystified by this foreign man who, unlike any other guy I had ever dated, seemed to both enjoy my company and know what he wanted, I simply said, "Okay."

On Wednesday he met me downtown near my office and took me to dinner, and then he demanded another "couple of drinks" after that. Then he negotiated another date for Friday.

Still no kiss. Bizarre. I would have called Thursday about it, since she was the white-boy expert, but I still wasn't quite ready to admit that I was dating a white guy. Also, I knew that Thursday would never let me hear the end of it.

I still wasn't quite sure how I had come to be in this situation. The Scot was so interesting and easy to talk to. And he was a master haggler. One date had turned into two. Two into three.

After a Friday night filled with a movie, dinner, and drinks, he had asked, "Now, what are the rules about sex in your country, which seems to have rules about everything?"

I laughed. "We haven't even kissed yet."

"Well, that's because if I get to kissing you, sweet girl, I've no plans to stop. So will it be tonight or after two more dates? I bought a few of your ladies' mags to research the subject. *Cosmo* says three dates, *Marie Claire* five, and funnily enough, your *Essence* didn't have any advice whatsoever on the matter this month."

Now I was really laughing. "You did not read *Essence*," I said.

"Oh yes, I did, and can I tell you that the black lassie at the Rite Aid gave me a right hard time about buying it. Her: Is this for your girlfriend? Me: No, it isn't. She's all: Why you buying *Essence* and that. I tell her, 'Well, I enjoy a nice read on top of the loo, don't I?' And she says, 'You strange.' Do you think she said this because I'm Scottish? Was it discrimination, Sharita?"

I was laughing too hard to answer, but after further negotiations, we settled on five dates before sex, but ended up in his bed after only four.

I had thought my first time with a white man would be different, but the only difference was that the Scot didn't put on any music before he started kissing me. The kiss was very good—direct and to the point, but tender enough to make me melt down below.

Apparently, he felt it, too, because he cupped the back of my neck to pull me deeper into the kiss with one hand and started unbuttoning my blouse with the other. "This is nice. This is verrae nice," he said, in between kisses. "I like this. I like it verrae much."

And that was all he said for a while. Neither of us were rock stars in bed, and there were a few awkward moments: I banged my shoulder against his forehead, eliciting a grunt followed by a chuckle. There was a moment of alarm when he went down on me, because this was first sex and I'd never had anyone go down on me on first sex. But the alarm soon passed, replaced by a building warmth as I ground myself against his mouth. Then just as things were starting to build up, he said, "Okay, then, let me just take care of this condom business . . ."

And then his face was above mine and he was guiding himself into me. His eyes closed and he let out what sounded like a sigh of relief when he got inside of me. "I don't want to take our Savior's name in vain, but Christ, that feels good."

I didn't mind. I felt the same way, and my eyes closed, too. Usually I started worrying at this point during sex, about whether I was moving my hips the right way or if my hair looked messed up from his vantage point. About not coming and if I'd have to fake it afterwards.

But I didn't worry with the Scot. In fact, worry was the last thing on my mind as my hips met each of his thrusts, my hands clenching his butt as that same delicious warmth started building up inside of me again. I ended up coming before he did. And when he slumped on top of me a few minutes later, we both had to catch our breath.

"Once again in the morning, then?" he asked before we fell asleep, facing each other, my right hand clasped inside both of his. This Scottish boy liked his negotiations. And four weeks later, I found myself engaged in yet another negotiation over Valentine's Day dinner.

"I tell you what," he said. "You can download a recipe for haggis, and I'll download a recipe from that Food Network show you're so keen about."

*"Down Home with the Neelys?"* I asked. Referencing the show sent a strange pang through my heart. Hosted by the most loving real-life black couple that I'd ever seen on TV, I found it hard to watch when I was between

relationships, because it reminded me I still hadn't found my match. The Scot and I had watched an episode together when we'd both had Martin Luther King Day off and had decided to spend it lying around his apartment.

"Yes, that one," he said. "They seem like a delightful couple, and I'm certain you'll like my take on their food."

I did not like his take on their food. He not only over-seasoned the Memphis-Style Catfish, he also put too much sugar in his peach cobbler and over-boiled the potatoes, which were supposed to be baked in the first place.

"I can't be blamed for it. I'm from a land where every laddie and lassie is taught to boil and over-cook our vegetables from childhood on. There's nothing such as a Brit that's capable of cooking vegetables in a flavorful manner. Even our celebrity chefs like Gordon Ramsay and Jamie Oliver are shite with veggies. This haggis, on the other hand, is the best I've ever had, and makes me want to send your version of the recipe on to ma dear mum. I don't know how you got the idea to put it over sweet potatoes and honey . . ."

"I found a recipe that said it's usually served over some kind of mash, and I thought sweet potatoes would be fun. Really, better than your mama's?"

"Well, she's no great cook, I'll have to admit. But truly, this haggis of yours is inspired."

If he wasn't so funny, he might be too bizarre to date. But it had been a lot of fun cooking next to him in my kitchen. And despite his botched dishes, dinner had been amazing, with him insisting that I come sit on his lap halfway through. "Why sit over there, when the candlelight's so much better over here?" he asked.

I found his reasoning suspect, but I did appreciate the way his kind gray eyes twinkled above his beard while I forked bite after bite of my haggis into his mouth. I had always known that dating was something you had to do in order to fall in love, an obstacle and a chore on the path to marriage. But until the Scot, it had never occurred to me that dating could also be fun.

# RISA

*L*ast Valentine's Day, I did the same thing that I'd been doing every Valentine's Day since Tammy and me broke up the first time: tried to convince her that we should be together.

My pitch stayed the same: It's time, I fucking love you, I would die for you. All that shit.

But her answer remained the same, too: I love you, but it would kill my family; please, Risa, don't ask me for things I can't give you.

This Valentine's Day, however, I was on the road, playing a show at some college in Montana. It was cold outside so I wore a fur bikini top, Raquel Welch style. The college kids loved it, and the guys from Yes, We Are were congratulating me on the wardrobe choice around the table at some college-town diner afterwards, when my phone lit up with a 310 number.

Here was the thing about 310 numbers: I always felt compelled to answer them, because in L.A. the truly important people always have 310 numbers. Agents, lawyers, music company execs, renowned plastic surgeons—they all seemed to go out of their way to make sure they were associated with the area code dispensed to Los Angeles's most expensive neighborhoods.

So I excused myself. Outside the restaurant, I cradled my iPhone between my shoulder and ear and pulled out a cigarette. "This is Risa Merriweather. What up, ho?"

"Were you really not going to call me back? Not even on Valentine's Day?"

Oh shit, it was Tammy. I hadn't been caught out with the call-from-a-different-number trick in a while. And I felt a little embarrassed for myself. "Hey, Tammy, this isn't a good time."

"Do you know where I am?" she asked. "In my bathroom, dry-heaving into my toilet. I've been here pretty much all day. It's disgusting. I'm disgusting." She started crying again. "I need you, and you promised you would be here for me, before you left town."

"Yeah, well," I took a drag off my cigarette. "I'm with some people. Gotta get back."

"Did you ever love me?" she asked me. "Or did you only love me when I was beautiful and sexy and didn't have cancer?"

"Oh, come on." I had planned to take the high road with Tammy, her being Dead Woman Walking and all, but . . . "How are you going to accuse me of not loving you? I asked you to marry me back in 2008 when it was legal, and you said no. If you had said yes, I'd be with you right now. But you said no, so guess what?"

"You know why I said no. I couldn't have . . ."

"See, I've been thinking about that. You keeping on saying that I know why you couldn't come out and that I know why you couldn't be with me publicly and that I know why you couldn't tell your family about us. But I don't know. I never knew. Because I gave up the Sweet Janes for your ass, and you wouldn't even hold my hand in public."

I didn't know how deeply I felt about this, but I was yelling now, so I guess I must have been pretty fucking mad, even if Tammy had cancer.

"Risa," she whispered. "I know I didn't exactly treat you right while we were together. But I don't have much time left. And I haven't told my family, so I'm alone. You're all I have."

Those words tugged at my heart. The image of Tammy dying alone on her couch with only some nurse she hired in attendance. That was a hard one to swallow. But I said, "No, Tammy, I've already wasted too much time on you. You only care about how other people see you, and all you've done is take from me. I can't let you do that anymore. Even if you're sick."

Tammy was crying again, and maybe this cancer was a good thing, because I had become pretty much immune to her tears by now. Pretty much.

"Risa . . ." she said.

"Call your family."

"Risa, please . . ."

"Call your fucking family."

I hung up. And after wiping away a few tears of my own, I flicked away my cigarette and went back inside.

# March 2012

Everyone complains about heartbreak. But heartbreak is like failure. It's nothing to be scared of, you can only learn from it. If you got your heart broken in your last relationship, congratulations. You proved you really know how to fall in love. Now dust yourself off and fall in love again.

—*The Awesome Girl's Guide to Dating Extraordinary Men* by Davie Farrell

# THURSDAY

*m*eeting with Davie Farrell in February changed my life forever.

At first I stood in the doorway, speechless. One of my earliest memories was meeting Michael Jackson backstage at an awards show. I'd shaken hands with Bono from U2 for goodness' sake, but standing there in that doorway, I became paralyzed with admiration.

If Davie Farrell hadn't waved me toward one of Mike's orange seats and said, "Sit down, darlin'," I probably wouldn't have ever gotten out of that doorway.

"Hi," I finally managed to squeak when I sat down across from her. "I can't believe this."

Davie grinned at me. "Neither can I. Mike called me to apologize for never telling me the truth about him and Tammy not really being together, and the next thing I know he's finagling a Valentine's Day session out of me for you."

I shook my head, annoyed and impressed with Mike at the same time. But then it occurred to me to ask, "Did you tell your husband and Tammy's sister?"

"No," Davie said. "James is my husband, and I try not to keep secrets from him anymore. But it's not my place to be telling Tammy's business."

So it sounded like Davie knew about Tammy being gay, but not about her cancer. Mike had kept Tammy's secret from her, despite the fact that Tammy might actually follow through and sue him for violating their non-disclosure agreement any day now. "Mike's very . . ." I trailed off.

"Don't finish that sentence. I can't talk with you about what you got going on with Mike. This is strictly a career consultation."

Davie's declarative statement filled me with a certain relief. The truth was I didn't want to talk about what I had with Mike either. I didn't want to label it, didn't want to analyze it.

"Mike tells me you're on some kind of big job search right now," Davie said. "How's that going for you?"

"No bites yet, but I'm looking hard," I said. "And I'm excited about entering a new phase in my career. I just have to figure out what that phase is, then figure out how to get a job in it—"

"Can I ask you what you originally wanted to do when you were a kid?"

"Well, I wanted to write," I said, surprised by her interruption. "But obviously that didn't work out."

Davie frowned. "What do you mean it didn't work out?"

"I mean I wasn't able to make a career out of it or anything."

"Let me stop you right there. Just because you're not successful at something doesn't mean it didn't work out. And it really doesn't mean you can stop doing it. If I'm guessing right, you've probably already tried to give it up and do something else, right?"

This conversation was not going at all the way I had expected it to. "Well . . . yeah, I mean . . . I tried stand-up comedy for a while."

"But it got boring, like every other job you've tried to do outside of writing. Then your mind started unraveling and your self-esteem plummeted. I bet it felt like you were going a little crazy, right?"

I gaped at her. The only thing she hadn't been right about was the "little crazy" part. "It was more like a lot crazy," I said.

"Suicidal thoughts?" she guessed next.

I narrowed my eyes at her. "Are you psychic?" I asked. "Is that, like, your trade secret?"

She laughed. "No, darlin', I just work with a lot of creatives. Now I want you to think back to the last time you wrote. How did you feel about yourself?"

"I was feeling terrible," I said. "Because I thought I had betrayed Tammy by sleeping with Mike."

"I'm not talking about all that outside stuff. I'm talking about you and the writing. How did that feel? Coming back to it?"

"Awkward at first, but then it was like riding a bicycle." For whatever reason I thought of my childhood home in Connecticut. The temporary relief that had filled me up when I had seen it for the last time after flying in from China. "It felt like coming home," I told Davie.

Davie leaned forward. "The majority of my clients have tried to do something else, only to find out that they couldn't. The fact of the matter is that we're all born to do something, and if that's what we're meant to do, that's what we've got to do until the day we die. Trying to replace it with anything else is a waste of time."

"But I'm thirty-one years old and I'm completely dependent on an actor who I have nothing in common with and who might get tired of me tomorrow," I said.

"So?" Davie said.

"*So* I've got to start building some safety nets. I can't be dependent on other people for the rest of my life."

"Why not?" Davie asked.

"Because that's not how I'm supposed to be. I'm a feminist. I hate that I've never been able to get by on my own. First it was my father; then my friend, Sharita, took care of me; then my ex-boyfriend, Caleb; and now Mike. I'm supposed to be a strong black woman. I'm supposed to be able to depend on myself. I want to be that kind of woman. I know I could be if I tried harder. I could be so much better than the person I am right now."

To me, this felt like a heartfelt statement, an inspired proclamation about the person I could be this time next year, if I put my mind to it.

But Davie leaned back and folded her hands on top of her stomach. "Yeah, you're thirty-one, so darlin', it might be high time for you to accept some stuff. You're a writer. You ain't independent by nature. And fate has set up one nice situation for you with Mike. Don't spit in its face. I thought we were really going to have to go through the ringer with this job situation of yours, but I've only got two words for what you've got to do now: Accept it."

Accept it. Those two words were ones that I had never considered before. Suddenly all the other paths I had been considering fell away, leaving only the original writing one. The one filled with money problems and living off boyfriends and borrowing money from Sharita and feeling like I would never be good enough to actually get paid for what I wanted to do with my life. A dark forest of a path filled with all sorts of monsters hiding in the trees and behind bushes.

*Accept it.*

Twenty minutes later, I emerged from the office.

"How did it go?" Mike asked me when I came back into the kitchen. He was at the table, reading the script for his next big-budget studio movie, which would start filming in two days. Frederic had left—probably in a huff—and the four pieces of cake were also gone, their empty containers the only evidence that they had ever been there in the first place.

I walked over to him and took his face in my hands. "I know you liked the cake, but, seriously, you're the one who gave me the best Valentine's Day gift ever. *Ever.*" I kissed him. "Thank you."

"Wow, what did she say?" he asked.

I shook my head and pulled him out of his seat. "Too hard to explain, and I still haven't given you the second half of your Valentine's Day gift."

"There's a second half?" Mike's eyes lit up and went to the refrigerator. "Is it ice cream?"

"No, it's dry cleaning."

"Dry cleaning," Mike repeated, confused and perhaps a little bit suspicious.

But a few minutes later his confused look was replaced with one of boyish delight, when I opened the door to his bedroom to reveal a uniform, complete with a white button-up shirt and a plaid skirt.

"I think it's time for you to finally bang your private schoolgirl."

"Is this authentic?" he asked.

I didn't have the heart to tell him that Choate didn't actually have schoolgirl uniforms and that I'd had to scour the Internet for one that wasn't obviously a Halloween costume designed to make grown women look like sexy schoolgirls.

Instead I started stripping out of the maxi dress that I'd worn down to breakfast. "You're going to have to dry hump me first, then if my parents don't catch us, maybe I'll let you put your thingy in me."

Mike stared at me for a long, serious minute. Then he said, "Girl, you out your damn mind. This is obviously the best Valentine's Day gift anybody's ever given anybody." He rubbed his hands together. "And you're the best girlfriend ever. Believe that."

I laughed and forced myself to stay in the moment, refusing to dwell on the fact that he had stepped us up to girlfriend-boyfriend without a formal conversation, and trying to ignore the sounds of a far-off engine revving, of a car crashing through a divider, of the anticipatory quiet before the inevitable drop.

Two days later, Mike left to begin shooting his next movie, a caper film about two security guards at the Fort Worth Mint "who decide to try to rob the hardest building to rob in the world—unless you're on the inside." It was set in Fort Worth, Texas, but it was being filmed in New Orleans, a place with decidedly nice tax breaks for film productions.

Caleb had left once or twice to meet with directors on remote film shoots and I had missed him a little bit, but this wasn't anything like that. While Caleb had called from the road every day that he was out of town, that wasn't enough for Mike.

He brought his usual dramatics to the being-apart situation. The first day he was gone, the doorbell rang and it was a deliveryman with a large vase filled with flowers from Mike. The note attached said, "Miss you." It was a very nice gesture and gave me a warm fuzzy. But then the next day, another vase of flowers came with a note that said, "Miss you," and the day after that another vase with another note that simply said, "Miss you."

"Are you serious?" I asked Mike on the third day. "You're not going to send me flowers every day you're gone."

"Why not?" he asked.

"Because it's a huge waste of money, it creates more work for your cleaning lady, and you really don't have to."

"You say I don't have to, but I'm thinking you might start missing me, too, one of these days. And when that happens, I want you to know that I miss you back."

See, the thing was that I had decided not to miss Mike. I was going to use the time apart to get at least three spec scripts in good working order and then I was going to start looking for an agent or at least a writing assistant job.

But that's not quite how things went. The spec scripts were coming along, but the not-missing-Mike was going terribly. At first the flowers had been cute, but then they transformed from nice gestures to constant reminders that though I lived in Mike's house and slept in Mike's bed, Mike himself was not actually there with me. By March, it hurt to look at the vases of flowers spread out on every available surface in the foyer and living room, so I stopped answering the door and let Mike's housekeeper, Griselde, decide what to do with them.

"Why aren't you signing for the flowers anymore?" Mike asked me toward the end of March.

"How did you know I wasn't signing for them?" I asked.

"Because the last two had something kinda cool attached, and you would have brought it up by now if you'd seen them."

"Hmm," I said, thinking that I was really going to have to learn some Spanish one of these days. That morning, Griselde, who didn't speak English very well, had tried to tell me something about the flowers. Assuming that she was asking to take some of them home or something, I nodded and smiled in the vacant way of all Californians who were too lazy to learn Spanish or even try to comprehend a domestic worker's Spanglish.

But going back over our one-sided conversation, I remembered Griselde saying something about a table. But which one?

It wasn't the end table in the foyer or the kitchen table.

"Try the one in the den," Mike said, laughing. He chanted, "Treasure hunt! Treasure hunt! Treasure hunt!"

"You could tell me what it said, you know," I answered, heading toward the den.

"Nah, I'm having too much fun doing it this way."

Sure enough, in the den there was a table with what had to be at least twenty small white envelopes on it. "They're here, but they're not in order. Can you just tell me?"

"C'mon, baby, that's not how I work. Sorry, I know it's hard for you writers to have to go off script," Mike said.

"My question has always been, why go off script? Can't you just read the lines as written, as slaved over by some poor writer . . . ?" I trailed off when I opened the eighth note card, which read, "Good news, the movie's been green-lit. Miss you."

"Wait, what movie? Our movie? Not our movie, right?"

"I like that you're calling it our movie, now. And yeah, our movie. What other movie would you care about being green-lit?"

"Well, I've always wanted to see an Ida B. Wells biopic make it to the big screen."

"So I'm assuming you're not excited about this."

I, for once, thought before I answered. "I'm excited for you?" I said, unable to come up with more.

"Your screenplay's going to be a movie," he said. "Be excited for yourself, too. Be excited for us."

An image of Mike at a craps table rolling a set of dice across my Rick T script popped into my head. He had gambled and won. I wondered how he would feel about "us" when we got to the boring part, when there wasn't a script to produce, after he finished playing the part of my father and the cutesy glamour of dating his daughter wore off.

"Didn't you say there were two big notes?" I asked, changing the subject. Five note cards later and I found one that said, "Miss you. SW1729"

I squinted at the card. "I'm not quite sure what I'm looking at here."

"That's the flight number for your plane from Los Angeles to New Orleans. It's leaving in two days. And it's one-way."

I didn't realize how much I had been missing him, until a smile near about split my face from ear to ear. "I can't wait," I told him. "I miss you so much."

My mother, I recalled after getting off the phone, also used to miss my father when he was on the road. They'd call each other every day. I could still remember all the postcards he sent from his concert stops. My mother stuck them to the refrigerator with magnets until the appliance became quilted with pictures of sunsets, famous landmarks, and cityscapes, until summer finally came back around and we were all able to travel with Rick T again.

When I had first started attending Choate, which was also a boarding school, I had wondered if my mother would pay the extra fee to have us stay on campus after Janine started her freshman year, so she could see my father more often. But then Brenda had come along, and according to my father, having family with him while he worked had become too distracting. They had argued about it, and my mother, who had transformed herself into a vegetarian pacifist, betrayed her ghetto roots, yelling with a finger raised in the air about how it had never been a problem before. "What's changed, Richard, huh? What's fucking changed? Or should I be asking who you fucking that's changed you?"

"I'm not. Don't accuse me of that," he'd say, sounding impatient and weary. Like my mother was pulling conspiracy theories out of thin air. "I'm older now, more professional. Most men don't bring their family to work. Keep your voice down. The girls will hear you."

They'd go on, my mom loud and brash, not the mom we knew at all, my father quiet and reserved, not the Rick T his fans knew.

In the end, Rick T got his way and started touring without us in the summers. I remained a day student at Choate, even after Janine joined me there. Rick T stopped sending my mother postcards from the road. And eventually my mother drove herself off a cliff.

I pushed away the image of that refrigerator full of postcards that all said, "I miss you." I reminded myself that Mike and I were just having fun. He might have called me his girlfriend on Valentine's Day, but we weren't getting married, and I wouldn't end up like my mom. There was absolutely no reason for the mild panic that popped off inside my stomach whenever I tried to focus on our long-term picture.

Two days wasn't a lot of time to prepare for a month-long trip, but I got all of my stuff together and even managed to fit in a trip to Target to stock up on a few toiletries that I'd need in New Orleans.

And lo and behold, who did I see as I was coming out of the checkout line but my old roommate, Benny. Seriously, I seemed to run into everybody at Target.

He was standing at the end of the checkout line, talking in Scottish to someone I couldn't see because the candy stand was blocking my line of vision. His tone of voice was moderate, but his eyes were laughing and, quite frankly, I had never seen my grumpy roommate in such a good mood. Was it a new girlfriend he was talking to? If so, I had to get a look at the woman who had transformed Benny from a grouchy troll and into a happy brownie.

Hoping that the girl spoke Scottish and could translate for me, I waved and called out, "Hey, Benny! What's going on?"

He waved back and said something completely unintelligible. It occurred to me that I'd also like to get his side of the story about the Abigail-Caleb reveal. Had he known they were having an affair of the heart? Did he even know they were together now? It didn't hurt so much to think about Abigail and Caleb now that I was writing every day and had my weird setup with Mike to distract me, and apparently Benny had gotten over his ex, too. Walking up to him felt like approaching someone I'd known in another universe, many lifetimes ago.

Which is why when I got closer and found a sheepish Sharita standing next to him, it took me a moment to put two and two together.

# SHARITA

9 hadn't exactly planned to keep Ennis from my friends. I'd just been waiting to see where things were going with him before I made any big announcements. But then weeks started streaking by and I kept on not saying anything. And it sort of felt true when Thursday had asked me a few days ago if I had met anybody new and I had said no, there was no one new. After all, Ennis wasn't new; we had been dating for three months now.

However, I began to see how bad this looked when my best friend ran us down at Target and didn't have a clue who Ennis was—outside of being her old roommate.

"What are you doing here? This isn't your Target," Thursday said to me.

"Um, we were just about to see a movie. So we came to get some candy beforehand," I said. I then proceeded to use all of my mental powers to telegraph to Thursday. "Shut up! Shut up! Don't let on that you didn't know we were dating."

My telepathic powers were apparently not that great, because Thursday said, "Oh. My. God. You and Benny are together? Are we, like, in the *Twilight Zone* or something? I'm seriously looking around for some kind of blinking portal or fuzzy lines to let me know that we've entered a different dimension. I thought you were Ms. Black Love to the day you die."

I found myself once again wishing that on my first day at Smith's orientation program for new students of color, I had decided to align myself with a regular black girl who had been raised by regular black parents as opposed to someone who had been raised with so much self-esteem that she thought everything that popped into her head deserved to be spoken out loud.

Thursday looked between the two of us. "So you and Benny are together?"

"Your name is Benny?" I asked the Scot, guiding us all to a space beyond the checkout line so that we wouldn't block traffic.

"No, I'm not fecking Benny. I'm Ennis, but she calls me Benny because she didn't understand when I told her my real name. Then Abigail picked it up because she thought it was a laugh, and between the two of them . . ." He shook his fist in the air. "But are you trying to tell me this is your friend 'Day'? How could she possibly be your best mate? You're so wonderful and she's one of the worst people I've ever known. And yea, before you ask, I'm including ma ex-girlfriend in that number."

"What's he saying?" Thursday asked me. "And when did you learn Scottish?"

"It's not a foreign language, Day," I said. "He's speaking English. You way overstated how bad his accent was."

"It's un-freaking-intelligible. Hey, did you tell Risa you two are together? Because if you told Risa and didn't tell me, that's so wrong."

"Risa? Is that the skinny bird with the harsh haircut?" he asked me. "I think I met her once at the North Hollywood flat."

"Yes, that's her. And how can you not have known that the girlfriend I mentioned that had a Scottish roommate was your old roommate? How many black girls do you think there are with Scottish roommates?"

"I was supposed to assume your best girlfriend was black, then?" Now his tone shifted. "I mean, I was never properly introduced to any of your friends, was I?"

"What's he saying?" Thursday asked again.

"Thursday, would you please stop? His accent is not that bad. I understand everything he's saying."

"Then you must have some kind of secret power, because I don't even understand how he's employed as a PA."

"He's not a PA, he's an assistant director."

"I was working a PA stint when I first met Abigail, but that was over three years ago," Ennis said. "I tried to tell her I'd passed the test and became an AD, but . . . this is really your best mate? Really truly? You know she used to make me write everything I said down. Refused to talk to me, except through a notepad."

"What's he saying?" Thursday asked yet again. "And why did he lie about being a PA?"

"Thursday. He tried to tell you, but you didn't understand."

"Why didn't he write it down?" Thursday asked, the picture of innocent confusion.

"Because he didn't appreciate having to write down everything he was trying to tell you."

Thursday chewed on that and then she said, "You really understand him? I mean really, really understand him? *Ni ye tingdong zhongguan ma?*"

"I have no idea what the last part was," I answered.

Thursday sagged a little, disappointed. "I asked if you understood Chinese, too. I thought your magical gifts might extend to other languages."

"Do you ken why I found it so verrae hard going to live with her?" Ennis asked, his good humor long gone.

"It was nice seeing you, Day, but we've got to go," I said.

"Wait, wait, wait, how long have you two been seeing each other?"

Oh no, this was what I had been hoping to avoid. "Three months," I mumbled.

Thursday cupped her ear. "First of all, did you say 'three months,' because I asked you, like, four days ago if you were seeing anybody and you were all, like, 'No'!"

"I didn't . . ." I rubbed my temple. "I didn't exactly say no. I kept it vague."

"Why?" Thursday asked as if Ennis wasn't standing right there and hearing all of this. "Usually you're telling me about new guys from the jump-off date."

"Thursday, we've really got to go. We have plans."

"Like secret boyfriend-girlfriend plans?" Thursday asked.

"We've got to go," I said, my voice turning edgy.

But Ennis said, "No, the movie's not for another forty minutes, and I, too, am curious about why you didn't tell your best mate about me."

"What did he say?" Thursday asked.

I leveled Thursday with a look that even she would understand meant that she was to stop talking now and go away.

Thursday raised her hands. "Okay, okay. I'm not going to chastise you anymore for pulling a Tammy. But you need to call me later."

"Who's Tammy? Is she the one with the cancer and the lesbionics that she was hiding for several years like a soap opera program on the telly?" Ennis asked.

"What did he say?" Thursday asked again.

Ennis and I did not end up going to see the sci-fi action flick, which we had been looking forward to all week, so much so that we had even decided to splurge on candy for the movie. This had been the fatal decision. Since we were both misers at heart, we stopped at Target as opposed to paying the markup at the movies. It had sounded like a great idea at first, but then Mike Barker had invited Thursday to New Orleans, and Thursday had brunch with a friend in North Hollywood, and, instead of going back to the West Hollywood Target, which was the one closest to Mike's house, she had decided to stop at the same Target as Ennis and me.

Now, I wasn't one of those people who thought God messed with folks just for the heck of it, but I did look skyward and shake my head with pressed-together lips as we came out of that Target. We had actually wasted more money by going to get the candy, because not only did we not go to see our movie, even though we had already paid for the tickets online, but Ennis also threw the candy in the trash can as we headed back to his car.

We drove in nauseous silence all the way back to his apartment, where I had left my car parked in front of his building.

"Here we are," Ennis said, pulling up right beside my car.

I stared gloomily at my lap. "Did you tell your best friend about us? I haven't met him, either."

"That's because he's back in Scotland. And, yes, I told him. I also told ma mum and ma sister and ma grandda. Am I right to assume you've told absolutely no one about us?"

"We haven't exactly had the boyfriend-girlfriend conversation," I pointed out.

"That's because I've done a good job of making it clear I'm crazy about you. I had hoped you felt the same. But I can see now I was wrong about that."

"Ennis, I'm not trying to lead you on or anything, I'm just confused, and I'm trying to figure out where we stand before I start announcing stuff. Just give me some time."

"No, Sharita. I know you Americans are big ones for giving each other *time,* but I'm thirty-seven years old. I don't want to 'play games,' as you all are so fond of saying. I want to settle down and have some bairns and live a happy life with someone who loves me as much as I love her. I won't settle for anything less. Now get out of the car, please."

"Ennis . . ."

"Get out of the car," he said again, his voice harsh and thick.

I got out of the car, feeling sullen and confused. That's what I got for dating a foreigner. He obviously didn't understand that in the States only stalkers and people with undiagnosed brain aneurysms pressured someone into calling himself her boyfriend after only three months.

Maybe that's what Ennis was. A crazy stalker Scot with a brain aneurysm. That would explain a lot . . . except stalkers with brain aneurysms didn't usually kick you out of their cars, did they? And they didn't usually drive away while you stared after them, right?

And when a stalker walked out of your life, it wasn't supposed to feel like he'd left a big gaping hole in your heart, was it?

Was it?

# RISA

I spent all of March bouncing from state to state, playing spring break concerts, because, for whatever reason, every college spring-breaked at different times and no one could quite agree on when. This would go on till late April, which was when Ipso! Facto! was scheduled to go back into the studio and I was scheduled to—well, I didn't know what I was scheduled to do yet. That all got decided tonight.

"Excited about the head of Gravestone coming out to see you?" The Lead Singer's Girlfriend asked. She was lying on my motel room bed, flipping through some art magazine.

I rock-star shrugged. Daniel Croisiere was planning to hit my set at the UNLV concert that night. So I had to bring it. But I didn't want to encourage The Lead Singer's Girlfriend by actually talking with her about my excitement.

Ever since I dropped Tammy, I'd been on a tear. I'd made out with groupies in front of her, ignored her texts, kept our increasingly rare sex sessions shorter and to the point, kicking her out afterward and telling her to go home to her boyfriend.

And in the way of all great rock star girlfriends, this only made her like me more. Whenever I had a hotel room on a non-travel day, she showed up at my door offering to keep me company before the show. "Where's your boy?" I asked . . . sneered, really.

"Oh, he's with the rest of the band. He doesn't care," she answered.

But see, he did care. The less I did to conceal that I didn't really like The Lead Singer's Girlfriend, the less she did to conceal how much she did like me. She openly flirted with me in front of him, throwing her head back and touching my shoulder anytime I said something clever. And I'd caught The Lead Singer himself staring at me a few times now, intent as if to silently ask, "What does she have that I don't?"

He was so on edge about her that he'd probably end up proposing to this chick any day now. And I would definitely not get invited on the next tour. So I needed this second deal with Gravestone to happen.

I couldn't lose both my career and my dream girl at the same time. Then I wouldn't have anything. So I ignored the nightmare girl on top of my bed, and I examined the desert sky outside my dusty motel window, and I choose a tangerine leather bikini top to match the polluted sunset. Then I went through the old motions of getting ready for the show, except it wasn't the same.

Not just because The Lead Singer's Girlfriend was lurking on the bed behind me, but also because when I tied the two suede straps behind my neck, a picture of Tammy flashed in front of me, pretty and laughing, like the first time we met and our eyes connected across the room.

When I tied the other two suede straps behind my back, there she was again, rolling around on top of her bed with me, giggling and telling me to keep it down, because Mike Barker was down the hall and she didn't want to wake him, even though she was paying him to sleep at her condo and pretend to be her boyfriend. When I'd first met Tammy, I had found her constant attention to the feelings of others lovable. But eventually it grew into a thorn. "How about my feelings?" I asked her during the big argument that got me kicked out of her condo. "You're so worried about your family. How about me?"

I was better off without her. I knew this. But when I pulled on my bright-green leather leggings, there she was, rubbing her naked breasts against my back as she fed me pieces of birthday cake—that was back when I would actually eat cake, when I was young and could stay thin easily, before she broke my fucking heart.

Half my head was shaved right now in an asymmetrical style, while the hair that remained was bleached out and dyed magenta.

"That hairstyle would look silly on anyone but you," Tammy said behind me in the mirror. This was another memory, from back in 2002, when I was one of the first black women to rock a fauxhawk. She'd looked at me looking at myself and said. "I wish I was brave like you."

I shook my head. Daniel Croisiere would be in tonight's audience and I was the opening act. It was time to stop being sentimental Lisa. Time to bring Risa out to seal a second album deal. I stared at myself in the mirror like I did every time I needed to channel Risa.

The second album, I decided then, could and would be better than the first. I had to show Croisiere what I was made of; I had to become Risa . . .

"I can't believe you still want me when I look like this," Tammy said the last time I saw her in person. The side effects of the chemo had loosened their grip on her, and she had tentatively shaken me awake to ask if I'd like to make out.

"Make out" was Tammy's code phrase for initiating sex. She could never meet my eyes when she made this inquiry, as if sexual desire were unseemly.

I responded to her request by immediately pulling her white baby-doll nightgown over her head and kissing her breathless.

"I can't believe you still want me when I look like this," she had said in the dark.

"Tammy," I said, turning her away from me and cupping one of her breasts with one hand and her pussy with the other. "You have the most magnificent set of knockers I've ever had the pleasure of viewing on a non-Photoshopped woman. I will always want you."

And she had laughed and said, "I love you." For the first time in years, she told me this.

And I knew if we could get past this cancer shit, I would come back from touring and she'd finally let me back into her life. But then she continued, "I just wanted you to know that, in case I'm not still here when you get back."

"You'll still be alive," I had said, because of the aforementioned growing-up-Catholic bullshit. "And if you need me, just call me and say the word. I'll come off the road."

She rubbed her crotch against my open hand. "Would you really?"

And I answered, "I would fucking do anything for you, Tammy."

Lisa was staring back at me in the mirror still. She wasn't purposefully withholding Risa and, to her credit, she looked rather helpless behind that determined brown gaze.

"Will you really always love me?" Tammy asked the first time I told her that, the first time the two of us hooked up after the big breakup. "Even if I never come out?"

We were floating in the afterglow of makeup sex, and I said, "Yeah, okay, why not?"

Tammy giggled. And I thought for the first time that if I could just make my post–Sweet Janes career work out, then Tammy would come back to me forever.

But like Thursday had said, it had never really been about the fame for Tammy. Now she had terminal cancer, and if I pulled off tonight's performance then I would be getting a second album deal, but I wouldn't have Tammy, and it was all just so very fucked up.

I hated Tammy, I really did.

I squeezed my eyes shut. Tammy ruined everything. The last ten years of my life, my self-esteem, my music career, which, let's face it, probably would have gone a little better if I had written about how much Tammy tore me up inside instead of not wanting to offend her in case she ever decided to take me back. Thursday had been totally right about her. Like that Ladytron song, that girl destroyed everything she touched.

And now she was destroying my career. Because after all those good-times flashbacks, another image burned itself into my brain: Tammy lying on the floor of her apartment. Dead and alone, because Thursday was right—Tammy would never stand up for me or anybody else . . . especially not herself.

And Tammy was also right—I had promised. And I might have been obnoxious like everybody said and I might have cussed too much and, okay,

I might have had an eating disorder. Whatever. But nobody had ever accused me of not keeping my promises.

I grabbed my short vintage rabbit-hair jacket and threw it on over my outfit, which I wouldn't be wearing on stage that night.

"Are we going to the venue now?" The Lead Singer's Girlfriend asked, closing the magazine.

"No, I'm going back to L.A." When I said this, I looked at her in a way I'd never looked at her before: gently. And she freaked out.

"I thought you loved . . ." She didn't finish, but her mouth set in a bitter line.

"Marry him," I told her. "He's good for you and he loves you. Also, he's so scared that you're going to leave him he probably won't make you sign a pre-nup so, you know, win-win."

I ignored her offended denials as I grabbed my wallet and headed for the door.

She broke off from accusing me of using her to ask, "How about your suitcase?"

I didn't answer. I'd already given her a good set of last words, and I wouldn't need most of those clothes anymore. They were my stage clothes and I definitely wouldn't be performing for a while after everyone found out I skipped out on the concert, and the rest of the tour.

They might even sue me, but fuck it.

The One had cancer. Seriously, what else could I do but go to her?

# April 2012

At the end of the day, love is a decision—the most important one you'll ever make.

—*The Awesome Girl's Guide to Dating Extraordinary Men* by Davie Farrell

# RISA

**M**y iPhone didn't have my full music collection or else I would have played that Roy Orbison song "I Drove All Night" on a loop during the four-hour drive in a rental car back to Los Angeles. Instead, I settled for Michael Jackson's greatest hits.

It was Saturday night, and the roads weren't too crowded. More people headed to Vegas than away from it. I sang along with Michael until my voice went hoarse and I was forced to listen to him, just listen to him asking how it felt to be all alone, like a stranger in Moscow.

Oh, Michael. I got angry at him, because if I'd had even an ounce of his natural talent, I would have lived forever, never dying, happy in my coal-black skin.

This thing with Tammy wasn't going to be anything less than awful. I could already tell.

I arrived at Tammy's condo a little after four a.m. As I got out of the car, I glanced at the clock and realized that it was April Fool's Day.

Ha.

No answer when I buzzed up on the box. I'd like to believe that this was because Tammy's family had come to get her, that she was lounging in some luxury hospice somewhere, blissed out on painkillers. But just in case . . .

I unlocked the lobby door with my extra key, which I kept right on my main key ring like Tammy and I were still in a relationship. As I made my way up to her apartment, I imagined her with her family, pretending to be straight until her last dying breath. She had been right about one thing: she wasn't exactly what anybody would call brave.

I knocked on her door. Once, twice, before letting myself in with my other extra key. The entire apartment was dark. No television light, nothing. Her family must have come to get her. And I would have left it at that, except it smelled horrible. Like lingering body odor, and food gone bad, and the staleness of not-having-been-open-to-the-outside-in-quite-a-while horrible.

I turned on the light and walked in for a look around.

Everything was a mess. There were Styrofoam delivery containers and empty junk-food packages everywhere. There was spaghetti sauce on the carpet leading to the living room, and a stack of pizza boxes near the couch. And as big as her family was on appearances, I'd figure that hiring a cleaning service would be the first thing they'd do after collecting Tammy.

I went to check the bedroom, which was also dark. But when I flipped on the light, I found the room surprisingly clean. The bed was neat and made. Except for a layer of dust, it looked like a Design Within Reach catalog layout. Odd.

"Is anybody here?" I called out to the empty room, already kicking myself for cutting out on my tour for a promise I hadn't really needed to keep.

Nobody answered.

I was about to turn off the light and go when I heard a scratching sound and a voice said, "Risa? Is that you?"

The voice was muffled and thin with sickness, but I could still tell who it was. I turned around just in time to see Tammy emerging from the closet. I loved irony, and my first instinct was to make a joke about her coming out of the closet. But then I saw her. Really saw her.

All of her beauty was gone, as was all of her softness. Her cheeks and her eyes were both sunken in and her ears looked big, almost to the point of drooping off her thin face. Her full breasts, which I'd worshipped every time we'd hooked up, hung saggy and much withered underneath her T-shirt. She was not wearing socks, and her missing toe screamed its absence.

The only thing that remained the same were her eyes, which were liquid with happiness.

"You came," she said; croaked, really.

"The front room is a mess. What happened to your nurse?" I asked her.

"I let her go," Tammy waved a dismissive hand in the air. "I was sick of having her around, looking at me."

"Tammy," I said, my voice monotone with horror. "How have you been getting to your doctor's appointments?"

"It's okay," she said. "I'm okay. I don't need to go to the doctor anymore. I've got medicine for the pain. So I really don't need anybody here. Just you."

"You didn't call your family," I said, so mad at her.

"They think I'm in the Maldives," Tammy said, rolling her eyes like her family members were just some silly rabbits and not people who were owed the truth. "I thought you were Veronica. She got suspicious the other day and came to check up on me. Luckily I heard her key in the door and got to the closet in time."

"She didn't think the messy living room was suspicious?"

Tammy chuckled. "See, you two never liked each other, but you totally think the same. She texted me about it immediately, and I told her I had a house sitter who was apparently taking advantage. That's why I thought you were her. She was acting like she might come back over here and kick my house sitter out herself if she could ever find him."

Seriously, I didn't know how I had ever come to be in love with someone this stupid.

"I just need to . . ." Tammy sat down to rest on the side of the bed, wheezing. "Too much exertion," she gasped, waving a skeletal hand to indicate that she was fine.

"I'm going to go clean up the living room," I said.

"Thank you for coming back." She looked up from her wheezing, skinny and pale and shiny-eyed. "It really does mean a lot to me."

I shook my head. As soon as I finished the fucking hazmat-level job that would be cleaning up her condo, I planned to do what I'd been refusing to do for almost a decade now—tell on Tammy.

# THURSDAY

I picked up Risa's call while walking toward the baggage claim area in the Louis Armstrong New Orleans International Airport, having just gotten off the red-eye from Los Angeles. "Hey what's up? Guess where I'm at."

"New Orleans," Risa said.

My mouth dropped open. "How did you know?"

"Because you're just pretending not to be in love with Mike Barker at this point," Risa answered, sounding bored. "Is he with you?"

"No, but he's meeting me at the gate. And by the way, I'm not pretending—"

"Sure, okay, whatever. Can you ask him for Davie Farrell's number?"

"Why? Do you need a career consultation, because her waiting list is, like, a mile long. She only fit me in as a favor to Mike. Wait, aren't you on tour? Why do you need a career consultation?"

"Actually, I kind of quit the tour. I'm back in L.A."

I shook my head. "Why would you quit your tour?" Then I answered my own question: "Oh no, you're back in Los Angeles for her, aren't you?"

"I tried to do it your way, Day, but . . . she has cancer."

"She used you. She let you dangle for years. Not weeks, not months, but years." An ache started up in my neck from having flown on a plane all night straight into this conversation. "And she doesn't care about anybody but herself. And let me just say, if you were in the same position, I don't think she would do the same thing for you."

"Day, I know she wouldn't, but do you get that she has terminal cancer? She's only thirty-three years old and she has terminal cancer. That's a big fucking deal."

My mother had been forty-three, only ten years older when she died. And yes, Tammy was dying, but Risa was being pathetic by going back to her after how Tammy treated her.

Then Risa said, "Anyway, she still hasn't told her family, so I've got to call them and tell them what's going on myself."

"Oh," I said, saddened that Tammy still hadn't told her family about her cancer. "I'll have Mike call you back with the number as soon as we're in the car."

"Thanks," Risa said. She sounded tired. Then she hung up.

I walked a little faster to get to the gate, even more excited to see Mike, who might be a recovering gambling addict and overly dramatic, but at the very least, acknowledged we were together, unlike Tammy, and now I'd come to find out, Sharita.

"What! Sharita's dating your ex-roommate's ex-boyfriend now?" he'd said the night before on the phone, when I told him about Sharita and Benny.

Unlike Caleb, Mike loved gossip. Oh, at first he had claimed that he hated it along with the paparazzi, like he was above such things, but whenever I mentioned something I had read in *Celeb Weekly* or on a gossip site, he was all ears, and then he would dissect it from an insider perspective. And he especially liked regular-people gossip.

"Crazy, right?" I answered.

"I thought she was Ms. Black Love," he said. Sharita's love life had been a topic of conversation between us several times before.

"So did I, but he had his arm around her like 'this be my woman.' I was all, like, 'Whaaaat???' It was crazy. Then Sharita was all, like, 'We've gotta go! We've gotta go!' Like rushing out of there would make me tease her any less."

"She must not have known who she was dealing with," Mike said.

"I know, right!"

Thinking back on that conversation as I came down the escalator made me smile . . . that was until I saw not Mike but Mrs. Murphy standing outside the baggage claim area.

"Where's Mike?" I asked when I reached her. An image of my father's mistress, Brenda, meeting my plane after my mother's death flickered across my mind's eye.

"Something came up," Mrs. Murphy said, averting her eyes. "He'll meet you in the hotel room."

"What came up? I thought he wasn't filming today." I asked, my Spidey sense tingling. Back when my father was still bothering to hide his infidelity from my mother, things "came up" a lot. Things that kept him on tour in exotic island locales for a few days past when he was supposed to leave, or things that kept him in the studio all night.

"I'm not sure," Mrs. Murphy answered, still not meeting my eyes. "Let's go gather your suitcase, shall we?"

Mike's "hotel room," as Mrs. Murphy called it, turned out to be a series of rooms housed within a space bigger than any apartment I had ever stayed in, including the two-bedroom one I had shared with Abigail in North Hollywood.

Mrs. Murphy let me in and left my suitcase in the enormous front room, which was done up in so much brocade and heavy curtainage that the *Gone With the Wind* theme music swelled inside my head as I searched for Mike in the five-thousand-square-foot (at least) space. He wasn't in the living room, or the kitchen. And I didn't find him in the master bedroom or in the large bathroom—though I did note the hot tub, and made a promise to myself to check it out with Mike later.

I dumped my suitcases in the bedroom, went back into the hallway and resorted to calling out, "Mike, are you here? If so, where are you?"

"I'm in here," Mike called back from behind one of the heavy wooden doors at the far end of the hall.

I jogged to it and opened it with visions of crawling over the desk and attacking him with kisses. And I might have done it, too . . . if Rick T hadn't been in the office with him.

He looked exactly as he had the last time I had seen him in person. Dressed in jeans, a simple T-shirt, Adidas, and a baseball cap. It was like walking into a room to meet my lover and finding a ghost instead. I froze in the doorway, trying to process what was going on.

Rick T stood up, his face a thundercloud of anger, and Mike, who had been sitting behind the desk, also stood up. He threw me an apologetic look and shook his head as if to say, "Stay calm, Thursday."

"You think sliming me in public's going to bring your mother back?" Rick T asked, waving around what I assumed to be the script I had written.

"You humiliated her, maybe it's time for you to see how it feels," I answered. Then I asked Mike, "What exactly is he doing here?"

"He said he couldn't reason with you, so he asked me to come down here to try to talk some sense into you," Rick T answered.

"That's not what I said." Mike shook his head again. "Rick is upset about the script, so we're talking about it."

"What is there to talk with him about?" I asked. "Didn't you buy the rights to his story? You didn't give him final script approval did you?"

"No, but I want him to be on board," Mike said. "This is his story."

"How do you expect me to be on board with this trash?" Rick T asked. He turned on me. "I don't have any kind of retirement, because I sent you and your sister to the best schools, gave you everything that money could buy, and this is how you repay me?"

"First of all, do you really expect me to feel sorry for you because you didn't manage to stay rich after Mom died?" My mother had been the one that, having grown up poor and never wanting to go back, kept Rick T's money working for us. She had invested it wisely and from what I could tell had set up what little retirement that Rick T had. But being friends with Sharita, I knew that keeping money in your bank account was a job, even if you were rich and especially if you were a musician. After Rick T married Brenda, according to Janine, they'd lived a fairly glamorous lifestyle, traveling, buying multiple properties, not paying attention to his financial portfolio even as his record sales dwindled.

"I'm so sorry that your mistress didn't turn out to be as good of a financial manager as Mom was," I sneered. "Second of all, it's not trash, it's not slime. It's the truth. Sorry again, if you can't handle the truth. Maybe think about not being such a dick next lifetime if you want super-nice scripts written about you."

"First of all, you think your mother was just a victim in this? She came from the projects and she ended up better off than she ever could have dreamed because of *me*." Rick T jabbed a thumb at himself. "Second of all, I was her prince. I saved her from that life. How about putting that in your smear campaign of a script?"

I had forgotten that my father also ordered his points, that I had, in fact, picked up the habit from him. A warm memory of us joking back and forth about my decision to attend Smith as opposed to his and my mother's alma mater, Columbia, came up unbidden. First of all, second of all . . . all the way up to us arguing tenth of all, laughing so hard that we could barely get our points out. We had been so happy back then, I thought with a small punch of regret, so proud of each other for being who we each were, so willing to tease each other and not really mean what we were saying. But that had been back then . . .

I pointed to the script that he'd been waving in my face. "Tell me one thing in this script that didn't happen."

"I only got a few pages in, but I can already see quite a few things that you left out while you were trying to paint me as a monster of ego." He ticked it off on his fingers. "First of all, you left out how I worked my ass off to get a record deal when your mama told me she was pregnant with you our senior year of college. You left out how I only stayed on the road so we could afford our mortgage and all the private schools we were sending you and your sister to. I haven't gotten to the part where your mother drives *herself* off a cliff yet. But judging from the rest of the script, I'm pretty sure you left out the seventeen stitches I had to get because you attacked me in my own home. And you left out how my ungrateful oldest daughter didn't even invite me to her college graduation—for the education I paid for." Like me, his voice grew colder the angrier he got. And also like me, the angrier he got, the meaner his words became. "You went to school to study screenwriting, and this crap is all you could come up with? Seriously, kid? I could be living on a tropical island right now if I hadn't wasted so much money on you."

"Rick, with all due respect—" Mike tried to intervene, to restore civil discourse to a situation that had exploded faster than he had probably thought it would with his actorly devotion to the power of positive thinking.

But I interrupted his bid for diplomacy with a raised hand. "You can't stand it, can you? It's just killing you that there's now going to be more than one person out there who sees through your act to who you really are. The only reason you ever bothered to try to make up with me was because I was the first one to stop liking you. Your career went to crap after she died— that's why you're not living on a tropical island now—and you know and I know that you deserved everything you got after what you did to her."

"I tried to make it right between us because you're my blood and I love you," he said. "And the only reason you didn't respond is because you're trying to punish me for your mother's death."

Tears of anger sprang to my eyes. "No, I'm punishing you for humiliating her. I'm telling the truth because you have millions of fans, and she only had me and Janine. While you were out on the road fucking your assistant and calling us once a day for maybe five minutes, if you had time, she was the best mother ever. And you treated her like she didn't matter, like she was some burden. So fuck you, and fuck your fancy schools. I wish you had been the one who died, you selfish piece of shit. I am my mother's daughter.

I stand righteous where you cut her down. I am the one person in this entire world that is on her side and not yours, and I will never forgive you."

The air between Rick T and me visibly cooled. He pointed at me. "First of all, I am your father. Don't call me out of my name. Second of all, don't talk about my wife like she was some groupie. I fell in love with her, and it's not her fault that I was already married. Third of all, your mother wasn't a saint. Just like you, she could be mean, and no matter what I did, she was never satisfied. But I stayed with her for you and Janine. So give me some credit there. Fourth of all, what happened between your mother and me has nothing to do with you, little girl. That was an A-and-B conversation, and I don't need your forgiveness for it, because it was none of your business."

It should be noted again that I had been raised by a pacifist vegetarian to be a pacifist vegetarian. My mother had believed words to be the most powerful weapons on the face of the earth and they were the only weapons we had been allowed to ever use. She wouldn't even allow us to kill bugs that we found in the house. I had lived in New York for three years while in grad school and had never even stomped on a roach because of the way my mother had raised me, but at that moment I clocked three things in the room that I could use to hurt this man.

I could stab him in the neck with the letter opener on Mike's desk. I could take the painting of the French Quarter off the wall and slam it over his head. I could grab the decanter of brandy, sitting on top of the room's small oak bar, and once again throw a piece of glass at Rick T's head.

But I suppose that I really was my father's daughter, because in the end I held myself still, despite the fury boiling within me, and said, "She was a human being, Rick. A sensitive and wonderful human being. I don't care if she didn't completely revolve around you the way Brenda does or if she nagged you more than you liked. She was a human being, and you didn't treat her accordingly, and that is my business. I didn't defend her back then, but I'm telling you right now, in the words of the project kids that my mom grew up with while you ate three square meals a day in Connecticut, don't you talk about my mama. Don't you ever talk about my mama. Don't you ever . . ."

My breath hitched and Mike must have come around the desk at some point, because he gathered me up in his arms, pressing my wet face against his chest.

"I know that you're both looking at this like a scorched earth kind of conversation," Mike said. "But by talking to each other about this for the first time, you're making progress."

"What?" I heard Rick T say behind us. "How is this progress? And are you two together?" Then before we could answer, "So that's why you threw away the first draft of the script, because she got to you."

I drew away from Mike, already seeing where my father was going with this, even though Mike could not. My father was the son of a preacher, a man who used to be able to convince millions of people at a time that the world view they'd grown up with was skewed, that privilege was bad, that their government didn't care about them, that the black people, who only made up twelve percent of our nation, were the most intelligent, beautiful, and powerful force on earth. Of course, he thought he could convince Mike to go back to the original script.

"Mike," he said. "I respect you. You're not the first person who has asked for the rights to my story, but I sold them to you because you're the first person I've respected enough to trust. I trusted you with my life, man. And I know that you don't think this is a betrayal, but it is. There are two sides to every story, and notice that while your first screenwriter flew out with you to actually talk to me, my daughter didn't even bother to call me and let me know she was working on a script. Thursday and I haven't spoken to each other directly since her mother's funeral. I'm not going to accuse her of using you to get to me, I just want you to consider that she might have an agenda."

Mike rubbed his chin, considering Rick T's words. And my father jumped on his moment of indecision, going in for the gentle kill. "Let's think about our two options. If you go with the original script, everybody's happy except for Thursday, who obviously has some unresolved issues with me and only wants to show one side of the story. If you go with Thursday's script, then I'm going to have to bring in my lawyers, and the press is going to be talking about how against this script I am. Thursday's going to get dragged through the mud; you know how mean females can get when it comes to the women their favorite male stars are dating. And if it looks like you're letting her run you, you're going to lose fans, which would be a shame after coming back from your gambling addiction."

Mike looked sideways at me, worry in his expression. Apparently, he did know how female fans could be. So far we had flown under the radar, because we didn't frequent places with paparazzi and because I wasn't famous, I was therefore not worth paying attention. At the only red carpet event we'd gone to, Mike's publicist had pulled me aside and asked if it was okay if Mike walked the red carpet alone. "It keeps the level of scrutiny down," she'd explained to me.

But living in L.A., Mike and I were both fully aware that the press could be snarky, creating a vicious feeding frenzy around any story if they sniffed blood. And now, my father was threatening to throw a bunch of bloody chum into the relatively peaceful shark tank we swam in.

"You're right," Mike said. "Thursday might have an agenda."

I stared at him, hurt that he would cave so easily to my father, though a certain part of me did understand how hard Mike had worked to get his career back after his gambling addiction got out of control. In just three years, he had gone from *Choco-Cop 3* to getting nominated for an Oscar. In 2010, one industry mag had named his comeback one of the ten greatest of the decade. No way was he going to throw all of that away for one script that he'd pretty much had to force me to write in the first place.

"Thursday might have an agenda," Mike said again. "But you wouldn't know that because you haven't read the script."

My mouth fell open, and Rick T, not being used to people who weren't his obstinate daughter daring to argue back at him, looked dumbstruck. "I don't have to read the script to know—" he started.

"See, that's where you're wrong," Mike said, bending down and picking the script up from where my father had tossed it. "You do need to read it, because you obviously don't know anything about your daughter. She fought me hard on writing that script. When I approached her about writing it, she was raw from a breakup with her last boyfriend that had happened less than an hour before. And even though she was desperate for money, she advised me against choosing her to write it, for the exact reasons that you're accusing her of. She said she hated you. She said she was too biased. She said that she wasn't the right person for the project. She said that, and then she went and wrote the best script I have ever read about a fellow black man.

"Sir, if anyone wrote anything approaching this about my life, I would be honored. So with all due respect, read the goddamn script. And if you still don't want it to get made when you're finished reading it, then I'll kill the project, even though it's already been green-lit. Because if you finish reading this, and you don't want it to get made, then you're a fucking idiot, and I don't want to play you in a film noways."

That all threatened, Mike pushed the script into Rick T's chest and walked out of the room, leaving me in the awkward position of sharing Rick T's shocked silence.

Rick T looked at the script, looked at me, looked back at the script again, and to my great surprise, took a seat, turned to page twenty-three, and started reading without a further word of protest.

Not knowing what else to do, I followed Mike and found him in the bedroom, standing there as if he had just been waiting for me to come in so he could say, "So that's where you got all that stubbornness from. I was beginning to wonder."

Now, I could have teased Mike about losing his positivity religion when he confronted Rick T, or I could have said, "Ultimatum much?" A few quips swirled around in my mind, but when I opened my mouth, the only thing that I wanted to say, that I needed to say, was, "I love you, too."

"You love me, too." He threw me a grin so cocky and sure that I wanted to slap him . . . and then kiss him afterwards. "And once again," he said. "Mike Barker gets what he wants."

# SHARITA

$9$had believed in black love for as long as I could remember. One of my earliest memories was watching *The Cosby Show* in the front room with my sister and mother and thinking, "Yeah, that's how I want my life to be."

I loved black men. Loved their lips, loved their eyes, the way they looked you up and down when they wanted to get with you, the rhythmic way they talked—even the ignorant ones—and their slow smiles, which usually revealed perfect white teeth, even if they had never known a dentist in their life.

Truth be told, I thought as I tied my hair up in my silk scarf the night after Ennis kicked me out of his car, I wasn't quite sure what I had been trying to do with the Scot in the first place. Sure he was funny and nice and smart and cheap like me, but he was also white, pushy, and foreign. Not my taste at all.

Despite this decision, it took me over three hours to get to sleep that night. And the next day at church, my mind kept on wandering to the point that I knew it would be useless to try to attend the women's Bible study group afterwards, so I went home.

Weirdly enough, today was the day I was supposed to have gone to church with Ennis. On our first date, he had casually brought up the fact that he had been attending church every week since his last breakup.

"It was that bad?" I had asked.

"No," he said. "But it made me see how far I'd gotten away from my roots. Right when I finished uni, I got involved in a business venture that I really needed to work out. So I started attending service at the little Episcopalian church up the road from my home and literally prayed that the venture would succeed."

"And did it?" I'd always been fascinated by stories about the power of prayer.

"As a matter of fact it did," he'd said. "I built a right nice nest egg, enough so that I could move to the States and have a wee bit of adventure. I stopped going to church, but after the breakup with Abby, I realized I'd prayed harder over that business than I'd ever had over our relationship. So I started going back to church after that. Once a week again, good and proper."

"And what do you pray for now?" I'd asked.

"Nothing in particular," he'd answered. "World peace, a new season of *Torchwood*, a Scottish Cup win for the Albion Rovers. Same stuff everybody prays for, I suppose."

Back then I had been charmed to meet a fellow single person who attended church on the regular. Today I just wondered what Ennis prayed for in church that morning.

I decided to take a nap when I got home. I was too tired to watch TV or go out or do any of the things I used to enjoy just two days ago when I was still dating Ennis.

I had almost gotten to sleep when the phone rang. I snatched it out of my purse, faster than I wanted to, hoping it would be Ennis. But to my surprise, I saw Nicole's name staring back at me on the caller ID.

"Hello?" I said, tentative, because we hadn't talked since the wedding.

"Sharita," Nicole said, her voice wobbling. "I didn't know who else to call."

"What's wrong?" I asked, fearing for the niece I hadn't met, but that, according to my mother, had been born beautiful and precious three months earlier.

"I'm tired," Nicole said.

"You're tired?" I repeated.

"Graham's working, he's always working. And I'm here with the baby. And I'm so jealous of him, because he gets to leave all the time. But I'm here twenty-four/seven. I don't even have time to get my hair done right, because weaves take too long. I just want to be pretty again."

"You're pretty," I said.

"No, I look so throw down, you should see how bad. And I'm bored. You have no idea how boring this is. They make it look fun in the movies, but it's not. It's so not. It's boring and it's disgusting. All she does is poop and spit up on me. I can't wear anything nice anymore. Not that it matters because nothing fits. I've only lost, like, five pounds."

"Maybe you could order something in your new size off the Internet while the baby is sleeping. And have you thought about getting a baby—"

"Don't even say babysitter. I've tried. But I don't trust anyone to look after her but me. And I know she'll freak out if she wakes up and I'm not there. I hate being needed like this. I keep on thinking that I should divorce Graham."

"What?" I said, barely able to keep up. Nicole was jumping around so fast.

"If I divorce him and we share custody, then he can have her for one week and I can have her for one week, and I get half of the year to myself to do whatever I want."

"If you're divorced, you'll have to get and keep a job to get by," I said.

"I want a job. A real job. Acting can go to hell. I want to go to an office and sit at a desk, and not have to take care of somebody who shits on me. I'm asking him for a divorce as soon as he gets home. Or should I get a lawyer first? You're supposed to get a lawyer first, right?"

Nicole sounded hysterical, and it surprised me how easily I fell back into the role of reasonable big sister—despite my little sister status. "How about instead of asking your husband who loves you and your daughter for a divorce, we fly Mom out there for a week or two."

"No," Nicole said. "I love Mom, but it was terrible having her here when Ella was born. She doesn't cook, says she doesn't remember how to change a diaper. All she wanted to do was shop. With what money? I don't know, since I had to pay for her to get here in the first place."

I stifled a smile, thinking about how Nicole had defended our mother the last time I had complained about having to pay for her to come out to

California, only to have her drag me to one shopping mall after another, adding brighter and brighter colors to her already ridiculously loud wardrobe. "At least you have money to fly her out," Nicole had said two years ago. "I wish I could see Mommy more often."

Now she knew.

"If Ella and I get on a plane today and come stay with you for a while, does that count as kidnapping?" Nicole was saying now.

Nicole, I realized then, hadn't gotten over on life like I'd thought. Yeah, she'd achieved black love, while I had not. And yes, her husband was well off and they lived in a fabulous apartment with their camera-ready baby. But Nicole was still Nicole. Easily overwhelmed, overly dramatic, weirdly drastic, and in constant need of her younger sister's guidance.

"How about this?" I said. "It's pretty slow here. How about I come out next weekend?"

"Really?" Nicole said, tears in her voice. "You'd do that for me, even though I'm a terrible sister and a terrible human being and a terrible mother?"

"You're not a terrible mother," I said.

"Yes, I am," Nicole said. "Women have been doing this for centuries and I can't handle it. Who decides to divorce her husband just so she can have some more time to herself? I'm terrible and selfish."

"You're not," I said. "If you were really as bad as you think you are, then you would have just done it. You wouldn't have called me first."

"I didn't want to have to call you," Nicole said. "That's what you never understood. I didn't want to ask you for money all the time. I didn't want to be a leech like you said I was at the wedding. I wanted to make it as an actor and pay my own rent. But Sharita, even when I'm trying my hardest, I can't do this life without you."

I put a hand over my heart, touched speechless for a second. "That's the nicest thing anyone's ever said to me," I finally said. "I can't wait to see you again, sister."

After hanging up, I realized what I needed to do. I went into my guest bedroom, which also served as my home office, and got out two manila envelopes, one of which I addressed to my sister. Then I went into my bedroom and got out my grandmother's pearls. I had always imagined wearing them at my own perfect black wedding, but now I could see that wasn't going to happen. I wrote my sister's address out and dropped the pearls in the envelope. Then I fingered the Sharpie I had used to write my sister's address and picked up the other envelope.

Scottish movies weren't like American ones. From what I had seen, they were usually pretty dismal tales about alcoholics and other tragic figures. And if there was any love story at all, nine times out of ten you could bet it wouldn't turn out well. The Scots didn't seem to even know the meaning of the words "romantic comedy."

Which is why Ennis was probably more than a little surprised when he opened the door to find me standing there with a sign written on the front of a manila envelope that read, "I'M SORRY. WILL YOU BE MY BOYFRIEND?"

The Scots weren't "a romantic comedy lot," as Ennis might have said, but that didn't stop him from opening his arms wide when he found me outside his door.

"Ah, wee Sharita," he said. "I prayed for this exact scenario in church this morning. How did you know?"

# May 2012

Don't worry about if a guy likes you. Worry about if you like him. You'd be surprised how long it takes some of us to figure out we never even liked the guy in the first place.

—*The Awesome Girl's Guide to Dating Extraordinary Men* by Davie Farrell

# THURSDAY

*A*fter the Rick T showdown, Mike and I went down to the hotel's five-star, Michelin-rated restaurant for a late breakfast. We lingered for a while, both wanting to avoid the Rick T elephant back in the hotel room, but when we came back upstairs, the study door was still closed, which meant Rick T was still reading.

"Say it again," Mike demanded as we re-entered the *Gone With the Wind* front room.

"Say what again?" I asked, knowing perfectly well what he meant.

"I love you," he told me. "It feels good to be able to say that without worrying about you freaking out and running away."

"I love you, too," I said, even though I could hear my mother's engine revving in the back of my consciousness.

We turned on a movie to pass the time while we waited. The red-eye, followed by the emotional fight, followed by a large breakfast must have tuckered me out, because I fell asleep, my head resting against Mike's chest. The next thing I knew, Mike was shaking me awake.

"Thursday?" he said. "Wake up, baby."

So I did, and I found my father in the room with us.

I sat up, feeling like I had been caught with a boy, taking my cues from the stern expression on Rick T's face. But then I remembered I wasn't in high school any more, and my dad was no longer my dad, just Rick T, a man I hadn't seen in person for over a decade before he showed up in Louisiana.

"My dad, your grandfather, tried to convert me on his deathbed," Rick T said. "Mom called me, said that he was dying, that he wanted to see me. I drove everybody over there. Remember that trip?"

I recalled my paternal grandmother complimenting everything but my dimples and nodded.

"I went in there, expecting some big apology from him, ready to forgive. But before I was even all the way through the door he was on me again, like he'd been holding his breath to make his next point since the last fight we'd had. He said, 'See what you done to me. All this fiddle-faddle, all this who-shot-Mary you been talking all over the devil box. My heart couldn't take it.'"

Rick T's mouth turned up into a bitter half smile at the memory. "I was like you, little girl, a smart-ass from birth. So of course I said, 'Last time I checked, rapping never gave anybody heart disease. A poor diet on the other hand . . .' Your grandfather got swole. You should've seen him hissing about how ungrateful I was, how I needed to turn my talent to God, how if I didn't, I'd be going to Hell and he wouldn't even spit on me from heaven. And you know what was crazy? He never listened to any of my albums. Preachers were like that back then. If music wasn't about Jesus then it belonged to the devil. He didn't care that I was trying to uplift black people, all he cared about was that I cursed while I did it and I wasn't using my voice to talk about God. He'd raised me to be Dr. Rick Turner Jr., like Dr. Martin Luther King Jr., and I'd been all set to walk that path. But then I met your mama and became a rapper instead."

He set the script down on the coffee table in front of us. "You should put that deathbed scene in there. If you put that in, I'll approve it."

There's this thing all writers get taught in grad school. You can't have your villain decide on his own that he's no longer going to keep fighting with the protagonist. Your hero has to earn everything she gets. And if the villain decides to stop being evil, it has to be because of something she did.

So having only recently returned to written words, the magical material that my mother had always assured me was all I needed to move hearts and minds, a sense of wonder crept into my voice when I said to my father, "Are you serious?"

He sounded pained when he said his next words, like this confession cost him something to make. "You know, when I first met your mom, we were both doing the poetry thing. I told my dad it was a hobby, but I would sweat over my lines for months, trying to get them just right. Same with homework. I thought my essays would be collected like MLK's speeches someday, so it'd take me weeks to do a five-page paper. But your mom—she didn't even use the desk in her dorm room. She'd write her essays in bed and get As. The first time we had sex, she turned over and wrote 'Thirty-Four Minutes' in fifteen minutes. Fifteen minutes . . ." He shook his head.

"Thirty-Four Minutes" had been the third single off of his debut album—swagger-free, and, according to *Vibe* magazine's End of the Millennium issue, the sixth-best rap love song of all time.

"People still come up to me talking about how much that song meant to them, and it only took her fifteen minutes to write it. You think I didn't respect her, like we were always the way we were at the end. But I respected her all right. I wanted to be her so bad. If I could have found a way to make us into one person, I would have. If I had her kind of talent, I'd be rich like Bono now." He broke off and folded his hands into a tight prayer fist before saying, "Your mom would have been so proud of you, pumpkin."

I went still, at that moment realizing that more than anything I wanted my dead mother's approval. "Really?"

"Yeah, I can see the way she raised you all over that script. That's why I'm going to give it my approval, but . . . but you can't keep on hating me," he said. "Maybe you're right. Maybe I did your mother dirty. Sometimes I wonder if my career tanked after she died because she wasn't there to guide me. Maybe this is my punishment for not having treated her better. Maybe I didn't appreciate her enough. I try not to think about it too much, because I'm old, and I already have enough problems getting to sleep at night.

"But estrangement—that's a powerful decision. I know, because I made it with my own father before you were even born. You have to decide that if that person you used to love died tomorrow, you'd be okay with never having forgiven him. After that deathbed conversation, I didn't even go to your grandfather's funeral. And yeah, maybe I was right about that. He was self-righteous, couldn't see all the good I was trying to do with my music, while these other vultures were eating rap alive with their nonsense. But I'm old now, and the music game forced me into retirement, so I have lots of time to think. I should have gone to his funeral. I was right to go my own way, but I should have forgiven him. I should have found a way to have a relationship with him, to let you and Janine have a relationship with your grandfather.

"Because the truth is that nobody's all good or all bad. Your mother wasn't perfect, but she was your mother, and she did good with you and Janine. I didn't do as good a job as she did, but I'm your father. I'm not all devil. You need to take the good parts of me and hold on to that, because you may not like me, but I'm the only parent you have left. That counts for something, even if you don't think it does."

After all of that, he folded his arms and waited for me to say something. And, despite ten years of telling myself that I had what it took to stay estranged from my father, I already knew that I had lost the battle. I didn't hate him anymore. I couldn't hate him anymore. It wasn't even possible to hate him anymore.

His rap was just too damn good.

So I picked up the script and said, "You know what, I will add that deathbed scene. That's good stuff." My writer's brain spun some more. "And the stuff about you going balls-to-the-wall to get a record deal after Mom got pregnant with me. That's good, too. Nice clock. I'll put that in."

And just like that, what had been complicated became simple. Rick T slept in the suite's second bedroom, and stayed on the next day, keeping me company when Mike went to set. We enjoyed beignets at Café Du Monde, visited a cathedral, studiously ignored the women pulling up their tops when the street turned into a reckless party at night.

I sat in the back seat with him when Mrs. Murphy drove him to the airport the following morning. He talked about Mike and me meeting up with him and Brenda in their Hawaiian condo the next Christmas. He was a snowbird now, and only spent the warm months in Connecticut. I told him I wasn't ready for Christmas With The Mistress yet. He told me not to call her that. She had a name. I suggested maybe he could visit Mike and me in California for Thanksgiving, if we were still together by then.

"You think you two won't be?" Rick T asked.

And I changed the subject, because it didn't feel appropriate to talk about the driving-off-the-cliff feeling that admitting to my love for Mike gave me.

After Rick T left, I took over the hotel-room office and wrote for the rest of the day. When Mike got home, we ordered room service and made love. And that's what we did for the next thirty days. Rinse and repeat, more boring than what anyone would imagine Mike Barker to be like. But, I had discovered, sometimes boring was good. Sometimes boring meant that you got your work done and he got his work done and at the end of the day, you were happy to be boring together.

I came to love our setup, and I would have stayed as planned until halfway through May, but on May second, Risa called while I was writing in the hotel suite's office.

"Hey, Risa, what's up," I said.

No answer.

"Risa, are you there?" I asked.

Still no answer. And I was about to check the connection, but then I heard several hitched breaths, and I realized that Risa was there.

She couldn't talk because she was crying too hard.

"Risa," I said. "I am going to the airport right now and I will book the first flight I find to L.A. I'm coming, okay? I'm coming."

"Okay," Risa said, her voice little more than a whisper. "Okay."

# RISA

*N*ot to accuse Thursday of being a bad friend, but she promised to call me back, and then she, like, never did. Meanwhile, I had to clean up Tammy's living room, throw open all the windows, and Febreze the shit out of it so it didn't smell like some teenage boy's nasty room.

When I went back to the bedroom, I found Tammy crumpled on the bed. My heart stopped, but when I put my finger under her nose, I felt air coming out of it. She was just dozing.

I decided to go over there. "There" being James Farrell's mansion in the Los Feliz Hills. Tammy had lived there when she first came back to L.A. after running away from me to New York. And I'd visited her there a few times in the first stages of trying to be friends. I surprised myself by driving there by memory, finding it easily despite not knowing the address.

"Hello, this be the Farrell residence," said a voice with a heavy Jamaican accent when I pushed the button on the speaker box outside the gate.

I recognized the voice as that of Paul, her brother's manservant, and I said that I was a friend of Tammy's and asked to talk to James. Paul buzzed me in, pushing some button inside the house that sent the metal gates sliding open with quiet efficiency. Not surprisingly, James remembered me.

"How's it going?" he said, greeting me himself at the door.

I told him that he might want to call his wife down.

"She's with a client," he said.

And I felt so bad for him that I decided not to prolong it. I said it straight, no prep. "Tammy's got terminal stage IV cancer. She's not in the Maldives. She's been lying to you since last July, and now she's in really, really bad shape."

"That's the sickest joke I've ever heard, and you need help," he said.

"I wish it was a joke," I said.

And he shook his head and said, "No."

Just "no," like him saying that one word and giving me a stern look would stop Tammy from having cancer.

I met his stern look straight in the eye, unblinking, and he sat down on the foyer bench and started saying it over and over again. "No, no, no. Not my baby sister."

"Can I borrow your cell phone?" I asked. Doing this shit was even worse than I thought it would be. Like, way worse, and I wanted to get it over with.

I found Veronica in his contact list. She also assumed I was joking. "I don't see why my sister thinks your antics are so funny," she said. "You're not funny at all." Her slightly Southern voice had such a declarative authority to it, you'd think she was the queen of something.

Again, I explained that I wasn't joking. I would be offended that so many people thought I could joke about something like this, but the truth was, I probably could have if it weren't happening to Tammy. I remembered, particularly back in January 2011, wishing out loud to Sharita that David Gall would get butt cancer and die sucking Ipso! Facto!'s collective dick.

That image was not so funny now.

I ended up driving James back to Tammy's place myself, and we found Veronica waiting for us inside Tammy's apartment.

She was bigger than I remember, not big like Sharita, but not skinny like me. But then I remembered that she had a kid about a year ago. She had hips now, and her cheekbones didn't look like they could slice through concrete anymore. It made her look more like Tammy. But then I had to correct myself. She looked like Tammy used to look. Before the cancer.

"She's not here," Veronica said when we came in. She looked like she was holding herself back from taking a gun out of her Chanel purse and shooting my ass dead. I, in fact, hoped she didn't have a gun in her purse.

"Did you look in the bedroom?" I asked.

"Yes, of course, and she wasn't in there either."

Oh, Tammy . . .

I led them back to her bedroom and threw open the walk-in closet's door. No Tammy.

I turned on the closet light. Still no Tammy. But then I spotted a toe sticking out from a row of evening gowns. Ironically, it was the foot with the full five toes that gave her away.

Whoever had said that all people want to die with their dignity intact had obviously never met Tammy.

"Come out, Tammy," I said. "I told them. Like you should have done a long time ago."

She didn't move, the evening gowns didn't so much as rustle. "Come on, Tammy," I said.

Still no movement, and I had to grab her by the foot and full-on drag her emaciated ass out from behind the evening gowns.

She shook her head furiously and put her finger to her mouth, both a demand and a plea. But I did what I had to do, dragging her out, even though she was silently screaming at me to stop.

However, at the end of the day Tammy was someone who has been raised to put her best face forward at all times. And she became all smiles for her brother and sister when I pulled her stumbling out of the closet.

"Hey, you two! Long time no see," she said with a cheery wave. "I don't know what Risa told you, but it's not true. It's just a flu and she was worried about me, and so she ended up worrying you needlessly. She's so silly."

Tammy laughed. Nobody else did. Maybe if her hair wasn't so short and thin and standing up on her head, maybe if she wasn't so gaunt, or maybe if her voice wasn't so obviously a bad, raspy simulation of her old one, they might have believed her even for a second.

But as it was, Veronica stared at her for about four long, horrified beats, before she broke down crying. "Oh, my God," she said. "Oh, my God."

James came over to Tammy and drew her into his arms. "Baby sister," he said.

I had read about the stages of grief for cancer patients in a pamphlet when I had taken Tammy to get chemo that first time: Denial, Anger, Bargaining, Depression, and Acceptance.

I had thought Tammy had gotten stuck in Depression, but now I could see that she'd been in Denial this whole time, because right before my eyes she went through three stages.

First she pushed James away and said to Veronica, "No, don't cry. You don't get to cry. You have a husband and a daughter, and I don't have anything but this cancer eating me up. Why are you crying when you're the one with everything? Stop crying."

Veronica was so surprised that she actually stopped crying. Her younger sister, I realized, had probably never spoken to her this way.

But then Tammy reversed on herself and said to them both, "I'm sorry I didn't tell you. At first I thought maybe I'd beat it. But then the doctors said it was terminal and I didn't know how to break it to you. Maybe I thought if I didn't tell you, I wouldn't have it. But maybe we can still fight this. Maybe I can make it another year. I'll try more chemo. I'll . . ."

But then her eyes shuttered on that small spark of fighting spirit. "Okay, no, I'm not going to fight. Why bother? It's terminal. I didn't get there in time. Maybe if I had gotten it checked out a few months earlier, but now I'm dying. Okay, I just am. I'm sorry if that upsets you, but I don't have the energy to fight with you about this. I just . . . don't. I'm so tired."

Then she crawled back into her bed and refused to leave it again.

This happened over a month ago. Since then, the Farrell family had called in all sorts of doctors, who all told them the same things: Yes, it was terminal. On television shows, there was always an experimental drug or radical course of treatment, but no, none of these were available for an African-American stage IV melanoma patient, not even a rich one. The cancer was too widespread for them to do anything but make her comfortable, which was what Tammy had already been doing before she went crazy and fired her nurse.

But the drugs couldn't take away all of the symptoms. Eventually, Tammy had to be given an oxygen mask to assist her with what was supposed to be the basic bodily function of breathing. She started sleeping less and less, because the drugs often wore off in odd increments of time and the pain woke her up. A hospital bed was ordered. Two full-time nurses were retained. I moved back into the condo.

Ever since Tammy broke up with me that first time, I had dreamed of being invited to move back into her condo. Literally, I'd had this dream and then woken up sad because it turned out to be wishful thinking with pictures. I had imagined that one day she would see me in a new light, deem me worthy of her, and apologize profusely for how she'd treated me. But when I moved back in, the Tammy of my dreams was gone. The woman who used to greet everyone with a big smile and sunny laugh was now barely talking to me or anyone else. Davie came by several times and did her best to bring Tammy out of her fugue. But Tammy's formerly generous reserve of optimism and goodwill had run dry.

I ended up having to take over her old role, coming into her room every morning and throwing open her windows and singing, "Wake up! Wake up!" like I was fucking Mary Poppins. I read to her from books that would have made me gag before but that seemed apropos now: *The Five People You Meet In Heaven, Love Song, Little Women* . . . sentimental shit like that.

In a last ditch attempt to bring back the Tammy I knew, I got her a boxed set of Disney cartoons. I planned a festival around watching all of the Disney princess movies in their entirety, from *Snow White* to *Tangled*. This took *forever*. A whole week, because Tammy kept on falling asleep. Moreover, it didn't work. The images flickered across her eyes, but nothing registered.

I told her that I loved her, whenever the two of us were alone. When the nurses were on break and there was no family visiting. These moments only happened once or twice a day, but I took advantage of them. "I love you," I reminded her.

She didn't answer.

But I persevered, because what else was I supposed to do? I had no career left. Gravestone had left me several angry messages culminating with a legal document that informed me I had been dropped from the label—just in case I was wondering if they'd take me back.

I went on ahead and gave up the lease on my apartment. I'd pretty much decided that after Tammy was gone, I would be leaving L.A. I was going to take what little money I had left from my deal and go to Merida, an artist community in Mexico. Merida was cheap as hell with a ton of expats who wouldn't mind that despite being raised in California, I didn't speak Spanish. I'd never been there, but I'd seen it on an episode of *House Hunters International.*

I had about thirty thousand dollars in the bank. My parents and my sister no longer spoke to me. And the only girl I'd ever truly loved was about to die. I'd never been so free. And I didn't want to rush Tammy into death or anything, but I was almost looking forward to life after her. I could already see myself in my little Mexican apartment, busking for extra dough wherever the rich American tourists went the most. Not changing my hairstyle every six months to stay relevant. Eating whatever I wanted. Growing old and not caring.

It was going to be awesome. I was going to be awesome. After Tammy.

But then May second came around and I woke up to the sound of Tammy arguing with Veronica. Now this was strange, because Tammy hadn't argued with anybody since the whole thirty seconds that she spent in the Anger stage back in April.

"What's going on?" I said when I came into her bedroom.

Veronica, who was standing over Tammy's bed, turned and glared at me. "I don't know what your game is, or how you convinced her to leave you all of her money. But I will fight you tooth and nail before I let you take advantage of my sister."

"What?" I asked.

Tammy took off her oxygen mask to wheeze out, "She's not taking advantage of me. I'm giving her the condo and the money to pay her back, because I've been taking advantage of her."

I froze. "Tammy, no, you don't have to leave me anything. It's okay."

Veronica totally cosigned on this. "Yes, there's nothing that she could have possibly done that would make her deserving of twenty million dollars. Listen to me, Tammy."

Tammy took the mask off again. "I want her to have it. All of it."

Veronica smoothed a hand over her sister's shorn hair. "Tammy, you're not thinking straight. The drugs, the cancer, they have you addled. I'm going to speak to our family lawyer tomorrow about giving me power of attorney."

Tammy took several inhalations from the mask before taking it off and saying, "Ronnie, I'm gay. Risa has been my girlfriend off and on for the last ten years. And the only reason—"

"You're not gay," Veronica said, cutting her off. "Risa's gay, but you're not. You're just friends."

"I'm gay, Ronnie. And the only reason Risa and I ever broke up was that I was too chicken to tell you. I wasted my life trying to be who you and Mama and the world wanted me to be. That's why I couldn't tell people about the cancer, because I didn't want anybody to see me like this, not even my family. I wasted so much time worrying about what other people thought."

Tammy had to stop because she'd run out of breath. She put the oxygen mask back on.

"No, you're confused. I know I kissed a girl once or twice in college myself. But I'm not going to let you throw away your entire fortune on some woman who has obviously been taking advantage of you if she's convinced you to will her everything you have."

Wow, Veronica sounded so sure of her negative assessment of me, I had to wonder if I was just imagining I'd been in love with Tammy this whole time.

But Tammy ripped the oxygen mask from her face and said, "Listen to me: I have let you boss me around all my life, Ronnie. All my life. But she is not 'some woman.' She is the love of my life. And she will get every fucking dime of my money, and if you don't let it happen, I will haunt you from my grave and make your life miserable. I swear to God, Veronica."

Having wheezed that, she put the oxygen mask back on and stared at Veronica angrily, sealing the threat.

Veronica was the first to break their glare-off. "I . . ."

She looked at me. "I . . ."

She looked back at Tammy. "I . . . fine. Whatever you say." Then she grabbed her Chanel purse and clicked out of the room in her stiletto heels. A few moments later we heard the condo's front door slam.

"Seriously," I said after Veronica was gone. "I don't want your money. I don't need it. Just hearing you tell your sister off is enough to sustain me for the rest of my life. I don't need food, water, or shelter. All I need to get by is that moment."

Tammy didn't laugh. Just took off the mask again and said, "You've got to stop smoking."

I nodded. "Yeah, I know. I will one of these days."

"Lisa." She called me by my real name. "Lisa, look at me."

I looked at her.

"You've got to stop smoking."

And though I'd been chain-smoking like a mofo out on the guest room's balcony to get myself through this grim shit, at that moment I somehow knew that I might as well flush the full pack of Parliaments I picked up last night down the toilet, because I was never going to touch a cigarette again.

"I don't want your money," I told her again. This was the truth.

"It's my penance," she said. "It's the only way I know how to make sure that everybody knows how much I really did love you. I'm sorry that it had to be this way for us, Lisa. I know it's all my fault."

I shrugged, the biggest rock star in the room. "Seriously, don't worry about it. I'm all about the forgiveness."

She nodded, and I think she might have been smiling behind her oxygen mask as she closed her eyes. Finally coming out of the closet had been exhausting for her. I let her sleep.

The plan was to call Thursday, because how could I not gossip about something like this? But when Thursday said hello . . . when my best friend, who in this crappy story's biggest twist was now in love with Tammy's ex-pretend-boyfriend, said hello, I found myself unable to talk around the salt rivers flooding out of my eyes and into my mouth.

"Risa," she said. "I'm going to the airport right now and I will book the first flight I find to L.A. I'm coming, okay? I'm coming."

"Okay," I said. "Okay."

About an hour later, Sharita showed up. She said that Thursday called, so she took the rest of the day off from work to come be with me. She held me like my mother used to hold me before I confessed that I was gay. "What's wrong?" she asked.

"She left me all of her money," I answered, sobbing.

And that was when I realized that Tammy hadn't been the only one in denial. In a way, her finally coming out sealed it. She was going to die. The One was going to die and there wasn't a goddamned thing I could do about it.

"Okay, we're going to pray on this," Sharita said.

And I loved Sharita so fucking much, because that was exactly what my mother would have said. I lay my head in her lap and let her pray over me. And I must have fallen asleep, because when I woke up, it was dark and I was alone on the couch.

I stood up and stretched. The apartment smelled like food again, but in a good way. Sharita must have been making something for lunch, or maybe dinner, since it was dark.

My hunch proved true when I went into the kitchen and discovered a pot of black-eyed peas simmering on the stove and a pan of cornbread in the oven. But Sharita was not in the kitchen.

I found her in Tammy's room. She was there with Thursday, who was holding Tammy's hand. Thursday, who had claimed to hate Tammy the last time we talked about her at length.

# EVERYBODY

The truth was more emotional than good breeding would allow. The truth was exhilarating. After years of hiding it, Tammy finally told her sister the truth, then she all but passed out, physically and emotionally spent. The truth, as it turns out, was also exhausting.

She dreamed of her first home in Houston, of large backyards, and afternoon teas, and pretty dresses, and seeing girls other than her sister naked as they changed in her room and then jumped into the pool she was lucky to have. So lucky, that Tammy's mother insisted Tammy throw at least three pool parties the summer before her freshman year of high school, inviting fellow teens from a list carefully pruned and added to by her mother with a blue-ink fountain pen. One of the girls at the first pool party, the daughter of a black Republican judge, who was said to be on the short list for a spot on the Texas Supreme Court, said that she also wanted to try out for the cheerleading team at the private school they were both scheduled to start attending in the fall. Would Tammy like to practice with her? Maybe she could come over, when there wasn't a pool party.

She was almost as light as Tammy, with thick black hair tamed into a tight and neat French braid. They seemed like a good fit for future best friends. Tammy, who had always been a giggler, peppering every sentence with a laugh—much to the consternation of her mother, who didn't believe that young ladies should be so silly—agreed to the judge's daughter coming over the next week. Dressed in tank tops and board shorts, they ran through a list of routines in the rec room, culled from their separate middle school squads.

"You're good, but you have to stop laughing," the judge's daughter told her. "You can smile, but you can't laugh like that."

Tammy covered her mouth, and giggle-proclaimed, "I can't help it."

"Stop," the judge's daughter said, getting closer.

"I can't help it."

"Stop." The judge's daughter was whispering now.

When the judge's daughter removed Tammy's hand and kissed her laughing mouth, it felt inevitable, like something Tammy had been waiting for her whole life without knowing it. She had kissed a few boys before that, chastely, nervously, but this kiss tingled, and this kiss made Tammy want to kiss some more.

She invited the judge's daughter back to practice again. Her mother approved, so much so that she decided to surprise them, bringing the ham salad sandwiches that their cook had made into the rec room herself. Her mother screamed when she saw Tammy and the judge's daughter, and dropped the silver tray. People came running, including Veronica and James, and the cook who made the sandwiches in the first place.

"What happened?" they asked.

Her mother stared down a red-faced Tammy, then said she thought she saw a bug, but it was just a shadow.

The judge's daughter was not invited to the second pool party of the summer. And they didn't end up at the same school. A congressional spot unexpectedly opened up during an odd-numbered year in Mississippi, where Tammy's father could run because the factory for Farrell Fine Hair was located in the district that he was being urged to represent. The family moved to Mississippi. And even though Tammy was no longer a giggler, had not in fact laughed since being discovered by her mother in the rec room, her mother continued to give her the same frosty stare that she used to give her for laughing at inappropriate times. Tammy suffered under this stare for the next three years, all the way until college. The frosty stare didn't relax until she brought Mike home for Christmas in her early twenties, when Tammy realized that if she wanted her mother back, she had to be exactly what her mother raised her to be.

~

Tammy woke up to find Thursday next to her bed, holding her hand. She wanted to tell Thursday why she did what she did. She wanted to explain that she wasn't hiding Risa but hiding herself. She wanted to tell her the truth.

But when she took off the mask, she used the little breath she had to wheeze, "I got a nose job when I was nineteen."

"I don't believe you," Thursday said, not letting go of her hand.

"Really?" Sharita, who Tammy now noticed in the guest chair, said.

"It's very subtle," Tammy said. "I had it done in Europe. I didn't want anyone to know."

"I never would have guessed," Thursday said.

"Me either," Sharita said.

Each word was a piece of pain, delivered with great effort, but Tammy felt she had to go on. "Thursday, I asked to meet you because I was jealous," she said. "Risa talked about you. I thought she was in love with you. I knew there were other girls, but I thought maybe she was secretly in love with you. So I told her that I wanted to have girlfriends, too. I asked to meet you and Sharita, because I was jealous of you. But when I met you, I got it."

"No, she's only ever been in love with you," Thursday said. "It's always been you."

"I know," Tammy said, the now-familiar nausea of regret rising up inside of her. "I was afraid that people wouldn't like me if they knew who I really was. I'm not like you and Risa. I need to be liked." Then Tammy realized, "I *needed* to be liked. I guess it doesn't matter now."

"We like you," Thursday said. "But we would have liked you even more if you'd been introduced to us as Risa's girlfriend. We would have said, 'She's great, Risa. Hold onto her.'"

*Hold onto her.*

Tammy wished for this alternative history, wished for it so hard, she was sure it must be unfolding in some parallel universe where she was with Risa, where she was brave, and not so self-conscious that she'd let a skin cancer go unchecked rather than have a doctor see anything ugly on her body. Where she was still living and living and living for many years more.

As if responding to her longing, Risa appeared at the door.

When Thursday saw Risa standing in the doorway, she gently set aside Tammy's hand and came over to her. They talked on the phone every week, but it had been nine long months since they'd seen each other in person. The longest they'd ever gone without seeing each other, since the day they met. And when they hugged, Risa felt every one of those two hundred and seventy days. Friends could be selfish and frustrating and, let's face it, all kinds of stupid at times. *But thank God I have them*, Risa thought. *Thank God.*

Tammy's coming out marked the beginning of the end. She went downhill fast after that. More doctors were called in, more drugs were administered. More family members showed up, including Tammy's parents, who were still married, but estranged and living in separate states.

"We didn't want to upset them," Veronica said when Risa asked why it took her and James so long to call their parents. "Our mother has been fragile since my father moved out. And we're not close to my father anymore. We didn't want to call them in until we absolutely had to."

The Farrell family, Risa imparted in whispered conversation to Thursday and Sharita, was very strange. Both alluring and off-putting. They tried to control each other, but they also kept their distance from each other. They lived very public lives, but tended to keep to themselves. They were, in a way, just like every other super-rich family, but not so much, because there were very few black families who had as much money as they did. They were, Thursday declared, thinking back to the New Yorker who approached Tammy on New Year's Eve, the black-American equivalent of royalty. And like royalty, they didn't gather everyone around a dying member of their family until that person was formally on their deathbed.

To Risa's surprise, Veronica introduced her to her mother as Tammy's partner. And when Tammy's mother said, "Tammy had a business?" Veronica said, "Partner as in her girlfriend."

Tammy's mother did not accept this. "Well, I don't want to hear about Tammy's business," she said. And then she proceeded to treat Risa as if she didn't exist for the time that she spent in Tammy's condo. Risa, who loved to be controversial but secretly hated actual confrontation, appreciated this.

In the movies, there were always speeches and declarations and people dying with dewy music in the background. In real life, death was noisy and unmelodic. There was lots of standing around and people saying things like, "Is anybody else hungry? Want to order some food?"

There was a lot of crying, but there were also a lot of stories, which Sharita was happy to bear witness to while Risa sat with Tammy and Thursday wrote in one of the back bedrooms. Stories like the time Tammy fell off the cheerleading pyramid, and the time Tammy insisted on dressing up like Sacajawea for a week after Halloween was over, and wasn't that just like Tammy to pretend to be in the Maldives when she was actually dying? Why the Maldives of all places?

Risa, who decided to stay by Tammy's side, lost track of time. As the days ran together, she eventually stopped reading to Tammy and settled for holding her hand. She listened to the machines, which were both administering drugs and monitoring her death. She remained unsure of which ones did which, only that they would do so quietly until Tammy died, at which point they would emit a loud sound to let everybody know that she had left the building.

It seemed to Risa that every day Tammy's sleeping heart rate got slower, the spikes on the monitor indicating that she was still alive getting farther and farther apart. She spent a lot of time watching that machine, and whenever Tammy was awake Risa made sure to say, "I love you," no matter who was in the room. Tammy had a tube down her throat now, so she couldn't talk. But she pointed to herself and then pointed back to Risa, which meant, "I love you, too."

Any day now, the nurses said.

James Farrell pulled Risa aside and thanked her for sticking by his sister. Davie Farrell pulled her aside and assured Risa that she wouldn't let the Farrells come after her or the money that Tammy was willing her.

Tammy's family went home at night and left Risa and the evening nurse in charge, but Thursday and Sharita stayed behind. They came every day to sit with Risa while she sat with Tammy. Sharita made sure that Risa's stomach stayed full and that she always had water in the large cup that Risa kept for herself on the nightstand beside Tammy's hospital bed. When she wasn't writing, Thursday talked with Risa while she watched Tammy, and when Sharita was not running all over mother-henning, she came into Tammy's room and talked with them, too.

Tammy's favorite activity had become lying there quietly, listening to them talk with her eyes closed, while she waited to die.

It was on the last night of Tammy's life that Sharita brought up the one and only class that all three of them took together while at Smith College: Afro-American Studies 100.

"Remember that one South Carolina slave legend we read about?" she asked.

Risa should've forgotten by now, but she remembered it right away. "Miss Missy."

However, Thursday had a more difficult time recalling. "How did that one go?" she asked.

Risa explained: "You know, Miss Missy's a slave, but she's always laughing and it's really weird. She falls in love with this big handsome Mandingo slave, but then the massa's son takes her as his mistress, starts raping her and shit. The Mandingo slave tries to save her, but then the massa's son shoots him dead. And then Miss Missy springs wings, because it turns out she's an angel. She picks him up and flies away to heaven. And the slaves tell everybody, but of course nobody believes them. But in South Carolina they're still like, if your baby laughs a lot, then it's probably an angel in disguise."

"Oh yeah," Thursday said. "I remember now. So do you think it was a mass hallucination or something? Too much tobacco got into their bloodstream?"

Sharita shook her head. "No, I think they really saw it. I mean, what are the chances of them all hallucinating the same thing?"

"Maybe it was the power of suggestion," Thursday says.

"I think they really saw it," Sharita said again. "And I'm bringing it up because Tammy's family says that Tammy used to laugh all the time when she was a kid. They were all saying earlier that she was the laughingest baby they'd ever seen and she kept it up until they moved to Mississippi."

Risa thought about that and turned to Tammy. "How about it, Tammy? Are you an angel in disguise?"

Tammy heard the question but could not answer, occupied as she was with the silent countdown on her life, on the last ten breaths she would ever take. Ten . . . *Risa* . . . nine . . . *I* . . . eight . . . *love* . . . seven . . . *you* . . . six . . . *Risa* . . . five . . . *I'm* . . . four . . . *sorry* . . . three . . . *Risa* . . . two . . . *I'm* . . . one . . . *sorry* . . .

A few minutes later, the machine that signaled one of Tammy's vital organs had failed and that she had stopped breathing let out a loud shrieking sound. The night nurse rushed in and pushed Risa aside. Sharita covered her mouth with her hand and put her arm around Risa's shoulders. And though Thursday did not believe in angels, she also came to stand beside Risa, putting an arm around her waist. They all stared at Tammy.

Waiting to see if she became an angel.

# June 2012

Go on ahead and make a list of all the physical qualities you want in your lifelong mate. It'll give you something to laugh about when you finally find him and he don't look anything like that.

—*The Awesome Girl's Guide to Dating Extraordinary Men* by Davie Farrell

# SHARITA

*E*ver since Tammy died, my own life seemed to be going by at lightning speed. There was making up for all the time I had missed at work. There were my now-daily chats with my sister. There was spending as much time with Ennis as I could squeeze out of my busy schedule. And there was helping Risa move again.

Risa had lasted a whole two days alone in Tammy's condo before she called Thursday and asked to move into Mike Barker's pool house. "I couldn't stay there," she told me while moving all the stuff that couldn't fit in the pool house back into a Silver Lake storage unit. "Too many ghosts, and none of them are Tammy."

Risa insisted it would just be for a couple of weeks, until Tammy's funeral, and then she was planning to go to some place called Merida.

"Where exactly is this place?" I asked.

"It's in Mexico," Risa answered.

"Where in Mexico?"

"In the Yucatan Peninsula," Risa said. "That's in the south."

"So you want to relocate to this place that you've never been to and do what?"

Risa shrugged. "I don't know. Live. Surf a lot."

"Like on permanent vacation?" I asked.

Risa put down the nightstand she was carrying and said, "Don't do that."

"Do what?" I asked.

"Shit all over my dreams," Risa said.

"I'm not trying to discourage you, I'm just asking you some practical questions."

"I know you are, and I'm asking you not to do it, okay?" She picked up the nightstand. "Let's go to the Griddle after this. I always wanted to try their pancakes."

Risa had been to the Griddle Café several times before, but she had never actually eaten there. This was her new thing these days, wanting to go back to every restaurant she had ever not eaten at, now that her taste buds were coming back after quitting smoking.

I both liked and didn't like this new version of Risa. On one hand, it was nice to not feel guilty about my own calorie intake when I ate in front of her. But on the other hand, Risa had become more direct, which was messed up, because before the big Tammy reveal I had already thought Risa had a pretty big mouth. Now it looked like she had been biting her tongue about a lot of things, including not really appreciating any of my sensible advice.

I set down the lamp I had been carrying. "I've been meaning to ask you for a while now. We have nothing in common. You think I'm too bossy, and I know you don't think I'm cool. Why are you even friends with me?"

Risa peered at me over her vintage designer sunglasses. "Really, you don't know?"

I shook my head. "How could I?"

"You," Risa said, pointing at me, "are just like my mother. Only better." She frowned. "Though now I guess I should ask why the hell your prude ass wants to be friends with me?"

I was laughing too hard to answer at first.

"What?" Risa asked.

"You're just like my mom," I said. "Only better."

Risa joined me in laughing. "Well, there you go."

So that took time. And my relationship with Ennis took time. And somehow by the time June 2012 rolled around, I had managed to squeeze in a visit to my sister and baby niece in New York, but I still hadn't found the time to take the vacation that I had vowed to take last October.

As if reading my mind, the night after I helped Risa move into Mike Barker's pool house, Ennis said, "Hey, I've been thinking. We should take a holiday together."

We were preparing for bed, Ennis already under the covers, and I was getting under them myself after tying my hair back in a silk wrap.

"A holiday? You mean like a vacation?"

"Aye, I could use some time on a warm beach with you."

He squeezed me when he said this, rolling the words into my neck.

"Where would we go?" I asked.

"Spain's nice. I've always fancied going there."

All sorts of practical questions piled up in my head, but then I stopped myself. If Ennis had always wanted to go to Spain, why not just go with him?

"Okay," I said. "When? I'll have to get a passport."

"Well, we've a hiatus coming up for the last two weeks of August. You'd have to get your passport expedited."

His answer surprised me so much that I turned over to face him. "Wait, you would be willing to fly during vacation season? That means we're going to have to pay premium."

"I ken what you're saying, and yes, it did give me a moment of pause. But you know, Sharita, sometimes paying premium is practical. For instance, we only get four hiatuses a year. The next one's at Christmas and the one after that isn't until the spring. Christmas prices are even more dear, and besides, I don't want to wait that long to give you this."

He reached into his right sweatpants pocket and pulled out a velvet box, opening it to reveal an understated diamond ring. "According to my American friends, big diamonds are the thing over here, but I didn't want to spend too much, because I could hear ya in the back of ma head saying it'd be better to invest that money in a college fund for our bairns, which is one of the reasons I love you and want you to do me the great honor of becoming ma wife."

I sat up, speechless. We had only been dating for six months. I hadn't expected a proposal so soon—to tell the truth, I hadn't expected a proposal at all. As many times as I had daydreamed about getting married and starting a family, with my dating history it had never even occurred to me to imagine getting proposed to. For a moment I panicked, my mind flashing to the composite of the perfect black husband that I'd had in my head since the age of fourteen.

He would be kind and practical. He would be handsome—but not so handsome that I would have to worry about women offering him their goodies every time he went outdoors. He would have a college degree. He would want children and a family. He would love God.

My dream guy had been fading for quite some time, but right before my eyes he was now starting to dissolve all together, and my heart reached out to him with a mental cry.

But then the Crystal Ball Vision I had been waiting for ever since I met Ennis chose this time to finally appear. I saw myself and Ennis outside a house in Ladera Heights. He was kissing our small son on the forehead and telling him to be a "wee good one" for his Aunt Nicole.

I saw him telling my sister that he would call as soon as the baby came. Then I saw him getting into a Honda minivan, where I was sitting in the passenger seat taking deep breaths with the contractions. "How far apart are we now, sweet girl?"

"Four minutes," I saw myself saying between gritted teeth.

I saw Ennis grinning at me. "Right then, better get a move on," he said, putting the minivan in reverse.

The rest of my life. That's how long this wonderful relationship would last.

And when I looked up from the vision, I found my imaginary black husband gone. And there was Ennis, holding the rest of my life in one velvet ring box.

# RISA

*S*harita called me at ten that night to tell me that Ennis asked her to marry him. A few thoughts ran through my head. Like who would have thought Sharita would be the first one of us to get married? Seriously, I had thought the gays would be given federal clearance to get married legally anywhere they wanted to in the United States before Sharita's doormat ass got a ring.

Out loud, though, I said, "You're going to make me wear a dress, aren't you?"

"You'd look so cute in a dress. I'm thinking something in a deep maroon," she said.

"Why, because it's the most boring color you could think of that would still be appropriate for a summer wedding?"

"Do it for me, Risa," she said, avoiding the question.

"How about a maroon tux?" I ask. "Or better yet, a sleeveless leather maroon blazer with a kilt? How hot would that be? If I wear that, you'll be seeing that shit on the runway next fall."

Being a rock star by nature, every time I came up with a new kind of outfit, I assumed that if anyone else copied that outfit in any sort of way it meant that a designer had seen me and stolen my idea for his or her collection.

I was not surprised when Sharita called me back a few days later to tell me that, on second thought, she and Ennis had decided to do a wedding without any attendants.

"It's going to be real small, just a little party in the backyard of the house Ennis grew up in. And it's already going to be such a hassle getting everybody from my side over to Scotland. We figured we'd just keep it short and sweet with just the two of us and a preacher."

"Fine," I said. "Be boring. But my bridesmaid look would have rocked the earth, son. I'm talking Scotland's first earthquake."

"Okay, I'm going now," Sharita said.

Whatever. I decided to wear the outfit I proposed to the wedding anyway and wondered how long it would take to find a sleeveless maroon leather blazer in the exact wine color that I was imagining. But then I remembered that I was rich now. I didn't have to hunt down a blazer. I could technically walk into a leather store and ask them to order me one special, or commission the whole outfit from one of Thursday's costume designer friends. In fact, if I wanted to mass-produce the look, I could fly to China and secure a factory to make ten thousand maroon leather jackets, tux ties, and kilts for me without going broke. And what?

It kept on hitting me anew, this rich stuff. Tammy's bank accounts had already been transferred into my name. She signed all the paperwork before she died. Her financial planners sent me a statement for the accounts, and it didn't come in a thin white envelope like my bank statements either. They arrived in several packages filled with sheaths and sheaths of papers for different accounts. Sharita has promised to help me sort through it all, but I'd already figured out that it all came down to one big "I'm rich, bitch!"

And that was going to take some getting used to because, technically, I could do whatever I wanted from now on. I could still go live in Mexico. Or I could go live in Europe or some magical paradise where lesbians were A-OK with the natives as long as their money was green. I was no longer bound to music as a life calling. Tammy was gone. My record deal was gone. I was finally free.

I thought about that for a while, and then I got on my Harley. I found what I was looking for in the back of my Silver Lake storage unit inside a dusty black case. I opened the case and there was my scratched-up acoustic guitar, exactly as I had left it when I switched to the electric guitar all those years ago. "Alrighty then," I said, like they used to say in the nineties, when people were still innocent enough to fall in love with catchphrases.

I picked it up, sat down on my old couch and start playing. "Tammy."

I didn't know that the song was called "Tammy" when I was playing it, or that the words coming out of my mouth were her eulogy. I wasn't even fully aware that time was passing, until I looked up and saw a security guard standing in the open entrance.

I stopped playing.

"You're not supposed to be in here too long. I'm supposed to kick you out if you're in here over three hours and not moving nothing."

I stood and started making moves to go, slinging the guitar onto my back like I used to in college, and closing up the case that it came in. I'd have to ask Thursday to come back with me for the case, but I'd risk the motorcycle ride home with the guitar on my back. Now that we'd been re-united, I was never going to let go of this beat-up guitar again.

"What's the name of that song you were playing?" the guard asked.

"It's called 'Tammy,'" I said, realizing the name of the song as it came off my lips.

"I liked it. Can I buy it on iTunes?"

I paused. Because I was supposed to move to Merida after Tammy's funeral, which would be the next day. Because I was supposed to have taken up surfing again by this time next week. Because I had no plans to be a rock star anymore. Because even if I did, I no longer had a record label to call home.

But mostly I paused because of something I had read in an exhaustive *Vanity Fair* article with the lead singer from an English rock band that was still touring even though its members were all over fifty and, by music industry laws, shouldn't even be relevant anymore.

"If you want to remain, you've got to pay attention to the common people," the lead singer of this band had said. "Who cares what rock critics think? If I was playing a song in a studio, and the janitor who's fresh off the boat from Africa comes through and said, 'Hey mate, I love that song, Where can I buy it? I want to hear it again'—well, that's how I know I've got my next Top 40 hit. People with shite jobs don't go out of their way to compliment the rich. So pay attention when they do."

I paused and I tried to memorize this security guard's face. He was Latino, maybe. Older, with a snub nose, crew cut, and a serious gut. I noted all of this, because I'd want to remember what he looked like when I told the story of how I meant to leave rock and roll, but decided not to because some random security guard complimented me on the first song that I ever wrote for my dead girlfriend.

Then I said, "I'm not sure when my debut album will hit iTunes, but keep on checking under the name Risa Merriweather."

# July 2012

I say this because I think a few of you need to hear it. Breakups happen, every day, for reasons much less dramatic than what you read in novels or see on TV. If this is the case with you, if it didn't work out—listen, it wasn't all your fault. But it wasn't all his, either. Learn from it and then let it go. Trust me when I tell you that you're both better off without each other.

—*The Awesome Girl's Guide to Dating Extraordinary Men* by Davie Farrell

# THURSDAY

*A*t Tammy's funeral, Risa sang a song so crazy beautiful even Tammy's ice queen of a mother, who did not in any way approve of Tammy and Risa's relationship, actually sniffled.

Risa spent exactly forty minutes at the after-party, accepting condolences and receiving compliments on the song, before she went back into Mike's pool house. Then she didn't come out again until late June, at which point she booked some time at a studio and a week later emerged from it with a demo that she sent straight to a few execs she had met from Gravestone's parent company, Jam Rock Records, with a note explaining what had inspired it and that they'd need to take it as is, with no changes.

Jam Rock offered her a very modest deal, with even less upfront than her original deal with Gravestone. Considering that she had made less with Gravestone than she had as the guitarist for the Sweet Janes, this was definitely a step down, and might have made me mad if I were Risa.

But Risa just shrugged. "That's okay, the album'll go big, and I'll make those bitches pay out the ass for the next one, which won't even be half as good. And even if it doesn't work out, I don't care, as long as I never, ever have to take another fucking note from David Fucking Gall."

But I had the feeling this wouldn't be an issue. The rest of the album was very good but, really, all she needed was "Tammy." That song would be going places, I could already tell. When I had heard it at the funeral, tears came to my eyes and I decided to visit my father in Hawaii for Christmas. Just like that, Brenda or no Brenda. I forgave him for everything right then and there, because it was that kind of song. The kind of song that could change your life. How could a song like that not find an audience?

"Do you think your pool house is magical?" I asked Mike over breakfast in early July. This was the day after Risa moved out, into a ramshackle house in Silver Lake right above the main drag of Sunset Junction.

"I'm beginning to," he answered.

I asked that not just because of Risa's record deal, but because of what had happened to me after I started using the pool house as an office.

In New Orleans I had mentioned to Mike that I had written something a little offbeat, "Like *Six Feet Under,* but funny and with black people."

"Send it to me," he said. "I want to read it."

So I sent it to him, and he read it in his trailer the next day and he texted me, "This is really good, baby."

Then a couple of days later he texted, "Diana likes it, too. She wants to shop it."

Diana was the executive in charge of Big Dog Barks, Mike's production company. So I spent the next few days e-mailing back and forth with her assistant, while we put together a treatment. Diana took it around and by June, Big Dog Barks made a deal with a fledgling cable channel that was known for its reruns but had ordered six pilots for two new original series slots, including *Down Home,* which was what we had decided to name my series. Diana had attached a burnt-out show runner who knew all the ropes of running a writing staff but didn't have much interest in the creative, and just like that, starting in September, after Sharita's wedding, we would be developing a pilot.

I was still a little stunned. It had all happened so fast. One day I was a starving artist, and the next day I was not. Which is why I asked Mike if he thought the pool house was lucky.

After the pool house conversation, Mrs. Murphy came in with the mail, most of which was for Mike.

"But this is for you," she said, handing me a card-sized envelope.

"It's an invite for Sharita's wedding," I said, opening the heavy linen envelope. "Do you want to come with me?" I asked Mike.

"Let me look at my schedule," he answered.

However, later that night he said the words that would send our boyfriendom-girlfriendom into a death spiral. We were swimming naked in his pool, not because he wanted to gamble, but because skinny-dipping might be one of the best forms of foreplay there is. And Mike who, before taking up with me had dated a stream of wannabe actresses with weaves they couldn't get wet, very much liked this form of foreplay. In fact we were playing an increasingly heated game of water tag when he had to go and ruin it all by saying, "We should think about doing like Sharita and Ennis one of these days."

"Doing what like Sharita and Benny?" I asked, more concerned with holding on to my now-joking mispronunciation of Ennis's name than the words coming out of his mouth.

"Get married," he said.

I laughed because I didn't think he was being serious. Then I stopped laughing when the look on his face told me that this had not been a joke.

"What's so funny about getting married?" He circled me in the water. Like a shark.

"I thought you were always like, 'I'm never going to get married,'" I said.

"I never said that."

"Yeah, you did. You were like, 'I'm just going to date cocktail waitresses and models forever. Yay, me.'"

"I think you're talking about George Clooney." An impatient, pursed-lip look came over his face. Like he was talking to a child. A really dim child. "You know I'm not that guy anymore. I don't gamble. I don't date women just because they're cute. I don't agree to stupid bets or sign non-disclosure agreements with rich gay heiresses. That's all in the past, because I've worked hard to turn my life around. You get that, right?"

I stopped treading water and let my feet settle at the bottom of the pool. Our sexy game of tag seemed to be over now.

"What exactly do you think we're doing here?" he asked.

I struggled to find an appropriate answer. "I don't know. Having fun."

Now he went still in the pool. "Ask me how many girls I've invited to live with me. Ask me how many girls I produced projects with. Ask me how many girls I've said 'I love you' to."

"Technically, I'm not a girl. I'm a woman," I said, because, you know, Smith.

"Ask me," he said, his voice dipping into growling territory. "And I'll tell you that the answer is zero. So maybe you're having fun, but I'm very serious about this. I want to get this pilot together and I want us to get married. That's what Mike Barker wants. We love each other. We're passionate about the same things, and the sex is great. What else do we need?"

I folded my arms. "You know who else loved each other, and were passionate about the same things, and probably had great sex in the beginning? My parents."

The night air, which had just felt a little brisk when we came down to swim, dropped into freezing territory. "We're not your parents," he said.

And my mom whispered, "*Don't be pathetic! Don't be pathetic! Don't be pathetic!*"

"Before I met you I was so fucked up. I couldn't get my life together. I went through guys like paper towels. I wasn't writing. I was crazy depressed. Since meeting you, though, everything's changed. I really like myself now. I like the person I am in this situation right now. But I don't want to end up like my mom, afraid to leave somebody who obviously doesn't love or respect me anymore."

"Thursday, I love you."

"I know you do now, and I love you, too, but—" I didn't know how to explain this to him so that he'd stop trying to turn this into a Hallmark movie where everyone simply overcomes serious emotional baggage with declarations of love. "Doesn't it bother you that we're not Davie-approved? She wrote a best-selling book of dating advice, and she helped you recover from a gambling addiction, but according to her book, we aren't a long-term match." I ticked it off on my fingers. "First of all, we had a tumultuous first six months. Second of all, we didn't meet in the summer. Third of all, you keep referring to yourself in the third person—that wasn't in the book, but it totally should have been—and fourth of all, we're complete opposites. That doesn't give you a moment of pause?"

Mike leaned backwards in the water, letting his feet float in front of him. "You really think we're opposites?"

I splashed and looked around his saltwater infinity pool, which fell off into a fantastic view of eastern Los Angeles. "Yeah, don't you?"

He splashed back. "Let's see . . . we've both dated a lot of other people before each other. You write the kind of roles I want to play. And we both have mothers who abandoned us."

I was so shocked that he would play that last card that he might as well have Tasered me. I mean, yeah, both of our mothers had grown up in the projects—mine in New York and his in Pittsburgh. But that's where the similarities ended. While mine had gotten out and made a life for herself with Rick T, Mike's had remained, gotten knocked up, and eventually succumbed to a crack addiction so bad that Mike had pretty much had to raise himself, supporting both of them as a drug dealer from middle school through high school, until he had somehow managed to get into Amherst on a full scholarship and leave Pittsburgh behind.

And yeah, both our mothers had died while we were in college, his from a drug overdose, mine from a car accident, but . . .

"My mom didn't abandon me," I said.

He regarded me with the same disappointed look he'd tried to pin on me when I was moving out back in December. "You know that's not true, right? She killed herself."

"Yeah, but . . ." I found myself without a good argument, and any remaining sensuality I might have still been feeling toward Mike evaporated in a blink. "My father—"

"Your father wasn't great, no, but you can't put all the blame on him. The drugs didn't kill my mom. She killed herself using them. And so did your mom. They abandoned us and they're dead now."

I finally broke down and told him the truth. "Mike, when I look at you, when I think too hard about how much I love you, it makes me feel like I'm driving off a cliff."

He gave me a sad smile. "Yeah, I get that. I've never done crack, but it feels like I'm carrying a crack addict around inside of me. But it's time to start giving ourselves some credit. We're not them. I recovered from my gambling addiction, and when you got hurt, you didn't jump over that railing. We both overcame and we found each other. That's what we have in common, that's why we should be together."

*"Don't be pathetic! Don't be pathetic!"* My mother was getting louder.

I stood there, refusing to let the infinity current or Mike sway me. "So you think that, as opposed to trying to find normal people without gambling addictions or suicidal tendencies, we should settle for each other because we're both really fucked up?"

Mike slapped the pool with an angry swipe of his hand. "You know what? I'm not going to lie. At first I thought it was kind of sexy that you didn't care who I was and were willing to walk away from me at the drop of a dime. You've been good for me, a challenge that I needed in my life. But it's a thin line between challenge and toxic, and if you can't figure out how to love me the way I love you, I'm going to have to let you go."

The way he loved me? What did he know about love? What did either of us really know about love? Anger rose up like a steam cloud inside of me. "Why are you trying to ruin this? We are so happy right now. You've got two productions in development. I'm writing for a living. We are both the best versions of ourselves that we have ever been. Why can't you leave it be instead of setting us up to fail earlier than we have to?"

Suddenly he was in front of me, my head cupped in his wet hands. "I promise you, I'm not like your mother. I won't leave you."

"See, you're not letting me talk. I'm not scared that you're like my mother. I'm scared that I'll become like my mother—"

"You're scared that I'm like your mother and that I'll leave you. I know, because I'm scared of the exact same thing."

The conversation had become too much. And after dropping a bomb like that, there wasn't much left to do but listen to the lapping sounds of the infinity pool.

If this were any other relationship, I would have dumped him right then and there. For presuming too much. For trying to psychoanalyze me. For believing that he could demand anything of me. If Caleb had pulled this mess eight months into our relationship, I would have tucked away my recurring farmers market dream and moved out, job or no job.

But I couldn't bring myself to dump Mike, and I realized at that moment that my list of reasons for not dating black men had been complete and utter bullshit. The real reason I hadn't dated black men before Mike, the only reason I hadn't dated them, was because I didn't want to be a black woman in love with a black man.

*"Don't be pathetic! Don't be pathetic!"* my mother chanted.

Black love wasn't sweet. It was humiliating and almost impossible for a black woman to disentangle herself from without serious loss of both pride and worth. And if a black woman married a black man? It was over. He could do anything he wanted. Cheat on her, disrespect her, impoverish her, and she still wouldn't leave him. Like my mother, she'd walk out on life before she ever walked out on her man.

Despite my Connecticut cadence, my liberated sexual attitudes, and my dating history, I was, at the end of this argument, a black woman. And black women, I figured out while in literal deep waters, weren't good at being in healthy love—especially when it came to black men. In fact, it made us pathetic.

I couldn't explain this to Mike—Mike who not only hadn't been to a farmers market during the current century, but had an assistant to do all of his shopping for him, and a team in place to make sure that he got exactly what he deserved out of every project, and a girlfriend who loved him too much to marry him.

*The rev of the engine, the crash through the divider, the quiet as we hung in the air.*

"Okay," Mike said after we had stood there quiet for too long. "You need some time to think about this. It's a little early, I know. But I'm going to ask you again someday. And if your answer's still no, then we're going to have to break up."

He swam away and got out of the pool. And when I joined him in bed over an hour later, he pulled me in for a long kiss, picking up where we had left off before the argument. True to his word, he didn't bring it up again. But he didn't have to. It hung over us now, lurked in every corner of the house.

And it was only a matter of time before that unspoken proposal tore the two of us apart.

# August 2012

I'll leave you with this. Love is a big decision. Take it seriously. However, the only thing more important than love is like. Think about that while you're dating. Do you like this guy? Like being around him? Like him as a person? Love is a decision, but like is completely natural, and at the end of the day, like is way more important than love. Remember that.

—*The Awesome Girl's Guide to Dating Extraordinary Men* by Davie Farrell

# SHARITA

There was a lot that Ennis and me didn't have in common. We were from two different countries, two different races, and two different backgrounds.

But then again, I thought as I walked toward the baggage claim in the smaller-than-I'd-expected Edinburgh Airport, there was a lot that we did have in common. We were both thrifty. We both suffered artistic sisters. His was a painter, living in London, because according to Ennis, "It's the most expensive place on earth, so of course my daft sister insists it's the only place she can live." Also, he had warned me that his mother might get a little handsy with the male guests or embarrass him in some other way at the wedding. "When she's got a few pints in her, there's no telling what she'll be doing." I had appreciated this quality in his mother because my own mother had a bad reputation for turning into the worst loudmouth at open-bar weddings.

Ennis had called the night before to tell me that he wouldn't be able to meet my plane. "Ma mum's insisting that we do the flowers and cake up right, and the morning your plane comes in is the only time I've left to meet with anyone else."

"I should have taken off work and come out to help you." I'd had a bunch of quarterly taxes to file for creative clients and hadn't come over with Ennis because I wanted to get as much work done as possible, so that I could really enjoy my first vacation in years.

"No, don't worry about it, love. They want me to look at a few pictures of some pretty flowers and taste a little cake. Trust me, there's nothing to it. I'm sorry I can't meet you. I'll be sending my best mate, Dale, round to meet your plane and he'll drive you in, if that's okay. I'll be done by the time you get here and ready to give you a big fat snog."

"Snog" might mean "kiss." At least that's what I hoped it meant.

I didn't realize until I encountered a group of people waiting near the baggage claim area that I hadn't thought to ask Ennis what Dale looked like. But to my relief, a husky redhead waved me down. "Look at this crush, will you? You must be Sharita."

I would have asked how he knew, but then, looking around, I could see I was the only black woman in the entire baggage claim area. "Hi," I said. "Thanks for coming to pick me up."

"Oh, no problem at all. Let's just get your luggage sorted out, and we'll be on our way."

Nestled into the passenger seat of Dale's black four-door car, I took in the gorgeous scenery while we drove to Ennis's childhood home, which, according to Dale, was just twenty kilometers outside of Edinburgh. Scotland, I was surprised to find, looked an awful lot like my image of Ireland, with greener-than-green grass in every direction I looked.

For the most part, Dale hummed along with English pop hits on the radio, but occasionally he'd point out a landmark. He seemed especially fond of castles, pointing to the stone ruins of one at the side of the road and saying, "That's a fixer-upper, innit? Ennis would have his work cut out for him with that one."

A few miles later he pointed toward a castle nestled high on a hilltop. "That's our main competition. They've got a few more rooms than us, and a full-on golf course."

"Oh, do you work in one of those castle hotels?" I asked.

Dale let out a big and hearty laugh. "Well, I try not to work myself too hard if old Ennis's not looking."

I found myself even more confused, but I didn't ask. The Scottish, I had found, had kind of strange senses of humor. Ennis was forever cracking these jokes and he'd have to take a long time explaining them to me, but I still wouldn't get why they would be considered funny in the first place. Nine times out of ten it ended up being a quote from some British sitcom I'd never heard of. Ennis quoted from one called *Father Ted* a lot. It had gotten so bad he made me promise to watch DVDs of it on our honeymoon so that I could start getting his jokes.

"It bothers me that you only laugh at what I say when I'm not intending to be funny." I had, of course, laughed when he said that and was met with an accusatory, "See what I mean!"

So I let Dale's confusing joke go, but then he turned down a narrow, woods-lined gravel road and pulled up in front of yet another castle.

"What's going on?" I asked when he came around and opened my door for me.

"Well, I'm going to take your suitcase up to your room, and you're meant to meet up with Ennis round back, but first you'll have to get yourself unbuckled."

"Unbuckled?" I repeated. "But I thought we were supposed to meet Ennis at his childhood home."

"Castle Craigh is his childhood home, now come out with you. I've got this suitcase and some other work to tend to."

I got out of the car. But I looked back at Dale several times as I approached the jaw-droppingly beautiful castle. And yes it was a real castle-castle, one that dated back to the fifteenth century, according to a plaque outside the large red wooden doors that led inside.

But once I got inside, I found what looked like a hotel, complete with two smiling front-desk clerks.

"You must be Mr. Craigh's fiancée," one of them said with a bright smile. "He's waiting for you out back. Just follow the runner here until you reach the back doors."

In a confused daze, I followed her instructions. At the airport, I had thought maybe Ennis and me had a lot of stuff in common, but now I was beginning to see I'd been wrong.

For example, when I thought of a backyard, I imagined a house with a big enough backyard to host a wedding. But when I came out the back entrance to Castle Craigh, I discovered that Ennis's version of a backyard looked like a postcard come to life, with acres of green grass broken up by English gardens and a pond. The whole scene was overlooked by a large gazebo, where Ennis was waiting, looking sheepish as all get out.

"Here's where we'll be doing the wedding," Ennis said as I walked up to him. "Or there's a sycamore tree over yonder. That might be nice, too."

He pointed in the direction of the tree, but I kept my eyes on him. "So you're, like, rich?" I asked, still not believing what all I was seeing.

Ennis came down the gazebo steps. "Not rich, no."

According to Ennis, his family wasn't rich. But his ancestors had been, and despite a few rough patches in their fortunes, the family had managed to hold on to the castle, with his mother converting their home into a bed-and-breakfast when Ennis was a little boy.

"Why did you think we were able to put your family and friends up for the weekend?" he asked, as if it were my fault for not figuring out that he lived in an actual castle sooner.

I shook my head. "I thought maybe you guys lived in a big house—not a castle. And, um, how did this not come up in any of the many long conversations we had before I flew out here? And isn't August, like, prime time for the wedding season? Did you have to kick a paying customer off our date?"

Ennis blushed and sat down on the gazebo stairs. "I might not have mentioned the castle because money became a rather large issue between Abigail and myself. She came home with me one summer, and once she saw all of this she didn't understand why I didn't want to live a more flash life. We were broken up less than a year later. I didn't want the money issue to come between us, so I didn't bring up my castle."

"Your castle?" I said.

"Yeah, ma mum formally handed it over to my sister and myself ten years ago. My sister wasn't interested in taking it over, kept pressuring me to sell it, so I scraped together some investment capital, bought her out. My mate, Dale, did his degree in marketing but didn't want to move to London or Dublin, where all the good marketing jobs were at the time, so he agreed to help me pretty up the grounds along with a small crew of men for free room and board. It took us a whole year to get it where we wanted it. And then Dale asked a few of his uni mates who had moved to London for some favors, and we got a couple of big names to marry here, and that was it. Within six years, we were a solid wedding operation, and the whole thing could be run without me. So I moved to Los Angeles. I never did love the Scottish winters, and I liked the idea of starting over with a different career of my own choosing."

I sat down next to him. "So let me get this straight. You're not rich, but you have enough money to do whatever you want for the rest of your life?"

"Sharita, I might have a few pounds in the bank, but I don't want to spend them on frippery. I see no reason to eat out at expensive restaurants every night or pay premium rents or go through money, like ma mum did, because we had it to spend. She nearly ran this place into the ground, and I would prefer to keep my money working for me as opposed to spending it on expensive weddings and a house larger than what we and two or three bairns would need."

He cast his eyes downward. "But I also didn't want to lie to you about my background, so I broke it to you this way. I'll understand if it changes your feelings about me. I think I'm practical, but Abigail thought me rather tight, so I'm giving you the chance to back out now if you'd rather a more flash husband."

He waited for my answer, but I just sat there, my own eyes cast downward as well.

"Do you mind telling me which way you're leaning?"

I spoke slowly. "Right now I'm thinking about grabbing my wallet and walking to the nearest town."

"This is my fault for not telling you sooner. I meant to, but things were going so well, and then it seemed like I had been keeping it from you for too long." Ennis looked like the saddest man on earth when he said, "But no need to walk. I can drive you, if it's a car to the airport you're wanting."

"Yeah, you're right, this is your fault," I said. "If it wasn't for you, I wouldn't want to go into town, find a stationery store, and start sending out thank-you notes to all my ex-boyfriends."

Ennis looked up from his feet, confused. "I don't ken your meaning."

"I'm so happy right now," I said, "that all I want to do is thank all the guys that were wrong for me. I am so grateful that none of them worked out, because they all led me to you. Does that make any sense?"

Ennis smiled, and it was a glorious thing to behold against the drab and gray Scottish sky. "I myself am mighty grateful to Abigail for dumping me. I never imagined I'd find a woman as tight with her money as myself, and I had a good feeling about us from the beginning. But I think writing your exes thank-you notes would be rubbing their faces in it. Not verrae mannerly."

I smiled back. "Yeah, I guess it wouldn't be. Thanks for keeping me grounded."

"Thanks for agreeing to be ma wife. You've made me the happiest man on earth."

"I feel bad for the couple we kicked out of our wedding date at such short notice."

He looped an arm around my shoulders. "Ah, no need to feel badly for them. I booked the date at the beginning of the year, on January second, actually."

I pulled away from him. "You set aside our wedding date the day after our first date?"

He shrugged. "You really do have to book these things early, don't you? All the spots get taken up and it's not good for a business if we start kicking customers off their dates, so I had to move quickly." He pulled me closer. "And like I said, I had a good feeling about us." He kissed me once, twice, then said, "A verrae good feeling."

# RISA

Sharita was fucking right yet again. I never did move to Merida. I was back in Silver Lake now, in a big two-story house with views of the Hollywood sign and a large two-car garage that I was having converted into a studio. If I weren't a rock star, it would be way too big for just me. But I am a rock star, and there is no such thing as way too big in the rock-star mentality.

I thought I had poured my heart out on the guitar-driven record that Jam Rock would be releasing before the end of the year, but apparently I had even more to say. I spent a lot of time on top of my roof, strumming my guitar and writing down lyrics as I thought of them.

I grazed all day on things I liked: olives, cheese, bread, hummus, and salami. I hadn't touched a cigarette since Tammy asked me to stop smoking. I often found myself watching DVR recordings of *Yo Gabba Gabba!* at four a.m.

I'd gained fifteen pounds, and despite the dull ache in my heart, I'd never been happier. Sometimes I even thought that I might be able to love somebody again. Maybe ten years from now, maybe ten months, maybe ten days, maybe ten hours. I didn't know. I was playing it by ear.

The day of the wedding came faster than expected. This was my first time traveling outside of North America. I had always imagined that my first time would be on tour as a rock star. And I was a little disappointed, but ah, well . . . there was always next lifetime. The next time I'd do this life shit right, I decided. I'd pick up a guitar even earlier, I'd marry the reincarnation of Tammy, because gay marriage would be legal by then, and I'd travel the earth with her by my side. Next lifetime.

As it turned out, Ennis was, like, a rich Scottish lord or something or other, and I'd be staying in his family's castle. Okay.

Thursday met me outside the hotel's graveled entrance and hugged me while a bellhop took my bags upstairs.

"Can you believe this?" she asked.

"No, I can fucking not," I said because, really, who fucking could? "Where's Mike?"

"He got called in for some pick-ups at the last minute," Thursday said. "So it's just us."

I was glad she didn't bring a date, because for the next two days it was like we were in college again. Nicole, her husband, Graham, and Sharita's niece did the whole tourist thing with Sharita's mom, while the three of us did a bunch of leisure stuff, like getting massages and having long meals in the castle's restaurant.

But mostly we talked about everything from politics to Tammy's death to Thursday's issues with not wanting to marry Mike.

"I mean, all I hear about are celebrities cheating on their wives, and falling off the addiction wagon," Thursday said. "Why would I want to sign up for that?"

She had a point, but Sharita said, "If one of us was involved with somebody who refused to marry her like you're refusing to marry Mike, you'd tell us to dump them."

"True," Thursday said. She got quiet and glum before saying, "Let's change the subject."

So we talked about stuff that wasn't Mike. Then suddenly it was time for the wedding.

Thursday and me weren't attendants, but we did help Sharita get ready. She looked beautiful in her lace sheath gown with her hair in a simple updo that I did for her the morning of, since Scotland wasn't exactly overflowing with black hairdressers.

"You look beautiful," Thursday said, echoing my thoughts.

Sharita looked at me. "Why are you crying, Risa?" she asked.

She asked because I wasn't exactly one to cry at weddings, but I couldn't tell her why I was really crying. I couldn't say, "Because this is it. This is where our friendship as we know it ends. No more sitting around, talking for the hell of it. You'll have kids. We'll probably never spend an entire day together again, unless we're at the Smith College reunion, and even then it won't be the same. This is the end of an era. The end of us. And I already miss you."

Instead I looked down at my kilt-and-maroon-leather-jacket ensemble and said, "I'm crying because I would have looked so dope walking down the aisle in this."

Everyone laughed and then everyone hugged. And I thought to myself, *This isn't so bad. We had a good run.*

A really good run.

# THURSDAY

$\mathcal{I}$ had seen some happy brides in my life, but I had never seen anything as radiant as Sharita's face when she walked down the aisle wearing Benny's blue-and-black plaid family tartan sashed around her lace-covered wedding dress.

She looked so content, so confident, like she knew that she was marrying the best person on the face of the earth. It filled me with both hope and jealousy. That's what I wanted, to face marriage with certainty and without one ounce of fear that the person I was agreeing to marry would smash my heart into pieces. Love was supposed to be solid and comfortable. Davie Farrell had been right. Love shouldn't be too much drama in the first few months. You shouldn't have to compromise your friendships for it—even if Tammy had harbored ulterior motives for wanting to keep Mike and me apart. Love shouldn't make you feel like you're driving off a cliff. There were so many things wrong with Mike and me, so many things that could go wrong.

*"Don't be pathetic!"* my mother reminded me in the wings of my mind.

No, I thought, as Sharita and Benny exchanged Scottish wedding bands, there was no way that I could marry Mike. So I think it was pretty easy to understand why my heart dropped into my stomach when I stood up to cheer after Sharita and Benny sealed their vows with a big kiss and saw Mike standing on the other side of Sharita's sister and brother-in-law.

Our eyes met and he smiled, mouthing, "Surprise," as a guy playing the bagpipe preceded Sharita and Benny down the grassy aisle.

Mike had finished the pick-ups in Louisiana earlier than anticipated. This never happened. "I mean, ever," he said. "It must be fate."

So Mike decided at the last minute to hop on a plane to Scotland and surprise me.

I was very, very surprised, but . . . "I'm glad you came," I said, and I meant it.

Since it was Benny's castle, we were able to use the private reception room despite our small number, and the castle's on-call DJ even came around to play some music. So even though there weren't that many people there to celebrate, after dinner and drinks and a heartfelt toast by Benny that I couldn't understand, we all ended up on the dance floor.

About ten songs in, just when people were thinking about going back to their seats (Sharita and Benny) or getting more drinks (Sharita and Benny's moms) or taking over the DJ duties (Risa), a Rick T song came on. This track was one of his few non-political ones. It was called "Challenge" and had been written by my mother specifically as an ode to b-boys. To this day, it could still be heard at breakdancing events across the world, and sometimes showed up in silly commercials or in movies where some kind of competition was involved.

"Are you ready for this challenge?" Mike yelled over the music, twisting into a classic b-boy stance.

I looked at him. "You know I'm Rick T's daughter, right?"

"And I'm playing him in the movie," he said. "I don't care who you are. I can take you."

Now these were fighting words. I mean, you could practically see a tumbleweed roll between us. Everyone stepped back off the dance floor to give us room, waiting with bated breath to see what I would do.

Well yeah, I loved Mike. And yes, I owed my entire career to him. But c'mon . . .

I wasn't going to let him talk to me like that.

With precise movements, I took off my heels. A cheer went up from the other people on the dance floor, and they gathered around us in a circle, watching as I proceeded to match Mike, move for every eighties move. We waved, we cabbage patched, we wopped, we backspinned, we roboted. And maybe I was Rick T's daughter, but Mike had grown up in a place where breakdancing was a way of life. We were too evenly matched, and when the song was winding down, there was, alas, no obvious winner.

I stood there panting and laughing and feeling so silly, and Mike looked like he was in the same boat, but he wasn't breathing as hard I was. In fact, when he hugged me to him, he was still able to talk. I knew this because he whispered two words in my ear. "Marry me."

*"Don't be pathetic! Don't be pathetic!"*

My heart sank, because I knew then that we wouldn't even get to have the remainder of our time in Scotland together. "I can't."

He stepped away from me. "Hmm," he said. Then he smiled, his lips tight, his eyes bitter. And he walked away. Just walked away.

The music was still playing, a mid-tempo track now: "Only You," an English electro-pop song from the eighties that I distantly recognized.

But no one was dancing. They were all looking at me.

"Is everything okay?" Sharita asked.

This was Sharita's special day. I didn't want to ruin it. I wanted to smile and be happy, because that's what my friend deserved. "I just need some air," I told everyone and ran out.

*"Don't be pathetic!"* my mother warned me.

Something weird was happening. I came to a stop outside the reception room, and put my hands on my knees. It felt like I was having a heart attack, my chest had so tightly constricted. And I felt cold, woozy, and nauseated.

*"Don't be pathetic!"*

But then the sound of Mike's laughter after we finished dancing came back to me, which triggered another memory. My last comic gig, and the random guy laughing in the back. I had thought it had been Caleb at the time, but I now knew that Caleb would never have laughed like that at a comedy show. He was too cool for that, too reserved to ever risk being the only one laughing at a bombing comedian's show.

411

No, it had been Mike. Of course it had been Mike. Mike who thought I was funny even when I wasn't. Mike who had believed in me even after I had given up on myself. Mike who had supported my writing career no-holds-barred, even before I'd known that I still had one in me.

My mother was screaming now. *"Don't be pathetic! Don't be pathetic! Don't be pa—"*

"Shut up, Mom," I whispered out loud.

The screaming voice in my head came to an abrupt stop, and I could feel her ghost staring at me from my mind's eye.

"You're dead," I told her with more fierceness than I have ever told anybody anything in my life. "But I'm still alive. And you know what? Who cares if I humiliate myself loving Mike? Who cares if I agree to marry him and it blows up in my face? *He's totally worth it.*"

I waited for the voice to say something back, but for once my head was quiet. My mother had nothing to say. And I realized what I should have realized years, months, even just a few minutes ago. I was the only one in charge of my life now.

I ran after him, up the stone stairs to our room. But he wasn't there. I ran back downstairs. He was Mike Barker, a huge black movie star; it couldn't be that hard to find him in a castle in rural Scotland.

"Have you seen Mike Barker?" I asked the lady at the front desk.

The lady eyed me suspiciously.

"He's my boyfriend," I said.

The woman pursed her lips. "Well, he's not on the premises right now."

"Where did he go?" I asked, panic rising in my chest. I had to fix this. Like right now.

"I'm not at liberty to say."

"I'm his girlfriend," I said again, hysteria closing in.

"Then you should know where he went, shouldn't you?" she said, with a prim look.

Let me say this: I loved my time at Smith, loved the company of women. But while there, I had often observed that women liked to play by the rules. And if you wanted a rule broken, you usually had to ask a man, in this case a man who hadn't been able to take his eyes off of my chest even as he was opening the door for me when I first came to the castle a few days ago.

So I took my barefoot self and my fourteen years of feminist training over to the doorman and said, "I will show you my tits if you tell me where Mike Barker went."

I wasn't sure if "tits" was a term they used in Scotland, but he must have gotten the gist, because he garbled something back in Scottish.

"What?" I said. "Speak really slowly, I don't understand Scottish."

"We sent him to the Hilton hotel in Edinburgh," he said so slowly that he could have been speaking in slow motion.

"Thank you," I said with the dignity of a queen.

Then I opened up the front of my shirtdress, lifted up my bra, and flashed him. "Do you mind calling me a cab, too?"

The clerk at the front desk of the Hilton wasn't nearly as prissy as the one at Benny's castle. "Oh, I'm sorry, love, you just missed him. He dropped off his bags and said he was going for a walkabout in the city."

A walkabout in the city. I wished I could call him, but my phone didn't work in Europe. Mike had offered to put me on his international plan, but I turned him down, not wanting to take on the burden of an expensive cell phone contract if we broke up.

Stupid, stupid, stupid. I had been so stupid about him.

I was about to start looking for an Internet café so that I could Skype him, when I rounded the corner from Lothian Road to Castle Terrace street and saw it.

I walked toward it, not quite believing what I was seeing. But as I got closer to the top of the street, I could see that yes, yes, this was a farmers market.

In a trance, I walked through the market, which was throbbing with tourists and locals alike, but in the distance I could see the back of someone's head. He was wearing a suit, like the one Mike had been wearing, and a fedora, like the man in my dream had been wearing.

And maybe this would be a case of me running down someone who wasn't who I thought he was, like in the movies, but I had to try. I pushed through the crowd, getting closer and closer to him. But the closer I got, the thicker the crowd got, and I realized that this was because he was Mike Barker, a movie star. Apparently, he had been swarmed, and he was signing autographs.

Everybody was shouting his name. "Mike! Mike! Sign mine!"

But my voice rang out above all of theirs when I yelled at the top of my lungs, "Okay, okay, I'll marry you!"

The crowd went still, then parted. And when it did, there was Mike. Looking at me, with someone's notepad in one hand and a pen in the other. He was smiling at me.

And I smiled back at him, before saying it again. "I'll marry you."

# August 1998

My editor begged me not to put this in here, but I feel like it's got to be said. I slept with my husband on our first date. I lied to him, and we darn near drove each other crazy. I wish I had followed all these rules, but I didn't. These rules work for most people, but they might not work for you. And if that's the case, I invite you to forget everything I have written here, and settle for aggressively being yourself. I trust that you'll figure out the rest. Because the truth is you're a grown woman, and at the end of the day, you probably don't need my advice.

—*The Awesome Girl's Guide to Dating Extraordinary Men* by Davie Farrell

# RISA, SHARITA, AND THURSDAY

*A* Spice Girls song played on speakers set up near the podium toward the front of the room, and Sharita found herself dancing a little as she and her new friend, Thursday, tried to find a table with two seats available at the closing banquet for Smith College's weeklong BRIDGE orientation program for students of color.

Though Sharita had warned Thursday several times that they were going to be late, Thursday had wanted to catch the end of a Rick T concert, streaming live from Belgium. And Sharita, feeling privileged to have met and befriended the daughter of one of her favorite rappers in her very first week at the elite women's college, had been too intimidated to speak up. Thursday was by far the most glamorous black person she had ever met. She had traveled all over Europe, Africa, South America, and the United States. She had even gone to Japan. Unlike Sharita, she shrugged off the beauty of Smith College's campus, saying that all the rich white institutions looked the same. She'd had dreadlocks since the age of ten and had never "been subjected to a perm." As far as Sharita could tell, she wasn't here on scholarship and she had only agreed to attend the pre-orientation for students of color because it beat sitting around the house with her sister and mother while her father was touring in Europe.

Unlike most of the other black women (not girls—Sharita had already been corrected on this several times) at BRIDGE, Thursday seemed to consider college a predestined right as opposed to a privilege. She had introduced herself to Sharita with a raised eyebrow and a sideways smile that mightily resembled a smirk. "You seem like one of those salt-of-the-earth black folk that my parents are always wanting me to get to know. Let's do them a boon and become friends."

Having never met a black girl—woman—who dressed like a hippie and talked like a rich white girl, a stunned Sharita agreed to this proposal of friendship, and they'd become inseparable by the end of the week. She would find out from older students of color in the coming year that just about every student of color that attended BRIDGE had the same "I met my best friend there" story.

But in Sharita's case, her new best friend had caused them to come in late to the end-of-program banquet. They had missed the speaker and were now having trouble finding two seats together at any of the round tables, which were all occupied by woman of color having passionate and intelligent conversations about matters both important and trivial.

Sharita was about to suggest that maybe they stand with their plates, when Thursday pointed to a table in the far corner. "There's a couple of seats next to Lisa Whatever-Her-Hard-To-Pronounce-Last-Name-Is."

"Um . . ." Sharita said. The truth was that she had never spoken directly with Lisa, but she could already tell she didn't like her. Sharita had nothing per se against lesbians. She filed it under the same situation as sex before marriage. The Bible didn't like it, but she didn't think it was something that would keep folks out of heaven or anything.

But Lisa wasn't like the other lesbians of color at BRIDGE. She wore men's cologne, she swaggered as opposed to walking like a normal girl—

woman! During the short introductions on the first day of the program, she stood up and said, "My name is Lisa Amoakohene. I'm from Cali. I have two plans in life: to be a rock star and to have kissed ten of you hot bitches by the end of the week."

To Sharita's astonishment, everyone, including the student BRIDGE leaders, who should have known better, laughed.

Lisa had concluded with, "Oh, and I have a tattoo my parents don't know about." Then she'd lifted her shirt and showed it to them.

Over the week, Lisa had gained a notoriety that had kept Sharita and most of the other black women in the BRIDGE program talking about but not befriending her. Thursday had been one of the few exceptions, shutting down one conversation about Lisa's copious application of Polo cologne with a sleepy-eyed smirk and a "Oh, I was raised not to judge, but I guess you all weren't brought up that way."

And now Thursday seemed eager for the excuse to meet the upstart Lisa, who, if the gossip was true, actually *had* kissed over ten of her fellow Bridgees during their short time there. She grabbed Sharita's hand and said, "C'mon, she seems like so much fun."

"I don't know . . ." Sharita said. "She'll like you, but I don't think I'm her kind of people."

"Like my mom always says, nothing beats a failure like a try. And for all you know, she'll love us and we'll all become lifelong friends."

Sharita very much doubted that, but before she could fully protest, they were at the table and Thursday was saying, "Hey, we haven't formally met. I'm Thursday, and this is Sharita. Mind if we sit here?"

Lisa regarded them both with slitted eyes for the longest time before finally saying, "Yeah okay, why not?"

# ACKNOWLEDGMENTS

So many people to thank . . .

My agent, Victoria Sanders, whose fierce passion inspires the heck out of me.

Melody Guy, who I suspected would be a real pleasure to work with—I suspected right.

Kelli Martin, whose enthusiasm for this novel made working with Amazon Publishing a delight.

My sister, Elizabeth Carter, my first reader and most steadfast "fan."

Gudrun Cram-Drach, who patiently reads draft after draft of everything I write and then gives me feedback that actually makes me enthusiastic to go even harder on the next draft.

Tara Armov, the Derby Doll who inspired me to put Risa on a motorcycle, and then walked me through how to do so.

Paul Ryan, who inspired me to put Risa on a surfboard, and then walked me through how to do so.

Dr. Patricia Perry, who originally told me the Bob Marley story and was kind enough to answer all my questions about the condition he and Tammy shared.

Brian Viehland, one of my oldest, dearest friends. You not only married my best friend, but you also never complain about the many architecture questions I send your way.

Georgie and Anika. I won't say why. I think you know.

My husband, Christian Hibbard, who makes it easy to not only write about, but also give thanks at the altar of true love.

# Acknowledgments

My mother-in-law, Mary Zimmerman, who I'm lucky to live with and even luckier to know and love.

My fellow Smithies. I'm so grateful to be a part of your rank.

And last but not least . . .

Thank *you* for reading this book. I super-hope you liked it.

So Much Love,
etc.

# ABOUT THE AUTHOR

ERNESSA T. CARTER

*E*rnessa T. Carter has worked as an ESL teacher in Japan, a music journalist in Pittsburgh, a payroll administrator in Burbank, and a radio writer for American Top 40 with Ryan Seacrest in Hollywood. Carter's also a retired L.A. Derby Doll (roller derby). A graduate of Smith College and Carnegie Mellon University's MFA program, Carter is the author of *32 Candles* and *The Awesome Girl's Guide to Dating Extraordinary Men*.

# Bonus Material
# MISS MISSY

*L*ittle befores Miss Missy was born, two other slave women been died giving birth. One mama den took the baby with her into the afterlife. The other mama done push for eight hours and whisper the name Elijah to Martha before dying from the all the blood coming out of her down there.

Martha be giving Elijah to Peter and his woman, Harriet. They other child been sold, so Martha say to them you take this one. Harriet don't give him back when Martha been put him in her arms.

Why Martha don't keep Elijah herself? Because Martha belly be full with her own baby. Her man, Thomas, been sold off for winter provisions. She say she tired. She say she can't be a mammy to her own and this dead slave's poor child. So she give Elijah to Peter and Harriet, and they take that there child.

"It gon' to be a boy," Martha be saying to them that ask after her own baby. She say he turn over and over whenever she lay down and he be swimming all around her stomach when she be getting the good word on Sundays. "The Lord done told me in a dream he be something special, like Mary been told of Jesus." That what Martha be telling us.

She ask us to say some dem prayers for her, because every slave know that a special baby be a difficult birth. We been already lost two mamas in the winter, and if Martha go on to the Lord, the slaves ain't going to have nobody to birth the babies no more.

But Martha be wrong. The birth ain't difficult and the baby ain't a boy. She be on the birth bed only a short time pushing, when a dark little thing slip out of her. And the baby ain't crying. She be laughing!

Martha take the baby from the woman that done caught it. "Dis baby girl be laughing," Martha say, eyes wide.

Yes'm, the baby got her eyes squeezed shut and her mouth curve up, with a sound coming out of her mouth that be happy. Even though she be black. Even though she be slave.

The two other slave women be nodding. "Dat's what it sound like," one them say.

"She laughing! She laughing!" the other one say.

They all be staring at the baby, fighting off the notion to laugh they own self.

Martha name the baby Miss Missy, because she be laughing when she come out and what name be funnier than that?

Slaves ain't got no reason to laugh. They lives be hard and they lives be getting took away, at any time, at any moment. There be some dancing in meadows on Sundays when we together to give praise to the New Lord for all He do and make, but even on that day, nobody be laughing.

Massa Green done give us this God who not going to introduce Himself proper-like until we done entered the afterlife, but we suspect the Massa can also be taking Him away if there be too much laughing with the praising, if it look like the slaves having too good a time. After service, we be putting our hats and head scarves and dark cloud faces back on, and we go on back to them tobacco and cotton fields—Massa Green grow both.

Even the touched slaves know not to laugh. They know not to get the overseer thinking they be having too much fun, not working hard enough. They don't want him to get to fingering his whip.

So how you going to explain Miss Missy? All she do is laugh.

Which be why we, the slaves of Green Plantation, done declared that child simple as simple can be. She start that mess when she be a baby and not one day go by we don't hear her laughing coming out the shack she be sharing with her mama. That laugh of hers be ringing out across the cotton fields, cuz she laugh every time she prick herself on the cotton's burly black stem. And heaven forbid she draw blood. She just 'bout fall over laughing, telling anybody that be standing near, "Look at what I's done. Lookatit!"

When her poor mama pinch her to keep quiet, cuz slave children ain't got no business being heard, Miss Missy be about laughing even louder. She say, "Mama, stooo-ooop."

Yes, she talk back to Martha. A few of the other mama slaves be fixed to slap that child for Martha. Martha too soft with her. She got three childrens took from her before Miss Missy, and she don't got the heart to train the girl to act right like she supposed to. So Miss Missy keep laughing and running and skipping like the world be a good place and she ain't a slave and like she got some reason for carrying on like she do.

Nobody be thinking she simple no more. We *know* she got to be simple. Not just simple. Simple and touched.

And maybe Martha be sending up a prayer for that. The only young slaves that don't get sold off when the Green Plantation full-up be the simple ones.

Miss Missy don't be getting sold when she eight, or when she nine, or when she ten, or when she eleven, or when she twelve, or when she thirteen, or when she fourteen—and now Miss Missy fifteen. FIFTEEN and she still be here.

Because she simple and touched. She be a big, tall girl, she got her daddy length, sure be. She work hard. Nobody else want to buy her with all the laughing, but it maybe ain't too hard on Massa Green to keep her, cuz she do the work good enough.

Martha get to keep her daughter. And rest us slaves, maybe we get to keep Miss Missy's laughter.

Even on the hottest days, the ones that kill a old-woman cotton picker where she be standing stooped over, even on these days, there be something about the laughter. It don't make us spit. It give us the other kind of feeling.

A feeling we ain't got no name for. But if we gonna call it something, maybe we call it joy. Though that ain't the exact right word.

Come time, everybody like Miss Missy. Even the mamas that think she need a good slap. Even the overseer maybe, because he never use his whip to stop her laughing. Even though if there ever be anybody needing a whipping, it be Miss Missy needing a whipping, black as a cave at night, with a laugh so light and free. It felt like maybe you could float away on it. More than one slave be imagining riding that laugh into the sky, over the trees, across the big river, and then north, north till we cain't see the plantation no more. North, north till we be free.

By time Miss Missy fifteen, the story come to be that the big Him God been take all the laugh supposed to be for us slaves and put it in simple Miss Missy, so we can be enjoying it without getting whipped for it.

"God be good," one of the old slaves say to me when I tell her this story we done made up. "Oh yes, God be good."

Saul be new on the plantation. Massa been traded him from a neighbor plantation that be needing a blacksmith for they horses. Our old blacksmith got sons that can be doing the blacksmithin' at our place, and Massa say he be low on young bucks, so he make the trade. The blacksmith's woman ain't happy about it. His sons ain't neither. Maybe they been thinking they daddy might get to die where he been learnt his trade.

But that ain't the case. One morning the blacksmith get took away in chains. And by the nighttime, there be Saul, tall, hard of body, teeth gleaming in the moonlight.

Maybe he ain't that smart either. Maybe Jesus done touched him, too, like Miss Missy. None us know what from what. But the main story be that he take one look at Miss Missy, and you can see him nose open up.

He be walking across that cotton field, like the overseer hadn't bint already told him where to pick and he be asking a woman in the row next to Miss Missy if they mightn't trade places.

# Bonus Material: Miss Missy

Before any us can warn him Miss Missy ain't quite right in the head, he be introducing hisself, like they at a white folks' dance, telling her his name be Saul and she sho be a pretty sight on such a hot, miserable day.

Pretty, he call her.

She look up at him with her rag wrapped round her head and sweat pouring down her face and she fall in love with him right back.

We can hear her laughing clear cross the field when she introduce herself as Miss Missy.

He say that sho is a special name.

And she agree it sho is.

She be fifteen. He reckon he be maybe twenty or there about.

And before we can tell them that slaves ain't know no romantic, Saul and Miss Missy be together. Always in the rows next to each other in the field. Always walking with they heads together in the nighttime. Always eating off the same metal plate when it come time to take supper.

They talk and they laugh and they ain't be like no slaves suppose to be. The overseer got his lips stretched real thin and he be making them work on opposite sides of the field. Tell Miss Missy to "Shut up, wench" when she try to call over to Saul on the other side of the cotton.

She look at that overseer, eyes just as merry, and she shut her lips tight. But she still be smiling.

And that night, she move out her mama's shack and go sleep near the fields on a stretch of grass. Nobody seen Saul and her talking that day, but they musta been, cuz Saul be moving out the men's quarters and he be joining her on her little pallet near the fields. And they don't be paying no mind to the grass that be damp and the mosquitas that be coming after them. They ain't thinking about how when the summer stop, the air going to be turning cold.

It be warm right now. And they be together. And everybody can hear Miss Missy laughing in the middle of the night. It be like a storybook, them two. The other slaves be telling and retelling the story to each other.

# Bonus Material: Miss Missy

They reckon Miss Missy gonna become big with baby any day now, and Massa gone be sell it, cuz he got enough slaves, but he ain't ever got enough gold.

A few of the slaves wonder loud if Miss Missy still be laughing after her blood been sold off like the rest of us blood done been sold off. But a few of us be hoping quiet that nothing bad happen to those two with the moon in they eyes . . .

Saul and Miss Missy. A dreamer maybe call them real romantic except for two things. The first thing be they slaves. The second thing be the Massa's son, who come back to the plantation some years after he bint sent away to boarding school up north.

The cost of buying a slave be rising every year, and that den created a new money pot for Massa Green. He start looking hard at the domestic flesh market. He ain't much for running a plantation no-how. His daddy was, but he ain't inherited none of that. So he leave dem fields to the overseer, and set about the business of breeding the slaves he done already got. He take dem big man slaves, and put them on top of the young girls. Sometime one man be put on top of three or four young girls a night. It get to be a system with the girls getting chose by who was how old and who was good about her monthlies.

But Massa didn't want too many heifers pregnant, because a woman pick cotton and tobacco faster without a baby in her belly. And it just so happen that when Saul and Miss Missy got to romancin', they was enough girls pregnant and they don't got to worry about getting selected for another season or two.

Saul and Miss Missy fall in love during the planting season. Then Saul and Miss Missy jump the broom come Christmastime, when slaves in every corner of the country get the whole day off. Miss Missy wear thistles in her hair, and a very old dress that the Mistress gave to a yellow house slave name Rachel to tear into rags. But Rachel done give it to Martha to be thanking her for delivering her a alive baby boy, whose daddy be the Massa. Rachel baby be so white, he and the Massa's real son—the one that be inheriting the plantation next—look like full-blood.

But they ain't that. The real son get sent to boarding school in the north when he be twelve. And the Slave Son get sent to the stables to help with the horses when he be twelve.

That winter and spring come and go, and Miss Missy's stomach stay flat, even though Martha been moved in with another old woman slave and been give Saul and Miss Missy her cabin to be making a baby in. We be hearing Miss Missy giggling in the night when Saul lay on top of her. We hear her every night laughing, but no baby.

And maybe one dem field slaves meet a house slave at the well, and they get to talking. And that house slave tell the Massa. Or maybe a overseer just take note, but Saul ain't one of the young bucks get chosen to breed that next summer. And Miss Missy ain't given over to breed.

Not having babies ain't tragic when you know they fixed to get sold, so maybe Miss Missy ain't too broke up about it. And maybe she keep on going like that for awhiles, laughing in the fields and giggling in the night.

But Grady, the slave that they be sending to the train station to pick up the Young Massa, saw it happen from beginning to end.

Grady say he fair don't recognize the real son when he go to get him. All pale skin and red hair and thin like a string, so you know he ain't been nowhere near a hard day's work in the important years.

"Young Massa Green?" Grady say. He ain't believing this pale man could be no kind of kin to our Massa, who got a belly big as a ripe watermelon.

"Yes," the man be saying back, according to Grady. Then he be pointing at his valise and get in the cart without saying another word.

Young Massa got them northern airs but good, he don't be saying a second word to Grady until they be pulling into the plantation, and the Young Massa point and say, "Who is that girl there?"

Grady look. It be Miss Missy running, skipping, and cartwheeling her way from the cotton field to the tobacco field. The cotton field overseer been got sick of watching Miss Missy and Saul flirt day in and day out, so he been sent Saul over to the tobacco fields. By the time Young Massa come along, slave folk been got used to Miss Missy running from the cotton field to the tobacco field at the end of a working day. 'Cording to the tobacco field slaves, once she been got over there, she be on Saul like they ain't seen each other in a score or two. Throwing herself in his arms, sometimes knocking him over if he ain't seen her coming. That girl know she can step up her acting a fool when it come to her man, Saul.

"That be Miss Missy," Grady say. He ain't one of them slaves that get all happy inside just cuz Miss Missy and Saul done got together sweet like they was. But maybe he ain't as grouchy as he supposed to be either, cuz just in case the Young Massa be offended by her happiness, he say, "She simple. And touched."

The Young Massa nod. Grady tell us he be looking down his pointy nose as Miss Missy do one cartwheel after another. Six in a row by Grady's count.

"Real simple," Grady say. "Real touched."

The Young Massa don't say nothing else, and Grady be thinking that the end of it, but two days later the news come down on a Sunday after church.

They be sending the Slave Son to tell Miss Missy the news.

"You going to be working in the Big House starting tomorrow," he say.

The Slave Son pretty of face and hard of body. But you cain't notice either because he keep his face right angry. You can tell from the get he going to be one of dem forever bitter 'bout him ain't being darkie enough to be a true slave and him ain't being white enough to be a true free. He tell Miss Missy the news like she done something wrong.

Miss Missy just laugh. She look up at Saul, who standing behind her in the door. "You hear that? I's going to have to run all the way from the Big House to the fields from now on when I'm through with work."

Another girl slave, Sarah May, happen to be passing by and when she see the Slave Son at Miss Missy's and Saul's door, she hide behind a nearby tree and eavesdrop, because as any white massa will tell you, eavesdropping be in the slave blood.

She tell us after that the Slave Son, who name be Jacob, but none us call him that, so the Slave Son 'cording to Sarah, he smile mean when he let Miss Missy know, "House slaves sleep in the house. Plus, the Young Massa ask for you specifically."

"Specifically." Miss Missy be confused. Her smile still on, but it be wobbling 'cording to Sarah May. Miss Missy look up at Saul again. "What 'specifically' mean?"

Saul, the happiest slave man any of us ever done had the grace to know, become the unhappiest one right before Sarah May's eyes. And before anybody can figure what he fixing to do, he step past Miss Missy and punch the Slave Son right between the eyes.

Saul be getting ten lashes for that. And by the time they be cutting him down from the whipping tree, Miss Missy be in the Big House on a pallet in the basement with the other house slaves, most of who be the unclaimed daughters of the Massa or one of the overseers. They don't talk about they daddies to each other or Miss Missy. They just be telling Miss Missy where everything be in the kitchen and let her know that she gone to be scrubbing all the Big House floors from now on.

Miss Missy sing a little song while she set to scrubbing them floors. Her singing ain't as pretty as her laugh, though. About halfway through the day another house slave kick over the bucket, maybe on purpose, maybe because she don't understand why Miss Missy, dark as night, no white in her, be in the place where only the most favorite slaves get to work. Or maybe she just don't understand why Miss Missy got any reason to be singing so happy. But if she think Miss Missy's singing be bad, you probably could have been knocked her over with a feather when Miss Missy laugh and say, "Time to get more water." And then she be skipping with the empty bucket through the house and out to the pump and smiling at the cold water tumbling into the bucket. "Hi, Water," she be saying with another laugh. "You sho is pretty on a hot day."

She say that to the water, just like she remember Saul saying it to her the first time they two meet.

Maybe Miss Missy got a plan that first day. Maybe she done already figure out how to see Saul on Sundays after church or during the dinner hour. But we ain't never gonna know, because when the work be done that day, just when Miss Missy be putting the rag back in the bucket, the house slave that done kick it over before, come to her with a crystal glass of whiskey.

"Young Massa take a whiskey in he bath. Myra already done heated the water for you. But she ain't going to do it again, so tomorrow night, that be your job."

The house slave shove the glass of whiskey into Miss Missy's soapy hands and walk out. I only know this because one the other house slaves tell me the whole story. She say she be the one that Miss Missy come up to after the kicking-bucket house slave walk away. She say Miss Missy say to her, "I'm supposed to take this whiskey to Young Massa, but I don't reckon where his room be."

Then she say Miss Missy laugh, like this be the funniest situation a slave girl ever be getting herself into.

I stand here ashamed, cuz I be one dem that sometime got to making fun of Miss Missy, cuz all she do is laugh and because she don't have the sense God gave a donkey to take serious what you suppose to be taking serious.

But that be before she stop laughing. Three hours after she take that whiskey up to Young Massa, she come out his room and she ain't laughing no more.

After a week of whiskey, she ain't even smiling. Three weeks, and she go'on right on ahead and stop talking unless spoken to.

# Bonus Material: Miss Missy

Innocent men done been hung on our plantation. Our girls be getting tied up to a bed, with a man they don't want put on top of them. Children be getting took out they mama's arms and sold to the highest bidder. But the end of Miss Missy's laughter bring out us crazy. The womenfolk walk around sadder and they be screaming at the menfolk for the littlest things. The mens be getting in more fights over nothing. One slave get stabbed by another slave, we still don't know why. Somebody say it might have been over a blanket. One of them said the other one done stole it, then the words, then the knife, then the death two weeks later from infection, then the whipping of the one that done did the stabbing.

Miss Missy not laughing be something awful.

And we all be trying not to be scared of a woman's not laughing, but we be scared. We got crows flying around our hearts. And we don't know what we go'on to do if she start crying next. It might break us. Break us even though we ain't thought we be capable of breaking any more than we already done broke cuz we be slaves. But that be before Miss Missy stop laughing.

And how Saul be taking this, you ask? That boy done start drinking a week after he hear Miss Missy stop laughing. He show up at the moonshiner's door with some boot polish to barter, asking for two jugs. Then the week after that, he be bringing the moonshiner a wooden comb that used to belonged to his mama. His fieldwork be suffering. The overseer hit him with a lash a few times, tell him he be needing to move faster. Saul pick a little faster, and he be back at the moonshiner's door by the weekend, this time with a scarf that Miss Missy done made for him last winter.

Last winter was when they still be happy.

It be the last thing of worth he got to barter. And them two jugs of moonshine going to have to do him.

It come down from the house that Miss Missy ain't fully there no more. She move through the days like a ghost now. They say that when she ain't moving, she be standing still like a small animal, like maybe that will keep Young Massa from seeing her.

This make us angry at Martha. If she been took our advice and done broke that girl like we said she ought when she was a young laughing thing, we wouldn't have to see this. We wouldn't have to care. Some us begin to hate Martha, think about not talking to her, like Massa's wife stop talking to him sometime because he say the wrong thing in front of guests or stay too long with Geenie, the latest slave girl he done took into his bed.

But we ain't the Massa's wife, and we fo sho ain't white, so we go'on about our business. Waiting, waiting . . .

The second to last jug of moonshine get set outside Saul door.

And one of them times at supper, Martha done surprise us by talking about it. "It like that David story," she say. "The one where he want that soldier's wife, so he send the soldier to war, so he can get him he wife. And the soldier die, and he get the woman. What her name be?"

"Bathsheba," somebody else say.

And Martha shake her head yes. "I should been named her Bathsheba."

Bathsheba a beautiful name. We all imagine Miss Missy in the Big House, cleaning them floors all day and bringing the Young Massa his whiskey at night, and we rename her. Bathsheba.

Some days later, Saul done finish that last jug of moonshine. Nobody surprised when he start screaming Miss Missy's name after drinking the last drop. "Miss Missy," he be yelling in the night. "Miss Missy!"

The sound send a evil spirit down all our backs. Later we say this why it took us so long to realize his screaming be getting softer, even though his emotion be getting louder. Else we would have stopped him from going to the Big House. We would have been about covering his mouth with our hands and pulling him back into his shack, and we would've sat on him until he pass out from the shine.

But we don't be realizing where he going. And by the time all of us field slaves get out our beds, cover ourselves and catch up with him, he be yelling outside the Big House.

# Bonus Material: Miss Missy

And both Young and Old Massas be out on the porch. With shotguns.

Miss Missy standing in the door behind the Massas, curled against the frame like the house be the only thing holding her up. There be light brown faces peeping out all the downstairs windows, and if you look up, you can see Massa's wife in one of them top windows. Only reason I see her is cuz I be praying to Lord God to make what be happening stop.

But most us don't look up. Most us keep our eyes on the Massas. And they guns.

"Get back to your quarters, nigger," Young Massa say to Saul in that strange northern accent of his.

Saul hold out his hand to Miss Missy. "You my woman. You come with me now."

Miss Missy don't move. She and a statue be twin sisters.

"You come here now," he say, waving the empty moonshine jug. "You my woman."

"Say one more word to her, and I will shoot you," Young Massa say. "She is mine."

"You come with me. You go where I go." Saul screaming now. "You MY WOMAN—"

The gunshot ring out in the night and Saul fall to the ground. His whole chest be gone. His whole life be gone, right before our eyes.

You ain't never heard night so quiet. We all be standing there, trying to take our eyes off Saul. But we cain't. Even the Massas be staring at him there. Now we all be the statues, and only Miss Missy be moving. She run down the porch stairs.

"Get back here," the Young Massa say, sounding like he be fixing to shoot her, too.

But Miss Missy don't stop until she get to her man. She drop to her knees and gather what be left of him in her arms. The ivory night dress that Young Massa done bought her get covered in Saul's blood and guts.

We wait for the tears, thinking that however bad we thought it would be, the tears going to be worse. But she don't cry. She laugh and laugh and laugh.

Then she say, "Oh, Saul, I am your woman. We can be together now. You done good, Saul. You done good."

And this is the part people don't believe when us slaves tell them what all happened, no matter how many us say it, they don't be believing us. But I'm telling you now that it happened. Happened just like we said, like us all said it did for the rest of our lifes.

Miss Missy be laughing, and then . . . the back of her nightdress be ripping, and out of her back come the largest pair of wings you done ever seen. They ain't white like they be in the paintings, they be gray and they be two times as long as she be tall.

And they be flapping. She beat them once, twice, and by five times, she be in the sky, hovering over us with dead Saul lying like a baby in her arms, and she be looking down at all us black faces in the moonlight. She still be laughing. And then . . .

. . . she look up to the sky and she fly up into it, taking her and Saul on home.

We stare up at the heavens long after we cain't see her anymore.

The Massas refuse to hear us talk a word of it after it all be done. Young Massa take a wife after that, and maybe become the first slave owner to not take a slave mistress, too. He get a reputation across the state for being a man of God, pious, and only us slaves be knowing it because of that night when he be finding out that he done raped an angel.

As for the rest us slaves, we spread the word. If you have a baby that laugh when she shouldn't and can't help but find the joy, even when her life be real serious, watch that one closely.

Miss Missy cain't be the only angel walking among us.